D1246477

riser

BECCA C SMITH

Published by Red Frog Publishing a division of Red Frog Media

Visit our website at www.redfrogpublishing.com

First published in 2010

ISBN 978-1-452-88907-8

Printed in the United States of America

Dedicated to my husband Stephan –
For making everyday an adventure and teaching me
what true love really is...
I love you.

Chapter Zero
Year: 2320

Okay, let me explain. My gift, or curse (I'll let you decide for yourself) to put it simply is: I can raise the dead. I know, sounds cheesy, but fortunately, or unfortunately it is true, and I don't mean just people. Basically, anything that had any kind of life: plants, animals, insects, plankton, *anything*, I can bring back. The only catch is, they're not really alive anymore they're just animated, like zombies I guess, but I control them. Plants are the easiest. My mom's garden is the prize of the trailer park, and she should take no credit whatsoever.

Animals and people are more complicated, maybe because there are so many working parts. I'm really not sure. My ability is still kind of a mystery to me. I have no clue why I have this power. It's not like I've ever heard of anyone else having this particular skill either, except in books and movies. I appear to be an anomaly in this world...

I was three-years-old when I knew I saw things differently

1

than everyone else. My pet goldfish, Larry, died and a black spinning hole appeared in the center of his body. I thought it was just about the coolest thing I had ever seen. When I told my mother about it, she gave me a look that I'd never forget. It was a mixture of confusion and horror. She simply nodded and made me promise that I would never under any circumstances tell anyone else about what I saw. I was instantly ashamed and scared at her reaction, but something in the way that she had said it made me keep my promise.

After that, I saw the black holes everywhere, from the tiniest dead insects, to the neighbor's dog when he was hit by a hover car (don't ask), to Ms. Thompkins when she died from a heart attack. The churning black masses had become second nature to me by then. At that point, I still didn't know *why* I could see them and I was scared to death to talk to anyone about it. I kept to myself mostly, afraid I would slip and say something to a neighbor or friend.

It was a very lonely childhood.

It wasn't until I killed my stepfather Bruce that I figured out that I could raise the dead. I never wanted to take Bruce's life: hurt maybe, kill no. And that was saying a lot seeing as he used to use my mom as a punching bag. He'd make me sit in the corner of our beat up trailer and watch him kick the living crap out of her. He'd laugh when I'd scream, he'd laugh when she'd scream, he'd laugh when *he'd* scream on the few occasions my mom fought back and actually inflicted pain on him.

Bruce was a jerk, but he didn't deserve to die, not like he did, not like how I killed him. I still can't believe it had been eleven years since it all happened. It felt like yesterday and forever ago all at once.

It was a day like any other day, Mom did some invisible transgression to piss Bruce off and he took it as a cue for another beating. Mom was having one of her comatose days, where I could tell she was just going to take it and hope that he got bored quickly from her unresponsiveness.

Bruce slammed her against the flimsy trailer wall of the kitchen with his beefy forearm. Tiny bits of ceiling floated down like snow on his greasy balding scalp. He sneered at her with glee, but she wouldn't give him the satisfaction of eye contact. She just kept her eyes down, arms dropped harmlessly at her side. Bruce went on a furious rampage. He punched her, pulled her hair, kicked her stomach, tried anything to get a response out of her, but she just lay there like a rag doll on the peeling linoleum floor.

Then he wheeled around to face *me*.

"NO!"

Finally, a reaction from my mother. Bruce was in ecstasy. He stormed towards me like an enraged bull. I could almost see steam coming out of his bulbous nose. Then WHACK!

I could literally feel every vertebra in my spine as all forty-five pounds of me slammed against the wall from the impact of Bruce's fist to my stomach. My world started to spin; everything was in blurred double vision. My mother's hysterical screams echoed in my head like a horrific nightmare. I couldn't focus.

PUNCH!

CRACK!

I could feel my nose crunch when he hit me a second time. It felt like it was running, but when I tried to wipe it clean my hands came away covered in blood. The combination of Bruce's frantic laughter and my mother's anguished screeches made it impossible to think clearly. I think I started to whimper at this point. My ribs were so bruised it hurt to breathe let alone move my chest to have a good cry like I wanted to.

These are the moments in life where you don't think rationally. In fact, you don't think at all, you just let your survival instinct take over. It becomes about you or your killer.

And I was no martyr.

I tried to blink fast enough to clear my vision.

THWACK!

My right eye started to swell from Bruce's backhand making it even more difficult to focus. At this point my mother, like a wailing Banshee, propelled herself onto Bruce's back and started pounding her fists onto any piece of flesh she could find. I could hear Bruce's low chuckle at my mom's feeble attempt to stop him. From the sound of his amusement I could tell that today was the most fun he'd had in years.

Taking short controlled breaths I took this moment of solace to re-gain my bearings. And that's when I saw it: a blurred swirling black hole in the corner of the trailer.

WHAM!

Bruce had thrown my mother clear across the room. Her body collapsed into unconsciousness as her head punched a hole through the trailer's wall.

I screamed a horrible, terrible scream: a scream that only a child could make whose world had just been crushed, whose mommy had just been smashed against a wall, leaving her daughter alone, defenseless, a scream that would make any human who possessed an ounce of parenting instincts come running, without thinking, without rational thought. And I couldn't stop. Even Bruce had to cover his ears from the onslaught of shrieking. But Bruce's instincts weren't to mother, they were to destroy and he started towards me.

And seeing him, fists raised, plowing forward, I suddenly felt inexplicably tied to that black swirling chasm across the room. I was a part of it. It was almost as if strings connected us together. And I did the only thing I could.

I made it attack Bruce.

At first I didn't know what I was doing, but I suddenly understood that I physically controlled the black holes. I was connected to them like they were an extension of my own body, like they were my own limbs.

Bruce bellowed in pain as we both realized at the same time what I had brought back to life.

A black widow spider, full of venom and ready to attack.

Over and over I made the spider tear its fangs into Bruce's body: his neck, his arms, his legs, his chest. Bruce swatted the spider, squished the spider, tore it in two, but nothing he did could stop it.

It was mine.

It was already dead.

He couldn't kill it again.

He fell to his knees. The poison was flowing through his body now. I could see a small black tornado forming in Bruce's chest.

Fear overtook every fiber of my soul as I realized what I had just done, what I was still doing. I dropped my connection to the spider instantly. It fell lifeless to the floor once more, the black void churning madly in its center.

I crawled over to Bruce's body, leaving a trail of blood from my broken nose. He was convulsing on the ground, his body seizing from the poison coursing through his veins. He was dying and there was nothing I could do about it.

"What did you do?" my mother's voice cut through the near silent grunting and gagging of Bruce's dying moments.

She had seen the whole thing.

"I..." I couldn't think of what to say. My mother looked relieved, guilty and horrified all in one condemning expression. I wasn't sure if she was upset about losing Bruce or that her seven-year-old child had just become a murderer. Bruce's eyes rolled back in his head. His last breath was rattling and eerily hushed. It seemed to last an eternity. As if the oxygen in his lungs didn't want to leave his body and clung to whatever life it could hold on to.

I stared into my mother's eyes. She couldn't speak. She couldn't move. A small line of blood trickled into her eye from a gash on her forehead, but she didn't flinch. She just looked into my eyes with a blankness more terrifying than any emotion could be.

"Chelsan..." she finally croaked. Her voice was gravelly from screaming.

That was all she could say. It was agony to see her so dead in the eyes, face, body... just staring. I would have given anything I had just to stop her from looking at me with those empty eyes. Her vacant stare felt like a howl of pain so excruciating I almost covered my ears from the silence. At least then I would have been able to hear my own muffled heartbeat. Any noise would have been better than the oppressive judging stillness.

And that was when I realized what I had to do. To break her out of this coma she was encasing herself into. I turned to Bruce. To his raging black abyss spiraling like a whirlpool deep inside his chest. And I switched him on. Just like the spider. He was a bit clumsy at first. I had to concentrate as hard as my seven-year-old brain would let me just to get him in a sitting position. But after a moment or two it became easier and easier and he began to feel like an extension of me. It was an eerie sensation as my thoughts mirrored Bruce's movements. I would think of his arm moving and it would move. I would think of him speaking and…

"Janet?" I made Bruce call to my mother.

His voice snapped her completely out of her stupor. She watched him in shock and overwhelming relief. "Bruce?"

And then I made him cry. Cry like he never could do when he was alive. I made him cry until his face and clothes were drenched with his tears. "I'm so sorry. I'm so sorry," I made him repeat over and over as he sobbed in the aftermath of the day's destruction.

Mom crawled over to the two of us, renewed hope in her eyes. Whether she knew what I was doing or not, she didn't say. All that mattered was that she wanted to believe it. She needed to believe it. I could see it in her face. I made Bruce embrace the two of us with a tenderness he was never capable of before. I was doing this for me as much as for my mother at this point. Feeling his strong arms around me, holding me close, affectionate, loving. It was the first time in my life I felt like I

7

had a father: a real dad. I nestled in closer. When my mom saw this she did the same. We both had contented expressions on our bloody bruised faces. I let Bruce sputter and jabber about how much he loved the two of us, how he would never hurt us again, how he was a changed man…

And he was.

After that day he became the best father anyone could ever ask for.

I still found it funny in a strange and disturbing way, that Bruce was a better father dead than he ever was alive. He was the easiest for me to control now because he was my first, and I'd had a lot of practice since then. It was almost as if he was really alive sometimes. But every time I watched his face go slack when he watched his holo-tv or he stunk so bad I had to puppeteer him in the shower, I remembered.

He was dead. Truly dead.

And it was my fault.

Chapter One

"Breakfast, Chelsan. Hurry before it gets cold. You'll be late for school." Speak of the devil, that was Bruce calling me for breakfast. "Chelsan, I mean it. I made you eggs!" Bruce's voice called through my door from the kitchen.

"I'm coming," I said with a sigh. Dead people could be so pushy sometimes. But I had no one to blame but myself. I made him say those things just like I made him cook my breakfast. I had been controlling him for so long, I barely had to think about it anymore. It was like I had a second body to do all the crappy things in life, like cleaning and cooking and anything else annoying. How nice is that?

Bruce is awake when I am and asleep when I am, too. Or at least "alive" anyway, I just make him kind of lie there until I wake up. I can't control him when I'm asleep. I wish. Think of everything I could get done!

I quickly dressed in my usual tank top, jeans and Chuck

Taylors (still popular after four-hundred years) and checked myself in the mirror. My hair was a mess so I ran a brush through it. I had been growing it out for the last three years now and it was just past my shoulders. I used to have a pixie cut that, unfortunately at the awkward age of fifteen made me look like a boy. So, three years later, I felt a little more feminine. It was chestnut brown and I soon realized brushing it was doing me no favors, so I tied it back in a high-ponytail. I had boring grey eyes (why couldn't they be blue?!), slightly fuller lower lip than upper lip, small straight nose, high cheekbones, and today, thank goodness, no zits. I remember having a pimple the size of a crater on my forehead just before school ended the year before that I didn't think I'd ever live down.

As I walked out of my room I blew a kiss to one of my many holo-pics of Jason Keroff (news reporter extraordinaire) plastered on my bedroom wall and entered the living room.

The new holographic-television was on as usual. Mom just had it installed and I was still getting used to the fact that the people were solid holographs as opposed to our old junky holo-tv where you could see right through them. Not to mention they'd flicker every five minutes making it impossible to really get into any kind of show. The only thing I could sit through was the news just because it didn't matter what the holographs looked like.

And there he was, the adorable reporter himself, Jason Keroff.

He worked for LA's own Channel 2 News and was a journalist for various magazines and newspapers. It was pretty embarrassing liking the guy that every other girl from the ages of nine to eighteen had a raging crush on.

But to be honest, thinking about Jason kept my mind off of my lost cause, Ryan Vaughn. Ryan was ridiculously perfect in every way… Stop!

Ryan was waaaaaaaay out of my league!

Jason. Jason. Jason.

He was reporting live on my holo-tv on location at a Virtual Reality Bar, about some scandal and such. (I never really did pay attention.) He was looking perfect, as usual, with his short cropped messy coal black hair, big green eyes, which would always feel like he was talking specifically to you through the hologram, slightly crooked nose that gave him that extra sexy "I just got into a bar fight" kind of edge, t-shirt and jeans with a nice dress jacket over the top, and a pair of Chuck Taylors. (Yes, I know, I'm a copycat.)

It was amazing how clear the holograms were on the new holo-tv. It was as if a ten-inch version of Jason stood in our living room, Virtual Bar behind him, hover cars flying over-head, all displayed on top of our entertainment stand.

Of course, no one knew how old Jason was. He kept that hidden from the press. He could be any age, really, since three-hundred years ago in 2020, a medical scientist named John Fortski found the cure for aging and put it in a tiny pill called, Age-pro.

Basically, this little white pill (if taken everyday) stops the aging process completely.

So if you take it at twenty, you're twenty *forever*.

You can still die, obviously: accidents, guns, murder, hurricanes, tidal waves, there's no pill for any of those things. But as long as you stay healthy and stay away from sharp objects, you could potentially live forever. I guess there used to be a bunch of diseases you could die from in the twentieth century, but after aging was cured supposedly the properties that were used for Age-pro were such a huge breakthrough in medical science that all of the killing diseases had a cure. But more importantly, they had preventative shots that everyone received as a baby so no one would die from some horrible illness.

People who had money were legally allowed to start taking Age-pro at eighteen, but people like us trailer-park-low-income types, usually started taking it when we were thirty. That was when the National Insurance kicked in and pretty much anyone could afford it. And let's face it, even people who had no money managed to find a way to get their hands on Age-pro. Who would want to miss out on immortality?

Jason was gone before I could really appreciate the crooked little smile he always gave at the end of each report and was replaced with boring Carleton Gordan, news anchor for the last hundred years not looking a day over nineteen.

Carleton droned on in his monotone, annoying voice, "Overpopulation has reached an all time high, and the death rate has dropped to a record low. The government commented this morning about its terraforming project on Mars, but no other word or solution has been made…"

"Come on, eat your food before it gets cold." Bruce pulled my attention away from the news.

"Sure, thanks, Bruce." I sat down at the rusty Formica-topped kitchen table where my waiting eggs rested. The smell finally reached my nose and my stomach grumbled in response.

"You better hurry, sweetheart, that rich school of yours

won't tolerate tardiness from a trailer kid." Mom came into the kitchen with her usual hostility toward the high school I went to. It was a private, richy-rich-school that we could never afford, but I worked at the ice-cream parlor off campus to pay the tuition that scholarships didn't cover. She wanted me to go to the public school about ten miles away.

But I physically couldn't. And I couldn't tell her why.

The first time I realized that my control of dead things had a proximity limit was when I was on my way to my friend's Aunt's house twenty miles away.

About five miles out, I got a call from my mother, screaming that Bruce had just dropped to the floor, dead. I cried hysterically until my friend's parents turned the car around. I concentrated as hard as I could until I could feel Bruce's black hole and brought him back to life. It was just shy of four miles away from the trailer park.

I knew then that I could never go beyond a four-mile radius of my home, or Bruce would become a corpse again. Not only that, but in the few minutes that I let him die for a second time, his body began to decay, as if it knew the exact date when he died.

Think if I left and let him die for good? He'd be a skeleton within minutes.

Luckily, he'd only rotted a bit on his upper arm and leg, so no one seemed to notice. Gross!

But this was my life, my existence, making sure all the dead things I'd brought back to life stay fresh so my loved ones weren't in excruciating emotional pain from their losses.

When I found out that the public high school was outside

my "safety zone" I looked for another school I could go to.

Only one was exactly three miles away, *Geoffrey Turner High School.*

A super elite, super expensive, private school named after the Vice President of Population Control, which was pretty much the most powerful position in the world, even more than the President, since population was the world's biggest concern today. He was the only man in the public eye who showed any sign of age. He was fifty when Fortski created Age-pro and Turner had been fifty ever since. I always tried to get a closer look at his wrinkles on the holo, but I think they did some kind of effect to hide most of them. He was a very distinguished man, always in a suit and tie, dark hair with flecks of white. His features were classic: straight nose, chiseled bone structure, strong chin.

Mom cringed every time I mentioned the fact that we had the same grey eyes. Even the shape was the same. In fact, she'd cringe every time I mentioned his name. She said it was because he was creepy to look at, being old and all, and not to *ever* compare myself to him again. And that was about all she'd say on the matter, but I suspected there was more to it than that. Vice President Turner must have done something political over the years to piss Mom off. Even though she looked thirty, she was about to have her fiftieth birthday soon, and Geoffrey Turner had been in office for over two hundred years. That was a lot of time to do something that my mom could hold a grudge for.

"Do you want to take the rest of your birthday cake for lunch?" Mom asked me as she was already packing it into my lunch box. I turned eighteen four days ago. I was the oldest in my senior class. It was always annoying starting the school year older than everyone else. By the end of the year everyone had caught up to me, but for some reason a year in high school was the equivalent of ten normal years. So for at least the first few months I'd be on the receiving end of jokes and condescending glares from all the seventeen-year-old seniors equating my "old" age to my intelligence or lack thereof according to them. I would say I couldn't wait to graduate and live on my own, but I knew if I left, Bruce would be bones and I still didn't think I could do that to my mother.

Mom handed me my lunch as she kissed the top of my head affectionately. She gave me her usual wink and a smile. Her way of saying she loved me. My mom was pretty gorgeous considering the time she began taking Age-pro. Her hair was brown like mine, but her eyes were light hazel. Her skin was ivory in color with a smattering of freckles across her nose and her body was perfectly thin.

She was thirty-one when she started Age-pro so she only had faint lines around her eyes, which I personally loved. Her face lit up when she laughed and the slight crinkles made her eyes sparkle. I used to think this was the reason my real father fell in love with her. I would sometimes imagine what he was like, what he looked like, what his voice sounded like. He died the day I was born and my mom didn't have any pictures of him. She said it was too painful a reminder. He was the love of her life and she always said it killed her the day he died. For some reason the way she'd say it always sounded like she meant it literally. Maybe that was why she ended up with Bruce, she

15

picked the complete opposite of my father so she'd never be reminded of him again.

"Thanks, Mom. I better go. I have to work at the shop after school today. I took a shift for Jenny," I told her between mouthfuls as I shoveled down a few more bites of Bruce's eggs. "I'll see you around seven." I kissed her cheek and ran out the door.

The flimsy aluminum door slapped shut behind me as I left the trailer.

I made my way to the Hover-Shuttle waiting area just outside the park. The Hover-Shuttle came every five minutes or so and could take you pretty much anywhere in the larger city of Los Angeles. The trailer park was pretty dead at the moment. Most of the people who lived there had blue-collar jobs that required getting up at the crack of dawn. I resigned myself to working at the ice-cream shop for the rest of my life if I didn't figure out what to do about Bruce. And that could be a *very* long time, an eternity possibly. An eternity of working retail! I hoped at some point I could be honest with my mom and make her understand what I did and let Bruce rest in peace. Yeah right.

I reached the designated steel bench to wait for the Hover-Shuttle. The waiting area itself was circular, like a fifteen-foot bulls-eye made of grey asphalt.

A few seconds later, I could hear the whizzing sound of the Hover-Shuttle coming my way. Closer and closer the rectangular metal box buzzed toward me. It was clunky and old, but most things that came to the trailer park were. Society pretty much wanted to pretend we didn't exist, so when it came to public works and transportation we were last on the list of repairs. That was what happened when there were twenty-seven billion people on the planet and over half of them were rich and demanded their needs came first. The other half of us did all the menial work and shut our mouths. No one wanted to stir the pot in fear that the National Insurance for Age-pro would be cut. If the government decided to cut the funding, they could push the age minimum to forty or even fifty!

The orange-yellow glow and the whirling of ducted fans from the belly of the Hover-Shuttle lowered to the center of the waiting area. The propulsion fans ran on hydrogen fuel cell technology, so to kill two birds with one stone, there were containers under the vehicles collecting the steam and water from the cells to later dump into recycling plants. There the plants would send the water to all sorts of places from drinking water distribution facilities to watering tanks located in most suburban neighborhoods for their greens. Anywhere and everywhere they could use it.

The metal on the shuttle was chipped and dented giving the appearance of a beat up refrigerator. The passenger door lowered to the ground with a loud CLUNK and turned into a set of grated metal steps. Skipping two at a time, I climbed up the stairs and entered.

The interior wasn't much nicer than the exterior. The seats were arranged like any public transportation: two rows of two-seaters with a middle aisle in between. There was only one other passenger besides me: a businessman, suit and tie, reading from his electronic reader, keeping to himself. I sat down near the front. The driver waited a few moments as if someone from the trailer park would come running up the stairs at any second. Or maybe he just counted to ten in his head at every stop. Whatever it was, at some invisible marker of time, he closed the door of the craft and we were off.

The humming sound of the Hover-Shuttle was almost deafening as we sailed toward *Geoffrey Turner High School*, the next stop. I looked out the window as we traveled and admired the landscape. Where the trailer park was stark and devoid of much vegetation, once outside its perimeter, the ground became lush with bright green grass and a field of California Oaks. Once the International Law of 2142 was passed requiring the planting of a tree every twenty feet, most places decided to re-plant near extinct trees like the California Oak. The law was passed as soon as everyone realized the down sides to Age-pro.

Overpopulation.

This basically meant we'd run out of oxygen if we didn't start evening out the balance of the world. More people meant *more* things, which meant *more* natural resources being drained, trees being one of the highest for paper alone. The first law to be passed was in 2068 that outlawed anything printed on paper. Electronic reading devices were already a popular luxury item back then, but they soon became a requirement if you ever intended to read anything. Only e-books were legal. But there just wasn't enough plant life on the Earth to sustain the amount of people inhabiting it so they had to make planting more trees a worldwide law. It was hard for me to imagine living on this planet without the amount of trees we had now. I loved trees. I loved getting lost in the forest with a good e-book or to just sit under the shade and have a moment to myself.

The Hover-Shuttle flew past the oak forest and I could see

my high school drawing near. It looked like something from a fairytale: early 1800s architecture (re-created of course: the school was only twenty-years-old) made entirely of brick and mortar, iron-wrought gates and ivy growing up the sides of the school like veins pumping life into the building.

I just wished the people inside it were as nice as the building was to look at. Being poor in a rich school didn't exactly lend itself to making friends. I had two people who were brave enough to socialize with the "leech" as I was so fondly referred to. And I truly considered them friends. Bill and Nancy. Bill was a sweetheart. He was loyal and simple in the kind of way that made it nice to be around him. He was also easy on the eyes with his perfectly messy brown hair, well-muscled body (I think the guy had a ten-pack if that was possible!) and a boyish face with long eyelashes. In the entire high school, his family was the richest by far! That was why they didn't give him much of a hard time hanging around with me. The one thing the rich kids had in common was the hierarchy of elitism. And since Bill could buy and sell almost everyone that attended Geoffrey Turner High, he'd get his usual kiss ass line of admirers every day whether I was with him or not. I always felt safest when I was with Bill since the worst kind of behavior I'd experience from the true nasties of the school was a total ignorance of my existence. When I wasn't with him it was an entirely different story. That's when the claws came out.

Bill and I met randomly sophomore year when I rounded a corner and slammed into his six-foot wall of a body. His stuff flew, my stuff flew, it was a mess. But the most tragic part about it was I broke my electronic reader, a lightning bolt shaped crack straight down the middle. Electronic readers weren't cheap mind you, I had to work double shifts at the ice-cream shop just to buy mine. I nearly cried between gulps of apologies. I thought I'd be crucified right then and there for daring to touch the precious Bill Merryweather, let alone knocking him on his butt. And without an electronic reader I'd have been kicked out of school for sure. I couldn't count the amount of times the school informed me, "Geoffrey Turner High is not a charity. If you can't purchase your own items, you will be excused."

Jill Forester (the ringleader of my torment for the last four years) was the first to kneel down and try to help Bill up, sending nasty glares at me about five times a second. Her hair was as black as her heart and she had bright green eyes that made her cruelly beautiful. Why are all the mean girls gorgeous?! She was thin and perfect and she knew it.

When she saw my broken reader she simply smirked and said, "Karma."

Karma, *this*! I wanted to say, but held my tongue and apologized to Bill again.

"You should be sorry." Jill couldn't help herself.

If ever I wanted to smack someone it was in that moment. But Bill did something I'll never forget. He shrugged Jill off and stood up. That alone caused a dramatic gasp from the crowd. He offered me his hand and smiled in a way that said, *don't listen to her. No harm, no foul, I'm fine.* I took his hand and he lifted me to my feet. He picked up my reader, handed it to me and genuinely looked like he was sorry. The group surrounding us already started to close in on Bill, shutting off any conversation, until I was standing alone in the middle of the hall with my broken reader. Later that day when I sat down in Geometry class there was a brand new, state of the art, grossly expensive, electronic reader lying on my desk with a card. The card simply said, "Sorry about your reader. Hope this will work for you. Bill." My heart had stopped. No one had ever done something like that for me before, especially someone as popular as Bill. He was really sticking his neck out on the social line for me. It was the nicest thing I had ever owned *and still own* to this day. I knew he had a ton of money and buying a reader was probably like spending a penny to him, but it was a kindness he was in no way obligated to do, and genuinely came from the goodness of his heart. Ever since then we've been close friends, despite Jill's agony over the union.

My friendship with Nancy was a different story. She was considered upper middle class which was still super rich compared to me, but not rich enough to give her the same respect that Bill had. We met freshman year when we were forced to be lab partners in Biology. She wasn't happy about it. I was new and everyone knew I lived in the trailer park before I even arrived on campus. That put me in the below filth category on everyone's radar though no one would openly admit this for fear of looking like the prejudiced jerks they were. I knew they'd come up with a "real" reason for hating me later, but as for the moment of my arrival, it would just be an unsaid loathing toward me. Nancy did the usual: rolled her gorgeous blue eyes and flipped her long locks of blonde hair, in annoyance of my presence, audibly grunting exasperation, all for the pleasure of the rest of the class. Just another perfectly beautiful mean girl.

When the teacher handed out the dead frogs we were

supposed to cut up, her face turned greener than their corpses. For me it was a room full of black swirling holes.

"Are you okay?" I asked.

Nancy tried to ignore the fact that I even spoke to her, but after a few moments she shook her head. "I don't think I can do it."

I didn't know what to say. I was afraid if I said anything she'd guffaw and tell me to shut up anyway, but as rude as she was to me, I could still see how much the frogs were upsetting her.

Then she spoke. Her voice barely audible, her face growing paler by the second, "I had a pet frog that just died... Jimmy."

She said it with such emotion and heartache, all my feelings of annoyance toward her melted away.

"I don't think I can cut into him." Even though her voice was a whisper her eyes were screaming with panic and anguish.

That was when I decided to use my gift. There was no way I could let this poor girl cut into what she saw as her pet.

"We won't be cutting anything today," I said and I popped every single frog back into existence.

It was pure and utter chaos. There were jumping frogs everywhere: on the desks, on the students, on the stools, on the floor. Screams and laughter mixed together like a symphony of bedlam. The teacher tried to wrangle the frogs into the garbage receptor, but since I controlled the frogs, that didn't happen.

"Open the windows," I said very calmly to Nancy, whose expression had done a complete turn around. There were tears of joy streaming down her face: joy and relief. Whether she knew exactly what I was doing or not, she didn't say, but she did know I was somehow responsible. She nodded and walked over to the windows, opening them wide.

I made the frogs jump and whiz toward the windows like moths to a flame and within seconds they were gone. All that was left was a very excited and amped up biology class. Nancy sat down next to me, wonder in her eyes, but she didn't say anything.

"Calm down, okay, calm down, get in your seats." The biology teacher tried to bring some semblance of order back to the room. "We won't be dividing into lab partners today, obviously… I need to sit for a second." The teacher had finally grasped what had just happened and he couldn't seem to keep it together. After he sat he said, "You can sit in your regularly assigned seats if you like. Just read chapters four and five, I'll be right back." He left the classroom without another word.

The room broke out into chatter and laughter at what had happened. Jill Forester waltzed over to Nancy and said in the most condescending and superior voice she could, "You don't have to sit next to *that* anymore, Nancy. Come over and sit with Joan and me."

I waited for the inevitable rejection from Nancy. I expected it and I honestly wouldn't have been offended. Social ladders in high school are tricky things. If you were knocked down a few rungs, it was really difficult to climb back up, and being friends with me would probably knock her off the ladder completely.

But Nancy didn't even flinch, didn't even hesitate, she just turned to Jill and said in a cheerful voice, "No thanks." Then without another word of acknowledgement to Jill she turned to me with a smile, "What are you doing after school?"

Jill was in shock, standing there as if she had just been slapped in the face. After a moment she seemed to recover. "Nancy, this is your last chance. I'm serious."

Still smiling, acting completely oblivious, Nancy turned to her. "Serious about what?"

Jill didn't have a response to the directness of the question. As if spelling it out would somehow expose her as the raging bigot she was. In one fell swoop Nancy had beat Jill at her own social game by either making her admit to her prejudice against me, or back out and fight the fight in some other way. People were starting to stare at this strange confrontation, so she decided to back away, but not without an evil glare directed at the two of us. She was always full of those.

Ever since then, Nancy and I had been best friends.

The Hover-Shuttle landed at the station on the outskirts of Geoffrey Turner High. It was right next to the black iron wrought gate that served as metal open arms to the school. I did love this school, despite the people in it that made my life torture. There was something so comforting about its presence that I couldn't quite explain. Maybe it was because I earned my right to be there. I earned the scholarships, I worked a part-time job, I made the grades, I deserved to be there. I wasn't born into it; I made it happen and I was actually a little proud of that.

I exited the shuttle without a word to the driver and made my way through the gate to the front courtyard. It was pretty much deserted since above me was the carpool platform with a long line of hover-cars dropping off students. Most of the kids liked being driven, but a handful of students drove themselves and parked in the designated lot behind the school. You had to be seventeen to get your hover license and most of the rich kids waited until they were eighteen since they enjoyed having drivers taxi them around everywhere. Bill was the only person I knew that actually had his hover-license.

The courtyard was green and lush with classic maples and a hedge fence surrounding the entire circumference of the area. Two rows of cherry blossom trees lined the walkway ending at the large arched oak door that led inside the school. My favorite time of year was spring when the trees become a forest of pink. There were benches scattered throughout to encourage students to study and socialize outdoors, but there were only a handful of us that took advantage of the space.

I walked through the oak doors and entered the bottom level of the school. The halls were quickly filling up as students made their way down from the hover platforms above. Mahogany lockers lined the hallways (no small feat considering the use of any kind of wood was limited by the law for environmental purposes) and white marble floors leading the way. I could only imagine the amount of money it took to maintain the beauty and quality of the wood and flooring with the wear and tear of high school students. Not that Vice President Turner had to worry about money. He was filthy rich and always had been, even before Age-pro. His family was old money, ancient money, like since the early fifteen hundreds kind of ancient.

When I reached my locker I opened the combination lock, pulled out my electronic reader and grabbed my fitted cardigan. Temperatures usually reached below freezing in Mr. Alaster's History class and I wanted something to protect me from the cold.

"Hey, did you read chapter eight?" Nancy suddenly appeared

at my side. She had grown a few inches since freshman year, but her hair remained blonde, long and gorgeous. I still had pangs of guilt when I realized how popular Nancy would be if she wasn't friends with me. She was truly stunning to look at, giant blue eyes: a delicate straight nose and perfectly bowed lips that were always pinkish-red in color as if she wore lipstick, but she was just naturally flawless. Her tight jeans and fitted top showed off her picture-perfect body. I always felt like the ugly duckling little sister when I stood next to her.

"Yeah, last night." I shut my locker and we began to walk down the hall toward class.

"Fill me in. I completely slacked." Nancy usually didn't do her homework and relied on me to keep her up to date. Her philosophy was that since she aced the tests what did it matter if she did the homework or not. She was one of those ridiculously smart people who never had to study for anything; everything came to her naturally. Somehow she'd manage to put all the pieces of the puzzle together just by looking at the question or the equation on the test. I, on the other hand, had to study for hours just to maintain my A status. If I didn't I'd lose my scholarships.

"We're just going over religious stuff since Age-pro," I told her.

Nancy rolled her eyes and made an exasperated groan. "Seriously? Haven't we covered that in *every class ever?*"

"I think we're going over the whole Voodoo thing today, so that'll be cool." I completely agreed with Nancy. The fascination of belief or lack of belief in religion since Age-pro was a topic that every teacher liked to discuss at some point in their classroom;

from literature, to biology, to history, to social sciences, even the math teacher had something to say about it! At least Mr. Alaster delved into the interesting stuff, like the transformation of Vodun or Voodoo from a religion to black magic.

"Watch out for Jill today. She's on a rampage and you're her favorite target." Nancy didn't seem all that concerned, but confrontations with Jill tended to get ugly and I knew she genuinely wanted to avoid it at all costs.

"What's she on a rampage about?" I asked. Sometimes knowing what was bothering Jill helped me figure out how to avoid complete and total humiliation.

"Her mom found out she was taking Age-pro."

I shrugged. Most of the kids here illegally started to take Age-pro before the eighteen-year-old restriction. The fear of wrinkles and cellulite overrode health and good sense. The reason there was a restriction at all was because the International Health Board ruled it dangerous to stop aging before a person had fully grown. It could cause massive complications later in life. There were extreme cases, like in 2143 the "Alice Rose incident." Basically, this woman, Alice Rose, had a baby and decided she wanted a *baby* forever, so she started giving it Age-pro. When she was finally caught, the baby was nineteen-years-old and still an infant. Alice was arrested and sent to prison. That was when everyone started realizing the dangers of Age-pro. They immediately made the eighteen-year-old restriction punishable by life imprisonment, which meant no Age-pro, which meant dying of old age. Who knows when Jill started taking it? She was damn lucky her mom found out about it and not the police. By trying to stay forever young she came dangerously close to living a mere eighty to ninety years.

"I'll steer clear," I said to reassure Nancy. I really didn't want to be in Jill's warpath today.

The bell rang and everyone started shuffling into his or her designated classrooms. Nancy and I arrived at Mr. Alaster's door and entered.

Jill sat at the back of the class with her usual crowd of admirers hovering over her like bees to honey. As soon as I walked in I looked away trying to avoid eye contact.

"Just sit down," Nancy said under her breath, which indicated to me that Jill was staring me down. It was amazing when you could actually feel people staring at you. I refused to look in her direction. Meeting gazes with Jill would only give her an opening to use me as her verbal punching bag.

I did as Nancy said and we both sat in our seats near the front of the room just as Mr. Alaster walked in. Mr. Alaster started taking Age-pro around thirty and had a thin, wiry frame with curly brown hair on top, making him look like a human carrot. He wore his usual brown cardigan sweater with round suede elbow patches, typical khakis and dress shirt, and, of course, his wire frame glasses. Let's face it, he looked the way you'd imagine a history teacher to look. Sometimes I wondered if he did it on purpose or if he really, truly liked to dress that way.

"Punch up chapter eight." Mr. Alaster's enthusiastic, buoyant voice filled the room.

I pulled out my electronic reader and brought up chapter eight like everyone else in the room. The title of the chapter read: "The Fall of Religion and the Beginnings of Elemental Experimentation." Snore. Though Mr. Alaster didn't seem to think so, he was, in fact, more eager than I'd ever seen him before.

"What did you think of this chapter? Any thoughts? Questions? Come on, guys, don't be shy, this subject is fascinating, trust me." Mr. Alaster's smile was almost contagious. He might actually be right if we hadn't already heard it a bagillion times.

"No one? Really?" Mr. Alaster didn't seem upset, only surprised at our lack of enthusiasm.

That was when Ryan Vaughn raised his hand. I looked away and tried to ignore his perfect face. It was too torturous liking someone I had absolutely no shot at. He was the resident whiz kid of Geoffrey Turner High, and I had an enormously embarrassing crush on him. Like I said, most of my crush on the reporter Jason Keroff was to keep my mind off of my doomed liking of Ryan.

Ryan's family was on the same pay scale as Nancy's, which put him in the upper middle class range. He was a popular kid only because he agreed to do other people's homework for the right price. Ryan's I.Q. was also fifty points above genius which put him as the smartest kid in school and rumor had it, in the world. Science scouts would come to our school all the time offering him jobs straight out of high school at the top research facilities in the world. Ryan didn't seem fazed by all the attention and no one knew if he took any of the offers.

He tutored me in math junior year and even though I was a social reject, he was still decent to me, which of course, made me like him all the more. I could barely speak when I was around him. He probably thought I was a complete idiot. Ryan was ridiculously cute and ridiculously brilliant. He kept his short, sandy-blonde hair in a kind of "planned messy" way and was taller than most boys our age (six-three). He was lean but muscular with big brown eyes and angular features. Okay, he was gorgeous, but way out of my reach. I seriously had a better chance with Jason Keroff than with him.

"Yes, Ryan." Mr. Alaster was thrilled that someone was participating, let alone the resident brainiac.

"Isn't all this *Elemental Experimentation* the same thing as religion? Just a bunch of mumbo jumbo made up to validate our existence." Ryan slumped in his chair and said this with a kind of arrogance that suggested he didn't have much conviction in his statement.

"That's a valid point, Ryan, but scientific Elemental Experimentation has tangible evidence that it truly produces results where as religion was always based on faith and imagination." You could almost see the saliva forming around Mr. Alaster's mouth from his passion on the topic. "The reason I'm so excited about this, guys, is because just this morning the Scientific Journal released the results of an extended study which began in 2247. It was run by a scientist named Lester Rankin who performed the Voodoo ritual of resurrection. He was actually able to bring a man back to life that had been dead for two days."

My interest immediately perked up. Nancy looked over at me with protective concern. We had never talked about the day I made the frogs come to life, but I could imagine she had wondered about it. And now as Mr. Alaster was telling me that there might be others who could do what I could do, I needed all the info I could get. I needed to download the Scientific

30

Journal pronto.

"For how long?" I asked before I could stop myself. My curiosity overtook my sensibility of speaking up in a classroom where Jill Forester resided.

"For how long what?" Mr. Alaster wasn't upset by the disruption, he genuinely was curious as to where my mind was going with this.

"For how long has Chelsan been a complete moron?" Jill chimed in from the back.

The class laughed on cue, but I ignored them as usual. I turned my attention to Mr. Alaster. "How long was he able to bring him back to life?"

"Aaah!" Mr. Alaster was thrilled with the racing thoughts I instilled inside of his mind. "For only a few minutes. And the man wasn't really alive, more like an animated corpse. According to the study, the longest they were able to keep the corpses mobile was a maximum of five minutes."

Interesting. Somehow this had to have something to do with my gift. Maybe I had performed this spell or ceremony or whatever it was when I was a kid and didn't even realize it? Maybe my mom or my real dad… maybe something genetic because they had done this hoochimimbober Voodoo thing? I couldn't stop thinking about all the possibilities. I needed to know more.

Ryan raised his hand again, perplexed. "Correct me if I'm wrong, but I thought Vodun was a religion."

Mr. Alaster's eyes lit up with excitement. "You are very correct, Ryan. *But* Vodun or Voodoo is no longer considered a religion because of its tangible elements. Many people no longer believe in the Vodun creator, Mawu, or, God, in Christian religions anymore. Only the people who consider themselves truly faithful, like the Christian Coalition, who segregate themselves around the world in tiny towns and refuse to take Age-pro still worship their God and practice the ritual ceremonies."

There were a few gasps from Jill and her lackeys in the back of the room at the thought of not using Age-pro *on purpose*.

"Paganism and Wicca were also categorized as religions in the past, but are now seen as Elemental Experimentation. In the twentieth century people thought of them as hokum because death was such a driving factor in the way that people lived. They were on this planet for such a finite time that the afterlife was far more important to them than the mere seventy to ninety years they were alive. Once the factor of death was taken out of the equation, people found that there were far more interesting things to explore. Suddenly finding out if these rituals or spells, as they used to call them, actually worked became a priority. Most of the population found that when you had eternity, your goals and ambitions changed."

This was where I started to tune out. Mr. Alaster was now getting into familiar territory that all of us had heard too many times to count. I looked over at Ryan and even he had zoned, staring at his reader as if he were following along with Mr. Alaster.

At that moment though Ryan's eyes unexpectedly met mine and he smiled slightly. I could feel my face flush and I quickly turned away. My stomach did back flips and I could feel myself break into a slight sweat. What was my problem? A guy who wouldn't say "hi" to me in the hallway smiles at me and I was completely falling apart. And to boot, I just realized that when I turned away I didn't exactly smile back. I probably gave him some kind of look of disgust. Typical. It didn't matter anyway, it wasn't like Ryan would ever *like me like me*. He was almost certainly smiling at the fact that some moron stared at him like a complete dork. I was such an idiot. What was more annoying than that was the fact that I desperately wanted to look at him again. Was I a masochist or something? Don't do it!

"What's wrong with you?" Nancy whispered to me with a look of concern on her face.

"Nothing. Not feeling well, must've been breakfast." I tried to cover up, but I could tell Nancy wasn't buying it.

"Is it the study?" Nancy's expression indicated that she really *did* know more than she was letting on. I could tell we were going to have a discussion about my gift very soon. And a part of me looked forward to it. After four years I could trust her. Besides, she obviously already put most of it together if she was picking up on my interest in the study.

"Yeah. We'll talk," I promised.

Nancy's face changed from concern to excitement. Between her and Mr. Alaster's enthusiasm I could barely concentrate.

Okay, I could barely concentrate because I desperately wanted to turn around and stare at Ryan. My brain was a mess. I couldn't wrap my head around why I cared? I tried not to think of Ryan Vaughn all that often. In fact, after our tutoring time, I tried to block him out of my head completely for fear of becoming a stalker. But it was very hard to forget the rare moments when his hand brushed up against mine by accident and it would send tingles all the way to my toes.

IT WAS JUST A SMILE! STOP IT! I needed to clear my head.

I needed to focus on something else.

"Maybe Chelsan would know." Jill's voice cut through my inner hysteria.

Know what? Great. I hadn't been paying attention *at all*.

"Chelsan?" Mr. Alaster smiled at me with eagerness.

"Yes?" I asked.

I could tell Mr. Alaster immediately knew I had no idea what he was talking about. His face fell slightly as if he couldn't fathom how anyone could not have been engrossed in his lecture.

"I think she was too busy drooling over Ryan to pay attention." Jill laughed. And the class laughed with her.

Was I that obvious? Oh man, if Jill noticed my red face and sweats, Ryan *unquestionably* did. Thank goodness I had resisted my urge for a second sneak peak!

"I wasn't drooling." Did I *really* say that out loud?! I wanted to crawl under my desk and die.

"I see." Mr. Alaster realized that this was a feud between teenage girls and didn't want to have anything to do with it. "Let's continue forward, shall we? What religions took the biggest fall after Age-pro?" He droned on and the class quieted down from Jill's outburst.

Nancy tried to give me non-verbal support in the form of an encouraging smile, but nothing would make me feel better. Nothing except making Jill feel just as humiliated. I searched the room until I found the perfect thing.

A dead fly on the windowsill.

I brought it to life.

I started slow, just an irritating fly buzzing around Jill's face. She discreetly waved it away. Then I amped it up. I made it fly directly in her ear. SWAT! I kept the fly in her ear as if her swat had injured him. This freaked her out to the point of standing up in class trying to rid herself of the fly now stuck in her ear. Everyone stared in amusement.

"Jill? What's the problem?" Mr. Alaster asked.

Here goes. The fly raced out of her ear and flew around her face, up her nose, out of her nose, in her hair, in her clothes until Jill was flailing her arms and whole body in panic. She looked like a frenzied animal being attacked by an invisible force.

"GET IT OFF ME! GET IT OFF ME!" she wailed.

I made it land on her cheek.

WHACK! Jill's best friend, Joan, hit the fly with her reader thereby smacking Jill directly in the face.

I made the fly fall to the floor, dead once more.

Everyone stifled his or her laughter for fear of Jill's wrath, but I smiled as broadly as I could.

I win.

"Jill, you may want to go to the nurse, your cheek is looking a little red." Mr. Alaster looked as though he was trying to hide his own amusement. A lot of the teachers in the school liked Jill less than I did. Her father's influence in the government made it impossible to give Jill anything less than a B. Our math teacher freshman year tried to give her a D and needless to say he was fired the next day and replaced with a teacher that let her pass with flying colors. The teachers that didn't hate her simply sucked up to her any chance they got. Owen Forester (Jill's dad) was second in command to Geoffrey Turner himself, which meant he had influence in over-population "perks." Perks that included owning more than one hover-car, landscaping that fudged the "planting a tree every twenty feet" law, free passes to Virtual Reality Bars, just to name a few. And Jill's favorite teachers always cashed in any chance they could.

Jill gave Joan a look that could kill and made her way toward the exit just as the bell rang for the class to end.

"Is it that time already?" Mr. Alaster seemed disappointed to let us all go. It felt like leaving someone in mid-sentence.

Everyone began to move out of their seats and exit the classroom.

"Wait for Joan to leave," Nancy warned me and we pretended to gather our things a little bit more slowly than we normally would. "Okay, she's gone."

Everyone had left, including Ryan. I didn't even want to think about ever seeing him again for fear of dying of embarrassment. Why did I have to open my big mouth?

Nancy and I headed for the door. "Do you like Ryan?" she asked.

I tried my best to act shocked and appalled. "No!"

Nancy laughed out loud. "You totally do! That's cute."

"Cute?" I complained in exasperated disgust. "More like tragic. Guys like Ryan don't like girls like me."

Nancy rolled her eyes and practically guffawed. "Oh, please! Girls like you? Attractive, smart *and* have a personality? You're right, you should just give up on guys right now."

"Easy for you to say. You have money."

"Ha! I'll give you some. See how much it makes a difference in your love life," Nancy groaned.

"Being friends with me is what's messing up your love life. You may not care about money, but everyone else does." Which was true though Nancy didn't like hearing it.

She opened the door and we entered into the crowded halls. And I ran straight into...

...Ryan.

I hit his chest full force. How could I not have seen him? How could Nancy not have warned me? Looking over at my best friend, I saw the triumphant smile on her face and knew she had done it on purpose. She had angled the door exactly so he'd be out of my view.

"Sorry," I sputtered.

Ryan smiled. I wished he wouldn't do that. It made my stomach churn in horrible ways.

"No problem. I actually wanted to talk to you for a minute. Can I walk you to class?"

My brain froze. What was that? Say something. Now would be the time to say something.

"She'd love to. Chelsan, I'll meet you later for lunch, okay?" Then Nancy eyed Ryan with a knowing smile, "Unless you have other plans," and she was off.

And I was alone. With Ryan. And I couldn't make myself say a single word.

Ryan's face seemed almost apologetic as if my silence was a reprimand for something he'd done. "You must think I'm a jerk."

Really? Nothing? I couldn't even make something up, like, 'nice shoes.' Anything?! It was as if my mouth was paralyzed.

"Look. I'm really sorry I started ignoring you after tutoring last year. Jill's crew made it difficult for me," Ryan admitted sheepishly.

What was going on? Was this some sort of horrible prank where I'd start being nice to him and he'd laugh and tell me what a moron I was?

"Are you serious right now?" Wow. I really said that. And I said it so rudely. Ryan looked like I had punched him.

He shook his head and actually seemed embarrassed. "You're right. I'm sorry I bothered you."

And he started to leave. To leave!

And I still stood there, like someone had turned me into a statue. Come on! Do something!

"Ryan, wait!" Good. That was good.

Ryan turned around and he actually had hope in his eyes. Real, honest hope.

"I'm not used to people being nice to me," I confessed with as much sincerity as I could muster.

Ryan's face was immediately ridden with guilt. "I'm sorry," was all he could say.

He said it so sweetly my gut twisted with sympathy. "It's okay. It's just that in the past when people have been nice to me, it's been because Jill put them up to it to humiliate me in some way."

"I'm sick of Jill and her team of morons." Ryan practically spat out Jill's name to my pleasure. "Can I walk you to class?" He looked at me with those big brown eyes and I hoped my face wasn't turning bright red.

"Sure." Was this really happening? I still couldn't wrap my head around it. It had to be some kind of trick. I resolved myself to not get too excited until I was sure Ryan was on the level.

"Physics, right?"

He knew my schedule, which could be very bad or very good. Bad because Jill told him my schedule, so this would all be a part of the plan, or good because he *knew* my schedule... which meant he actually paid attention to what I was doing and where I was going.

"Yeah." Good. Cool and not too desperate. Like I wasn't about to vomit from nerves.

"Chelsan!"

I turned around to see Bill standing in front of Ryan and I like he was the Sheriff of Nottingham and Ryan was Robin Hood.

"Is he bothering you?!" Bill was actually angry. I had never seen him like this before. I was so surprised by his behavior I didn't know what to say. Unfortunately, he took that as a yes.

Bill slammed Ryan up against a set of mahogany lockers, pinning him with his arm. "Leave her alone." Bill was a couple inches shorter than Ryan, making him six-one, which was nothing to scoff at, but he was much more muscular and Ryan looked like a fly trapped by a spider.

My mouth had literally dropped. And as much torture as it was seeing Ryan wrongfully accused, it was almost a little exciting to see Bill so protective of me. I knew we were buds, but I didn't realize how far he would go to keep me safe. He was actually being violent. The angriest I had ever seen him was when Jill rigged it for him to be Homecoming King, and even then he had barely raised his voice.

"Bill. He's not bothering me, I swear! Let him go." I finally found my voice.

"Are you sure? It looked like you were about to throw-up."

Seriously? That actually showed?

"I'm sure. He was just walking me to class."

Bill let Ryan go with an apologetic shrug, but his eyes were still fuming.

Ryan, meanwhile, had let this whole event take place without so much as a peep or a struggle.

A crowd had formed and everyone waited with anticipation as to what would happen next.

Ryan straightened his shirt and combed his hand through his hair as if contemplating what his next move should be. Then he turned to me and did something that made every fiber of my being melt and tingle all at once.

He kissed me.

I felt like I was going to explode and collapse. There was no way my knees were going to function much longer if he kept this up.

Ryan pulled away, his hands cradling my face. He smiled. "See you later."

And then he was gone, down the hall, past the shocked observers and out of sight.

My whole body was shaky, including my brain. But as out of control as I felt, I didn't want the feeling to end. In fact, it just hit me that Ryan was gone. Hey!

"Chelsan?! What are you doing with Ryan Vaughn? Are you guys dating or something?" Bill looked at me with an emotion I couldn't quite place. One second it looked like anger, the next like I had killed his puppy.

The bell rang for class to start. The crowd dispersed, heading to their respective classes.

"No, Bill, Ryan and I aren't dating."

"Then why did he just kiss you?" Bill returned to his calmer demeanor as if me admitting that Ryan and I weren't dating comforted him in some way.

"I dunno, maybe because you slammed him against the lockers? He had to save face somehow." Damn it! That was probably it! It wasn't me that he wanted, he just didn't want to look like a wimp in front of the school. Uuugh! I felt like crap now.

Bill's face flushed with embarrassment. "Sorry about that. I really thought he was messing with you."

"It's okay. At least I know that you'll always have my back." And I meant it. Knowing *that* was the only thing keeping me from crawling into a hole and dying right now.

"Always."

The halls were empty.

"Better get to class." I smiled at Bill and he smiled back.

"I'll pick you up from work and drive you home. What time are you done?"

"Nine o'clock."

"See you then." Bill hurried toward his class until I was alone in the hallway.

With a deep and loud exasperated sigh, I made my way to Physics, knowing that the rest of the day would be spent re-playing Ryan's kiss. Well meant or not, it was still achingly unforgettable.

The rest of school was highly uneventful. At lunch, Nancy made me give her a play by play of the Bill and Ryan showdown. She was most interested in the kiss, which apparently had spread throughout the high school pipelines like wild fire. I didn't go into too much detail, but I admitted that it was nice.

Nancy seemed a little disappointed by my lack of enthusiasm, but I didn't want word to get around that I was as flustered about it as I was. The only nice thing about the whole dramatic event was that Nancy appeared to have forgotten all about the conversation we were supposed to have about my gift. A small relief. I knew it was coming, but at least I wouldn't have to deal with it today. It would give me a chance to do the research about this new study myself and hopefully have more answers.

Besides, I was still paranoid about the whole Ryan thing. I needed more information before I moved forward. Ryan may want to have nothing to do with me after Bill smooshed him against the lockers. Most likely he was licking his wounds and would never see or speak to me again.

Probably for the best.

I took the Hover-Shuttle to work. *Mel's Ice Cream and Sodas.* It was still within my safety zone of the trailer park and it also happened to be the a popular hang-out for students from my school. They just loved to come in and have me serve them (like having money didn't already equip them with a hefty superiority complex over me).

Mel's was located on a beautiful cobblestone road lined with maple trees. Even though the need for roads and highways weren't necessary since all the vehicle traffic was sky level, they were still used as landing stations, decoration for shoppers, and more importantly, historical landmarks. I had to play sick my sophomore year when my history class took a field trip to a freeway called the 405. Supposedly, when people still drove land cars it was one of the busiest streets in the country and, according to my teacher, it was mainly a parking lot in its busiest times. As over-populated as our planet was, traffic wasn't really a problem since we had seven levels of hover airspace. Sometimes there were so many hovers above one area that it looked like cloud cover, blocking out the sun completely, 'But at least the cars are moving,' my mom would always say.

Mel's was one of the many little shops that were reminiscent of small cottages. The rooftops were thick clay tiles that gave the street the appearance of something out of a storybook. I had to admit there were worse places I could spend eternity.

I entered the shop, which was packed with people. I nearly cringed when I saw Jill sitting in the corner booth with her pack of hyenas. There was no way I going to avoid a confrontation with her. Not after the whole *Ryan* thing. She'd feel like I was encroaching on her territory.

I made my way past the red and white striped booths and black Formica-topped tables, lifted the flap of the bar, dropped it behind me, waved at Roger behind the cash register and walked into the back of the ice-cream shop.

Mel, the owner, sat at his desk in the corner doing paperwork with his usual large grin. He was heavy-set in a jolly way, balding (a rarity, but Mel started Age-pro at thirty-five and he was scared of hair implants), with small features that made him look like someone placed a tiny face on a large round canvas which happened to be his mug. Mel was just about the nicest person

I'd ever met. He considered his employees his family since he had none of his own. I'd do anything for Mel, including taking Jill's abuse so as not to disturb the other customers. Oh boy. Better mentally prepare.

"You okay, Chelsan? You're not catching what Jenny has are you? Just terrible, she's been puking up a gut for two days now. You'd think with all the diseases they've cured, the flu would have been one of them! At least you can't die from it, I suppose, but still... I sent matzo ball soup to her house this morning. I hope she gets better soon." Mel looked very disturbed at Jenny's bad health.

"I'm fine. I better get out there. Roger looks like he's going to explode."

Mel chuckled and nodded toward the giant-sized fridge next to me. "Better pull out more shake mix. I think we're running low out there."

I nodded, went into the freezing refrigerated chamber, grabbed a twenty-pound container full of shake mix and headed back to the melee of the shop.

Roger finished helping a customer and turned to me with a groan that could only come from someone who has worked in the service industry. Roger was a few years older than me and lived at a trailer park a couple miles away from mine. He was a good solid guy, always helped anyone in need, volunteered for just about anything: someone you could count on. His brown hair was short and curly, his face delicate, almost feminine-like in a pretty-boy kind of way. Very popular with the ladies. Even Jill would sometimes stoop to flirt with him.

"How long has it been busy?" I asked.

Normally, it wouldn't get crazy for another couple of hours.

"Since your school let out. I gotta warn you, I've been hearing your name come up *a lot*. Especially from your favorite." He nodded toward Jill.

"Yeah. Long story." I really didn't want to get into with Roger. He'd find the whole thing amusing, of course, but if Jill overheard me talking about Ryan, she'd find some way of turning it against me and embarrass me somehow. "I'll tell you later when it's not so crowded." I gave Roger a meaningful glance and he nodded in understanding.

"Gotcha. Don't you think it would have been easier if you went to regular school like the rest of us?"

"You have no idea, but Geoffrey Turner is one of the top schools in the country." I gave Roger the usual spiel. I had it memorized. I literally had a double life, the *fake* one where everyone thought I was an over-achiever that planned on going to the best schools and would have an amazing career, and the *real* one where I brought dead things to life and couldn't step out of a four mile radius from my home or my jerk step-dad would drop dead and rot on our trailer floor.

"I know. And just so you know, us *park people* are *really* proud of you. It's always an inspiration to see someone succeed and get out."

Roger smiled with pride, like he was living vicariously through me. My heart dropped slightly. There were a lot of people in the parks who saw me as an inspiration. I didn't want to think of how disappointed they'd be when I ended up staying at the ice-cream parlor and doing nothing with my life.

"Hey, no pressure. Relax, you look like you're going to cry."

I obviously hadn't perfected the art of hiding what I was thinking. I definitely needed to work on that. "I've just had a crazy day."

"You're killing me! What happened?" Roger salivated for the gossip.

"Later. Trust me."

"So, trying to sleep your way into money." Jill's voice came out of nowhere. How did she sneak up on me like that?

I turned to face her and there she was with Joan at her side sneering at me.

"Do you need a re-fill on that shake?" I asked in the most sickly sweet voice I could muster.

"Yes, but I don't want your dirty hands touching my glass. What's his name here will do just fine." Jill gave Roger the empty glass and he took it with a wink of encouragement to me.

"What do you want, Jill?" I wanted this to be over.

"I want you to stay away from Ryan Vaughn. Stick to your own kind, like *Shake Boy* here." Jill grew angrier by the second. I couldn't fathom why she hated me so much. She had everything: money, power, good looks. Why was she always so focused on making my life miserable?

Roger returned with Jill's shake and handed it to her. He had his back slightly turned so Jill couldn't see his lips and he mouthed to me, "Ryan Vaughn?" Then he made a face of genuine approval. "Nice."

I almost wanted to hug Roger. He was a friendly lifeline in the midst of attack.

"Okay. Will do. Is that all?" I raised my eyebrows in emphasis of the desire to end this.

Jill stood there, frozen in body, but eyes livid. I had seen that look before. It was the same expression Bruce used to make before he...

PUNCH!

Right in the face. Jill actually punched me! And it hurt!

"Oh crap!" Roger was stunned.

Even Joan and the rest of Jill's crew looked shocked.

And just when I thought that Jill had recovered from her freak-out, she leapt over the bar and tackled me to the floor.

This time I was a little more prepared, but not much. It was amazing at how awkward fighting actually was. In your mind you can imagine how you'd be, what you'd do, how you'd defend yourself, but when someone was actually on top of you, wrestling you to the ground, your basic instincts kicked in.

Fight or flight. Those are pretty much your two options, and as I knew from Bruce, mine was fight.

I grabbed Jill's wrists to stop her hands from wrapping themselves around my neck. Her face was distorted and snarling from anger. She had finally reached her limit. With the combination of being caught taking Age-pro, the fly that practically devoured her, Bill's protectiveness of me and Ryan's kiss had finally sent her over the edge.

Once I had a good hold on Jill's arms I used my whole body to flip her over so I was on top and...

BAM!

I punched her hard in the face.

That was when I felt the strong arms of Mel pulling me off of Jill's body.

Joan quickly ran around to the other side of the bar and

helped Jill up, yelling, "YOU should fire her! She attacked Jill!"

"I did not! She punched me and then Amazon'd it over the bar!" I couldn't believe Joan was actually trying to go there.

"It's true, Mel, Chelsan didn't do anything but defend herself." Roger was obviously having none of Joan's shenanigans either.

"Like I would ever stoop to fighting!" Jill caught on to Joan's tactics. "And I have a room full of witnesses who will back me up." Jill smiled at me, regaining her evil calm and turned to Mel with as much malice as I've ever seen from her. "And if you don't fire her, my father will be coming down here and closing up this fine establishment, so I suggest you rid yourself of the scum that works here."

Mel looked like he wanted to kill Jill himself, but I knew Jill would make good on her promise of destruction. I turned to Mel before he had a chance to decide. "It's okay, Mel, I'll leave."

Mel's face burned with fury. He wheeled on Jill, but I stepped in front of him before he'd do anything he'd regret, and whispered so Jill couldn't listen. "Don't. You'll lose everything."

Mel did something then that I didn't expect. He hugged me and bent close so only I could hear, "I'll fix this." He pulled away and turned to the room full of staring customers. "Nothing more to see here. Go back to your business."

Everyone pretended to do just that, but there were still flickering glances of curiosity from the audience.

I gave one last look at Roger and could tell he was still enraged at the unfairness of it all.

"I might just have to press charges." Jill embraced this ruse full force now.

I turned to her with as much fury as I could evoke. "Then I might just have to report your Age-pro use to the proper authorities. It stays in your system for at least two weeks after you stop. All they'd have to do is a blood test." I totally lied. I had no idea if Age-pro stayed in your system or not, but from the horror on Jill's face, neither did she. "Even *daddy* can't get you out of that one," I added for measure.

It was the equivalent of another punch.

Jill fixed her hair and straightened out her clothing. "I suppose you being fired is enough punishment."

I shook my head and left. I had another semester's tuition due later this year and without a job there was no way I could pay it. Jill knew that. And then it hit me.

She had planned the whole thing.

That was why the shop was so full. Full of witnesses she controlled. I should have known something was up. She was waiting for me to hit her back and I fell for it. Though that look of rage on her face was as real enough, and Joan acted pretty surprised when Jill punched me and leapt over the bar. Jill probably expected me to punch her first when she made the comments about Ryan and when I didn't bite she couldn't let the opportunity pass. I was still an idiot, but whether I hit her or not, she would have made everyone swear that I did, so it was pointless even thinking about it.

I made my way to the Hover-Shuttle stop which was located at the end of the street. I'd have to let Bill know that I didn't need that ride after all. I pulled out my cell phone and started to dial.

The phone rang a few feet behind me. I whirled around to

see Bill holding his phone and smiling.

"You think a fist fight between you and Jill wouldn't be on every cell phone in our school in milliseconds," Bill laughed with amusement. "Come on. I'll take you home."

"Thanks," was all I could say. I had to admit it was nice seeing him there. Bill was quickly becoming a rock of support I didn't think I could live without.

"Tell me you got some good licks in." Bill tried to lighten my mood.

"I wish I could have done more." I smiled back at him.

"We're a pair today, me with Ryan, you with Jill."

"I seem to be the common denominator in all these equations."

"Something worth fighting for, I'd say." Bill leaned down and kissed the top of my head.

I was shocked. As innocent as it seemed, Bill had never touched me, let alone kiss me. And as surprised as I was, it was actually kind of nice. Unexpected, but comforting. I smiled up at him and gave him a playful nudge in the gut. "Let's just agree not to get into any more fights from now on."

"Agreed." Bill put his arm around me and gave me a supportive squeeze. It wasn't like the fire I felt with Ryan, but it was just as powerful. Like the fierceness you feel with a friend you know you'd do anything for. A surge of intense loyalty came over me and I squeezed Bill back.

"Thanks for picking me up. I really needed a friend."

"Any time."

We arrived at his hover-car without mishap and he opened my door for me like he always did. I sat inside while he smoothly

50

walked around to the driver's side and slid into the car. He started the car and we were off.

"So, fired, huh?" Bill cringed.

"More like quit. Mel looked like he was going to throttle Jill himself for giving him an ultimatum like that. I didn't want her dad messing things up for him."

"If I could help you I would, you know that, right?" Bill was so sincere it made my heart hurt.

"Yeah, I know. Thanks, Bill."

"You need money? I think her plan was to get you to have to drop out due to lack of funds," Bill said this so quietly I had to strain my ears to hear.

"I figured. But I can't take your money. I'll figure it out somehow." The last thing I wanted to do was owe someone money. Especially since I was doomed to work crap jobs for the rest of my life. I'd be indebted to him *forever.*

"I wouldn't expect it back, if you're worried."

Did he just read my mind?

"But I, personally, would *have* to pay you back and that's why I can't. Thanks though, I really appreciate it."

"The offer will always be open if you need it." And he left it at that. Just like Bill: never pushy, never overbearing, just simple and to the point.

We arrived at my trailer and he lowered the hover-car to the ground. Bill quickly exited and ran around it to open my door.

"Thanks," I replied, a little embarrassed. He was being extra polite, probably because he felt bad about the whole Ryan debacle. I stepped out of the car.

"Try not to think about it." Bill tried to make me feel better.

And then he hugged me.

What was going on?

I hugged him back and pulled away, punching his arm to try and re-establish our normal buddy behavior. "See you Monday."

His face registered disappointment, but he hid it with a smile. "See you Monday."

Bill got in his hover-car and flew away.

"I thought you two were just friends," my mom's voice sounded from the doorway of the trailer.

I turned to face her and she looked angry.

"We are. What's your problem?" I didn't like the tone she was using to talk about Bill.

"Get in here."

I sighed and walked into the trailer. I kept Bruce sitting in front of the holo-tv and intended to keep him there during this soon-to-be painful conversation.

"Bill is a nice guy," I defended. I had this argument with my mom about five times a month. For some reason she didn't like Bill. Any time I'd mention him she'd ask me if there were any other boys at school that I liked. My reply would always be a groan and a giant no, but it was as if she knew I had a hopeless crush on Ryan and wanted me to do something about it.

"I know you think so, but I don't trust him. I see the way he looks at you. Aren't there any other boys at school that you like?"

SEE?!

"Mom, he doesn't look at me in any way but friendship." Which was true. Though he did just kiss the top of my head and that hug felt a little too tight.

"I saw that. I know you don't feel that way about him and you should tell him. Maybe he'll leave you alone after you deflate his ego a little."

"Charming, Mom."

"Well… wait a minute. What are you doing home so early?"

Uh oh. Here came another painful topic.

"I quit."

"Good. I don't like you working *and* going to school."

What? Not even a *why?* Or what happened? Just: *Good.*

"Good? I have no idea where my tuition is going to come from now." I was a little angry at her response.

"You'll just have to go to public school like the rest of us did," Mom responded with an air of pleasure.

I couldn't even stomach the rest of the conversation. "I'm going to bed."

I stalked past her and went into my room, slamming the flimsy aluminum door. I pulled out my reader, searched the directory for the Scientific Journal and downloaded the study Mr. Alaster referred to about resurrection.

After a few minutes my eyes grew heavy and I couldn't keep focused on what I was reading. I pulled my comforter on top of me and laid my head on my pillow, falling instantly asleep.

Chapter Two

I awoke to the sounds of clunking and clacking from the kitchen.

"Mom, seriously?!" I yelled through my wall. She was about to go fuss around in her garden and she was arranging her tools. The reason I knew this was because it had become an annoying Saturday tradition that would never fail to wake me up. She hated it when I slept in late. It was some kind of strange pet peeve of hers.

"Oh, did I wake you? Sorry, sweetie," her muffled voice came through the wall.

"Sure you are," I mumbled into my pillow.

My mother also knew that once I was up, I *was* up. I couldn't go back to sleep.

I suddenly thought of the Science Journal's report and I had a surge of excitement course through me. Maybe I could find some kind of clue as to how I had my powers. But the last place

54

I wanted to read was in this dingy trailer. I suddenly thought of the perfect place, just outside of the trailer park, where no one ever went, where I could just be by myself and concentrate on the report.

I wore the same clothes as yesterday and I seriously debated on not changing. I wouldn't see anyone from school anyway. "Is it hot outside?" I called to my mother.

"It's already eighty-five degrees," she called back.

Shorts it was.

Grabbing a pair of cargo shorts from the floor, I quickly changed into them and replaced the tank top I wore for a sleeveless fitted top. I slipped on a pair of flip-flops, headed toward the kitchen, blanket and reader in hand.

Mom was arranging her bucket full of gardening supplies, about to head out front. "You going somewhere?" she asked thoughtfully.

"Just over to my tree to read."

Mom knew the spot.

She smiled, "Well, have fun. You should take some toast or an apple with you. Lunch won't be for another few hours and you'll be starving."

"Thanks, Mom." I grabbed an apple and left the trailer.

Walking through the trailer park, I felt a rush of contentment. This truly was my home and everyone in it felt like family.

A black swirling hole came running toward me as I recognized Buster, a golden retriever that belonged to a little girl named Katie. This was the dog that was killed by a hover-car. The driver was drunk and swerved down too low to the ground, clipping Buster's head, killing him instantly. I knelt down and scratched behind Buster's ears. I made sure that he acted like he enjoyed it thoroughly.

Katie ran up to us slightly out of breath. "Buster! No more running away! You almost died last time!" Katie's long blond locks were tied in a neat ponytail. She had no idea he had actually died that day. When he was killed, everyone in the park came running out of their trailers from the screams of anguish flooding out of Katie. I just couldn't bear to see her giant brown eyes filled with such sadness and despair, so I kept Buster on my own leash and Katie had been happy ever since.

"Hi Katie, Buster looks good." I made Buster turn and lick Katie's face until she giggled and fell to the ground from his onslaught of affection.

After I was sure she'd had enough attention, I had Buster stop so she could regain her composure. She laughed when she said, "We're going to play Frisbee today."

"You guys have fun. I'm off to go read." I scratched Buster's head for emphasis.

Waving at Katie I walked to the outskirts of the park, a smile still on my face.

It took a while to arrive at my favorite spot. It was a field of rolling hills smattered with wild flowers and a large willow tree resting on top of the highest peak. The tree was a haven of shade on a particularly hot day. The only thing that could possibly break up the heat wave were the darkened clouds I could see on the horizon. Unfortunately, the clouds were making the air thick with humidity, but at least my willow tree would give me some comfort.

I walked up the incline of the color-filled hill leading to my tree. The flowers were gorgeous this time of year. Every color imaginable covered the landscape making me feel like I had stepped into a painting. Most people steered clear of this area because *with flowers came bees,* and lots of them. There was even a hive in my lovely willow tree. Thousands of these fields existed all over the world, another part of keeping the planet green and well oxygenated. I never minded the bees; they pretty much kept to themselves and if they buzzed around me, it was only out of curiosity, not the malice that most people assigned to the poor species. Even if you were stung, it was not like it was a life or death situation, unless you were allergic or something. But as many times as I'd frequented this spot not once had any bee killed itself by stinging me.

I pulled back the long hangings of leaf-covered branches that draped to the ground from the top of the willow. My private fortress. The buzzing of the beehive added a nice hum of life to the day. I laid my blanket on the ground, plopped down on my stomach and pulled out the reader.

I scrolled down to the Scientific Journal and brought it up on screen. I decided to start from the beginning since all the science mumbo jumbo went completely over my head last night. I had to admit, even awake and well rested I was having trouble understanding the terminology of the report. Words like neurotoxins and membrane proteins were cluttering the pages. I had to use the built-in dictionary just to read through two sentences. After the first pass, what I gathered was this: using certain forms of Voodoo rituals (i.e. ceremonial garb, prayers, herbs, blood, not specified whether human or animal, yuck) they were able to bring back the corpse for up to five minutes.

No matter how hard I searched, I couldn't find anything that explained my power. It wasn't like my mom performed Voodoo. And my dad died before I was born. It was disheartening and I immediately felt defeated. Was I some random fluke of nature? Some misstep of evolution? I had no answers. Maybe I was missing something. I resolved myself to asking Mr. Alaster on Monday. Possibly he'd have some insight that I couldn't see. I could never tell him my secret, of course, but in a round about way I could at least find out what he knew. Not much, I'd guess, but it was worth a try.

Flipping through the pages of my reader, I found a news clipping of Jason Keroff. He droned on about Vice President Turner and his crusty old body and I didn't pay attention to the rest. I simply admired his adorable smiling eyes and that sarcastic smirk he was so good at.

And suddenly, Ryan popped into my head. The spontaneity of his kiss. The dirty blonde mess of his hair. Uuuuggh! He was ruining my perfect crush on Jason. It took me weeks to forget about Ryan after his tutoring ended, and that was a professional relationship. Now that he added a kiss in the mix (which could have been totally insincere) it was going to take me much longer to block him out of my head now.

I quickly thought about my strategy of how to avoid him at school. It worked before, it would work again. No talking, no close proximity and above all, no eye contact! It was those eyes that pulled me in every freakin' time and I was mad at myself for wanting to believe, even if just for a second, that he actually might like me. That was the biggest mistake I could ever make. I had to make him the enemy or I'd never get through this.

Always remember, he ignored me and brushed me off last year. And even though he apologized, I had to believe that it wasn't heart-felt. Guilty feeling, maybe, but lying about it all the same.

THUMP!

I grabbed my head in pain. It felt as if someone had just hit my forehead with a steel hammer. What was that?

THUMP!

I began to panic. Was I dying? Was this some sort of brain hemorrhage? What was causing me this intense pain? It felt like an axe jammed into my brain and split it in two.

A green mist appeared in front of me, blinding me, seeping into my head through my nose and ears and mouth. I screamed in fear until the green fog started to clear and suddenly I was in the trailer park standing in front of my mother. She was in her garden, choking from the same green smoke. I reached out for her, but my hand went straight through her body as if she was a ghost.

Then I realized, I *was* the ghost.

I was at two places at the same time.

My body was still under the willow tree, but some other form of me was back in the trailer park watching my mother drop to the ground, coughing from the smoke filling her lungs.

I looked around and the green mist was everywhere and everyone in the park was choking and collapsing to the ground.

"Chelsan?"

I watched as a ghost of my mother stepped out of her writhing body.

"Mom! What's happening?" I couldn't hide the panic from my voice. Either I had fallen asleep and this was the worst nightmare I'd ever had, or something very unexplainable and weird was going on.

THUMP!

I cringed in pain and when I looke up, my mom and I were in an empty room. "Mom? What is going on?"

She wouldn't answer me. My brain squeezed with agony. I must have been having some kind of seizure and it was causing this insane delusion.

"I wanted to show you before it's too late," Mom spoke to me and her eyes met mine. There was a kind of desperation to her expression I couldn't quite put my finger on.

"Before what's too late?"

THUMP!

"Make it stop!" I cried out from the torment and suddenly Mom and I were in the most extravagant mansion I had ever seen. Almost every item from the stairway, to the tables, chairs, even the frames on the wall were all gold. It was like stepping into Fort Knox, melted down and molded into a house.

"Where is this place?"

Mom put her finger on her lips to quiet me and pointed.

I noticed a very pregnant version of my mom standing in front of Vice President Geoffrey Turner and his wife, Roberta. Uh oh.

Roberta was a Feline. A genuine cat lady. I had only heard about Felines in history class. Back in the early two-thousands (before Age-pro) women and men used to have surgeries to literally lift their skin off their skulls and pull it back to get rid of their wrinkles and sags. Gross. As a result the more they did it the less human they looked until eventually they started to resemble cats, hence the term Felines. On top of that they'd inject themselves with some kind of paralysis drug to freeze their faces in place. It was a horrendous sight; I had only seen pictures, but standing there in front of this woman with her long black hair pulled back tightly in a bun, midnight colored eyes and shiny-stretched-back alabaster skin, made me cringe.

Looking at mom was a relief to the eyes, in her early thirties, fresh, vibrant, beautiful. The complete opposite of a Feline. Mom had obviously started her Age-pro by then and her face was timid and scared. She stood next to a man and my heart nearly jumped out of my body. I was positive with every fiber of my soul that it was my father. He had my eyes and my lips. I nearly choked from the emotion at seeing him.

The scene was surreal, as if watching it on a holo-tv and hitting pause. All four figures were frozen in time as if we had stepped into a three-dimensional photograph.

This was so confusing, why was my mom talking to the Vice President? What were they doing in his mansion? And then it hit me…

"This is your memory."

Mom reached out and touched my face, nodding once. "I know about your gift."

My eyes widened. "You what?"

"I need to show you everything I know."

"But why now?" I asked. Still trying to figure out what was happening.

"Just watch."

It was like she hit play. The four figures started moving.

WHACK! Geoffrey Turner slapped my father so hard, he

actually fell backwards.

"HOW COULD YOU FRANKLIN?! After all these years?!" Turner roared in outrage.

I turned to the ghostly image of my mother to see her reaction, but she simply watched the scene in front of her, expressionless. As if these were events she had played over and over in her mind, eventually becoming numb to them.

"I LOVE HER!" My father screamed back. "AND I LOVE THE BABY SHE'S CARRYING!" He took a deep breath to calm himself and looked at Turner pleadingly, "She's your grandchild, father. Doesn't that mean anything to you?"

What? Did he just call Vice President Turner his father?

My mom from the past began to cry hysterically, holding her swollen belly, trying to regain her self-control. My father immediately supported her with his arms, keeping her steady.

"She's trash, Franklin, look what she did to you?! You know what must be done," Roberta replied quietly, but far more deadly than Turner's slap to the face.

My father's eyes seemed to pop from genuine terror. "You wouldn't dare," he hissed.

"You're back now and we forgive you, but we won't let you *mate* with this trash. These are the consequences you have to pay." Geoffrey Turner reached out and touched my mother's belly. "She'll be coming soon, I'd say my good-byes if I were you."

That seemed to crack whatever composure was left in my father. He punched the Vice President so hard in the face that he flew back five feet to land on his gold coffee table.

CRACK!

I cringed as I realized some kind of bone snapped in Turner. Roberta wheeled on my parents.

And then the most frightening thing I had ever seen happened…

Roberta's eyes turned a deep solid purple. Out of her mouth a large boa constrictor slithered its way to the floor and moved with lightening speed toward my pregnant mother.

"Mom," I spoke in a quiet, frightened voice.

"Keep watching," was all she said.

My dad grabbed a gold statuette from the mantle and threw it as hard as he could at his mother. It hit with such terrifying impact that Roberta crumpled to the ground with only the sound of the THWAP to her head. The snake vanished only milliseconds from my mother's feet…

…THUMP!

I clenched my hands over my head from the tortured agony of the returning…

THUMP!

The surroundings started to swirl and change once more. I didn't know how much longer I could take the throbbing pain. My mind was racing and sluggish all at once. I wanted to vomit, but I could literally feel the disconnection between my body and this strange form I was currently in.

Red, orange and black churning colors swarmed around my eyes with dizzying force.

In an instant everything was in focus.

Mom and I stood next to a ten-foot bonfire. It was the only source of light in the pitch black dead of night. The flames licked up the side of a silhouetted cliff face and the sound of crashing waves filled the unnatural silence.

I saw Geoffrey Turner and Roberta standing in front of the fire. Their faces were painted like skeletons and they were dressed in long black robes embroidered with intricate tribal designs.

Their eyes were inhumanly pitch black and they began chanting unintelligible words. The fire responded in turn, flames rising higher and higher, crackling and snapping like a furious counterpart to the spine-chilling peace of the night.

Roberta's feline face was monster-like in the fire's glow. In her hands, she held a picture of my mom. She threw it into the flames and the fire roared in answer.

Turner reached down and picked up a cruelly serrated knife with symbols carved into the handle. He screamed in a kind of tortured pleasure as he tore into his arm with the saw-toothed blade. Blood poured from his wound into the fire.

The fire was alive with what could only be described as ecstasy. Flames leapt into the darkened sky. Turner's voice was hoarse and crackling as he said, "The mother and child will die."

Turner's wound closed like an imaginary zipper zipped his skin back together, forming a large white scar. Both Geoffrey and Roberta's eyes cleared.

WHOOSH!

The flames instantly extinguished and we were all plunged into darkness.

THUMP!

Ow. Seriously, ow.

Mom and I were in a delivery room. My delivery room.

There she was, dead on the gurney, and me, the baby me,

dead in my father's arms.

The doctor was there. He placed one hand on my father's shoulder. "I'm so sorry."

When my father didn't respond the doctor shook his head in sympathy, "I'll give you a few moments."

The doctor left the room.

I was stunned by the memory. I turned to my mother. "But how?"

"This is how it happened," she answered and looked at me. Her eyes were filled with tears and then she turned back to the memory.

As soon as the door swung shut my father took a deep breath and placed my corpse on top of my mother. He leaned down and kissed Mom's lifeless body.

I gasped as my own father's eyes rolled back in his head and when he stared down at the two of us, they were solid red like a nightmare. He grabbed a scalpel from a nearby tray.

"I give my life for theirs."

And he slashed his arms and throat, dropping on top of our cadavers with a thud. His blood sparked and cracked as it seeped into our skin and clothes.

SNAP! The baby me's eyes popped open and she breathed in life.

As the last vestiges of life left my father, his eyes began to swirl black, like the holes I could see in dead people. Faster and faster it spun until it twisted its way out of his eyes and into mine.

In that moment, my mom of the past, gasped for air underneath my father's dead body.

"That was how you got your power," Mom responded quietly next to me. I could see this memory was the most painful for her to watch. There were tears in her eyes as she saw herself on the gurney screaming at the sight of my father's corpse.

Doctors rushed in, shock on their faces. They quickly removed my father and grabbed the crying baby to make sure I was okay.

The scene froze in an eerie melee of chaos and blood.

"Why didn't you tell me?" So many things were racing through my head. If she knew all along what had happened, why was she just now telling me? And in *this* freaky way, and getting back to the original topic, *how* was she showing me this? What was happening?

"I'm not done."

THUMP!

I really wished the thumping would stop already. I could handle the visions, but the thump, thump, thump, was going to make my head explode, literally. The environment began to transform once again, colors melting into each other like an impressionist painting until our trailer slowly came into view. We were inside and I gasped at what I saw.

We were in the memory of the day when I first used my gift. Bruce threw my mother of the past into the trailer wall. I almost started to panic when I knew that I was about to watch myself kill him. The seven-year-old me was screaming at the top of her lungs and suddenly Bruce was being taken down by the black widow. It was sickening to watch. It was one thing to reflect in a memory, but seeing it in front of me like this, like a voyeur watching some gruesome snuff film, was unbearable.

66

"Stop it, please," my voice was barely a whisper.

It was as if she hit pause again. She froze the scene just as Bruce dropped to the floor from the spider's poison.

"You knew I brought him back?" I could hardly believe it. My self-imposed prison was all a lie. She knew and let me do it anyway. I felt betrayed and hurt.

"It was necessary." Mom still wouldn't look at me. She just stared at the frozen memory in front of us.

"Necessary?! Why didn't you tell me you knew? You know I have to stay near him, or he'll rot." I still couldn't believe that she truly understood the facts of the situation.

She looked at me, her eyes filled with sadness and regret. "Just trust me, Chelsan. It was necessary."

"Mom. What is going on?" I couldn't take this anymore, and I needed to know what was happening.

THUMP!

"MOM!" I cried out from the pain.

And we were back in her garden in front of the trailer. The green smoke was layered in a thick fog blinding my view of the park. All I could see was my mother on the ground, choking. It was surreal standing next to a ghostly version of her and watching as her body on the ground was writhing in agony.

"I'm dying," she confirmed.

I looked around in panic. "No. I can save you!"

THUMP!

"I can't take that noise anymore! Make it stop!" I screamed.

"It'll stop soon enough. It's what's keeping us linked together right now."

"MOM! I'll go back to the park, I'll save you! Let me go!"

I was sobbing now. Keeping us linked in this strange way was stranding me under that damn tree. I could be half way back to the park by now.

"Promise me something, Chelsan." Mom looked at me as seriously as I'd ever seen her.

"Anything, Mom, just let me go help you!"

"Promise me you won't bring me back."

I caught my breath. And I knew then; she was really dying. "The thumping..." my voice broke from emotion.

"It will end soon." She tried to comfort me.

I knew in that instant that the thumping was her heart beat. It was the only thing that would tie us together. No! I could barely keep it together.

She nodded and then smiled through tear-filled eyes. "I love you, Chelsan. Promise me."

I could only nod in response.

"You must keep safe. Your Grandfather will be coming, and he *will* try to kill you. You were meant to die today. He won't stop until we're both dead."

THUMP!

And I was back under the willow tree.

I gasped for breath as I was slammed back into my body. The pain to my head was gone as soon as I returned. And I screamed for it to come back again. The alternative was far more excruciating. She was dead. My mother was truly dead. I could feel it with that last thump of life.

Feeling returned to my body and I ran as fast as I could through the willow branches, across the field of flowers and straight into...

…A nightmare of unimaginable proportions.

The whole park looked as though it had been hit by a tornado. Trailers were smashed, overturned, destroyed beyond recognition. The green smoke was gone, dissipated by the time I got back to the park.

But only *my* eyes could see the most terrifying picture of all. A sea of swirling black holes of people I knew and loved. My heart nearly stopped when I saw *her* just as I left her in the vision, my mother, lying dead amidst her demolished garden. A garden I had kept flourishing and alive for the last ten years. I couldn't bear it. I couldn't stand to see her like that.

I raced past the twisted metal and corpses to reach her side.

All I had to do was reach into her chest and bring her back. She'd be with me, forever. I couldn't live without her. I didn't want to. I needed her.

"I'm sorry, Mom. I have to," I whispered in her ear.

Every part of me fought the compulsion to break my promise and use my gift, but grief does terrible things to people and I couldn't think clearly anymore. In less than an hour I lost everything. She was my everything. I could barely breath. I could barely function. And then I did it.

Mom's eyes fluttered open and she looked at me. There was nothing there, just emptiness.

Her soul was gone.

I had violated her soul.

I immediately dropped my connection with her black hole and she fell to the ground once more. I quickly turned my head and puked all over the smashed petunias. I collapsed in a heap on top of her and something inside of me broke. I couldn't stop crying. My eyes felt like they would swell shut from the amount of tears pouring out of them.

Then I heard a noise that disturbed the agonizing silence. Sirens and the whizzing of hover-cars coming my way. I peered up from Mom's body to see what looked like a swarm of over-sized bees heading straight for the trailer park.

It was the press and emergency crews. I looked down at the crushed flowers and plants of my mother's garden and I knew she wouldn't want anyone to see her pride and joy like this. I concentrated as hard as I could in my heartache and slowly began to repair every inch of Mom's legacy. I made every flower bloom whether it was their season or not, every tomato was the richest red, yellow and orange, every peapod was bursting with marble–sized peas, every tulip, petunia and azalea were the most vibrant colors imaginable. By the time I was finished the garden was more gorgeous that it had ever been.

The onslaught of hover-cars reached their crescendo as they came to a halt a hundred feet outside the park. In a matter of seconds, I was surrounded by reporters, paramedics, firemen and police. Cameras flashed, people's voices melded into one loud shout, the buzz of hover-gurneys moving around from victim to victim. My head was going to explode from the assault on my senses. There were about two hundred camera crews all crowding around the most news worthy sight there.

The lone survivor.

Me.

Fantastic.

The voices slowly started to separate from each other in an annoying attack.

"Were you here when the tornado hit?"

"Is this your trailer?"

"Do you know the woman you're standing over?"

"Are you the only survivor?"

Too much. Too much. I instinctively scooted in closer to Mom as if she could protect me from all this. But I was truly alone.

"She's my mom." I found that when I spoke, every single person in the area quieted down to hear my response. "What tornado?" Mom didn't show me any tornado. It was some kind of green smoke. Tornados didn't give off smoke.

"Clear the way. Clear the way." Two paramedics swooped in and before I could respond they had hovered Mom away in a gurney.

"WAIT! That's my mom!" I cried out. I stood up and tried to take on the crowd full force to get my mother back.

"We'll take good care of her," one of the paramedics called over his shoulder and they were out of my view.

The pack of reporters closed their ranks, making it impossible for me to cut through.

"How sudden was the tornado?"

"Did you hide somewhere?"

I wanted them to all go home and leave me alone. "There wasn't a tornado. Something else killed them. Some kind of green smoke."

There was a roar of chatter almost like a rhythm.

"What kind of green smoke?"

"Are you suggesting that *smoke* caused this kind of damage to these trailers?"

Their voices became a single chatter yet again and I couldn't tell one reporter from the next.

"I don't know… I… my mom…" My head started to spin. Go away! Can I see my mom? Leave me alone! All the things that I wanted to say, but I found that my tongue was locked in place from being overwhelmed.

"Were you close?"

Did he really just ask me that?

"THAT WILL BE ENOUGH!" a voice came roaring from behind the press.

All eyes, including the firemen, policemen and paramedics turned to the largest man I had ever seen. I recognized him right away, the Mayor of Los Angeles, Norman Bradfield. Everything about Mayor Bradfield was round: tummy, face (including the three chins he was sporting) arms, legs, fingers, toes, everything! He had a kind and warm face on the holo-tv. He always reminded me of Mel and that made him great in my book, but in person he had a slyness to his gait. He was a shark, I could tell right away.

Everyone moved aside as he walked toward me. All the reporters made room for his eminence. It was as if they all sensed a photo opportunity within their grasp and they drooled in anticipation.

"Leave this poor girl alone," his voice boomed. At least, this, I agreed with. "She just lost her mother!"

Okay. True, but the way he said it made my skin crawl. He had absolutely no *real* emotion behind his words. He said them for affect only, no true sympathy or care about me and how I might feel. I had seen Jill pull the same kind of manipulative tactics all the time on teachers and other students; a fakeness I had developed a kind of radar for over the last few years. And this guy made Jill look like an amateur.

To prove my point, the Mayor actually leaned in close to me and gave the cameras the cheesiest, most over-the-top look of concern he possibly could. I wanted to vomit again, this time on his perfectly shined shoes.

"Now, now. From the looks of it, this girl was the only one who survived this terrible tragedy." Mayor Bradfield's voice was so loud it carried all the way to the furthest reporter.

"She says it was green smoke."

"She said there was no tornado."

I watched the Mayor's face very carefully to see what his reaction would be, and I wasn't disappointed. There was a brief second of what could only be described as panic. I knew something was going on here, and my mom died before she could tell me everything. She was so focused on letting me know all her secrets (and my own) that she didn't even think I'd want to know how she died in the first place. It was vital that I found out. What if this was a new kind of bio-terrorism, or some kind of natural disaster created by Mother Nature to control the population? What I *did* know for sure was that it wasn't a tornado. I was less than half a mile away. I would have felt it, heard it, seen it, something!

"This girl is obviously confused." Mayor Bradfield recovered with a smile that stretched so far across his face I didn't think he could speak. I was wrong. He must practice. "Were you knocked out in the tornado?" He placed his hand on my shoulder as if to comfort me, but he was squeezing quite a bit of pressure on me

73

to the point of… ow!

I removed his hand with an exerted shove, which caused a slight gasp from the swarm of press. "I was just over that hill and there WASN'T A TORNADO!"

I could barely hear anything from the uproar I caused. The Mayor put his hand back on my shoulder with so much force I was paralyzed where I stood.

"You see! She wasn't even here! How would she have seen…" He leaned down to me so only I could see his face. His eyes were raging at me. "What did you say you saw?"

With every chubby finger clamped down on my shoulder in a vise of warning, I spoke quietly, "Green smoke."

Mayor Bradfield turned to the press with his glorious fake grin on his blobish face. "Aaah, yes, *green smoke*. She was probably seeing the tail end of that tornado!"

I cringed and I could tell from the reporters' reaction that they ate up every word he said. It was so frustrating not having proof. But who was going to believe a trailer girl over the Mayor of Los Angeles? I suddenly had a flash of petty brilliance.

I concentrated as intently as I could, though it was difficult with the Mayor's hand now a permanent clamp on my shoulder.

It was enough. I had been doing this one the longest….

…Bruce walked out of the tangled metal that used to be our trailer.

It was like a lion's roar when the press saw him. This was more excitement than anything so far. Here in front of them was a true witness to what really happened. And lucky for me, I controlled every word that came out of his mouth. I was tempted to bring a few others back too, but that would be too

74

much to take on. Bruce would do just fine.

In all the upheaval Mayor Bradfield's grip loosened and I tugged away from him to run into Bruce's open arms. "Daddy! You're alive!" I made sure my voice carried out to the cameras and press.

It was complete and utter chaos. Camera flashes, screaming voices, and the Mayor like an island in a sea of madness, staring daggers at me.

"Sir, sir, was it a tornado?"

"Did you see anything?"

Bruce stepped forward with his arm wrapped around me. Everyone was silently anticipating what he would say. "I didn't see a tornado. All I saw was green smoke."

Take that Mr. Mayor.

Between the Mayor and I, we were making the Media's day. They acted like they hadn't seen this much excitement in years. And the more I thought about it, the more I remembered a lot of *natural disasters* like these, but they always seemed so straightforward to me, now it made me wonder.

Mayor Bradfield used the bulk of his body to maneuver himself in the spotlight once more. He pulled out a holo-tape. My heart leapt with anticipation. Holo-tapes were small devices that projected holographic images from a satellite. We'd be able to see *exactly* what happened, like a security camera from space. "Let's see the truth for ourselves, shall we?"

He activated the device and a holographic image of the trailer park appeared in front of the watching audience. It was just like before I left it to read under the tree. My eyes welled up with tears when I saw my mother in her garden, not a care in the world, not realizing she was about to die. And then…

A tornado.

An actual tornado touched down in the center of the park. It ripped through the trailers like they were made of paper, smashing them to obliteration. Bodies were flown around and torn apart in a terrifying spectacle of torture and destruction. Just as suddenly the tornado dissipated into nothingness, gone as quickly as it came. The holo-tape ended with an image of me running to my mother's side in the garden and soon after the cavalry arriving. There was no green smoke. There was nothing of what my mother let me see.

And then I noticed something…

The garden in the holo-tape was still ruined and destroyed. I looked behind me at the vibrant, gorgeous garden I had fixed for my mother and then again at the satellite feed. They didn't match.

This was much bigger than a simple tornado. I decided in that moment to shut my mouth. If the Mayor could manipulate a holo-tape then there were bigger players at work here. This had conspiracy written all over it and I intended to figure out what was going on.

"I must have just missed seeing it touch down," I pretended to confess. Then I made Bruce wobble a bit as if he had hit his head a little too hard.

Mayor Bradfield turned to me again so the press couldn't see. "Right decision." Then he whirled around, open arms, open face and with, crinkled-in-concern-eyebrows, motioned to two paramedics. "Help these two out, would you? They've been through quite an ordeal." After posing for one more picture with us, the Mayor started toward the middle of the park. "Come. Let's see the horrendous damage this tragedy has caused."

And the swarm was off, following the Mayor like ants chasing after food.

The paramedics gave us a once over and moved on to their hover-gurneys, lugging the bodies to their vehicles.

I felt a tapping on my shoulder. I turned around and came face to face with…

…Jason Keroff.

Gulp.

He was even more gorgeous in person, but standing in my mother's garden with *zombie* Bruce sitting amongst the flowers I didn't feel anything for my childhood crush. Jason leaned in to me and whispered in my ear. "You're in danger. Take this."

I felt something slip into my hand, it felt like a square piece of metal. "That's my contact info. Call me. Landline only. No cell."

And he was gone. Off to join the rest of the journalists.

After all these years of being infatuated with this man, seeing him only reminded me how much of a fantasy it really was.

My mom was real and the most important person in my life and now she was gone forever. It made meeting Jason hollow and uneventful. I wanted to cry, but I knew that it would immediately become a photo op for the media so I held it in and waited for them to leave.

I didn't have to wait long. With a bigger than life wave to the cameras, Mayor Bradfield entered his hover-limo and whizzed away to wherever Mayors go. The paramedics loaded the last corpse in their hover-trucks and with barely a minute passing, press, paramedics, police and firemen were gone, like they never came. I was completely alone with a drooling Bruce. I rolled my eyes and decided to do a little investigating of my own.

"Hey! Chelsan!" I turned around and nearly burst into tears when I saw Nancy running toward me. Her clothes were dirty and she looked pretty scuffed up. Seeing her made my heart swell with emotion. I didn't realize how much I needed a friendly face until I saw her coming straight toward me. Before I could move to embrace her, she tackled me to the ground in the biggest bear hug I had ever experienced. "Chelsan! You're alive! They've completely closed off the park for miles, but I crawled through the back fence and seriously, I was like a ninja, I stayed as low to the ground as possible, I'm a complete mess, but I got here..." She was rambling and I loved every second of it.

"Nancy, I can't breathe." Her hug had turned into squeezing every last breath out of my lungs.

"Oh, sorry. I'm just so relieved to see you alive! They said on the news there were no survivors when the tornado hit. They did a life scan and everything! How did they miss you?!"

"I wasn't in the park, I was reading under the willow." Uh, oh. If they did a life scan and someone was really paying attention they'd know that Bruce was *really* dead. I couldn't focus on that, yet. If Jason thought I was in trouble then I'd have to keep that piece of information on my "potential danger" list. Now that I knew Vice President Geoffrey Turner was my grandfather and what he was capable of doing to his own family, I had to be on my toes. Mom warned me he'd be after me and now Jason Keroff was cautioning me, too. I needed to be prepared for anything.

"I've always hated that tree! All the bees! But I'm completely grateful for it now!" And then she noticed Bruce. "Oh Bruce! I'm so glad you made it, too!" She turned to me. "So lucky." Her face suddenly went from relief to horror. "Your mom?" Nancy said it so cautiously and carefully it took away some of the pain I felt when she mentioned her.

I simply shook my head and Nancy hugged me again. "I'm so sorry, Chelsan."

I pulled away from her and made a decision in my head. I needed help and Nancy had more than proven she was someone I could trust explicitly. "Look Nancy. It's time we had that talk."

Nancy's eyes widened, but she nodded as if she knew exactly what I was talking about.

"Nancy, Bruce is dead. Really dead, like eleven years dead."

Nancy looked over at Bruce with shock and curiosity. "The frogs were dead, too, right?" I could tell she was already making calculations in her head.

"Yes. I can bring back anything that's died. Like this garden: it was smashed and destroyed when I got here, but it was my mom's and I couldn't let…" I choked. Thinking it and actually saying it aloud became much harder than I thought. I needed to keep my head clear for my mother's sake. She had warned me that my life was in danger and if I fell apart now, I didn't think I could ever recover. I wouldn't care if I lived or died if I let my grief overwhelm me, and my mom wouldn't have wanted that. It was why she showed me what she did. To protect me somehow. To warn me. And it was up to me to figure all of this out.

Nancy hugged me once more. Despite me telling her that I

was a defect that essentially made zombies, even plant zombies, she still wanted to be my friend. She pulled away and looked at Bruce. "So, nothing's going on upstairs? Or is he really alive?"

"No, nothing, I control all of it. That's why I didn't bring back my mom," I lied. I couldn't admit to what I had done. It made me feel dirty thinking about it.

"Good call." We sat there in the garden, facing each other. "I kind of figured it was something like that, but I didn't want to say anything because... well, because if I was wrong you'd think I was a psychopath," she admitted apologetically.

"I didn't tell you for the same reason."

"Ever since the frog thing, I've been doing some research on the subject. There have been more cases than just the Science Journal's report on the Voodoo necromancy. There are Egyptian, Wiccan, Indian, all sorts of places that have spells. Which one do you use?"

"None of them. I was born with it, or re-born, or I don't know. This is going to sound even crazier, but before my mom died, she took me back, back to her memories or something. It's why I know she wasn't killed by a tornado." I was still trying to process all this.

Nancy looked just as interested. Nothing I said seemed to faze her. She had obviously been thinking about this for a long time. Three years, I guess. The frogs made more of an impact than I originally thought.

"What did she show you?"

"My grandparents didn't want my mom and me to live, so they did some ritual so that we'd die when I was born. It worked and my father killed himself over our dead bodies, doing some spell or ritual and boom, we were both alive again and I got my powers." At least that was what it looked like from what my mom showed me. I couldn't be certain that I wasn't completely insane and delusional, but from the look on Nancy's face at least I wasn't the only one.

"Okay. When we get back to my place, you'll have to tell me *every* detail of what you saw. We can look it up and see exactly what spell they used."

A warm glow spread through me. It was like a comfort I had never felt before. Not only did Nancy believe me, she was helping me. It felt really nice knowing someone had my back. Like all this was real instead of the giant secret I'd been keeping my whole life. I felt liberated.

"Okay. That sounds good."

"How does it work, exactly? Your powers, I mean." She was very business-like as if she had an encyclopedia in her brain and she was scrolling down it to find the perfect information to help me.

"I see black swirling holes in dead things and I can connect to them and control them like puppets."

"That's freakin' sweet." Nancy started to laugh and I felt a pang of doubt. Please don't tell me she was placating me this whole time. No, no, no, I couldn't take that. "Did you make that fly attack Jill yesterday? That was classic."

Huge sigh of relief. I even laughed a little myself. "Yeah."

"Nice." Nancy was simply thrilled, and I could tell she was relieved I was finally telling her the truth. She had been waiting for it for a long time. Nancy looked around at the destruction of the park. "We should get out of here. Clean-Up will be here soon."

Clean-Up. An organization "dedicated to cleaning up the World's disasters before you have to!" Once the authorities had left a disaster area, Clean-Up came in and pretty much wiped the vicinity clean and planted trees or fields of flowers, like the one up by my willow tree, which basically meant I was running out of time.

"I have to find out what happened." I couldn't leave yet. There had to be something here to tell me the truth.

"How?" Nancy stood up and helped me to my feet. I kept Bruce sitting in the tulips, slumped over.

I scanned the area and noticed something very interesting. "They're all dead."

"Yeah... these are things we know already." Nancy's voice was laced with concern.

"No, I mean, flies, rats, bees, cockroaches, spiders all of them." This had to have significance.

"Wouldn't a tornado kill everything?" I could tell Nancy was asking to help with the thinking process, not to try and prove me wrong.

"It would definitely kill most of them, but *all?* I just wish I could *see* what happened." So frustrating!

"Can't you use Bruce or something? If you can control his movements why couldn't you see through his eyes or something?" I obviously had a bewildered look on my face because Nancy immediately appeared abashed. "Sorry, I don't know how this whole thing works."

"No, no. I just never thought about doing something like that before," I confessed. My mind raced. Was that possible? Could

I actually play back what Bruce saw when he was experiencing *the tornado*? I decided it was worth a try. "I'm going to try it."

Nancy's eyes lit up with excitement. "Cool. Tell me what I should do."

"Just keep an eye out for Clean-Up. This may take a bit. I'm not sure what I'm doing."

Nancy gave a mock salute and her face was filled with anticipation of what would happen next.

I made Bruce stand and walk over to me.

Nancy let out a small gasp of excitement. "Sorry," she mumbled.

I reached up to Bruce's face and placed my hands on his puffy cheeks. I could still see the tiny bits of rotted skin under his stringy hairline from when I had left my four-mile radius and let him die the second time. I needed my mind clear of any distractions, so I closed my eyes and began to concentrate as hard as I could. "Okay, Bruce, show me what you saw."

Nothing.

I tried not to think of what must be going on in Nancy's head right now.

Stop it!

Focus.

Come on, Bruce. I shut everything out, sounds, movement, smells and lastly thoughts…

…a red neon glow filled the inside of my head like a psychedelic balloon bouncing around my eye-sockets. Small pinpoints of light appeared in the far distance. I instinctively moved toward them, or soared toward them would be a better description, until the tiny bits of light began to take form.

Suddenly, I stood in my trailer next to Bruce. He sat in his recliner watching the holo-tv and everything was as it was before the destruction.

I did it. I was actually there, or some part of me was there anyway. I looked down at what I thought would be my body, but there were only wispy shreds of the same red glow I saw before. I had no corporeal form. I was simply an observer. It kind of creeped me out, but I didn't want to become distracted and break out of what I was accomplishing. I hurried to the window and then I saw her...

...my mom. She was in her garden watering the roses. She had a sweet smile on her face as if all was right in the world. I wanted to scream and warn her, tell her she was about to die, but I had to remind myself I wasn't really there. This was just Bruce's memory.

Green smoke oozed across the ground of the trailer park like a devouring snake swallowing the life out of everyone there. People coughed and choked, dropping to their knees, falling to their deaths.

Mom saw what was happening and her face crumpled. She looked up at the sky and closed her eyes. I knew she was connecting to me under the willow tree in that moment.

Flashes of yellow moved through the trailers and I squinted through the green fog to see what it was. It didn't take long to recognize a HAZMAT suit and the men inside of them. Strapped to their backs, were two-foot canisters connected to spray nozzles and they were spraying my neighbors and mother with poisonous green toxin.

This wasn't a tornado.

This was an extermination.

I was about to jump out of the memory when the sound of crunching metal tore through my senses threatening to knock me out of my head. A large hovercraft, the size of the park itself was acting like a kind of magnet, collapsing and crunching the trailers like they were crumpling up a wad of fabric. Within seconds the park looked like it did when I found it. As if a tornado had destroyed it.

A large ramp from the hovercraft lowered to the ground and the men in the HAZMAT suits shuffled their way inside.

And then they were gone. The ship moved so fast I could barely see the blur as it zoomed out of sight. The green gas dissipated and I watched me from the past run up to my mother in her garden. I saw myself about to bring my mom back, as I reached inside her body to her black hole, as I grabbed onto her essence and…

I jolted myself out of Bruce's head.

I could barely breathe. Nancy's arms grabbed onto me and held me up for support. Bruce had fallen backwards, crushing the tulips.

"Are you okay?" Nancy's voice was frantic with worry.

"I'm okay. I'm okay." I took in deep breaths, trying to re-gain my bearings. "I saw…everything."

I turned to make eye contact with Nancy. Her demeanor relaxed a bit when she saw that I was coming back to myself. "What did you see? You only had your eyes closed for five seconds."

"Really?" Really? It felt like forever. Or at least as long as the memory lasted, but I still had no idea how this worked,

85

let alone that I could even do something like that. It made me wonder what else I could do?

"Yeah. You got all rigid and then, wham, you were gasping for air. I thought he tried to suck you in, or kill you, or something. It was really freaky looking." Nancy seemed scared.

"It was very weird, but it felt a lot longer for me than that. Look, Nancy we have to get out of here. I'll tell you everything when we get out of this place." I suddenly felt panicked. Whoever these guys were, they could always come back to kill stragglers. Especially a straggler who went on international television claiming this wasn't a tornado, but green smoke! No wonder Jason Keroff said I was in trouble. He knew something about this. I needed to contact him. Maybe he could help me.

"It wasn't a tornado, was it?" Nancy asked in dread.

"No, it wasn't. Nancy, I don't think you should get involved in all this. I think I may be in BIG trouble." I started to really worry for her safety.

"Oh no! You can't tell me in one sentence that you'll spill everything and in the next say you can't tell me anything! That's just cruel. We're going to figure this out *together*. No more keeping stuff in. It's not good for your complexion and don't think I've forgotten about that crater that stayed on your forehead for a week. If you had just confided me in the first place you could have been pimple free." She smiled now and I found it contagious.

"Got it. Acne free life from now on. But seriously…"

Nancy placed her finger to my mouth to shut me up. "I don't want to hear it. Let's get out of here before we end up with a California Oak on our heads."

"Yeah about that... I don't exactly have a place to stay." I was officially homeless and Nancy's house was seven miles away, which was why I had never been there before.

"You'll stay with me, dummy." Nancy started to walk away toward the edge of the park.

It wasn't long before she noticed I hadn't budged.

"Come on, Chelsan. Don't give me the whole 'I can't possibly accept' speech, you're staying with me and that's final."

"Um, Nancy..." I didn't know how to tell her.

"What? Clean-Up will seriously be here any second."

"Bruce." It was all I could sputter.

"Leave him."

"But, I was just on TV, they all think he's alive." I had my one shot to free myself of Bruce once and for all and I blew it for my stupid pride.

"So? Trust me, Chelsan, natural disasters are lame TV, no one will remember."

"But Clean-Up will see the body. They can't re-form an area until it's clean."

"Look, Chelsan, he's a ten-year-old anchor you don't need hanging around your neck. What about the willow? You're never going back there again."

Yeah. She was right. It was time. Time to say good-bye to Bruce. I nodded and made Bruce follow Nancy and me to the flower fields and my willow tree.

Knowing it was the last time I'd ever be here made me sad, but I couldn't say that a part of me wasn't a little relieved at the same time. Bruce would be out of my life forever. I could live my own life now. I wouldn't be tied down to an eternity of puppeteering.

And I didn't want to be in the place that would always remind me of the moment I lost my mother forever.

"Should we just leave him here?" I could tell Nancy was wondering why I wasn't moving.

"Give me a minute."

"Sorry."

I made Bruce sit with his back propped up by the tree trunk. He looked peaceful. I was controlling the bare minimum. Now that I had no one to fool, it felt wrong to make him act *normal*. Like I was abusing him or something. The real Bruce was a vicious monster so I guess we could call it even.

"This may gross you out. You might want to close your eyes or turn your back or something," I warned Nancy.

"I'm good. Do your thing." Nancy looked morbidly curious, but I knew after what she was about to see, she wouldn't be so quick to want to participate anymore.

Okay. Here goes. I reached into Bruce's fiery black hole that I had known so well over the years and...

...disconnected from it.

What happened next was revolting. Bruce's skin looked like a million flesh eating bugs were devouring him in a giant feast. Gooey glumps of blood and tissue slopped to the ground, revealing Bruce's bones underneath. The rest of his flesh oozed off his skeleton to create a chunky indistinguishable pool of blood and skin. But even that began to turn grey, then black, then disappear into the ground all together.

I could hear Nancy gag behind me, but as much as I wanted to do the same, I couldn't keep my eyes off of Bruce.

It all happened within seconds. One minute my stepfather was sitting under a tree, the next a pristine white skeleton. All traces of blood and flesh gone as if they had been consumed whole.

Then we both heard it at the same time.

"Clean-Up," Nancy muttered quietly. She looked dazed at what she just saw.

"We're far enough away. Let's go see." I wanted to get her out of there. I knew her *researching* and her actually *seeing* might make her change her mind about helping me. It made my power more real than anything else so far.

It terrified me, and gave me such a profound sense of guilt. Bruce was such a horrible person before he died. I never even thought about how I was violating him as a human being. I should have just let him die that day.

We walked from out of the willow's protective branches, leaving Bruce behind.

Clean-Up was a group of seven skyscraper-sized hover-trucks. Two of them were storage vehicles, equipped with giant magnets that picked up all the trailers, scraps of metal, anything and everything that was magnetized and stored them inside their steel bellies.

The third truck lowered itself to the ground and hundreds of ten-foot steel blades shredded the dirt below, loosening it for planting.

The fourth, fifth and sixth hover-trucks carried the plants (in this case it was indeed oaks) and dropped each tree to the ground, roots down, until they were shoved deep into the tilled soil.

The last truck carried a mixture of water and fertilizer, which was dumped on the freshly planted trees like a heavy rain, hardening the earth and securing the roots.

Twenty minutes later, Clean-Up had left and a forest of oaks stood in front of us. The trailer park was gone forever, just like Bruce.

Just like my mom.

"The quarantine should be down now." Nancy's voice sounded so quiet after the noise of Clean-Up.

It was like my home had never been. The wafting smell of wet foliage hit my nose as if it had been raining for days.

"Let's get out of here," I said just as quietly. "Are you sure it's okay if I stay with you?"

Nancy nodded. "Don't worry about my parents. They'll want to take care of you."

I had no idea how Nancy's family would really feel about letting a trailer girl stay with them even if it was just for a little while. But the truth of the matter was, I had no idea what I was going to do or where I was going to stay for the long haul. I was essentially homeless with no family, except...

...For some reason it hit me in that moment. Vice President Geoffrey Turner, the guy that my school was named after, the guy that everyone worshiped was my *grandfather* and the killer of my parents and everyone in this park. I didn't know exactly how to feel about that.

"Um, Nancy?" I figured I should tell her everything. We were walking through the newly planted trees, the ground hard and wet. Pieces of clothing and non-magnetic items lay half-buried in the soil. Over time all of these things would deteriorate altogether from weather and abandonment, leaving no trace of their existence.

"Yeah?"

The sound of the Hover-Shuttle whizzed above our heads. The driver would never have to stop here again. I didn't want to think about it.

"Um.." I wasn't sure how to broach the topic.

"You don't have to say anything, Chelsan, you've been through more in the last hour than most people will ever experience in eternity. When we get to my house you can rest and have alone time and then we can talk."

I realized in that moment that Nancy had reached her limit of *new information*. I'd have to tell her about gramps later. And to be honest, I felt like I could sleep for days. "Okay, later."

After about an hour of walking (I was suddenly very impressed with Nancy; she must have ran the entire way through trees, fields and foliage to get to me as fast as she did) we arrived at a Hover-Shuttle station. It was right next to the largest shopping mall in California.

The entire structure was made of multi-colored plexiglass from the walls, to the doors, to the flooring. It consisted of five dome-shaped buildings making the whole place look like rolling hills of stained glass. Built on top of a canyon-sized crater, it was hard not to have a moment of vertigo when looking down through the colored plexiglass floor.

The crater was a mile deep and with all its crags and fissures it was stunning to look at. The mall had been around for over two-hundred years and supposedly was one of the most structurally sound buildings ever made despite the fact that it was basically covering up a large hole in the earth.

There was always a loud humming at the mall from Hover-Service. Since all packaging was banned in 2070, Hover-Service took over everything.

Basically, once you paid for an item (you did this by sticking your thumb on a scanner and typing in your seven digit pin number that was linked to your account), it was then sent in a large hover-box and delivered directly to your house. Hover-Service traveled in a lower air space than regular traffic so whenever you were near a large shopping area there was constantly a mass of metal boxes whizzing twenty feet above your head.

It didn't bother most people, but it still bugged me. I guess I didn't shop enough to make it apart of my "sound" vocabulary.

"Uh, oh." Nancy nudged her head toward the end of the cobble-stoned street.

Jill was there with her cronies. She hadn't seen us yet and I didn't plan on her having the chance. "Let's duck into the mall. I really can't deal with her right now."

"Good idea."

Nancy grabbed my hand and led me through the first door we could find which happened to be a shoe store.

Nancy dropped my hand and her eyes lit up, completely forgetting I was there. Shoes were Nancy's thing. Her solution to everything was pretty much to buy a new pair of shoes. According to her, she had nearly a thousand pairs. I couldn't even imagine how much space that would take up: probably the size of my trailer. Or not anymore... Uugh. I didn't want to think about it.

Fortunately, the colorful melee of the shoe store was a distracting rainbow of eye candy. All the shoes were displayed on the same colored plexiglass that the mall was made from and it made it hard to differentiate between all the different types of footwear.

"Nancy, shoes later. We should get to the other Hover-Station on Fourth Street."

"Right. Completely." She was already focused on a particular pair of sandals. "Just let me check the price real quick."

And before I could utter a word she was making a b-line to the shoes.

"Nancy," I grumbled under my breath and joined her by the sandals. "Really? My mom just died and you want to buy shoes?" I was tired and grumpy and frankly, I needed to bawl my head off.

Nancy's voice was almost shaking and her eyes welled up with tears. "I'm so sorry, Chelsan."

My heart squeezed in pain. I knew Nancy wasn't trying to be insensitive, she simply didn't know how to cope.

"It's okay. I'm still in shock, I think." I nodded to the foot wear. "Go ahead and buy some shoes."

Nancy wiped her eyes and shook her head. "I needed to pretend everything was okay and normal for just a second. But it isn't, is it? Nothing will ever be okay again." Then she hugged me.

I was about to lose it. Pulling away, I took a deep breath to steady myself. "Let's get to the station."

Nancy nodded and motioned to the exit. "Is the coast clear?"

I cautiously looked out the doorway for any signs of Jill. So far, so good.

"Hey."

I turned to the voice and the small tapping on my shoulder. Oh boy.

There, standing in all his perfect glory was Ryan Vaughn. He combed his hand through his hair in an almost nervous gesture. Was he nervous? In front of me? Considering I still hadn't uttered a word, I realized I was pretty anxious, too. Even after everything that happened today, Ryan still made the butterflies do hang-gliding flips in my stomach. I didn't know what that meant, but it made me nauseous.

"Hey," I replied all cool-like. At least I made something come out of my mouth.

"I saw you on the news. Are you okay? Where's your dad?" I knew people would notice Bruce was gone! "I was really worried. I'm just glad you're okay." Then he touched my hair in an almost unconscious manner. I nearly died. I physically tingled all over. I really was going to vomit now.

He pulled back his hand as if he'd touched a hot burner. "I'm sorry. I didn't mean... I'll leave you alone."

I wish I could control what my face looked like. Why did I always manage to make him think that I thought he was a leper?! It wasn't this hard when he was tutoring me. Probably because I could just ask him questions about the homework and I was content to listen to him speak. We never did get too personal. And why did it always take me so long to respond! If the situation were reversed I would be in excruciating torment right now. Wait a minute, I was.

"No, don't leave." Do something! Grab his hand or arm or

something! I fumbled my hand toward his hand and somehow managed to slap his arm. The crater underneath our feet seemed like a really good place to be right now. "Sorry. I'm just still... I don't know." I didn't want to talk about what happened at the trailer park with him or with anyone. It was too painful. And in that moment, I was suddenly very grateful to Ryan. Even if it were for just a few seconds, he made me feel something other than anguish over my losses. At least Ryan torment was torturously good in some ways when I didn't act like a complete moron.

"Well, you didn't need to slap me though I probably deserve it." He was smiling. It was a relieved, endearing smile that made his eyes sparkle. It made my insides rise in temperature about a hundred degrees.

It was infectious. I smiled back. "Sorry."

Ryan placed his hands on my arms to grab my attention and force eye contact. "Do you need a place to stay?"

I was shocked I didn't explode right there.

"Sorry, I.Q. boy, she's staying with me." Nancy chimed in with a knowing smile and a quick look of *good job* to me.

Ryan released his hold on me and actually looked relieved. I wasn't sure if I liked that response or not. Especially the part of him letting me go. "I just thought, well the news said... never mind. Nancy's perfect."

"What did the news say?" Nancy was concerned.

"Nothing. I'm just glad you could take care of her."

He said it so sweetly even Nancy's face fluttered a little. "Of course I'll take care of her. Speaking of which, look at my clothes. I look like I just crawled out of the jungle. I need to change."

"Let's just go somewhere where there aren't any humans."

"Too late." Ryan nodded his head toward a swarm of lights and cameras.

Before I could run in the opposite direction they were on us like the leeches they were.

"Chelsan! Chelsan! Is it true you're staying with the Merryweathers?"

"Is Bill Merryweather your boyfriend?"

"Where is Mr. Merryweather?"

I looked at Ryan and Nancy in shock. Nancy seemed surprised by the onslaught of reporters and their questions, but Ryan appeared more sheepish than caught unawares. He glanced down at me with what could only be described as embarrassment.

Nancy caught on pretty quick as well. "I guess *this* was what was in the news, *Ryan?*"

"I…" Ryan was at a loss for words.

"Coming through," a familiar voice rang through the crowd of press.

And there was Bill, smashing his way forward to get to me, his face wracked with concern and relief at seeing me. He shoved clear of the flock and hugged me fiercely. "You're staying with me," he announced in my ear.

Out of the corner of my eye, I could see Ryan's face fall. And even though I was grateful for Bill's concern and friendship, I suddenly wanted to comfort Ryan and explain to him that Bill and I weren't like that.

I pulled away from Bill. "Bill, thank you so much, but I'm

staying with Nancy."

Bill's expression was one of awkwardness and disappointment. "But my parents already announced that you were staying with us."

"She just lost everything she's ever known and you're concerned about what the press might think about *you*?" Ryan stepped forward and grabbed my hand, holding it firmly. There went my knees again, I was shocked I was still standing. Why did I fall apart every time he touched me?

"No. I didn't... you're right, of course, Nancy is a perfect choice." In Bill's effort to hide his horror of what he was accused of, he didn't even notice Ryan's hand holding mine.

The press did though.

"Is *he* your boyfriend?"

"Did you break Bill Merryweather's heart?"

"Bill, I know you didn't mean it that way." I wanted to repair the look of pain in Bill's features.

"You guys better get out of here. Nancy, my hover-limo is out front. I'll stall these guys."

"Thanks, Bill." I smiled as sincerely as I could and Bill tried his best to look reassuring.

"I'll call you later," he said, though there was doubt in his eyes.

"*Come over* later, stupid." Nancy punched his shoulder and shook her head. "Just because she's not staying at your house doesn't mean you can't see her."

This seemed to brighten Bill's mood although at this point he couldn't stop staring at Ryan clasping onto my hand possessively. "Seriously, get out of here. I'll catch up to you later."

"Thanks." And we were off, running for the exit. I could hear Bill's booming voice keeping the press at bay with 'a surprise announcement from Merryweather Corporation,' it was a much juicier news bite than a trailer girl surviving a tornado. I'd have to make up for humiliating him later.

Ryan was still holding my hand and it was starting to feel like the most natural thing in the world. And in my chemistry-induced stupor, I wondered if I could surgically attach my hand to his.

The mall doors practically flew off their hinges from the amount of force Nancy used to open them. She was in protective mode now and wanted to make sure I didn't have to endure any more public scrutiny today. That and she kept muttering 'this is all my fault, stupid mall,' under her breath, which meant she was guilting hardcore. Normally, I'd try and comfort her, but frankly, all I could focus on was Ryan's hand in mine.

"Over here." Nancy spotted the hover-limo first and Ryan and I followed her toward the thirty-foot black stretch monster parked a few yards away.

Jill and her clone Joan stepped in front of the passenger door, blocking our way into the limo.

"This is Bill's limo, if you get in, I'll call the police." Jill's arms were crossed and her face glowed with superiority.

"We have his permission, Jill." Nancy practically spit on Jill's feet.

"We'll just have to wait for him, won't we?" Jill smirked. "Who knew that losing your trailer park would turn you to a life of crime?" Jill laughed, but Joan's eyes widened slightly as if even she was a little surprised at Jill's words.

It was impossible to believe that Jill could actually be that cruel. I underestimated her hatred for me. I could see in her eyes she was enjoying my pain, she was thriving on it.

"Get out of our way," Ryan spoke with such venom that even Nancy and I were taken aback.

"Holding hands, I see. I never took you for a trash lover, Ryan. I'm just glad I never let you kiss me on our *date*," Jill directed the last part at me. And I admit, it stung that Ryan went on a date with *Jill*. "You're just sloppy seconds, trailer girl."

Nancy apparently had had enough. "You heard the man, get out of our way!" She shoved Jill with some force.

Jill fell to the ground in horror and disbelief. Joan helped her to her feet and from the look on her face she wanted to stay out of it.

"Come on." Ryan opened the door of the limo and led me inside.

Nancy scooted inside and slammed the door shut. She turned to the driver. "Take us to my house, Gary."

"Everything okay out there?" Gary asked as he put down his electronic reader and brought the hover-limo to life.

"Yeah. Just get us to my house and away from here." Nancy sank back into the seat next to me and leaned her head against my shoulder in exhaustion. "Sorry I tried to buy shoes."

I laughed. The first real laugh I had since everything happened. My adrenaline was amped up to about a billion and I knew the crash would be coming soon.

Ryan turned to me and put his forehead to mine. He reached up and touched my face with his hand in a protective manner. My heart couldn't take this. I may have been eighteen, but I was going to croak of a heart attack any second now. His eyes were so intense as they met mine. "Jill's the trash, that's why she hates you so much. Don't ever take anything she says seriously, okay?"

I could only nod. My voice box would probably squeak something unintelligible anyway. I wanted him to kiss me so badly in that moment, but I knew I'd probably end up missing his mouth entirely and slobbering on his neck or something. I was such a clueless idiot when it came to boys.

Ryan pulled his hand away and placed his arm around me and included Nancy in the embrace since she was already asleep on my shoulder. We must have looked like quite the threesome to Gary, but he didn't say a word; he just drove the hover-limo towards our destination.

It only took a few minutes for the hover-limo to arrive at Nancy's house. Her street was a typical upper-middle class neighborhood. Perfectly coifed grass separated the parallel lined mansion-sized houses. It used to be cement streets and driveways separating their property over two-hundred years ago, but once hover-cars took over, the need for suburban roads became obsolete and if it wasn't a landmark or shopping center it was replaced with grass. In dry, hot places like California, large water silos were set at each row of houses (covered from view by trees and foliage, of course) and an endless process of water-filtration and recycling took place to constantly keep the grass watered and green. Residents were required to empty their fuel cell tanks from their hover-cars into the silo to keep the water fresh and replenished.

Gary landed the limo with ease on the hover-pad in front of Nancy's house. "Here we are."

"Thanks, Gary." Nancy was alert and awake now as she opened the door of the limo. "Come on, Chelsan, let's go tell my parents you're staying."

"What about Ryan?" I asked, not wanting to part from him yet.

"I live a few houses down across the street. I'll come by later." Ryan pulled his arm out from under me and gently nudged me to the exit.

I couldn't fathom that he was still near me, that he still wanted to have anything to do with me. I kept on waiting for him to laugh hysterically and tell me it was all a big joke. I really barely knew the guy and yet it felt like we'd known each other forever. I wondered if that was how it was for my mom and dad. I'd never know.

All three of us stood outside the limo as Gary lifted the limo up into the air and out of sight.

"Well… I'll see you later," Ryan said quietly. He actually looked shy and insecure. It made me wonder if he had been like this when he was tutoring me and I was just too oblivious to notice.

"Okay. See ya. Thanks for everything." Okay. Awkward. Neither one of us was sure what we should do next. I think he was debating on whether or not to kiss me, but he was obviously going through some kind of battle inside his head because he just stood there. And I just stood there. And Nancy just stood there.

"Yeah, okay, bye Ryan." Nancy had a lot less patience in this matter. "Chelsan, let's get inside before any more reporters show up."

Ryan settled for a wave and a slight nod of his head. "I'll come by tomorrow." And he sauntered off to his house.

I felt Nancy's hand grab mine and pull me toward her front door. "Come on, crazy girl. You'll see him soon enough."

I let Nancy lead me to her abode. The structure itself was one of the most modern I'd ever seen, but I hadn't been able to leave a four-mile radius my whole life, so that wasn't saying much. Her house was essentially three white stucco stories stacked on top of each other like a three-step staircase. Windows lined each wall, promising a bright interior and the glass was already tinted a dark brown to block out the sun for the day, making it impossible to see inside.

I felt a pang of nerves as Nancy opened the steel front door. Most people had steel doors and sometimes steel window shutters, essentially making their entire house a fortress. With Age-pro promising immortality, no one wanted to risk dying from a random crime or natural disaster, so making one's home impenetrable became a priority to the general public. Especially for the rich.

We entered her house and I was amazed at the impeccable décor of the bottom floor. The entry way was painted in soft golden tones to compliment the terracotta tiling beneath us. Directly after the foyer was the living room with a giant life-size holo-TV playing the news. It was like watching a play it was so crisp and life-like. A giant wrap-around black vinyl couch faced the TV and Nancy's parents' backs were to us watching the news cast.

"Mom, Dad," Nancy greeted her folks and I could sense the hesitancy in her voice.

Nancy's parents immediately turned to see the two of us standing in the entryway. I was put at ease right away when the two of them came running up to us, concern oozing off their faces, like true parents.

"Chelsan, are you okay? We heard everything on the news. We saw you too, young lady. Look at you, you look like you went on a safari. Go change your clothes."

This all came out in a worried rush from Nancy's mom, while her father hugged Nancy as if he hadn't seen her in days.

"You went through the blockade, didn't you?" her dad mumbled in her ear. "I'm so proud of you."

And then I was suddenly being slammed with a hug from Nancy's mom. "You poor dear." She held on tight and in that moment I fell apart. It was too close to having my own mom embracing me. I started to cry. And the harder I cried the tighter she held on. "I'm so sorry. We'll take care of you. You stay here as long as you want," she kept reassuring me and it made me feel safe and devastated all at once.

"Give her some air, geez, Mom," came Nancy's voice right next to me.

I relaxed my death grip on Nancy's mom and she pulled away from me, tears of sympathy in her eyes. "George, get us some hankies."

George hurried to the end table next to the couch and grabbed a few handkerchiefs from a small stack and brought them back to the two of us.

"I'm Vianne, by the way, and this is George, but you probably already knew that." She smiled as she wiped away her own tears and blew her nose for measure. "And I mean it. As long as you need or want to, you are welcome here. We've heard so much about you from Nancy. It's just so lovely to finally meet you. I just wish it had been under different circumstances." She kissed my cheek.

It almost made me break again, but I wiped my tears clean from my face. "Thank you. I really appreciate it."

"Your step-father is welcome here as well, where is he?" George was making sure I knew my whole family was wanted. They had obviously seen my fiasco in front of the press with Bruce. My mind went blank. I didn't know what to say.

"He died, Dad. Of complications," Nancy quickly interceded.

Vianne's hand went straight to her mouth to cover her shock. "We didn't know. The news didn't report it. I'm so sorry, Chelsan."

"I think I need to lie down for a while." All I could think about was collapsing and turning my mind off, even if it was for a little while. It was taking too much energy to breathe, let alone carry on a conversation of cover-ups and lies to people who genuinely wanted to help me.

Nancy grabbed my hand. "I'm taking her upstairs to my room."

"Good night. Let us know if you need *anything*," Vianne said over our shoulders.

"Night. Thanks again," I barely called out as Nancy dragged me up a spiraling wrought iron staircase leading to the next floor.

A long hallway greeted us with the same terracotta tiling as the foyer. The walls were Spanish yellow stucco and the doors were darkly stained oak. There were six doors total and they were all closed. Nancy opened the second one on the right and we entered my dream room (which happened to be Nancy's).

First of all, it was huge! At least the size of one of our classrooms at school. Blue seemed to be the color of choice in terms of decoration, from the bed, to the carpeting, to the walls, all different shades of the same deep ocean blue. The entire back wall was lined with shoes. Nancy wasn't kidding; she literally had hundreds of pairs. It was like she had a shoe store in her own room!

And then there were the holographic-pictures, and I had to stifle a laugh. The wall facing her bed was covered with holos of Jason Keroff, all with the same serious expression he always had on his face when reporting. She must have downloaded them from the same place I did, since I was seeing a lot of the same ones that I had.

Wait a minute.

Jason Keroff gave me his contact info.

He told me I was in danger. He knew about the exterminators. Or had suspicions anyway.

"Okay, so I'm obsessed, but so are you, so don't give me that look." Nancy had seen my horrified stare and misinterpreted it as shock from seeing her shrine to Jason.

"No. It just reminded me…" I knew Nancy needed to sit for this, so I led her to the bed and plopped her down. "Nancy, don't freak out, but Jason Keroff was with the press at the trailer park. He told me I was in danger. It was like he knew what really happened. He gave me his contact information."

"Okay, hard not to freak, Jason Keroff, seriously? You've got Ryan and Bill, Jason is mine."

"Focus, here, Nancy. And I don't really have Ryan or Bill."

"What were you saying about focus?" She smiled knowingly at me and then her tone turned serious. "Right. What *really* did happen anyway? You didn't tell me."

Sitting on the bed next to Nancy, it unexpectedly hit me that she knew absolutely nothing. Not who my grandpa really was, not about the green smoke, not about Jason Keroff. I had some explaining to do, so I started at the beginning and told her everything, all the way from the very details of my grandparents' ceremony, to what really happened at the trailer park. Nancy's eyes widened to the size of saucers in a few places and I could tell she was holding her tongue (a mammoth effort for her). When I was all finished I was more exhausted than I thought possible. And even though Nancy was just bursting with questions, she obviously saw this, too.

"You need to sleep," Nancy observed as she squeezed my hand with encouragement. "I'll interrogate you tomorrow." She smiled.

"Sleep sounds really good. Do you have a sleeping bag? I can set up over there." I pointed to a particularly nice corner in her gigantic room. It was a mass of pillows and looked exceedingly inviting.

"Oh no! Are you joking? Do you think I'm Jill or something? My bed is a double King! No way are you staying on the floor, you're sleeping up here in my nice fluffy bed." Nancy seemed almost appalled.

The bed was bigger than my room in the trailer and it felt ridiculously comfortable. "Thanks," was all I had the energy to say. I almost blacked out on impact when I lowered my head to a pillow.

I could barely hear Nancy saying good night as I drifted off to sleep.

Chapter Three

The whole morning was spent answering all of Nancy's questions. She was the most fascinated by the fact that Vice President of Population Control Geoffrey Turner was my grandfather.

"The one time I wish I could flaunt something in Jill's face," Nancy grumbled aloud. "If she knew that her daddy's head honcho was your grandpa! The most powerful man in the *world*! It's too juicy!"

"Not that juicy. He tried to have me killed, remember? And *me* living meant his only son dying."

"Yeah, but Jill doesn't know that!"

"Nancy, telling Jill anything is basically telling Turner." I could see Nancy's gears churning, trying to find a way to rub this in Jill's face, but I had to make sure she kept it between us two.

"Yeah, I guess you're right," Nancy groaned.

We sat in her back yard on a swinging bench secured between two trees. She lazily pushed it with her foot causing it to swing crookedly.

Nancy's property seemed to stretch on forever once you reached the back. There were several trees and lots of foliage in the main yard and in the back was a thick row of forest running down the entire street. I knew this was only an illusion of course. Each block of houses had a line of trees eight to ten rows thick in their back yards to follow with the Environmental Code of Oxygen policy.

The kind of trees also showed how expensive the neighborhood was, the lower middle class, had bamboo, Nancy's was pine, and zones as rich as Bill's were cherry blossoms and bonsais. It was weird how everything was so divided by how much money you had. Trailer parks like mine didn't even have tree policies, we just lived near wild flower and oak disaster zones so it made the planting of forest rows like Nancy's moot.

"What about the ritual? Does it sound familiar to you at all?" I asked, wanting to bring the conversation back to figuring out how I had my gift in the first place.

"I can think of a couple of things. I'll transfer some of the books I found to your reader so we can both get in research mode. I'm more interested in your father's spell. He somehow managed to manipulate Turner's hex and flip it back on himself. Sorry."

She must have seen me cringe when she mentioned my father's death. Up until recently my father was just an imaginative figure that died of natural causes when I was born. Now, not only knowing, but seeing my mother's vision of the way that he died, it was difficult not to be upset. "Don't be sorry. I want to figure this out. I just didn't know how hard it was going to be."

"We'll do this one step at a time. The first thing we need to know is *exactly* what spell Turner used. Then we can deal with… the other stuff."

We searched all morning in our readers. Nancy found some things, but there'd always be one thing different in the ceremony. And it wasn't a simple thing like candle choice or the kind of knife he used, it was sacrificing a goat or severing a limb. So needless to say we'd have to search elsewhere. I asked if Turner could have made up his own spell, and while Nancy thought that might be possible, she still wanted to find the base spell he used.

"This is very powerful mojo we're talking about here, Chelsan. This isn't your run of the mill curse. He *made* you and your mother *die*. That's as serious as it gets." Nancy leaned back on the vinyl sofa. We had moved to the living room once the Recyclers made their rounds on her block. Their machinery was so loud sucking up all the garbage from each house it made it impossible to concentrate. I knew I shouldn't complain, everyone's garbage ended up in Clean-Ups' fertilizer and mulch trucks, but listening to a giant vacuum cleaner sucking up slurpy garbage made me a little queasy.

"Why do I get the feeling that a spell that powerful wouldn't be found in a library download?" I began to feel like this was hopeless.

"I know, right? There has to be some way we can get access to books like that." I could tell Nancy was frustrated as well.

"Maybe I should call Jason?"

"Yes, please." Nancy immediately perked up. "He'd definitely have access to stuff like that."

I smiled at Nancy's enthusiasm for calling Jason Keroff. I almost wanted her to do it. The thought of picking up the phone and dialing his number made my palms sweat. "I'm kind of nervous," I admitted to Nancy.

"Don't be. He asked *you* to call him. It's not like you're some kind of stalker that tracked down his number and are trying to get a date. Your mother and your entire neighborhood were just exterminated and he wants to help you. You are the one in control, okay?"

Nancy's speech gave me some confidence. I had to stop thinking of Jason as someone better than me just because of who he was. I kept reminding myself that when I met him yesterday, I didn't feel anything. I wasn't nervous, I wasn't excited, I was just blank. That was good. I had to pull on that, if I had any chance of making this phone call without barfing.

"Okay. He said no cells, just landlines." I took a deep breath as Nancy practically squealed reaching for the phone receiver. I grabbed it out of her hand and put it against my ear. "I'm so nervous," I blabbered. I couldn't hide it, especially not from Nancy.

"Do you want me to do it?" Nancy was serious and concerned. I could tell she genuinely felt my pain, but as tempting as it was, I knew I had to be the one who called.

"No. Thanks though. I really should do this. Here's the number." I flipped up the metal device Jason gave me and a 3D hologram of his number popped up and rotated slowly like it was on display. Nancy quickly dialed and I held my breath as I

111

could hear his ringer through the receiver. Don't be home, don't be home, don't be home...

"Jason Keroff."

Uggghh. Major butterflies. "Um, hi, this is Chelsan, the girl from the trailer park. You told me to call you." I said this so fast, I wasn't sure if he could understand me.

"Chelsan, hi. Did you call from a landline?" His voice was warm, but had an edge of caution to it as well.

"Yeah, I'm at my friend Nancy's house."

Nancy leaned in to me as close as she could be without toppling me off the couch. Let's face it, Nancy was definitely in swoon city. She could barely contain her sighs and squeals of delight and I had just started the conversation.

"Okay, look. I don't want to talk on the phone. Can you meet me tonight at Alby's Bar and Grill at the Riverside mall? Say, seven o'clock?"

I took the receiver away from my ear and placed my hand over it so Jason couldn't hear me. "He wants to meet at Alby's."

Nancy's eyes bugged out of her head. "Tell him YES! What are you thinking?"

I put the receiver back to my ear. "Yeah, that sounds good. I'll see you then."

"Be careful, Chelsan. I mean it." Jason sounded intense and it made the pit of my stomach sink even further into the terrified zone.

"I will, thanks." And I hung up.

"You didn't say *bye* or anything?" I could tell Nancy was beyond excited and she could care less on how the conversation ended. "I'm going with you by the way."

"Of course." I decided it wasn't worth an argument and besides, I really didn't want to go alone. Jason said to be safe, and being safe meant having back-up.

"When are we meeting him?"

"Seven o'clock."

"That gives us plenty of time to get ready. It's three o'clock now, so maybe we could go shopping." Nancy's head was spinning now.

"Nancy, I don't want to go shopping. I want to find out as much information as we can before we meet Jason." I just couldn't get excited about meeting Jason like Nancy could. Jason equaled facing the fact that I really *was* in danger, and staying here at Nancy's I actually felt safe. I didn't want to lose that feeling.

"Okay, no biggie, I have plenty of stuff here. Let's get back to the readers." Thankfully, Nancy didn't seem upset at all, she was just excited to be meeting Jason.

The thought of the meeting tonight made my belly do flip-flops and not in a good way. I concentrated on my reader. It was an article on a Voodoo ritual involving the slaughtering of a goat. Why goats? What did goats ever do to anyone? I put the reader down. "You're right. Jason would have access to better stuff than this. We should plan our strategy."

Nancy's face lit up as she put her reader down. "Strategy as in what we're wearing or as in what we're saying?"

I rolled my eyes, but smiled. "You, seriously, have a one-track mind."

"I know, I'm sorry." Nancy smiled back.

The doorbell rang.

"Saved by the bell." Nancy jumped up from the couch and made her way to the front door.

I stayed put, but peeked over the couch to see who it was.

And to my shock, Joan, Jill's lackey, stood at Nancy's doorstep.

"And why shouldn't I slam this door in your face?" Nancy looked like she was about to punch Joan right there.

Joan looked over her shoulder constantly. "Could you just let me in, please?"

"Are you insane?" Nancy was in shock. "What would possibly compel me to do that?"

Joan was serious as she stared Nancy in the eye. "Trust me, Chelsan will want to hear this."

Nancy was genuinely taken aback. She glanced over at me for instructions.

"You can let her in," I replied quietly. I was curious as much as I was suspicious.

"Fine, but if this is a trick, I have no qualms about kicking your ass." Nancy threatened and I appreciated her loyalty.

"It's not a trick," Joan responded as she hurriedly walked inside Nancy's house. "Trust me, I don't want to be here either, but I thought you deserved to know what I know, considering what happened to you and your family..." Joan said with genuine sympathy.

"Know what?"

Joan sat down across from me.

Nancy sat next to me so she was facing Joan as well and she could give her dirty looks when needed.

"Okay," Joan began, still glancing over her shoulder as if someone would show up at any minute to catch her in the act

114

of being seen with us. "Okay. About yesterday."

"Yes?" Nancy was more impatient than I was.

Joan was one of those girls who could be physically glued to Jill and no one would notice. It was almost as if she had no personality of her own, she was essentially an extension of the monster. In fact, I think this was the first time I had ever heard her say more than three words aside from her outburst at Mel's when she was trying to have me fired. Why was I listening to her again?

"I don't know if this means anything, but it's been nagging at me and I thought you should know." Joan fidgeted nervously.

I was skeptical at anything Joan told me and wondered if she was nervous because she genuinely had important information or because this was the longest she had been away from Jill.

"Just spill it, geez, Joan, you're acting like a spaz." Nancy was at the end of her patience and frankly, so was I.

"Fine. The reason why Jill was blocking you from Bill's limo was because her dad told her to," Joan confessed quietly.

"What?" Uh, oh. I didn't like where this was going.

"Yeah. She got a call from him at the mall, saying you were there and not to let you out of her sight. He said he had direct orders from Vice President Geoffrey Turner." Joan made another sweep of the room with her eyes as if it was bugged and she'd be arrested on the spot.

Nancy and I exchanged worried glances.

"Say something. You guys look like you knew this was coming. Did you hear what I said? Geoffrey Turner, the most powerful man in the world, wanted Jill to keep an eye on you! That's not a good thing, let me tell you." Joan was apparently disappointed in our lack of reaction, but I didn't want to reveal too much to her in case this was a way of finding out what we knew.

"Thanks for the info, Joan, we'll take it under advisement. Now leave, please." Nancy was on the same page I was.

"I wish I hadn't told you." Joan was livid.

"What do you want from me, Joan? Thank you for telling me the most powerful man in the world is sending orders to his slave's daughter keep an eye on me? Thanks." I really didn't feel like trying to make Joan feel good about her decision to betray Jill. I was glad she did it, but she was still a bully that had been causing me havoc my whole high school career.

"Fine. See if I ever help you again!" Joan stood up and stormed to the front door, slamming it on her way out.

Nancy and I had to laugh at the dramatics.

"She's going to go tell Jill, you know," Nancy declared in a more serious tone.

"Yeah," I agreed with a sigh.

Nancy shook her head, "There's nothing we can do about it now. At least we know more than we did."

"He's probably having your place watched."

"Good to know. We'll have to be extra careful when we sneak out tonight to meet Jason."

"We're going to need a ride. The Hover-Shuttle seems too *public*. He'll have people looking there for sure." I tried to narrow down a plan.

Nancy was almost excited by the prospect. "This is like espionage. We're literally spies working against the government."

"Nancy, seriously, you're way too happy about all this. Hello?

My life is in danger."

"I know, but it's still exciting." Nancy went to the window next to her front door and peered out. "Joan's gone. She lives kind of far, I wonder if she had someone bring her here."

"You mean like Jill?" I asked what I thought Nancy was implying.

"She's been Jill's second limb since I've known them. I can't imagine her doing *anything* of her own accord."

"Me, either. Still." I let the thought linger.

"Oh crap!" Nancy leapt back from the window and scurried to the couch.

"What?!"

Nancy smiled, "You'll see in about two seconds."

There was a knocking on the door for the second time today.

"Who is it?" I asked Nancy, since she obviously knew.

"Why don't you get it?" Nancy picked up her reader with a Cheshire cat grin.

"Nancy?"

Knock. Knock. Knock.

"Are you going to get that, or what?" Nancy wasn't budging.

"Fine," I uttered and rolled my eyes for measure.

I stood up and made my way around the couch at a leisurely pace.

"Hurry up. He might leave."

He? Uh, oh. It was either Bill or Ryan, and at this moment I didn't know who I wanted it to be. Bill meant comfort and reassurance. Ryan meant butterflies and hot flashes. Okay, I was leaning towards Bill for the simple reason of keeping the contents of my stomach from making a projectile force out of my mouth.

I reached the door much quicker than I preferred and opened it slowly.

Ryan.

Breathe.

"Oh, hi, Ryan." Wow. That was the coolest I'd sounded yet.

"Hey. How are you?" How was he always cooler? It was as if he was in tune with everything I said and somehow managed to be that much more relaxed and laid back than I could ever be.

"Come on in." I opened the door wider to let him through.

Ryan came in and I shut the door behind him.

"Ryan! Hey, how's it going? Come sit over here with us," Nancy called him over.

She acted way more excited than was necessary. I guess that was what I got for letting her meet the crush of her lifetime tonight.

Ryan made sure that he sat down next to me on the couch, and even though the couch was huge, he sat so our legs were touching. Nancy tried to hide her obvious amusement by handing Ryan a reader.

"We're doing research, dig in and help us, genius."

My eyes met Nancy's with a strike of horror. Ryan didn't know about anything! What was Nancy thinking? My face must have turned dead white because Ryan didn't take the reader he looked at me in sudden concern.

"What's wrong?" The worry in his eyes was enough to make me almost forget Nancy's blunder. Almost.

Nancy figured it out quickly enough. Her face was actually red. She pulled back the reader and turned it off. "I'm sorry. I didn't even think. I forgot he didn't…" Nancy was at a loss for words.

Know was the end of that sentence. Although a part of me agreed with her. It felt like Ryan knew everything already. Like he was in on all the secrets and yet he wasn't.

Ryan glanced back and forth between Nancy and me and he placed his hands up in surrender. "I have no idea what's going on, but this is really weird." He turned to me suddenly upset, "Do you… oh man, I'm so sorry. You don't like me, do you? You must think I'm this clingy jerk. I'm going to go."

Ryan stood up, face flushed, tail tucked between his legs and I nearly had a panic attack.

"Ryan, stop!" I said that a little too loud.

"No, it's okay, Chelsan, I get it. I'm a jerk. Seriously, I get it." Ryan was genuinely hurt, and for no reason. I had to tell him.

"Ryan, sit. Please. I like you, dork." Just the way I always imagined telling him. Ugh.

It was enough for Ryan, he smiled his *heart-wrenching* smile that always gave me goose bumps, and sat down next to me. Even closer than before. "Then what is it?"

"There are some things you need to know about me."

And I told him everything. I didn't mean to. I started out thinking I'd only tell him what he needed to know, but by the end of it I guess he needed to know everything because I hadn't left anything out.

By the end of the conversation, instead of revulsion (as I fully expected), I saw wonder and awe in the way he stared at me. And he was definitely staring. Then his expression turned sad.

119

"I'm really sorry about your mom. She was a really nice lady," Ryan stated quietly.

At the mention of my mother, that familiar lump of anguish stuck itself in my throat. "Thanks." Then it occurred to me, "You sound like you met her?"

Ryan's face flushed red. "I did. About six months ago," he paused as if unsure if he wanted to finish this story. "I came by your trailer one night to see you. I guess you were at work, but she invited me in and made me a chocolate shake."

I was shocked. A: my mother *never* told me, and B: Ryan came to see me at *my* house! "What?"

"Don't be mad. She promised she wouldn't tell you and by the look on your face, she obviously kept her word. I didn't want to freak you out. I just wanted to apologize for ignoring you all the time. But I wanted it to come from *me* and not second hand from your mom." Then he smiled. "She gave me some really good advice."

I was going to ask him exactly *what* that advice was, but I decided that was between the two of them. No wonder she was so judgmental of Bill. She had obviously picked sides once Ryan had come to see her. He must have been the *other boy* she kept on hinting at. That was so Mom.

"I'm glad you got to meet her."

"Me, too." He smiled, "Do you think you could show me how you bring something back to life?" he asked a little shyly.

"Sorry, no dead things in here." Nancy punched Ryan's shoulder in a joking manner, but there was definitely some protectiveness packed into that punch. It was Nancy's nice way of saying, '*don't make Chelsan perform like a monkey you jerk.*'

120

"It's okay, Nancy. I would need proof, too, if someone told me all this." I tried to reassure Ryan and Nancy, but Ryan's face fell. He looked like I had kicked him.

He turned to me so we were eye to eye. "I believe you. You don't have to prove anything to me. I was just curious." He turned to Nancy, rubbing his newly smacked arm. "And I deserved that."

"No, really, it's no big deal. Here." I searched the room for anything dead. There was a particularly large cockroach, but I decided to keep insects out of this, Nancy would freak. And then I saw the perfect thing.

A small houseplant that was on its last legs. It was some kind of flower plant, but the petals and leaves were brown and dead. I walked over to the small pot (it was only a few inches high) and brought it over to the couch. I connected to the plant's swirling black hole and brought it back to life. Green leaves and vines grew higher, larger, fuller than this plant had ever dreamed, and white silky flowers bloomed from every corner. When I was done, a two-foot masterpiece stood before us.

Ryan's mouth had dropped and even Nancy was taken aback. I think it was good for her to see me bring life back to something as opposed to the nightmare I had left her with when I disconnected Bruce from his black hole.

"Wow." Ryan had finally spoken.

"Yeah," Nancy chimed in.

"I can put it back the way it was," I volunteered. I started to feel uncomfortable. What would Ryan say if I brought a human back, I mean, hearing about it and actually seeing it were entirely two different things. Nancy had been exposed to

Bruce, but I think she was in some kind of denial about that. I didn't want to scare them off. "Guys, *wow* and *yeah*, not very encouraging." I decided to take the honest approach.

Ryan put his arm around me and gave me a little squeeze. "You just became even cooler, and I thought you were just about the coolest person I'd ever met."

"Don't put it back. My mom will love it. This was her favorite, but she over-watered it to death." Nancy took the relaxed approach at this point.

"Okay. Just tell her I gave it to her as a thank-you for letting me stay with you guys." I turned to Ryan, his words hitting me like a ton of bricks. "You thought I was cool?"

"I think you're the *dork*." He smiled at me and then reached over and took my hand.

Somehow *dork* never sounded so good.

"Knock it off," Nancy said with a roll of her eyes, but I could tell she was happy for me. "Don't let Bill see you do that." She threw that in for measure, which made Ryan scoot in closer to me and made my stomach ache.

I still wasn't sure how Bill felt about me, but I wasn't an idiot. I could tell there was definitely more than friendship on his mind. And as much as I really liked Bill, I didn't feel the same kind of excitement and fire for him that I did for Ryan. How could I go from no prospects to two of the most sought after boys in my school liking me? And even after all the attention both of them had been giving me, there was still a part of me that didn't believe they *really* liked me. Like it was some form of "primitive-animal-ape thing," where as soon as one showed interest the other one became all territorial and mistook it for feelings for me. So really neither one of them liked me, they just needed to win the competition over my affection.

And then I was bummed again. That was probably it. I hated my mind sometimes. I always had to make a good situation turn into some logically horrible one. I never could believe that good things could happen to me and I didn't know how to break that.

"I'm seriously impressed. I'm not freaked out or anything." Ryan let go of my hand and put his arm around me and I literally had goose bumps. It was scary how much power he had over my physical being. I had to be careful I didn't let him have that much control over my mind as well or I'd soon become one of those lame girls that did everything their boyfriend did.

I could tell Nancy thought the same thing as she shoved her reader in Ryan's hands. "Do something useful, Ryan. Aren't you supposed to be some kind of genius? We need access to files that we can't download from the public server."

Ryan pulled his arm away from me and held the reader with both hands. "You mean restricted files from that study Mr. Alaster told us about?"

Nancy raised her eyebrow in interest. "That would be a great start. Yes."

"Can you do that?" I asked. My interest was piqued. All Nancy and I could find was the article published in the Scientific Journal and there weren't any details as to how the experiment was performed or any of the trials leading up to the actual resurrection. If we could read the entire report maybe we could get more accurate answers and figure out why I was the way I was.

"Yeah, no problem. What else do you need?" Ryan was eager

to impress.

"We're trying to figure out what kind of spell Mr. Vice President used to kill baby Chelsan, but all we're coming up with is the basics." Nancy was worked up now. If Ryan could do what he said he could we could potentially find out what had happened to me.

"We need to be careful about what we hack into. If Turner is keeping an eye on Chelsan and you then he's keeping an eye on Bill and me as well. We're the only people that have been around you in the last twenty-four hours." Ryan turned to me as if the next thing he was about to say was going to be difficult. "You need to tell Bill everything, too. He's in danger now just by being your friend. And…" He paused and swallowed hard, "He's a good guy."

"Wow." Nancy raised her eyebrow, impressed. "Look at you, all mature." Nancy was serious as she looked at me, "He has a point, Chelsan."

I knew they were right, but I felt like I was starting to lose control over the situation. If I ever had any control at all.

They would help me even if it meant they were in danger.

I couldn't live with that.

And in that second I made a decision.

The only way to protect them was to leave them.

What was I thinking involving people I care about anyway? They could end up dead and it would be my fault. I'd never be able to live with myself. I was so selfish!

"You're right. Why don't you call him and have him come over." Bill *did* have the right to know. He needed a heads up. "Be right back." I stood up.

"Hang on. Your Chuck's are untied." Ryan pointed out and reached down to tie the laces of my shoes.

For some reason it threw me off a bit, it was such a small gesture, but it made my heart skip a beat. I smiled at him and wanted to say good-bye but I walked to the bathroom instead. They couldn't follow me in there and I knew it had a small window leading to the side yard. I would have to do this quick.

I entered the bathroom and took a deep breath. I tried not to panic. I didn't want to be alone. It was terrifying, but I wouldn't be able to live with myself if anything were to happen my friends. I guess Jill was right to a certain degree, I didn't belong with the students of Geoffrey Turner High. I was trouble.

The window was about twenty inches in height and twenty inches wide, so it would be a tight fit, but doable. Unlatching the lock, I slid the window open as quietly as was humanly possible. I squeezed my body through the opening with surprisingly no sound at all and dropped to the soft grass below. Half-crawling, half-running, I hurried out of Nancy's side yard and once I was at a safe distance I ran full force down the grass street. It was still wet from watering and I almost slipped a few times, but I finally made it to a Hover-Shuttle station a few blocks away without any injury.

There were a few others waiting with me, but they didn't pay me any mind. I looked like a local kid waiting for a ride to the mall. Come on! Where was the stupid shuttle! I knew as soon as Nancy and Ryan found out I'd escaped they'd start an all out search for me, and I wanted to be as far away from them as possible. I had to go where they'd never guess I'd be. And I needed to find a phone to call Jason and make a new meeting place otherwise Nancy and Ryan were just going to show up at Alby's and all this would be for nothing.

Finally! The Hover-Shuttle arrived at the station and I clambered inside it as if the police were after me. I sat down on an aisle seat so no one could see me from the window. I wasn't sure where I was going, I just wanted to GO! I knew that if Nancy and Ryan caught up to me, I wouldn't be able to refuse their help. Especially if Ryan worked his Voodoo mojo on me. That was what it felt like anyway. How could one person make my entire body and brain go completely numb! It was a little frustrating to say the least. I knew I wouldn't be able to leave them again. I wasn't strong enough. Jason was my only hope now. Hopefully, he would steer me to...

...to what? What exactly was I expecting from this guy? I was trying to live moment to moment because when I actually sat down and thought about the future I was instantly queasy. What could I possibly do to save myself from the most powerful man in the world? If Turner really wanted me dead, wouldn't I be dead by now? So what was he waiting for? Maybe he was worried someone would find out he was my grandfather and tie him to the murder? Or maybe my dad's death made him change and he really wanted me back in his life? I just didn't know anything. I felt so lost and utterly alone, my choice or not, it sucked.

What if he knew about my power?

The thought had been flitting around my head since my mother's visions, but it finally solidified itself in that moment. He could want me alive to use me, or study me, or I don't know.... My mind was going a mile a minute. I needed to

126

relax, take a deep breath and find a phone. Baby steps. The Hover-Shuttle traveled into downtown Los Angeles. A surge of excitement flowed through me. I had never been to the city, I had never been anywhere because of Bruce. Everything I had ever seen on holo-tv, I could actually see with my own eyes. I felt like a hermit that finally decided to leave the house for the first time.

I peered over the shoulder of the person across from me to see out the shuttle's window at the oncoming skyscrapers in the distance. Downtown Los Angeles. It was the most stunning view I had ever seen. It was an island of steel surrounded by an ocean of trees.

At first glance, the buildings seemed clumped together in what appeared to be a chaotic mess, but upon closer inspection there was meaning to the madness.

The outer circle consisted of water dumping silos for all the hover-vehicles flying into the city to deposit their fuel cell tanks, making it easy to water the surrounding foliage that stretched for miles in every direction. Just past the silos the first set of steel and glass made up the smaller-sized outer ring of buildings that looked like a circle of miss-matched teeth.

There were five other rings of varying sized skyscrapers leading to the center of Los Angeles, a giant, three-hundred foot in diameter, metal cylinder that was at least a thousand feet above all the other buildings. It was used as a hover-pad landing area, but *how* someone was to get down from the twenty-eight-hundred foot tall structure, was a mystery I was about to find out.

The Hover-Shuttle swooped up to the hover pad on top of

the cylinder and landed with ease in its designated area. The door clunked open and everyone started to file out. I slowly stood up and walked out of the shuttle last.

I expected huge gusts of wind from the height we were at, but it was completely devoid of any draft or even a breeze. There were Hover-Shuttles and cars landing everywhere in a constant buzzing and whizzing of sound, but it was calm, as if we were in the eye of a storm.

I noticed a slight blurring of sky every time a car or shuttle came in to land and realized it was a kind of force field set in place to protect people and vehicles from weather. I had only read about technology like that in school. I had never seen it in person.

I might never go to class again.

It hit me hard. I hadn't thought about that.

But, if I was supposed to stay hidden, it wasn't like I could go back to school. Great. I was officially a high school drop-out. As much as I used to complain about homework and class, I realized I was actually going to miss it. And even though my motivation to go to one of the best schools in the country was to keep Bruce alive, it still meant something to me that I was accepted into a school like that. Now that was over. No. I couldn't think like that. Maybe when I talked to Jason he'd be able to clear things up for me so I could go back. I didn't know where I'd find the money for tuition, but I'd discover a way somehow.

Focus. I needed to find a phone.

I watched where everyone was headed and saw several hundred mini-platforms all along the outer edge of the circled roof. I saw as someone would stand on the platform and be sucked down the building. It must be some kind of elevator tube. Another thing I had only heard of before, but had never been in.

I took a deep breath, good thing I wasn't scared of heights.

I waited in line for my turn as I watched people pop out of view as soon as they stood on the platform. The lady in front of me wore her screaming daughter like a spider suit, the girl's grip was so tight. I couldn't blame the girl. We were essentially on top of a mountain about to be propelled down to the ground in a tiny vacuum tube. My stomach started to churn. I had to keep reminding myself that people did this everyday and I had never heard of any mishaps. I had seen one of these elevator tubes on holo-tv, but it always looked like fun. Or it was so quick I didn't think much of it at all. But standing in line waiting to be sucked down the abyss, I really wanted to vomit.

The lady and her tormented child stepped onto the platform in front of me and...

WHHOOOMP!

They were gone, crying and all.

Me next.

I swallowed hard and shuffled forward.

"Come on, kid, we don't have all day!" the jerk behind me yelled in my ear.

"You go." I couldn't do it yet.

He shoved past me and with a roll of his eyes...

WHHOOOMP!

He was gone.

"Are you waiting for someone?" the next woman in line asked me.

"No. I'm just… I've never done this before," I confided.

"You want me to go with you? It's better in pairs for your first time." She looked like she was thirty so I knew she wasn't a rich jerk.

"That would be great, thanks," I sputtered.

"Move it, ladies!" The man behind us shouted.

The lady smiled at me, encouraging. "Don't listen to him. Everyone is always in a hurry. Here."

She grabbed my hand and moved me forward. "Gotta do it quick, or you'll never do it."

I nodded and squeezed her hand a little harder than I should have.

She looked at me and gave me a wink of confidence. "One, two, three."

And we stepped on the square platform.

WHHOOOOSH!

We flew down the tube at a ridiculous speed, but it was completely exhilarating! The wall in front of us was glass and the city whizzed by us in a blur of silver and black. Two seconds later a door slid open and we were street side. A digital clock directly over the door began to count down from five.

"Quickly, unless you want to go back up." The lady pulled me out of the tube and onto the crowded streets of Los Angeles.

"Thanks again," I said to the lady.

She nodded and waved. "Any time, dear."

And she was off, heading up the street, pushing her way through the large throngs of people.

Cities were one of the only areas in the world where they actually kept the old pavement and concrete in tact. There wasn't a lot of concrete in the world anymore. I could feel the heat from the sidewalk through my shoes, which was both comforting and weird, not like the cobblestone in front of Mel's. It was like flooring with grit.

I decided to walk in the same direction as the lady that helped me and scanned the area for a payphone. (They made a big come back fifty years ago!) I didn't have to go far. I found one on the corner of Olive and Sixth Street, right in front of Pershing Square. I had only read about the place, but it was far more impressive in person. Even the holos didn't do it justice.

It was lined with forty-foot pines acting as sentries to Los Angeles' oldest park. It had its own water silo in the North West corner to keep the vegetation vibrant and breathtaking. Roses of every color imaginable, giant seven-foot sunflowers, red-orange hedging, plants and flowers I had never even seen before made up the inner square. In the dead center of the park was a perfectly coiffed square of the brightest green grass I had ever seen.

According to what I'd read, every summer and spring they'd have outdoor concerts and in the winter they'd bring in an ice-rink for skating. It was also the one place I'd seen so far that wasn't entirely packed with bodies. For some reason it seemed like everyone had a quiet respect for the place of beauty and didn't want to see it trampled by foot traffic.

I picked up the phone and was about to place my thumb up to the money scanner when I realized that if Turner *was* looking for me I would be giving him a giant flag as to where I was. I put my thumb down and looked around for a volunteer. The large shuffling crowd of passer-bys looked like the last thing they wanted to do was stop, so I scanned the park. A man sat at a bench, head bent over his electronic reader. I walked over to him with as friendly a smile as I could muster.

"Hi. I don't mean to bother you, but is there any way you could thumbscan the payphone for me? I'm all out of credit and I need to call my dad."

The man sighed heavily as if I was asking him to lift one of the skyscrapers towering above us. "Yeah, fine," he muttered, annoyed, but willing to help.

I'd take it.

He walked over to the payphone and scanned his thumb.

"Thanks," I said, wanting him to leave, but he just continued to stand over me.

"Well, call your dad. I want to make sure this isn't for drugs or some virtual reality bar scam," he sneered at me.

Okay, so he was paranoid. I could understand that, but I hoped Jason would play along.

I pulled out his number and dialed. The man looked at me suspiciously, obviously upset I had to look at a number. I guess he figured if it were my dad I'd have the number memorized. I turned to him, "He just got a new cell phone." I probably shouldn't have tried to over-explain, but I tended to crack under pressure when I lied.

The phone rang once. "Hello?"

"Dad? It's Chelsan." *Please, please, please remember who I am.*

"Smart girl. Is Harry Dalop standing over you?" Jason's voice sounded amused and I was instantly relieved. Jason must have some kind of caller I.D. and the guy next to me, Harry, apparently, showed up on it.

"Yeah, I ran out of credit again. I can't meet you at seven, can we meet at seven-thirty, somewhere closer?"

Evidently, Harry had heard enough of the conversation to feel content with his decision to help me out and went back to his reader on the bench.

"Okay, he's gone," I whispered.

"We have to go on the assumption that Turner has put out a voice recognition alert on your dear old pipes so let's make this quick. Where are you?" Jason was all business, which put me ill at ease. I wanted to be the only person paranoid; I needed an anchor of calm if I were to get through this.

"Downtown. I wanted to keep my friends out of this and they knew where we were meeting."

"Gordo's Virtual Reality Bar off of Pico and Central. Seven-thirty." Click.

The suddenness of Jason hanging up the phone made me jump a little, but I took a sigh of relief. At least, Nancy, Ryan and Bill wouldn't know where I was going. And a virtual reality bar was as seedy and sleazy as they come. The complete opposite of Alby's Bar and Grill at the Riverside mall. I had an instant pang of fear going to place like Gordo's, but the more I thought about it the safer I felt. It would be the last place Turner or anyone would expect me to go.

I looked at the digital clock on the payphone: six-thirty. I had an hour. I decided to head over to Gordo's to get a feel for the place. I wasn't sure how long it would take me.

Once I started walking off the beaten path, there were fewer and fewer people, only the distant sound of whirling hover cars above to keep me company. The closer I came to

Gordo's the dirtier and more rundown the area became. The trailer park looked like the Ritz Carlton compared where I was now. Cluttered metal lay in clumps in alleyways, stacked up to eight feet high. It felt as if I was walking through the dumping ground of Los Angeles. No wonder Jason chose this part of town. Geoffrey Turner wouldn't be caught dead at a place like this.

I turned onto Pico and saw the blazing holographic sign of "Gordo's Virtual Reality Bar," hovering over the square metal building like a cloud. There were no signs of windows anywhere on the structure, only one opened door in the front with an attendant waiting for customers. I couldn't find a clock anywhere so I had no idea what time it was. I figured I'd wait inside. I knew I was early. It felt like a good thirty-minute walk over here, which meant I had a half an hour more before Jason arrived.

I took a deep breath and marched up to the entrance of the bar. The attendant was a guy dressed all in black with a pencil-thin mustache that made him look like something out of a villain encyclopedia. Appearance-wise he was mid-twenties, which, judging by his occupation, put him in the category of black market Age-pro or actually in his mid-twenties, you never knew. He was skinny like his mustache and smiled at my approach.

"We don't get very many pretty ladies that often. What brings you here? Street fight? Mugging?" He paused for emphasis, "Murder?"

"None of those. Just meeting someone here." I tried to sound as casual as possible.

Virtual reality bars were humanities solution to working out all their pent up aggression. When Age-pro hit the market, I guess society used to be full of violence and war, but when given the option of living forever, people didn't want to be killed or locked up in prison where they'd have to live a life without the anti-aging pill. But according to leading scientists in human genetics, humans needed to satisfy their violent tendencies hence the creation of virtual reality bars. A place where you could be anywhere or anyone and kick the crap out of something. Virtual reality technology had been around for over three hundred years and hadn't changed much.

"Are you sure? You look so innocent on the outside, but I'm sure there's a demon ready to jump out of you."

Was that some sort of pick-up line?

"No demons, just meeting someone." I didn't really want to engage in the conversation he thought we were having.

His face fell a little as he smoothed his creepy mustache with his hand. "Go on in. Bar's down the hall to the right."

I moved past him without a glance or a word. I was afraid he'd ask me to thumbprint, and then Turner would know where I was. I figured this was probably the reason why Jason picked this place. It didn't look like they thumbprinted people that often.

Once I entered the building, I had to walk down a long corridor lined with glass doors. It was hard not to peek in at the inhabitants of the padded virtual rooms. It would have almost been comical, if it didn't make my skin crawl. Everyone dressed in the official blue spandex suits made for comfort and flexibility. Each suit was laden with sensors to make the experience as real as possible. To top off the outfit was a black helmet contraption with a visor that made the whole virtual experience happen.

There was an array of padded props in each room, I guess depending on the individual fantasy of the person inside. The first lady I passed was literally strangling a life-size dummy. She pounced and throttled the poor stuffed person like she wanted to rip it into a million pieces. She screamed a triumphant and terrifying screech that chilled me to my bones.

After that, I diverted my eyes from the rest of the rooms. It felt as if I witnessed a crime the way that she strangled the stuffed man. And knowing that to her eyes, she was really killing someone, somehow made the virtual reality experience a little too *real* for me.

I hurried past the rest of the doors and turned right. There was a run down bar waiting for me with exactly zero people in it. Only the bartender was there, wiping down the counter out of what looked like boredom. His face perked up when he saw me. I couldn't tell if he was a letch or if he was just happy to see someone at the bar.

"What can I get you?" he called out to me with a large smile. He was a heavyset man with dark circles under his eyes and a five o'clock shadow. He appeared to be in his early-twenties, another black market Age-pro would be my guess.

"Nothing. I'm just waiting for someone. What time is it anyway?" I asked as I walked over to the bar.

He didn't seem to mind that I wasn't ordering anything, he just looked happy he had company. "It's..." He looked at his watch, "Seven twenty-five. Who ya'll meeting?" His smile hadn't left his face since I had walked in the room and it was beginning to creep me out a little.

"Just a friend." I tried to sound as casual as possible, but I could feel myself sweating slightly. I really wished Nancy were here. She'd have this guy wrapped around her finger and I could just sit back and watch and not have to participate in any kind of social behavior. I wanted to order a water just so I could have something to fidget with, but I couldn't thumbprint, Turner would find me in a second. It was completely awkward sitting there at the bar with absolutely nothing to do but wait.

"Awfully strange place for a rich girl to meet someone," he leered at me. It was so grotesque and repulsive I flinched instinctively.

"I'm really eighteen, I'm not rich." He had assumed I was wealthy because I looked eighteen. And from the expression on his embarrassed face, the thought had never occurred to him that I actually *was* eighteen.

"Whoa," was all he said. He suddenly found that the other side of the bar was where he wanted to be at that moment.

Apparently, my age really freaked him out.

Good. I was thankful that he left me alone.

"Would you like a drink?"

I whirled around to see Jason Keroff smiling an annoyingly cute lopsided smile at me. "Good girl, keeping away from thumbprints. You must be parched."

"Yeah, a little." The butterflies Jason gave me weren't the same as the ones Ryan did. This was more like being nervous because I was about to give an oral report in front of class. I tried to remember yesterday when I was devoid of any emotion whatsoever at seeing him just to remain calm in his presence.

Why was I such a freak?!

Jason motioned to the bartender. "Two waters, please."

The bartender didn't even acknowledge me as he slid the two glasses of water in front of Jason and I.

Jason turned to me, still smiling. "What's up with him?"

"I think my age scared him a bit."

"You told him your age?" Jason's smile faded. He looked worried.

"I didn't tell him my name or anything. He thought I was a richy and hit on me. It was gross," I shared, hoping I hadn't done anything wrong.

"Well..." Jason trailed off as if thinking of some horribly long math problem in his head. "It's probably fine."

"So what *is* going on? I'm not even sure what I'm doing here. I'm freaking out. My mom is dead, my whole trailer park is now an oak forest, my grandpa is Geoffrey Turner..." I began my panicked rant.

"Wait. What was that about Turner?" Jason interrupted me with wide eyes. He searched the surrounding area as if he was expecting an army to suddenly appear from out of the shadows.

"Um..." Oh yeah, I hadn't told him that part of the story yet. "Yeah, he's my grandpa."

"Does he *know* he's your grandpa?" Jason was actually sweating at this point.

"I don't know." And that was the truth. I really didn't know. "What can you tell me about what happened to my mom?"

"First off..." Jason pulled out an object that looked like a stylus and placed it on the bar counter in front of us. He hit an invisible button and the whole thing lit up blue like a glowing mini-cylinder from space. "This is a frequency jammer, just in case someone has this place tapped."

The blue glow lit up Jason's face in an almost eerie way. I felt as if we were in some kind of covert spy mission huddled over the gadget that would turn into a weapon if needed. Unfortunately, reality wasn't that far off from my fantasy. "That thing doesn't blow up, does it?" I couldn't resist asking. No more surprises for me thank you very much.

Jason's eyebrow lifted in what I could only describe as amusement. "No, it doesn't blow up." Jason leaned in close so there was no chance of the bartender overhearing. "Listen, you mentioned the green smoke. Tell me everything you and your step-dad saw. Is he with your friends? Is he safe?"

"No, he's dead." I didn't know how much I could share with Jason yet, but the look on Jason's face went from concerned to panicked in about two seconds.

"They got to him already? You're in more danger than I thought. We have to think about this." Jason shook his head as if he had some kind of tick.

"No. He died eleven years ago." I let that hang there for a second. I wasn't ready to tell Jason my secret yet, but at the same time, I couldn't let him think that my grandpa or the government killed Bruce or whomever else he thought did the deed.

"Wait. What?" Jason was genuinely confused, and a little bit put off, as if he thought I was messing with him.

I needed to show him. It was the only way I could leave no doubt in his head that I was telling the truth. I searched the room.

There was a dead fly a couple of feet away on the bar. "Will that device block any surveillance cameras as well?" I asked, just to be cautious.

Jason's eyebrows crinkled in genuine fascination at this point. "Yes. Why?"

"Just sit tight." I jumped off my stool and grabbed the dead fly, bringing it over to Jason. I plopped back on to my stool and placed the fly in front of the blue glowing device. "Dead, right?"

Jason nodded, his interest apparently piqued from the curious sparkle in his eyes.

I reached into the fly's black swirling center and made it fly around the frequency jammer. It did somersaults, spins, twirlies, everything I could think of and then when I was certain I had made my point I let it drop to the bar with a slight thwack.

Jason swallowed hard and was silent for a good two minutes. My palms were definitely sweating. I wanted to say something, but I couldn't think of what to say. I wish I knew what Jason was thinking, but his face was unreadable.

"I brought Bruce out and made him say that about the smoke because the Mayor didn't believe me." There. I broke the oppressive silence.

Jason nodded slowly. "We're so dead."

"Yeah." It was really starting to sink in that I was in way over my head.

"I'll tell you what I know." Jason talked slower as if he was in shock.

Which, let's face it, he probably was. Before he came here, he was most likely thinking he was going to help some poor teenage girl who accidently witnessed something she shouldn't

140

have. He wasn't prepared for the granddaughter of the Vice President of Population Control who could raise the dead. I was shocked myself that he was still here. But he was a reporter and I'm sure the juiciness of the story far outweighed the danger for him.

We'd see, I guess.

"Let's start with the green smoke," he began, "I've been trying to uncover this story for years, fifty to be exact. I've only been a reporter for a little while. I was a lab assistant for forty-five years at the International Laboratory Sciences Institute." Note to self, he was definitely over the age of seventy, Nancy would freak, she thought he was around our age. "Our purpose was to find new ways to help the environment and population problems such as developing hydroponics for crops and finding new chemical treatments for re-generating plants. I was good at my job and moved up through the ranks. The higher up the ladder I went the more disclosure contracts I thumbprinted until I was dealing with chemical solutions that by my calculations would kill effectively and efficiently rather than re-generate life.

"When I started asking questions, I was terminated immediately. Three attempts were made on my life soon after I was fired. That's when I became a reporter, just to put myself in the spotlight so it would be more difficult to kill me without people noticing. I admit, I tried my hardest to become the 'teen idol,' anything that would make me more valuable and harder to kill." He paused, taking a deep breath. "Your... grandpa..." He shook his head and ran his hand through his black wavy hair. "We're so dead."

"So my grandpa is *exterminating* people?" I tried to keep

141

Jason focused. He seemed to do better when he was focused.

"Yes. Your grandpa's definition of population control is literally that... he controls the population by killing off people he feels the public won't miss. He takes run-down areas like trailer parks and comes in with his armies of poisons. Poisons I helped create." Jason couldn't make eye contact with me when he said the last part.

He was ashamed of himself. I could tell immediately. "Hey." I reached over and squeezed his hand supportively. He let his eyes meet mine, but they were full of guilt and horror. "I don't blame you. If not you then someone else. All I know about my grandpa is that he's one stubborn determined guy. If he wants something done, he won't stop until he's succeeded." And in the spirit of the moment, and the glowing blue of safety, I told Jason all about my mother's vision and the ceremonies that led to my unique talent.

Jason responded with a raise of the eyebrow, as if remembering something he had tucked away in the back of his mind. "I know what he did to you..."

Before Jason could finish his sentence the bartender swooped over and smashed Jason's frequency jammer with a baseball bat. It was so sudden and violent Jason and I couldn't move for a good three seconds. Jason was the first to respond with cat like reflexes, grabbing the bartender's bat and yanking it away.

The bartender didn't even struggle. He just placed his hands up in supplication and nodded toward the doorway as if trying to communicate some hidden message to Jason.

And apparently Jason understood this strange language of bats and nodding because he turned to me and grabbed my hand. "Jig's up. Gramps has found you."

This froze my insides as if someone had poured liquid nitrogen down my throat. "He's here?"

Jason carefully led me off the stool and toward the back door of the bar, away from the entrance. "Chances are the big man himself isn't making an appearance, but his extermination squad is here."

"The poisons?" I gulped. I didn't want to die the way my mom did. It was somehow more terrifying than the act of dying itself.

"No, worse: guns." Jason tried the back door, but it was locked. He looked at the bartender for help.

The bartender shrugged almost apologetically and then screamed, "They're in here!"

"Great." Jason took matters into his own hands by letting go of mine and using his strength to slam the bat onto the door handle. It smashed into pieces. He kicked hard and the door's wood splintered enough to fly open.

Gunfire cracked loudly from behind us. A few stray bullets lodged themselves into the wall. Jason took my hand once again and practically threw me into the adjoining room, which happened to be one of the virtual reality padded cells.

The man inside didn't even notice we had interrupted his fantasy. He was throttling a stuffed dummy with every ounce of energy he possessed. Jason pulled me toward the exit, swinging the door open and throwing us both to the ground of the hallway beyond, just as another round of gunfire whizzed overhead. I managed a quick look back just in time to see the poor man in the padded cell turn into Swiss cheese from the onslaught of bullets ripping through his blue spandex suit and the dummy he was strangling. He was dead before he even knew what had happened.

I screamed. I couldn't control myself. I had seen way too much brutality in the last two days and my brain couldn't take it.

Jason pushed me forward. We were half-crouched as we ran through the hallway. More men with guns appeared in front of us and started firing. Jason shoved me into another padded cell with a woman punching the wall in front of her. Glass shattered into a million pieces as the rain of bullets tore through our room, killing the lady in front of us, her black spinning hole already formed before she hit the ground.

Jason searched the room for another exit, but the only door was the one we came in. I could see the poor man riddled with bloody holes across the hall from us, his black chasm swirling madly.

"No way out," Jason said, holding the bat in front of us protectively, then shrugged at the obvious futility of it.

"I can help." I had to try something.

The gunfire had stopped. Orders were barked out to the other soldiers. They thought we were dead and they were coming in to collect the bodies.

Screams from the other inhabitants of the virtual reality bar echoed outside our room. They had obviously heard the gunfire and were running out of the bar for their lives.

I only had a few moments, maybe less before the soldiers turned the corner and saw us huddled in our rattrap. I took a deep breath and connected to the lady's black hole in front of us. Just like Bruce, I kept reminding myself.

Footsteps crunched over the glass…

… almost to our door.

I made the lady run up to the doorway.

Gunfire tore through her, shredding pieces of skin, causing them to slap against the wall and floor. I still couldn't see any of our attackers. I knew as soon as they saw us alive they'd shoot us instantly. They were at close range, but I made the lady move closer to them. And then I heard the distinct call from one of the men.

"Zombie 442! Take proper aim!"

Zombie 442? Apparently this wasn't the first time this gun crew had seen an active dead person.

I angled myself so I could see what I was doing and made the woman grab the gunman's throat that stood closest to her with frightening impact. His face was already turning blue. I could feel her hand squeezing the life out of this soldier and it terrified me, but I couldn't stop either. All I could think about was keeping his gun from blowing us away. Bullets tore into the woman's head from all sides, as if they thought this was the key to finishing her off. In a matter of seconds she was completely headless, just a pulp of cracked neck bone was left. Vomit. Yes, vomiting sounded like the right thing to do at this point, but I had to save Jason and myself first.

I made the woman throw the man she was strangling down the hallway where most of the bullets had come from. There were actual shrieks of panic and a clattering of metal with a resounding thud of men smacking the floor and walls. I must have had her throw him pretty hard. I had never used my power

145

that way before and I had to say it was making me a little dizzy and excited.

Now that all the soldiers were out of view I needed to see what was going on. I was a blind puppet master, and Jason and I wouldn't be safe until we could get out of this building. I took a sneak peek over at Jason, whose eyes were round with fear.

He made quick eye contact with me. "That's way different than a fly," was all he could sputter out.

"I'll get us out of here, I promise," I lied. I had no idea if that was even possible. I started to think this was it for me. I was going to be responsible for killing my celebrity crush. At least I wouldn't have to feel guilty for long.

Then I remembered what I did with Bruce. When I made him show me what really happened at the trailer park, and I thought I could do something similar with the first man they had killed.

I sought out his black hole and linked myself to him.

Okay. Body parts check, now for the hard part.

I put all my energy in trying to focus on his sight.

POP.

Whoa.

I could see through his eyes *and* I could see through mine.

At the same time.

Talk about instant migraine.

I closed my eyes to eliminate any confusion (and headaches).

From his viewpoint, I was in the room we had just abandoned. I was still aware of my own body back with Jason across the hall. It was totally surreal. I made the man stand up and walk to the doorway. Gunfire tore through him as soon as I made

146

him enter into the hallway. They were aiming at his head, so it was like trying to see through a snow storm with all the bullets hitting his face. Damn, they hit his left eye. I had one eye left. I made a quick count. There were four of them and they were all wide-eyed with fear, unloading their guns into both corpses in front of them.

I realized at that moment I was still controlling the woman as well.

I needed the man's functional eye so I made him put his arm out protectively and let them shred his arm until it was just bloody pulp and bone. I didn't care as long as I could see. I focused my attention on the woman, using the man as a lookout and her as my weapon.

I made her headless corpse leap forward, grabbing the first gun she could get her hands on. It was very awkward, using *his* eyes and *her* body, it made my perspective all wonky. But from the looks on these soldier's faces, they were halfway to peeing their pants, so I took full advantage of their freaked-out status. I could feel that she had a good grip on the handgun. I made her rip it from his hand and point it at the four combatants. Their bullets were tearing through what was left of her flesh, and I felt like I was starting to lose control of her.

I made a note that maybe my gift was somehow tied to skin or something, I would need to tell Nancy right away. We could look it up. Then with a pang of anguish, I remembered I would probably never be able to see Nancy again. Maybe Jason would help me if we survived, but my corporeal self couldn't help but feel him cowering next to me like a baby. I couldn't blame him, I guess. This was definitely some gruesome stuff. If I hadn't been keeping a dead man alive for the last eleven years I might not have fared as well either.

I tried to make the woman squeeze the trigger of the gun she was holding, but I couldn't do it. Physically I could, but mentally I wasn't ready to shoot anyone. I logically told myself that if I didn't kill them, they would most definitely kill me, but after killing Bruce when I was seven I just couldn't do it. I wasn't a murderer even if it was self-defense. I was better than that. I had to think.

I made the man leap forward as fast as I could manage (which was ridiculously fast by the way). Controlling him was about ten times easier than controlling the woman since he still had most of his body in tact. I made him snatch another gun from one of the men and bash the soldier over the head with it. He fell into one of the other goons, unconscious. I felt guilty, but at least he was still alive.

"Retreat!" one of the men screamed. His voice was shrill and breathy. As much action as I assumed these men had seen, apparently they hadn't seen this.

I watched from the man's corpse as the soldiers backed away, guns drawn, one of the combatants potato sacking his unconscious team member over his shoulder. And they were gone.

Out the front door.

I made my one-eyed corpse follow them out to make sure they were truly gone. I had him aim his gun at the retreating soldiers as they jumped in their hover-hummer, dumping their fallen compadre in the back and whizzing away out of view.

I instantly dropped my connection with both corpses. My

head was spinning. I had never done anything like that before and it literally drained me of most of my energy. I felt like I hadn't slept for ten days straight. I turned to Jason, my eyes drooping. I knew I would crash soon and we needed to get out of there before the soldiers returned with back up to finish us off.

"We have to get out of here," Jason said as if reading my thoughts.

"Yeah. I'm not sure I can stay awake," I managed to slur out.

He nodded and his previously horrified looks had now turned to determination and protectiveness. Jason picked me up like a baby and carried me out of the building and into the abandoned parking lot.

"Great." Jason shook his head in anger.

"What is it?" My mouth felt like it couldn't open properly and no matter how hard I tried I couldn't seem to keep my eyes open.

"They towed my hover. We're going to have to walk. *Can* you walk?" Jason could see that he was asking the impossible. "Of course you can't, you just managed to make two zombies fight Turner's thugs," he mumbled more to himself than to me, but then he smiled his signature roguish smile and looked at me. "Impressive by the way."

I could barely enjoy the compliment, but I managed a weak smile. Or at least I think I did, it was always impossible for me to tell what expression I was making my face accomplish. Especially when I was this tired. "It's….good…" Don't know what that meant, but I was trying.

Then I heard the whirling fan of a hover car. "They….

they're...coming..." I tried to make my mouth and voice function normally.

"It's not them. Maybe we can hitch a ride, looks like they're coming to the bar." Jason carried me over to where the hover car landed. "Hey, we need help."

Maybe I was imagining it, but I swore I heard Nancy shriek. I tried to pry my eyes open. I must have been delusional. Wishful thinking. In my tired stupor I really wanted my best friend with me.

"What did you do to her?!" It really did sound like Nancy.

"Nothing. Look, we need a ride. We really need to get out of here, NOW!" Jason was feeling the pressure and the panic as time was slipping away.

"Don't you yell at me! Just because you're some famous reporter doesn't give you the right to use and abuse my best friend!"

It *was* Nancy. Please don't be a dream. Please don't be a dream. Even though I knew now more than ever that having my friends around me was a possible death sentence to them, I couldn't help but be selfish. I needed Nancy. I needed Ryan. And I needed Bill.

"Best friend?" Jason was confused now.

"Nancy?" I managed to squeak out.

And suddenly I was being taken out of Jason's arms, into someone else's. My stomach managed to perform the impossible back flip as I realized Ryan had grabbed me from Jason. His face was worried and flushed. It was like a full on battle with my eyelids to stay open. Ryan was ridiculously gorgeous.

"I knew you'd try something. I managed to put a tracer in

your shoes before you took off. It took a while to track you down, with all the crowds and then there was some kind of frequency jammer messing with the signal." I heard about half of that. I couldn't stop staring at his lips moving. I must have looked like an idiot.

"We better get you out of here." It was Bill's voice. Bill had come, too.

"Bill." His name was easier to say being only one syllable.

"Yeah, it's me." Bill's hand touched my hair and I hoped it wasn't my fatigued state, but he looked fine with me being in Ryan's arms.

"In the car. Let's get out of here." Nancy had taken charge like she always did.

"Let her go to sleep. Trust me, she needs it," Jason said to the others.

I felt Ryan's lips touch my forehead and then everything went black.

Chapter Four

"Chelsan, wake up. It's time for school."

Bruce? Were the last three days all a terrible nightmare? Sure, I'd still have to take care of Bruce the rest of my existence, but that would be paradise compared to what I'd been through. It made sense. I mean, being Vice President Turner's granddaughter? Extermination of trailer parks and zombie fights? Really? It had to be a dream. And best of all that meant my mom was still alive...

"Mom?" I opened up my eyes in expectation of seeing my drab trailer wall.

I was in Nancy's room.

My heart sunk. All of it actually happened. Mom was truly gone. My eyes welled up.

"Hey, you okay?"

That was when I noticed that Ryan was lying next to me!

I was immediately self-conscious. I must have looked like a

152

complete disaster because he kept on staring at me.

"You look beautiful." Ryan brushed his hand against my cheek and smiled.

I decided to throw caution to the wind and I reached up and held his hand in mine. Not as bold as Nancy probably would have been, but I was pretty wimpy when it came to boys I was fast discovering. Ryan didn't seem to mind, he snuggled in closer so we were forehead to forehead.

"Were you here all night?" I asked.

"No. I just snuck in the window this morning. No one knows I'm here, Nancy would freak. I'll climb out when she comes back up," Ryan whispered. His breath was minty fresh and I realized with sudden horror my breath probably smelled like the sewer.

"I think I need a mint." Wow. I amazed myself at what came out of my mouth.

Ryan didn't even blink as he reached down in his jeans pocket and pulled out his personal metal gum container. He took out a piece of gum and placed it in my mouth. This guy really made my mind turn to jelly.

"Better?" he asked with a smile and put his forehead back to mine.

"Better." I needed to get past this "school girl crush mode" that made me paralyzed around him. "Why do you like me?" I blurted out.

And to my surprise, he just smiled. "Anyone would be crazy not to like you."

"Then everyone's been crazy my whole life. You're the first one." Being a leper at school was pretty much common knowledge.

Ryan rolled his eyes. "I know *a lot* of guys who like you, they're just too scared to do anything about it because of Jill."

"Yeah, right." I couldn't believe him. I saw the way people looked at me, like I was going to eat their pets or something. Jill didn't have that kind of power. Did she?

"You don't even know how beautiful you are, do you?" Ryan's hand stroked my cheek again and then he turned serious. "Ever since I tutored you last year I wanted to be with you, but I let my fear of being a social outcast make all my decisions for me."

"But you're so popular. No one would have cared who you dated." I was both excited to hear him say that he liked me since last year and hurt that he didn't like me enough to do anything about it.

He leaned in and kissed me.

Mush. Pure mush. I couldn't think straight. All I could do was kiss him back. I didn't want to stop. The more we kissed the tighter I held onto him.

Eventually he pulled away. His stare was so intense I couldn't keep eye contact with him for very long. It scared me how much I liked him.

"I shouldn't have cared what people thought." Ryan's face was full of hurt and embarrassment. I could tell it was a decision he had struggled with.

"We could have kept it secret." We could have. No one would have needed to know. And I certainly knew how to keep a secret. Until recently anyway.

He held my face with both hands so I had to look him straight in the eye. He was almost angry he was so passionate.

He accentuated every word, "I would *never* disrespect you like that."

"It wouldn't have been disrespectful. I get it. People don't like me because I'm trailer trash. I wouldn't expect you to…" I couldn't even finish my sentence. He silenced me with another kiss.

Ryan pulled away. "You are *not* trailer trash. You are the most amazing human being I've ever met. You can do things with your mind that scientists all across the world have been trying to do for centuries. You're the smartest person that I know, *and* you're drop dead gorgeous. And I love it when you make that confused little face of yours. You get this cute little crinkle on your forehead." He was smiling by then and it made my heart spin. "And I'm shocked that you'd even be interested in me. I'm a weak jerk for not telling everyone to *F* themselves when I wanted to ask you out. I treated you like crap and I don't deserve you." He was hurt again.

"Hey." I held his cheeks in my hands like he did to me. "Don't beat yourself up for trying to fit in. If I thought I had a remote chance of having a *normal* high school existence, I wouldn't date you either." I smiled at my own joke, but Ryan wasn't having it.

"Don't brush this off. I was mean." Ryan was more serious than I'd ever seen him.

"Okay. I get it. But that's over now. Everyone pretty much knows we're going out. You made that quite clear last Friday."

"Why are you trying to make *me* feel better for being a dick?"

"Fine. Feel like crap, just don't break up with me." A part of me liked the fact that he was beating himself up about the way he ignored me, but another part of me just wanted him to shut

155

up already and kiss me.

Ryan smiled. "I'm never going to break up with you. In fact, even if *you* break up with me, because you probably will you know, I'm very boring, I'll stalk you forever."

I snuggled in closer. "Boring? Yeah right. You're only the smartest kid alive. I'm surprised my grandpa hasn't snatched you up to enlist you in his services."

"He's tried." Ryan looked at me cautiously. He wasn't sure how I was going to react and I could tell he was scared.

"What do you mean he's tried?"

"You know how I get recruitment offers on a daily basis?"

"Yeah?" It was crazy how basically the whole *world* wanted a piece of Ryan. When someone tested off the charts like Ryan, it made him a very popular guy. He received job offers from every science research lab in the world. When he was eleven years old he figured out the missing piece of some unsolvable math equation that had stumped mathematicians for centuries. It was no wonder Turner wanted him.

"No. I don't mean he tried to recruit me recently. He tried to recruit me when I was eight. Three years before I solved Trildion's theorem." Ryan paused, "Chelsan, Turner kidnapped me."

I couldn't say I was surprised considering what my mother showed me in her visions. Turner was ruthless and kidnapping kids to serve his interests seemed on par with what I knew about him already.

"He must have had access to my test scores. That was the first time I tested above the genius level. Some men in suits arrived at my house two days after I took the test and told my parents that I was selected for a special government program for the gifted." Ryan paused.

"You don't have to tell me…" I could see how hard it was for him to continue.

"No, it's alright." His face was determined. "Anyway, my parents asked me if I wanted to do the program and I told them 'no.' When they told the men my answer they said it wasn't an option and took me anyway. My mom was screaming, my dad tried to tackle them with a fire poker, but one of the men pulled out a gun and put it to my head. That stopped them in their tracks. I was shoved into their hover-limo and taken away." Ryan swallowed hard.

"I'm so sorry." I did the only thing I could think of to make him feel better, I kissed him gently. "How did you get out?"

Ryan took a moment to re-group then looked me in the eye. "I was taken to some sort of research facility. It was a giant single room with ten-foot ceilings and row upon row of computers and electronics. There were kids my age everywhere either on the computers or strapped into virtual reality gear poking the air in front of them like they were writing on a chalkboard or something. That's when I met Turner. He came over to me and welcomed me to the facility. He said he'd been watching my test scores for a while and that this would be more of a home to me than with my parents." He paused thinking, "He scared me more than anything, Chelsan. It was like I was talking to the Bogeyman. He looked at me like he was the hunter and I was the prey. My instincts kicked in and I started to cry. I lied and told him that I had cheated on all my tests. I told him how I stole the tests from my teacher's computer and memorized them, that was why I didn't want to come here because I knew they'd find out about me. I couldn't tell if I had convinced him or not, he just stood there staring at me as if judging whether or not I was telling the truth. I told him that I'd study hard and I'd try and prove that I could be smart. If I could memorize the tests then maybe I could actually learn what was on them. I hoped that by pretending that I actually wanted to be there, he'd believe my lies more. After staring at me for what felt like an eternity, he sent me back home. My parents and I were so relieved, and when I told them what happened they said I should mess up my schoolwork to back up my lie. Just to be safe.

"The men in suits came to the first couple of tests, waiting to see my scores. I made sure that I missed half the questions. Eventually, they stopped coming all-together and I felt safe again. I slipped back into my normal behavior and started to forget all about Geoffrey Turner." Ryan took a deep breath.

"About three years later, I was in math class and the teacher put Trildion's theorem on the board. He gave us all a crack at trying to solve it, not expecting any true results since we were all eleven and no one had solved it in three hundred years. But I just saw the answer, you know? That's how things work for me. I see problems and equations and the answers just form in my brain as if they were already written down for me. My teacher flipped out. He called the news. I was the poster child for geniuses. They had a national dinner for me with the President and everything.

"That's when I saw Turner again. He looked at me from across the room with such venom and hatred I nearly pee'd my pants. I was suddenly grateful for my teacher announcing the fact that

I solved the theorem to the world. I think Turner would have taken me again if it had been kept quiet. The only interference we've had since is the government telling my parents in no uncertain terms that I was to go to Geoffrey Turner High. To keep an eye on me, I guess. I'm still scared of him. And now knowing what you told me about what happened to you and the exterminations, I don't feel so ashamed about that anymore. Any sane person *should* be afraid of Turner." He stopped and looked at me.

"I'm related to him. The man is a monster and we share the same blood."

"You're nothing like him. I'm telling you, I've looked into his eyes. That guy is as evil as they come." Ryan cupped my face with his hands again and kissed me. "I just wanted you to know my history with him, and a little bit of who I am before you decide I'm a boring idiot." And he smiled his disarmingly charming smile.

I smiled back, then a thought hit me. "What do you think he wants all those kids for?"

Ryan shook his head. "I don't know. I've been trying to block it out of my memory for so long, I never really thought about it."

"We should. I'll tell Jason, maybe he knows something."

Ryan looked away, his face suddenly distant.

"What's wrong?" Oh boy. He thought he could handle Turner being my grandpa, but I bet he couldn't. What happened to him was too traumatic.

"Do you like him?" he asked quietly.

What?

"What?" I had no idea what he was talking about.

"Jason Keroff. I know you had those holo-pictures of him before you actually met him, and he obviously likes you…" Ryan trailed off.

I covered my mouth to hide my laugh.

Ryan didn't find it funny at all. He started to sit up in Nancy's bed, preparing to leave.

I quickly grabbed his arm and pulled him back down so we were forehead to forehead again. "No. I don't like Jason Keroff. I only started liking him to keep my mind off of you."

Ryan eyed me suspiciously, but I could see the relief in his eyes. "Really?"

"Yes, really." I played on his guilt strings for fun. "I mean, after you ignored me as soon as I didn't need tutoring anymore, what was a girl to do?"

Ryan kissed me again. The kind of kiss that made the hair on the back of my neck raise and my toes tingle.

I pulled away. "And how did you know I had holo-pics of Jason anyway?"

Ryan's face turned red. "When I met your mom. I could see inside your bedroom. They were kind of plastered everywhere," he teased.

"Stalker." I smiled.

"You know it." He kissed me again.

We heard a noise outside Nancy's bedroom and he pulled away.

"Better go." Ryan snapped up from bed and headed for the window.

"Nancy won't mind. Stay." My mind was still numb from his

kiss and the last thing I wanted him to do was leave.

"She wouldn't, but her parents would. Better to come through the front door." As if he couldn't stop himself, he ran over to me and gave me a quick kiss. Then he leapt to the window, opening it wide.

And he was gone, out the second floor window before I could say good-bye.

I wanted to giggle uncontrollably from the amount of excitement pumping through my veins. Ryan really liked me. For once in my life something was actually going my way.

The door opened and Jason Keroff walked in.

Lame.

Me of three days ago would have killed for this moment, but a lot can happen over a seventy-two hour period, and seeing Jason there was a cruel wake-up call to last night's events.

"School. Come on. You're going." Jason barked out orders with a grin. It was rather irritating.

"School? Are you joking? Where's Nancy?" I groaned and threw back the poofy comforter that was the down fluffiness of perfection.

"I'm right here." Nancy came in like a goddess. Her hair and make-up looked as if she had stepped out of a fashion magazine and her outfit of jeans and a tank fit her like a glove.

When I saw her, I wanted to tell her everything that just happened with Ryan, but Jason was there so it would have to wait. I ran across the room and hugged her as hard as I could. She nearly fell over from the force and smiled.

"Good to see you, too." Then she pushed me away and smacked me on the arm.

"Ow." I massaged the place where she hit me.

Nancy waved her finger in front of my face in a threatening manner. "Don't you EVER try and leave again! I don't care if you think you're saving the world! We are a team! I knew the risks from the beginning and I don't care, got me?!"

"I didn't want any of you to get hurt," I admitted rather sheepishly. I felt as if I was being grounded or something.

Nancy placed her hands on my shoulders, making forced eye contact with me. "Promise me."

A warm feeling of relief and comfort overwhelmed me for a second. Nancy was the very definition of a best friend. And I knew in that moment she'd risk her life for me. Frankly, she already had, just by being near me.

"I promise, Nancy, geez." My lungs were suddenly squeezed of every last drop of breath as Nancy crushed me in one of her bear hugs. She let go and I gasped for air with a genuine laugh.

"We were so worried. You should have seen Ryan, he was a crazy man trying to find you." Nancy rolled her eyes.

Hearing about Ryan made my stomach churn with excitement. I wished he didn't have that kind of control over my mental state of being, but there was nothing I could do about that. I just had to come to terms with the fact that Ryan made my head spin. Waking up next to him was like a dream. He genuinely liked me. Oh boy, there went the stomach again. I had to stop thinking about him.

"And *this* guy." Nancy nodded her head toward Jason who now sat on her bed. "He's a complete waste of time. What was he thinking getting you all shot at like that?" she spoke in an almost flirtatious way.

To my surprise, Jason smiled back at Nancy with just as much *flirt* as she was giving. "I got her out safe, didn't I?" Jason stood up from the bed, eyeing Nancy with interest.

I flipped out. "You got *me* out safe? Me? Was that when you were huddled in a ball? Or when you were sucking your thumb until I made all the men with *guns* go away? Was that when you *saved* me?"

Jason's smile didn't budge. He even looked at me like he was endeared by what I had to say. "I didn't suck my thumb."

"Might as well have," I mumbled angrily under my breath.

Jason scuffed my head like I was a five-year-old. "You saved my life and I thank you very much for it. Are you happy now?"

I remembered what he had started to say before our attack last night: *I know what he did to you.…* "You said you knew what Turner did to me last night! Did you mean it? What did he do?" I was charged with excitement.

"Oh yeah that." Jason motioned around the room indicating that it may be bugged. "I can't remember."

My heart sank. I'd have to wait until later, until we could talk in a secured location. It was so strange that people could actually be listening to our every word. And if Nancy's house was bugged, then I had to assume they had heard everything I said to Nancy and Ryan for the last two days, which meant Turner would know about my power. And he'd have heard the conversation Ryan and I just had. I should have known better. I really hoped Jason was wrong.

Jason saw the panic in my eyes and leaned in to whisper. "I have something with me that will let me find the bug. Leave it to me, okay?"

Nancy must not have liked the intimacy of our conversation because she stepped in to say, "Get ready for school, Chelsan. We have to leave in ten minutes."

"I'm not going to school! You're both insane!" I was still a little panicked by the whole situation.

I suddenly noticed all of Nancy's holo-pictures of Jason were mysteriously absent from her wall. "I see you took all of your…"

That was all that came out of my mouth before Nancy shoved her hand over it to shut me up. "Seriously, get ready."

I pried her hand away and crossed my arms in a final attempt to keep my ground.

Nancy shook her head and looked at me seriously. "Chelsan, it's the best place for you. We have to keep you as public as possible. School is the safest place you can be right now."

"Did you guys discuss all this while I was sleeping?" I had to admit it made sense, but for some reason I was grumpy and more than that, I was just plain scared. If it were up to me I'd hide in Nancy's closet all day (probably where she hid all of Jason's holo-pics). *Keep you as public as possible...* It made me think of Ryan and what he told me about staying in the public so Turner couldn't kidnap him. I decided to tell Nancy and Jason everything right there. If my grandpa were listening it wouldn't be anything new.

Nancy seemed way more interested in the fact that Ryan had snuck in to be with me (like a true friend would) but Jason's face scrunched with worry and what was worse… recognition.

"I've heard about those although there's never been any proof. Conspiracy theorists call them *I.Q. Farms*. I'll find out what I can." Jason's brain was already spinning with a plan.

Nancy grabbed my arms and shook me lightly in exaggerated exasperation. "Now get ready. My mom is making a special breakfast for that loser." Nancy hid a smile.

"And this *loser* is very hungry, so I'll see you two later." Jason winked at Nancy and strode out the door with a confident swagger.

As soon as he was gone, Nancy nearly screeched with excitement. "Did you see that? He totally digs me."

Her excitement was infectious and I cracked a smile. "He definitely perks up when you're around. I think he's scared to death of me. You should have seen how he flipped out when I ..." I didn't know if I was ready to tell her what I had done last night. I was suddenly afraid she'd never want to see me anymore.

"He told us everything, dork. You don't have to hide anything from me to protect me. I've told you before, we're in this together, okay?" Nancy gave me a quick hug and a reassuring smile.

"It was pretty crazy." I sighed in relief and made her lean over so I could whisper all the details I could remember about the incident last night, including the fact that the less flesh corpses had, the harder they were to control.

Nancy whispered back, "You should write that down for Jason. Give him something more to go on." Nancy walked over to her closet and tossed a pair of jeans and a t-shirt on her bed. "Wear that. My wardrobe is officially yours. And if you don't tell me every single detail about Ryan showing up in *my* bed, I'm going to have to kill you."

"Thanks." As I changed into the outfit I gave Nancy a play-

165

by-play of this morning. She squealed in all the right places and high fived me when I told her that he liked me ever since he tutored me last year.

Nancy eyed me up and down as if inspecting a piece of meat. "Perfect. Ryan and Bill will be at each others throats by noon." My eyes must have grown round with horror because Nancy shook her head. "I'm kidding! I just meant that you look great."

"I think you should know; Jason is at least seventy-years-old." I wanted to tell her before she started liking him too much. Most people didn't care about age differences since almost everyone looked the same age anyway, but I wanted to give Nancy a heads up just in case it bothered her.

"Actually, he's ninety-five!" From the way her eyes lit up, I guessed Nancy didn't care at all. "It's so romantic. I always wanted to be with an older man and Jason is... well... he's perfect."

"You certainly insult him enough." I smiled at her doey eyes. I'd never witnessed Nancy liking *anyone* before, mainly because no one would go near her on the account of being my friend. Seeing her so fired up about someone was nice. It made me feel like life was normal, even if just for a second.

"We're just flirting. He knows I don't mean it. Besides, I think he likes it. What a freak," she said with a grin that had no signs of leaving her face any time soon.

"All right, crush girl, let's go to school." I smiled.

"Crush girl? You and Ryan are the ones who are finally speaking after a year of pining over each other. At least I'm being bold." Nancy was almost offended, but her grin stayed in tact.

"Fine. I'm crush girl, you're slut girl." I ducked before Nancy could hit my head with a laugh.

Nancy laughed with me and put her arm in mine as we walked to her door. "Hopefully school will be uneventful and boring. I need to have at least one day of relaxation."

Great. Now I knew I was in for trouble. Might as well dare the universe to spit on us. But of all the places I could be right now, school did appear to be the safest. Jill would seem like a good friend compared to what I had been through the last couple of days.

"Can we eat something? I'm starving." I knew we were short on time, but I needed a full stomach to face the day.

"Sure. We can watch my mom fumble over every word with Jason. I swear she's driving him crazy!" Nancy rolled her eyes.

"Unlike you." I couldn't resist.

"I'm driving him crazy in *other* ways." Nancy squeezed my arm with a small laugh.

We walked down the winding stairs and made our way through the house to the kitchen table. Jason was there with George and Vianne fawning over his every word. It was kind of cute. Jason was the oldest by far of the entire group. George and Vianne were only in their forties, though everyone at the table looked eighteen.

Vianne's eyes lit up when she saw us enter. "Girls, sit down. Have a quick bite."

The doorbell rang at that very moment.

George stood up as if being with three girls and Jason put him at his limit of tolerance. "I'll get that," he mumbled under his breath as he hurried to the front door.

Nancy and I sat down across from Jason who was stuffing a

cheese omelet in his mouth.

"Jason here, was just telling me how brave you were last night, Chelsan." Vianne smiled from ear-to-ear.

I nearly choked on my toast. Did Jason really tell her what happened? My mind raced. She obviously seemed fine about the whole thing, proud even, but the more people that knew my secret the more danger they would be in. I was about to respond when Jason cut me off.

"If Chelsan hadn't noticed that mugger and called the cops, that poor lady would have been breathing through a tube the rest of her life." Jason smiled eagerly at me.

So proud of himself. What an idiot. Why would he even make that up?

"Anyone would have done the same." I jammed a fork full of scrambled eggs before I was forced to say anything more.

Jason's annoyed eyes met mine. "Vianne was just asking why we came in so late last night. Filling out paper work, giving our statements. It was a good thing Nancy was there for support. I know Chelsan really appreciated it."

Oh. Maybe he wasn't such an idiot.

"Anything for my girl," Nancy said with a grin.

"You guys ready?" Bill's voice came from behind us.

I turned around in my seat. Bill was there with his usual smile to greet me. I felt a rush of emotion when I saw him. Bill had really been there for me from the moment he gave me a brand spanking new electronic reader to picking us up last night at the virtual bar. Nancy and Bill really were my best friends. I never knew how much they cared until my life became the current nightmare I was living. It was hard for me to accept that Bill may have feelings for me other than friendship. I had to admit there were times where I was tempted because of how safe he made me feel, but I truly didn't feel that way for him. I cared about him so much I almost wish I did like him, to spare him any hurt. I didn't want to be the jerk that broke his heart.

Bill grabbed a piece of my toast and shoved it down his throat. "We're going to be late."

"We're coming, we're coming, geez Bill," Nancy teased.

"You guys have your stuff?" George asked from the hallway. He walked in followed by Ryan.

My heart jumped in my throat and I suppressed the urge to laugh. Ryan didn't miss a beat. Aside from the quick wink, he acted as if he hadn't just spent the morning with me upstairs.

"I was just talking to Ryan here and he was telling me about the new hydro-converters they installed at the school. Pretty state of the art stuff," George said as if he was incredibly impressed by Ryan's knowledge. "I might want to hire you when you graduate." George patted Ryan's shoulder like a proud father.

Nancy guffawed. "You and everyone else on the planet! Dad, Ryan's already had about a million offers from the top science research labs in the world. Get in line. He's the kid who solved Trildion's Theorem. Duh."

"I appreciate the offer, but I'd like to try college first," Ryan added diplomatically.

Regardless of Ryan trying to let George down with grace, he still looked pretty humbled and embarrassed. George probably thought he was being generous, but Ryan's I.Q. put him above and beyond any job George could offer him at the Science Corp. It was basically considered the lower end of the science community, like making hydrogen fuel cells for cars and appliances and such. Good money, but not much respect in the science world.

Ryan walked over to me, his sandy blonde hair ruffled in all the right places, and kissed my forehead. My knees nearly buckled.

"Hey." I tried to hide the shake from my voice. I kept on flashing to this morning when he held my face in his hands...

"Hey," he said in an 'oh so cool' tone. How could he do that so consistently?!

"Seriously, we're late." Bill's voice deflated the mood.

I looked over at him and I could tell he was trying to hide his irritation at my obvious feelings for Ryan. I wanted to make him feel better, but I didn't know how, and I figured the more he saw us together, the easier it would eventually be.

"Okay, I'll get my stuff," I replied as nicely as I could to Bill, which appeared to make a visible improvement in his expression. It went from angry to shaking his head in exasperation.

"Already ahead of you." Nancy walked over to the counter and tossed me a backpack. "Your reader is in there."

Vianne, George and Jason walked the four of us to the front door.

I turned to Jason before we left the house. "Are you going to be here when I get back?"

Jason leaned in to whisper in my ear again, which made both Nancy and Ryan completely annoyed. "I just wanted to make Nancy jealous. Think it's working?"

"Yes. Now answer my question." I couldn't believe I ever had a crush on this man-whore.

"Of course. We're in this together. I'll research as much as I can about Turner *and* about your special gift. When this place is clean, I'll tell you everything I know about the ceremony he performed. We'll figure this out, get you safe. And get me safe while I'm at it." Jason pulled away with a grin.

Ryan grabbed my hand territorially and threw one last look of 'aggressive boy speak' over at Jason. It didn't faze Jason at all. He walked back into the house with Nancy's parents.

As we climbed into Bill's hover-car, Nancy leaned in close to me. "What did he say?"

I sighed. This was going to be a long day.

Driving to school was actually nice. I sat there quietly while the three of them filled me in on what our cover story was. It was basically what Jason had told Nancy's parents with a few added details. Bill seemed to have accepted my power with as much enthusiasm as everyone else had. His only issue being that he hadn't seen me do it yet. Ryan told him all about the plant I brought back to life and the two of them actually bonded. Well, if my curse can bring my boyfriend and one of my best friends together then bully for me, I guess. Boyfriend. It had a nice ring to it.

And during the whole ride over, Nancy would always manage to bring the conversation back to the topic of Jason.

I couldn't help but smile. These were the people who were going to stick with me through everything no matter how hard or how ugly. And I suddenly felt extremely lucky. My mom would be so happy for me.

Bill drove his hover-car into the designated parking area for students. It was about half-full.

"I'd prepare myself if I were you, Chelsan. We'll keep you surrounded." Bill was in strategic mode and I wasn't sure why.

"What do you mean? I thought it was going to be safe at school?" Maybe he was just being cautious.

Bill exited the car and opened the back door where I sat. He leaned in and smiled at me as if I were a naïve idiot. "Chelsan, your whole trailer park was demolished and your mother died, people are going to treat you differently. There may be press as well. This is a big story. Especially since you go to this school, you're the only person of *meager means* to have been accepted. I'm surprised Jason isn't on this."

I stepped out of the car with a grumble. I knew he was right, I hadn't thought about *those* kind of consequences I was so focused on the *someone trying to kill me* part. "This is going to suck."

Nancy came around and gave me a supportive squeeze. "It'll be fine. Mostly people will just stare and feel sorry for you."

"Keep an eye out for Jill. If Joan was right about Turner giving Jill's dad orders, who knows what she'll do to you." Ryan had positioned himself next to me and I felt his hand wrap around mine like I belonged to him. If everyone was going after me today, I wanted his hand permanently attached to mine.

We walked through the school's third floor entrance to a melee of flash photography and screaming reporters.

"Here we go," I mumbled under my breath.

I couldn't believe the amount of people that swarmed around me like locusts. Nancy, Bill and Ryan quickly formed a circle of protection around me acting like my own personal guard dogs.

"CHELSAN! CHELSAN!" The press shouted my name, edging closer. I felt like a celebrity.

Bill leaned down so I could hear him from above all the ruckus. "Reporters aren't allowed in the classrooms. We just need to get you to Mr. Alaster's."

Nancy took the lead and literally shoved anyone who was in our way, including students. Most of the inhabitants of Geoffrey Turner High never gave me a second thought except to spit on me or shove me on Jill's orders, but now they looked at me like stunned deer. I couldn't figure out if this was good or bad. Their expressions certainly didn't give me much help. I was like a slow moving hover accident that they couldn't keep their eyes off of.

We inched our way toward Mr. Alaster's class on the first floor. The whole time questions were shouted from the reporters around us. Mostly, they wanted to know about the tornado and the mysterious green smoke I claimed to have seen. Others asked about Bruce and where he could be located. So far, nothing of real panic. I could ignore them in good conscious. I wished that this story would get old and they'd leave me alone soon.

Just as we were about to enter Mr. Alaster's class, the entire press corps stopped in their tracks as if someone had hit them all with a stun gun. They appeared to be listening to something.

Ryan leaned in with a sigh of relief. "It's their ear pieces. Stopping like that means that they're all getting some breaking news story. This might just be your lucky day. For them all to be silent like that, the news will be pretty big."

I took a deep breath of thankfulness as Nancy reached for the door and started to open it. Hopefully, whatever it was that they were listening to was way more interesting than me.

A slow buzz of excitement started at the end of the hallway and came to a roar in a matter of seconds. But instead of deserting me like I expected them to, they shoved their way closer, eyes alight with the fire of a burning story.

They screamed at me all at once, desperate for me to answer, but I couldn't differentiate what any of them were trying to ask me.

"Come on." Nancy shoved me inside the room with Ryan squeezing my hand harder than before. Bill came in with us even though he had Calculus first period.

And just as Nancy shut the door in the reporters' faces I could hear one reporter above the rest. "What do you think about Vice President of Population Control Geoffrey Turner coming to meet with you today in person?!"

Nancy slammed the door shut and looked at me with horrified eyes.

Gulp. What was that?

My whole body went numb. Turner's coming to meet me? Today?! My mind reeled and I thought my brain was going to explode.

Mr. Alaster was suddenly in my face, full of concern and sympathy. "Let's get you to your seat. I can't believe you actually came to school today. You should take it easy. We can send your work home with Nancy," he uttered this in a rush. Mr. Alaster apparently wasn't used to the news being right outside his door practically salivating through the window. It was like watching cats in front of a mouse hole, waiting for me to come back out so they could pounce.

I let Mr. Alaster lead me to my seat even though it meant

174

parting with Ryan's hand. Ryan didn't even let poor Ernie Gelson have a choice when he made him switch seats so that Ryan could sit next to me. Nancy, of course, sat in her usual seat, on my other side, and Bill stood awkwardly behind me.

Mr. Alaster patted Bill on the shoulder. "You may go to your first period now, Bill. I have things under control here."

Bill gave me a last look of encouragement and then braved his way through the door. Roars of questions greeted him and most likely a team of them would follow Bill all the way to Calculus as well.

I noticed Jill and Joan staring at me from their desks a few seats back. It was hard to say what was going on in their little pea brains, but whatever it was it didn't look favorable to my cause. Jill was downright hostile. Which wasn't exactly new, but the way she looked at me made me worry. She knew something and I wanted to know what it was. Maybe it would help me prepare for Turner's visit today.

I tried to breathe evenly and slowly. Turner wouldn't kill me today, not with all these witnesses. Unless, he made it look like an accident. I could hear the headlines now: "Geoffrey Turner consoles survivor when she accidently falls down a flight of steps…"

Jason said it best: I was *so* dead.

I had to stay ahead of the game. I had to be smarter than him, like my dad when he flipped Turner's spell back on itself and saved my mom and I. I had to keep reminding myself that I had a power that Turner couldn't touch.

I swallowed in dread.

Maybe he could.

I thought about the soldiers yelling "Zombie 442." I thought about the green smoke. I thought about my mother's vision of Turner's arm slicing open and then sealing back up with an ugly white scar…

He had powers. Or access to them.

And they may trump mine.

I just didn't know.

I didn't want to start sweating in a fit of panic in front of everyone in the class so I settled on taking deep breaths. And besides, I couldn't give Jill the satisfaction of seeing me in such distress. She was probably on orders to spy on me and I didn't want to give Turner any indication that I was scared to death of him. And I was.

Mr. Alaster kept on glancing at me but pretending that he wasn't. And although I could tell he was concerned, it made me more nervous.

"Settle down. Settle down. I still have a class to teach despite all the excitement," Mr. Alaster said to an already quiet class. His mind was so focused on the reporters outside he hadn't even noticed that the classroom was silent. "Click your readers to page four-hundred and six." And he delved into a long and boring lecture that no one really paid attention to. Half the time I don't think even he was listening to himself, his eyes kept roaming from me to the frosted glass square of the door and the silhouetted forms of the press on the other side.

The click of the PA system made Mr. Alaster jump slightly.

"Oh! Everyone quiet! An announcement!" Mr. Alaster waved his hands as if we were all screaming loudly.

Again, no one was talking. If I weren't so terrified, I'd actually

176

find his behavior kind of funny.

The Principal's voice crackled through the speaker hanging over the door. "May I have your attention please?" A pause then a deep breath, "It has come to my attention that Vice President of Population Control Geoffrey Turner will be gracing us with his presence at our school today. This will be the first time he's made an appearance here since the grand opening twenty years ago so I expect all of you to be on your best behavior. His sole mission is to express his condolences to one of our very own, Ms. Chelsan Derée after the tragedy that destroyed her home and family. Our hearts go out to you, Ms. Derée. The assembly will be after class. Have a good day and get back to work."

I could feel all eyes on me. I wanted to disappear from sight. I stared at the surface of my desk, hoping Mr. Alaster would break the tension by finishing his boring lecture on the history of paper. Instead I heard the grating voice of my worst enemy a few seats back: Jill.

"Maybe Chelsan would like to share her feelings. Losing your mom must be excruciatingly painful. Why don't you tell us about it?" Jill sneered.

I tried to rationalize how anyone could be that mean. Some kind of trauma? Horrible parents? Massive insecurity? Or just plain evil. All of the above probably.

Ryan turned around in his seat and gave Jill a look that silenced her immediately.

Mr. Alaster stepped forward so he was in direct eye contact with Jill. "If I hear one more crass and vilely inhuman comment out of you again I *will* be requesting your leave from this establishment! My job be damned, I will not tolerate your archaic, bullish behavior in my class again!"

Whoa.

Jill froze. She was completely stunned.

I had never seen Mr. Alaster that angry before. It was one thing to hear Jill say horrible things to me, I was used to that, it went into my 'Jill filter.' But when Mr. Alaster put her comment into perspective on how mean it really was, it suddenly made the loss of my mom too real at that moment. It was like when you're hit in the head by a ball and you're in kind of a shock until everyone comes up to you and asks if you're okay. And the floodgates open. That was exactly what happened. I just started to cry.

Apparently, even Jill didn't have anything snide to say about that which was almost a disappointment. If I could turn my emotion to anger, I could stop crying! This was so embarrassing! I covered my face so no one could see me, but mostly so I couldn't see them staring at me. My mom was everything to me. I still couldn't believe she was gone. With all the danger and excitement of the last few days I was able to shove back most of my anguish over losing her to simply survive. But hearing Jill and Mr. Alaster put it out there, I felt so bare and dirty almost. Like I needed a long shower to wash away my feelings of being exposed to the public about something so personal. It was hard enough that my mom died.

I felt Ryan and Nancy huddle around me like a protective circle of hugs. It felt nice and I began to calm down. "I'm okay." I found myself mumbling through my hands.

"Take your time, Chelsan," came Mr. Alaster's sympathetic voice. He'd probably be fired when Jill's father heard about what he said to his daughter. But I'd always be grateful to him for standing up to her.

I took a deep breath and pulled my hands down away from my face. "I'm good."

Ryan and Nancy tentatively sat back down in their seats, their worried eyes still on me. The class was silent, watching. I looked up at Mr. Alaster imploringly. *Please start talking about something that doesn't involve me,* I begged him in my head.

He seemed to catch my drift because he cleared his throat and continued his lecture on paper. The minutes dragged by painfully. Part of me wanted class to be over so I could run away from *the stares*, and the other part of me didn't want it to end because I'd have to brave the press corps that pawed at the door waiting for me to exit.

The bell finally rang and I felt my heart leap into my throat. I could hear the rustling of reporters outside. Jill stood up first followed closely by Joan. She hadn't said a word since Mr. Alaster basically told her to shut up, and surprisingly didn't appear all that upset by it. This, of course, made me worry. She was up to something. I had known her long enough to know that.

Jill and Joan were out the door and swallowed whole by the crowd of reporters. The rest of the class slowly started to file out as well, leaving me, Nancy, Ryan and Mr. Alaster staring at the doorway with trepidation.

"Assembly time," Mr. Alaster stated what we were all thinking.

"Yup," I agreed as I tried not to make eye contact with any of the screaming news people.

Ryan grabbed my hand and locked his fingers tightly with

179

mine. "We got your back."

Nancy wrapped her arm around my free arm. "We won't let him touch you."

"Chelsan, I'm here if you need me. And if those screaming monsters are too much for you, you can always sneak in here for protection. They can't enter a classroom under any circumstances. Okay?" Mr. Alaster managed a small smile of encouragement.

"Okay, thanks," I replied shyly. Who knew Mr. Alaster could be that cool?

"Yeah, thanks, Mr. Alaster." Nancy was genuinely grateful, too. "Actually, we need a few moments. Before we go out into *that*."

"Of course. I'll leave you three alone." Mr. Alaster didn't even blink. He headed straight for the door. "Move aside! Move aside!" He shoved his way through the press, pushing a little bit harder than he probably should have. He turned around and gave us a quick wink.

Ryan and Nancy both turned to me, game faces on.

"You ready for this?" Ryan asked, though I could ask the same of him. He looked petrified.

"We could always duck out the back," Nancy suggested, but we all knew that was impossible.

"I'm good. Let's do this." I tried to sound as pumped up as possible though it was the complete opposite of what I felt.

"So, no plan?" Nancy crinkled her nose in concern.

"Nope."

And with that, I charged ahead, Ryan holding my right hand, Nancy clinging to my other arm.

I felt as if I could dive on top of the reporters and they'd carry me to the assembly hall like I was at a rock concert it was so crowded. They all screamed at me again.

"Over here!" I heard Bill's voice above the rest and I tried to find him in the crowd.

The sea of people parted before us like a human pair of scissors except instead of blades it was two lines of men in dark suits and sunglasses. The reporters shoved up against the wall of men, but their defenses held strong. At the end of it all was Bill with a silly grin on his face.

He half ran over to us and nodded to the men in suits. "Money comes in handy sometimes. When I told Dad about how the press was hounding you, he sent a whole team of his best body guards over here."

"Wow. This is just what I needed. Thanks, Bill." I let go of Ryan and Nancy and hugged Bill as hard as I could.

The reporters still yelled, but at least they couldn't touch me. The guards barely flinched as the press tried to tear them apart to get to me.

Ryan pulled me away from Bill by clasping my hand in his again. It made my heart pound knowing how jealous he was, but Bill had really pulled through and I wanted him to know how grateful I was.

Bill shrugged at Ryan's obvious territorial behavior and motioned us forward. "They'll get us to the assembly hall."

The men closed ranks forming a twenty-man circle around us and we made our way comfortably toward the assembly hall.

"I didn't want to show you this, but I think you should know." Bill turned to me cautiously.

"Just show us, Bill." Nancy was having none of it. She was in one of her *get to the point* moods.

Bill pulled out his cell phone and popped up a holo-video for us. It was me in Mr. Alaster's class, crying like a baby. Uuuggghh!

"That's why Jill said what she did. She was trying to provoke you for this video." Ryan shook his head angrily.

"Yeah, well, I was dumb enough to fall for it," I groaned.

"Dumb? The most horrible, horrendous thing that can happen to a person happened to you, *two days ago*! I think there would be something wrong with you if you *didn't* cry!" Nancy appeared more outraged at my response than about the video itself.

"Turner probably told her to do it. It's all about the story and spin for him. He'll make sure that everyone knows you're too distraught to be a reliable witness, and with your step-dad gone, no one will believe you about the green smoke. He's just covering his bases," Ryan said and then kissed my cheek. It instantly made me feel better.

We arrived at the assembly hall without incident. The room itself was the biggest in the school. The ceiling was forty feet high and made out of a solar frosted glass that adjusted to the light outside, keeping the assembly hall the same day-like brightness no matter what time of day it was.

Painted yellow walls complimented the dark-stained brown of the stage and fold out chairs were placed in neat rows for all the students. The main focus of the room was the stage that made up the entire back wall and came up about five feet off the ground. Maroon velvet curtains normally framed the theater like a picture, but today they remained closed, probably hiding my grandpa behind them.

The press was only allowed in the back of the room so we were safe as soon as we sat down in our seats. After making sure we were okay, the bodyguards stood against the wall waiting for us to finish so they could keep vigil once more.

Bill and Ryan sat on either side of me while Nancy took the aisle next to Bill.

I could see the holos of me crying on almost everyone's phone. It was completely surreal. The only part of the video I could stand to watch was when Ryan and Nancy hugged me. I gripped Ryan's hand harder and he stroked my hand with his thumb in response. My toes tingled in delight and it made waiting for the assembly to start more bearable.

Bill leaned down to my ear, "My dad said you can have the guards as long as you need them. Turner won't be able to get to you."

I wanted to tell him that if Turner wanted to *get to me* there was absolutely nothing any of us could do about it, but I didn't want to say anything to upset him. Especially since he'd gone through all the trouble to bring his dad's bodyguards here.

Ryan squeezed my hand to reassure me and kissed my shoulder.

"You don't have to prove that you guys are dating. I get it," Bill fumed. Apparently, he wasn't as cool with Ryan as I had hoped.

"Are you sure about that? You seem pretty set on the fact that you still have a shot with her." Ryan turned to Bill, just as angry.

"Guys, please don't do this." I tried to calm them down, but neither one of them heard me.

"Here we go," I heard Nancy groan. "Boys."

"Well maybe that's because I've been friends with Chelsan *publicly* for three years now! I wasn't the a-hole that was afraid of what people might think!" Bill's nostrils actually flared.

I sat in the middle of the two of them holding my breath.

"You're so rich no one cares what you do!" Ryan's hand squeezed mine to the point of pain.

"Ow," I said, but he couldn't hear me.

"Nancy isn't rich and she didn't care what people thought!" Bill roared.

The people that were already staring, now stared even harder. Even the press tried to take pictures of this feud.

"Don't bring me into this," Nancy chimed in, but she knew it was a futile effort.

But Bill's comment worked like a slap in the face to Ryan. His grip loosened on my hand and his body slumped in defeat. "You're right."

And to my surprise, Bill actually seemed sorry. "Forget it. I'm just jealous."

Neither one of them could look at each other.

Nancy rolled her eyes and crossed her arms. "You two are idiots."

"Can I say something?" I wanted to clear the air.

"No," all three of them spoke in unison, which made them all smile.

"Fine." Maybe letting the two of them have it out was enough. I'd probably make it worse anyway.

Principal Weatherby walked up to the microphone in the center of the stage. He was a bald portly man who had the thickest handlebar mustache I had ever seen. His face was always a rosy pink color, which gave the impression that he was forever embarrassed. Weatherby appeared to be in his late twenties, but everyone knew he was one-hundred and sixty-seven. He helped build this school. It was his pride and joy.

More nervous than usual, Weatherby's shaking hands grabbed the microphone stand in front of him. "Quiet down. Quiet down." He cleared his throat as everyone in the room stopped and gave him their attention. "It is my honor and privilege to introduce the namesake of our school, Vice President of Population Control Geoffrey Turner!" He yelled the last bit since the room had already exploded in applause.

I think we were the only four who didn't move a muscle. We all waited in anticipation of what would happen next.

We didn't have to wait long. The curtains behind Principal Weatherby began to part. I had been right. Turner stood on stage behind the curtains, probably watching me. He walked toward Weatherby with a plastered smile on his face. Some of the students oooh'd and aaahh'd, not just because they were seeing the most powerful man in the world, but because he actually looked old.

Age-pro was invented when Turner was in his fifties and not many people of that era were very public. It was one thing to see the Vice President on the holo-tv, but entirely different to see him in person. He had wrinkles around his eyes and creases on his forehead, his body seemed normal, but his hands had brownish spots and blue veins that you could literally see from where I sat. It was a bit of a shock for everyone. Old was worse than poor for the general public. Being poor myself, I might have had sympathy for the old guy, but I knew what he was capable of. I tried to block out the images of him slicing his arm open or of his wife and the boa constrictor oozing out of her mouth. Aaaah, my grandparents. No wonder I could raise the dead, look at my genes.

Five others followed after him and I craned my neck to get a better look at them…

"I'm dead…" I croaked.

Nancy, Ryan and Bill all looked at me for something more, but I couldn't utter another syllable.

"What's wrong?" Ryan asked anyway.

I was breathless with disbelief.

Standing behind Turner were five people…

…Five *dead* people.

Their black swirling holes mocking me from my seat.

"His staff…" I tried to keep the squeak from my voice.

"What about them?" Nancy talked to me like I was four to try to calm down.

"They're dead. They're all dead." I could literally hear and feel my voice shake.

My three friends had no words. Their eyes opened in amazement and they watched me as if they waited for me to say I was kidding.

I wasn't.

Someone else could do what I could do. Maybe a lot more than someone, maybe lots of someones. My mind whirled and whirled until I thought I was going to puke on Ryan's lap.

"Chelsan!" Ryan turned my head to his with his hand. "They're calling you up to the stage."

186

Everyone gawked at me. I took a deep breath. I seemed to be taking a lot of those lately. Worst of all, I peered up at Turner, curious and horrified all at the same time. His eyes bore into mine. I could feel the hatred emanating there, boiling, in fact, so much so I had to turn away. I had no doubt in my mind; he knew exactly who I was and he wanted me dead. I tried to rationalize in my head how I could ever escape this mess. There was a count down happening and I had no control over when it was going to hit zero.

I stood up on shaking legs and made my way to the stairs on the side of the stage. The most important thing I could do was to keep a clear mind and try and think of a plan. First things first, if someone was keeping these corpses alive and kicking, I needed to find out if I could take control of them myself? I walked as slowly as I could so I could experiment. I concentrated and tried to link myself to the dead man closest to me who typed something in his reader.

Nothing. He kept typing.

Okay.

Again. Maybe I was nervous. Of course I was nervous! Concentrate.

Nothing.

But I sensed something new this time. It was as if there was an invisible wall completely covering his black hole. It was literally a barrier of some sort and I had no idea how to break through it.

This was not a good sign.

I found myself on stage standing in front of Turner and his zombie staff.

His smile was forced, but no one noticed.

Turner held out his hand for me to shake and I obliged cautiously. His hands were soft but firm in their grip, his eyes found mine, his smile cunning and cruel. My head churned again. I thought I was going to pee my pants in front of the school. (*The world* actually, considering all the cameras were focused on us.) This guy really had a hold on my fear button and he was pressing it over and over. That was when he went in for a hug.

As he tightened his arms around me, he leaned in to my ear. "Hello, Granddaughter."

That could have been a loving moment in life if Geoffrey Turner wasn't completely evil.

Turner pulled away with an even larger grin than before. The roar of the crowd egging him on. I was amazed that I was still conscious.

He turned to the microphone. "It is with great pleasure that I award Chelsan Derée with a full scholarship for the rest of her stay here at Geoffrey Turner High School."

More roars from the crowd.

Turner droned on and on about the tragic events that led to my mother's death and my home being destroyed.

It gave me time to process. Paying my way through school indicated that he wasn't planning on killing me soon. Or maybe it was an alibi. I needed to discuss this with my friends. But in the mean time, I needed to stay on my toes around this guy. And I needed to calm down! I was letting my terror rule me and I wanted to keep my head clear. Think this through, logically and calmly. I could use any dead thing in my near vicinity to hurt him if need be. That was good. Just because these five corpses were out of my control didn't necessarily mean I was screwed. To keep my mind focused I found a dead mouse's black hole inside the assembly hall wall. I attached to him easily, made him run a little, even threw in a jump. Okay, that meant Turner didn't control every dead thing in the surrounding area. Just these five guys.

I glanced back at one of them. A lady with black-rimmed glasses and blonde hair pulled back in a tight bun. She wore a pants suit and held a briefcase. She even fidgeted for goodness sake! Whoever controlled her was really good. A thought hit me. Maybe someone wasn't controlling her. Maybe this was more like the Vodun ritual Mr. Alaster told us about from the Scientific Journal. If that were true how were they controlled? There had to be some way. I needed more information. I tried connecting with her black hole, but she had the same protective wall that the first man had.

Quick test. Yep. They all did. Great.

My mind ripped back into the present moment when I heard Turner say, "I'm going to meet privately with Ms. Derée in Principal Weatherby's office to take care of all her needs. Thanks to the press for coming out here and thank you to Principal Weatherby for such a kind welcome. Good day to you all."

Privately? Uh, oh.

I searched the audience to see Nancy, Ryan and Bill giving me looks of encouragement, but I could tell they were more scared than I was.

I was dizzy with all the deep breaths I was taking, but it somehow calmed my stomach. I barely heard Principal

189

Weatherby excuse the students. Their shuffling out the door was another step closer to me being alone with Gramps.

"Ms. Derée?" Turner held his hand out for me to follow Principal Weatherby.

Weatherby turned to me with an expression of genuine concern. "Don't worry, Chelsan, we've restricted the press access to my office. They won't bother you."

I smiled, but inside I thought that I'd kind of like the reporters around now. Maybe I could convince Principal Weatherby to stay with us. "Principal Weatherby?"

"Yes, Chelsan." I'd never seen him so worried about me. He was usually warning me that if I didn't have the money for this school I was no longer welcome. I guess with everything that had happened to me, he was feeling a little guilty.

I walked up next to him so that Turner and his staff were trailing us by a few feet. I spoke quietly so only Weatherby could hear. "I'd feel more comfortable if you stayed with me. I'm too nervous around the Vice President." I glanced back to make sure Turner didn't hear.

Weatherby placed his hand on my shoulder supportively. "I hear you, Chelsan, but I can't argue with the man. He wants his time alone with you. Don't worry, it won't take long, he has a busy schedule. He just wants to go over some contracts with you so he can set you up financially. Great man, Geoffrey Turner."

Yeah, he's peachy. Oh by the way did I mention he wants to kill me? Okay, thanks for your support. Bleh.

I was on my own. I could deal. Hopefully.

We were at Weatherby's office in no time.

"Thank you, Principal Weatherby, we'll only be a few moments," Turner said with his usual grin.

"I'll just be in the teacher's lounge when you're through." Weatherby shook Turner's hand, gave me an encouraging wink and headed toward the lounge next door.

"After you." Turner held the door for me and I walked through trying not to shake too much.

Turner entered with his staff. One of his men closed the door. When everyone was inside, the five corpses lined up against the wall.

Weatherby's office was pretty large with a six foot oak desk near the back and brown leather furniture. The throne behind the desk (and it seriously looked like a throne, over five feet high, two feet wide, mahogany trim with grommet punched leather) was a statement of how much Weatherby thought of himself. There were holo-pictures everywhere on his wall of Weatherby with some celebrity or political figure. It was almost like a shrine to himself and how many people he'd met over the years.

Turner sat in Weatherby's seat of power and motioned for me to sit across from him in the puny wooden chair reserved for visitors. "Please sit."

"I'll stand." Better to stay on my feet.

"Suit yourself." Turner nodded his head to one of his staff and the woman with the briefcase walked over and laid it on the table. "Thank you, Marion. Could you close the curtains, please?"

Marion didn't say a word as she walked to the large window overlooking the cherry blossomed courtyard and closed the heavy brown curtains. Only the overhead lights from the office gave any illumination to the room.

"So." Turner let that hang in the air for a good two minutes.

"So," I repeated back, trying to figure out what he was going to do next.

"I finally meet the murderer of my only son."

And there it was. He really *did* blame me for my father's death.

"No chance of this being a heartfelt family reunion then?" I figured I'd throw that out there.

"No chance," he replied and my blood temperature dropped forty degrees.

"If you had given your blessings instead of your curses, he'd still be alive." Wow. That was bold. I was really impressed with myself.

Until I saw the look on his face.

I had never seen so much loathing in a person's eyes before. Not even Jill's and that was saying a lot. Maybe I should have kept my mouth shut. But maybe I shouldn't have. Something about this man made my skin crawl and I realized it wasn't fear, it was a revulsion that spread through me to every fiber of my soul. If he knew who I was then the attack on the trailer park was intentional. It wasn't random, it was purposeful and targeted. He was finishing the job he started eighteen years ago.

"Trash." He said it so quietly and with so much venom I almost flinched instinctively.

Minutes passed with agonizing slowness as we stared at each other from across the room. His dead staff motionless, watching.

Turner focused his attention on the briefcase and opened it

as if we were in the middle of a business meeting. He pulled out an electronic reader and he punched up a contract, sliding it to me on the desk.

"Thumbprint, there. It's your money for the rest of the year." I could tell he was detached at this point. Maybe I could get through this meeting alive after all. Come to think of it, it was crazy for me to think he'd try anything in such a public setting. How would he explain my dead body after he just had his *private* meeting with me? I had been so worked up on the possibility of an attack I hadn't stopped to really think about the practicality of it all.

"I'm going to read it first, thank you." My body and mind were starting to relax a bit. He wouldn't hurt me. Not today anyway.

"Be my guest." Turner leaned back in the giant chair folding his hands comfortably over his stomach.

I read the contract fully which didn't take long since it consisted of two paragraphs. Nothing in it suggested anything of foul play, just a brief summary of how much money I was to receive minus the costs of tuition and materials. It was actually a hefty sum; I'd be able to live out the rest of the year in comfort. If I wasn't killed first, and therein lied the rub. I thumbprinted the document and it instantly deposited the cash into a savings account. Sweet.

"Can I go now?" I asked hoping he'd say yes.

"No."

I tensed up. The way he said it chilled me.

Slowly, Turner stood up from his seat and walked over to me. "You'll be leaving, but it won't be alive."

I took my chance.

I whirled around with as much speed as I could muster and bolted for the door. Two of his staff members grabbed me before I even made it a foot. I tried to scream. They covered my mouth, blocking any sound to signal for rescue.

Turner placed a finger on his mouth and smiled wickedly at me. "Are you going to be quiet?"

I nodded my head, knowing no one was outside anyway. Weatherby had made sure that we were to be undisturbed at all costs. That cost was *me* apparently. The man let his hand off my mouth.

"You must be able to tell that my staff here is *special*." Turner mocked.

"You mean dead? Yeah, I noticed." I could feel my eyes roll.

"You'll be like them soon. It's a quick ceremony, and then you'll be under my control," he stated, very pleased with himself.

I hadn't thought about this outcome. Of course. He could kill me and no one would know the difference because everyone would still think I was alive. Everyone except my friends, they'd know, but who cared at that point? How was I going to get out of this? A question I asked myself a lot these days. Stall. Stalling was good, and then maybe I could think of something in the mean time.

"Do you control them?" I asked not expecting a real answer.

Turner laughed. "You sense my little barrier do you? Tell me, do you know *why* you can't break through it?"

Oooooh, so condescending. I hated that I was related to this guy, but what was worse, I knew he knew more about my power than I did and that was just annoying.

"I know more than you think." I said it with as much conviction as I could muster.

And to my surprise, Turner actually paused in doubt. "What do you know?"

Things started to click in my head and I decided to make a gamble. "Everything Jason Keroff knows. He's been staying with me at Nancy's." I fished to see if he had Nancy's house bugged.

And it paid off.

"That boyfriend of yours may have found a way to block our listening devices, but it won't matter in about ten minutes." Turner glared at me.

Ryan. Why didn't he tell me he had blocked Turner's signal? It didn't make sense, but regardless of how the signal was blocked, the end result was Turner hadn't heard anything that happened at Nancy's. And that meant, he only had the virtual reality bar incident for his information on me. Didn't know what that meant yet, but I knew it was important.

"Syringe," Turner spat out. He was really going to do this.

The woman called Marion went to the briefcase and pulled out a syringe full of clear liquid.

"It's a quick poison, you won't feel any pain. Unfortunately." His eyes were actually sparkling with that last statement.

Panic. This was a good time to panic.

She leaned in to inject me with the poison.

Struggling was out of the question I was so paralyzed with fear. I was going to die. I was seriously, unequivocally about to die.

The needle was about to touch my neck when…

...I acted on instinct just as I had when I was seven with Bruce and the spider.

THWUMP!

It felt like a tearing of flesh as I ripped into the black holes of all five of the dead bodies. The invisible barrier that kept me out was obliterated. My whole body flushed with the power of it. I almost wanted to burst out laughing from the rush.

I made Marion pull back the needle.

Turner's face fell in disbelief. "Marion! Inject the girl!"

I reached into the two men holding me and made them grab Turner instead.

Turner was too shocked to react properly. He looked at me with horror in his eyes. "Impossible!"

"Oh, it's possible, Gramps." I gained my footing and for the first time I knew I would survive this round.

I made Marion point the needle at his neck. I had no intention of killing him, but I wanted to escape this office unscathed.

"Stop! I order you to stop!" Turner tried to order the corpses, but I had full control.

"You're going to tell me a few things, or I'm going to have Marion, here, inject you with that poison. Remember, it works both ways. I can bring you back, too and I have no problems with the authorities finding your dead body later in your own bed," I said coldly. I was right, too. I could end this now. He'd never bother anyone else ever again. All I had to do was let Marion inject him. We could all walk out of there and no one would know the difference.

Except me. I'd know. I just couldn't do it.

I wasn't a killer.

196

Without warning, Turner's eyes rolled back in his head and the whites turned a deep crimson. He spouted out words that I didn't recognize and the air started to charge with electricity. I began to feel my grip on the corpses' black holes start to wane. I had to think fast. I would lose control over the dead people very soon.

So, I did the only thing I could think to do.

I disconnected their spinning holes from their bodies, like I did with Bruce when I left him under the tree.

I leapt back from the corpses that dropped to the floor like rag dolls.

This jolted Turner back to reality, his eyes normal once more. He glared at me with an almost awestruck expression.

The five people deteriorated to different levels of grossness before our eyes. Marion was still juicy (that was about the nicest way I could describe it). Two of the men quickly turned to skeletons and the last two were a grayish blue color and smelled really bad. And I mean *really bad.*

That was my cue to leave.

Before Turner could perform some crazy mojo on me.

"You explain it," I said and left the room as fast as I could.

I waved at Principal Weatherby as I passed the teacher's lounge and practically ran back to class. I didn't look back once. I didn't have to. I knew Turner had his own mess to clean up.

I hurried into Physics and sat down in a seat near the back. My teacher, Ms. Norbert, nodded to me in greeting, but continued with her lecture, not wanting to disturb her lesson plan. Sitting there without Ryan, Nancy or Bill bordered on torture. I wanted to tell them everything that had happened, but most of all I just wanted to be around people who cared about me. My meeting with Turner ran through my mind over and over again. It hadn't sunk in yet how close to dying I had come.

About five minutes later the loud speaker came on. Principal Weatherby's voice sounded shaky and disturbed. "The school is closing for the day... and maybe the week... I...I... please walk to the carpool or parking areas in an orderly fashion. Your parents will be informed when you can... come back... good day."

Everyone gossiped immediately about the strangeness of Weatherby's announcement and the nervous trill of his voice.

"Settle down, class," Ms. Norbert instructed with firmness. "Now form a single file and do as Principal Weatherby says. Read chapters eight and nine in your readers while you have some time off." Students made their way to the door. "I'll be giving you a test on both chapters when you get back so no slacking!" She added with a note of authority and the class groaned in unison.

I made sure I was the last to leave. My heart raced. I would have given anything to have been a fly on the wall when Weatherby walked into his pristine office and found five rotting corpses on the ground. Especially, since they were alive and kicking ten minutes before. I imagined Turner would be making a massive pay-off to Mr. Weatherby's bank account; that, and I was sure a clean-up crew was on its way, hence the shooing of children.

When I reached the door I sighed in relief when I saw Bill and his twenty bodyguards waiting for me. The look on his face was a mixture of relief and worry. "Are you okay? What happened?" Bill went in for a hug and I hugged him back. It felt so reassuring and nice after everything I'd been through I almost wanted to cry.

"I'm okay," my voice sounded muffled as I muttered this directly into his chest.

I pulled away and gave him a reassuring smile. "I only want to tell it once. Let's find Ryan and Nancy and get out of here."

Bill nodded and talked to one of the bodyguards. "We're headed to the parking lot."

We made it to the hover-car without a stitch. Ryan and Nancy were waiting for us both with the same look Bill gave me before. Apparently, they were just as worried about me as I was. And rightfully so, it turned out.

When Ryan saw me amidst the circle of guards he pushed through (or I should say he was *let* through, these guys were pretty impenetrable) and held me close. "We were so worried," he whispered in my ear.

"Really, I'm alright. Let's just get in the car," I reassured Ryan, but I didn't want him to let me go. As soon as he pulled away from the hug, I grabbed his hand in mine. Aaaaahhhhh. Everything good now.

Bill sent the guards packing while we all climbed into his hover-car. "We didn't even need them. The press was sent off campus a few minutes before Weatherby's announcement."

Once we were all situated inside (I sat with Ryan in the back seat while Nancy rode shotgun), Nancy turned to me with impatient wide eyes. "Now, spill! What happened once you left the Assembly Hall? Details!"

I told them everything that had happened, from the invisible walls around the staff's black holes, to their rotting corpses on the floor of Weatherby's office. I left nothing out. The three of them sat in stunned silence.

"No wonder Weatherby was freaking." Bill was the first one to speak.

"That's so gross." Nancy was creating the visual in her head.

"It was terrifying. I thought I was going to die." I needed to say that out loud to make it real for me. So far the last few days felt like a nightmare I couldn't wake up from.

Ryan put his arm around me and let me rest my head on his shoulder. "You're with us now."

"You definitely gave Turner something to think about." Bill shook his head in amazement.

"You kicked his ass is what you did," Nancy chimed in, impressed herself.

"It wasn't me, by the way," Ryan said out of nowhere.

"What do you mean it wasn't you?" I asked.

"Blocking off Turner's listening devices at Nancy's. It wasn't me."

"Oh. I kind of knew that, but who did?" I wondered aloud.

"We'll figure it out when we get there. Maybe Jason will know." I couldn't help but notice the slight trill in Nancy's voice when she mentioned Jason.

After a few minutes, Bill pulled up to Nancy's abode and parked his hover-car in the landing zone.

George and Vianne walked out of the house to greet us, their faces wracked with anxiety. As we exited the car George squeezed Nancy with a hug that made her gasp for air.

"Geez, Dad, what's up with you?" Nancy asked as he released her.

Before he could respond both George and Vianne hugged me within an inch of my life.

"We've been sick all day worrying about you four!" Vianne said in her usual *mom* tone. "Get inside. We have a lot to discuss." She looked at me pointedly.

Uh, oh. What did Jason tell them?

Once we were inside we all sat down in the living room. Jason was there with a mug of coffee smiling at all of us like he was in a pleasant mood. "Now don't panic," he started the conversation, "but I told George and Vianne here everything."

My face must have turned two shades whiter because Vianne reached out and grabbed my hand. (The one that wasn't already taken by Ryan.) "It's okay, Chelsan, we know everything and we're not going anywhere, and neither are you. This is your new home now, permanently. No arguments, you hear me?"

She waited for me to nod and I did. I was so surprised I couldn't speak.

"Before you say anything George and I have known about people with your *talents* for ages. Vice President Turner has been developing re-animation rituals for the last two hundred years. Of course, no one knew it was successful. The article in the Science Journal three days ago was the first proof anyone's ever seen, until you." Vianne squeezed my hand for reassurance.

"How did any of this come up today?" I asked, wondering how on earth this could enter into a casual conversation.

Jason grinned, "I was scanning the house for bugs when

George caught me. He told me there was no need for that and then he showed me just about the coolest device I'd ever seen, for a reporter anyway." Jason pulled out a glowing red ball the size of a baseball.

Ryan whistled low. "Is that what I think it is?"

George sat up in his seat like a bright-eyed kid being praised for his accomplishments. "What do you think it is?"

"It looks like a SDS device, but on crack. Can I have a look?" Ryan was extremely excited by this SDS device especially when Jason handed it over to him. It was perfectly round and had its own inner glow that pulsed every few seconds or so.

"Is this why Turner couldn't listen in on our conversations?" I asked.

"Precisely." George acted as if we were in a classroom and I gave him the correct answer.

"You have a guarantee that it works?" Jason realized he didn't know what happened today.

I filled them in.

"Oh you poor dear." Vianne patted my hand in concern. "We always knew Geoffrey Turner was up to something. Jason, the only way to protect Chelsan is to get that man behind bars."

"Let's think on this a little more before we go jumping the gun," Jason cautioned. "I don't want to get any of us hurt."

"Shouldn't we do something?" Bill spoke up. "Money isn't an issue and my parents said they'd help."

I think Bill wanted to make it clear that he was important in this equation. I wanted to reassure him that his friendship was all I needed, but being a guy I think he needed to prove his worth in other ways.

"First things first. I found out a few things today." Jason leaned forward. "Most importantly, I'm pretty sure I was right about what ritual Turner and his wife used to kill you and your mother."

As tired as I was, this immediately piqued my interest. "Really?"

"It's called *The Ritual of Vortex*. From the fire, to the picture, to the serrated knife, to the arm slicing, all there. No one has ever proved that it has worked, it's a myth that goes back hundreds of years which was probably why your father was able to reverse it." Jason grew more and more excited as if he had been waiting all day to tell us everything.

"What *did* my dad do to us? Did you find that out?" I asked, as excited as he was.

"That, I'm not clear on, but I think your father made it up. He must have known about the properties of The Ritual of Vortex and figured out a way to reverse it. Brilliant, actually." Jason was impressed. "Except for the dying part, it was almost flawless."

Nancy smacked him on the arm.

Jason's face turned to me apologetically. "I didn't mean…"

I waved my hand for him to stop. "It's okay. Just continue."

Jason cleared his throat from embarrassment. "Sorry." He paused to gather himself, "Anyway, your dad reversed the spell but I'm assuming the mojo involved was still active after he… passed… and what made you and your mother come back to life, also gave you your gift."

The Ritual of Vortex. It sounded like something out of a sci-fi movie. Magic so powerful it not only killed my mother and I, but also gave me my gift (with my father's interference). "Why me? Why didn't my mom get any powers?"

Jason shrugged. "I don't know. Maybe because you were a baby? It could be anything really. I also found out more about the Science Journal's report. The stuff that they didn't release. A possibility that may explain why you lose some control over corpses with less …flesh." Jason almost sounded queasy at the prospect. "The subjects they used were actually brought back for over three hours. A part of the experiment they didn't report was the fact that they sprayed the bodies with acid over the three-hour period. The more they destroyed their flesh, the less they could control them, until eventually the bodies collapsed."

"That is so disgusting," Nancy said aloud and I had to agree with her.

"It's not definite proof, but it gives you more to go on than before." Jason raised an eyebrow with another thought. "I also found out a few things about I.Q. Farms as well." He looked pointedly at Ryan.

Ryan's hand tightened in mine.

"Most of this is from rumors and my *conspiracy theorist* contacts, but now that we have a living witness sitting in front of us, I tend to believe it. Basically, Turner started these *farms* going on the research of Larotte Fielding in 2133 that believed children's minds, from the ages of seven through ten, were capable of far more than we ever realized. If utilized properly, there was nothing their intellect couldn't solve or discover. Let's just say Mr. Fielding was arrested and sentenced to life without Age-pro when they discovered his research laboratory where he had kidnapped thirty-three kids and performed experiments on their brains. Supposedly, Turner picked up where Fielding left off. No one has ever seen one since, but like I said, there are still people who believe they exist. And now Ryan is an eye-witness."

I looked over at Ryan sympathetically. He tried to hide it, but I could tell he was frightened. The boy who got away.

"What about that thing the soldiers said; zombie 442?" I asked trying to change the subject.

Jason shook his head. "Nothing. Some military code. And if there is actually a *command* in the military to respond to what you did, it means our world just opened up to a whole lot of chaos. It proves that there are more people like you out there, or at least more who can bring back the dead. Your innate gift may be unique to you. I just don't know."

Everyone was quiet after that.

Too much to process.

"I'm really tired," I admitted. Sitting there with everyone hearing about the kind of trouble we were in made me feel guilty beyond words. And the guilt soon became exhaustion.

"Of course, sweetie. Go get some sleep," Vianne comforted.

"Sounds good. See you guys later."

"I'll walk you up." Ryan wasn't about to let me go that easy and I didn't want him to either.

"Okay." I smiled.

Nancy gave me a wink of approval as we made our way upstairs to her room.

When we arrived at the door I turned to Ryan and leaned my head against his chest. "This is my stop."

Ryan reached down and held both my hands in his pressing his forehead onto mine. "You want me to come in with you?"

"Yes, but I want to sleep and if you're there I won't be able to." I knew that for a fact, the boy made me too crazy for sleep.

"Okay, but I'll be downstairs if you need me." He leaned in and kissed me gently on the lips.

"Go, before I change my mind." I disengaged my hands from his and entered Nancy's bedroom. I shut the door behind me before I actually *would* change my mind.

Her bed looked so ridiculously comfortable with the fluffy down comforter of awesomeness. Single-mindedly I walked over to that paradise of cushions ready to drop and sleep for fifteen hours.

I suddenly felt a hand clasp over my mouth.

I tried to struggle, but the person behind me pinned my arms with his free hand. He was so strong. I searched for anything dead in the room to distract him, something, but the room was clean. My hands were quickly tied together with what felt like leather cords.

I stomped my foot on the ground to make some noise, but the carpet muffled all sound.

No. It can't end like this, I kept on repeating in my head until I felt the sharp prick of a needle in my neck and all my surroundings became a blur. *It can't end like this*, I thought one last time before everything went black.

Chapter Five

Tuesday September 21, 2320

...I slowly came to. My brain was throbbing and I felt like puking. I couldn't clear my head no matter how hard I tried. Whatever was injected in me was still working its drugtastic wonders. I tried to move my hand, but it wouldn't budge. I realized, through my drug-induced stupor, that I was tied to a chair.

I screamed. Well, I wanted to scream, but I think it came out as more of a garble.

A bright glowing ball of light dangled from the ceiling, but I couldn't make out any details. I could only assume it was a light bulb.

Footsteps clacked on what seemed to be a wooden staircase. Okay, good. My head cleared slightly. I needed to concentrate, break out of this fog. Where was I? Who took me? Was it Turner? After the mess I left him in, I wouldn't be surprised. Who else could it be?

I looked through my bleary eyes to see the silhouette of a man walking toward me. I couldn't see his face, my sight was too blurred, and the angle of the light made him look like a walking black shadow of doom coming toward me.

"Hey." I attempted to speak, but my tongue felt like it was made of lead.

"Not time to wake up, my sweet," the silhouette said. His voice was low and terrifying. I couldn't put my finger on it, but every instinct in my body told me I was a dead woman.

I felt the prick of a needle in my arm.

"No." I didn't even know if that came out properly my mind was starting to fuzz up again.

I made one last lame struggle before the blackness overtook me again.

Wednesday September 22, 2320
…W…w…where…?

Thursday September 23, 2320
PRICK!

Ouch. W…w..hat?

I was awake again. I puked all over the floor.

Why was I feeling better?

I glanced over at where I felt the prick and saw through my blurred vision a tube plugged into my arm. An I.V.? How long had I been here? I looked down and noticed he had taken my shoes and socks off and my ankles were tied to the chair as well.

"Sleep, little one, I'm not ready for you," the man's voice was almost a whisper and sounded like the reaper coming to claim another victim. He injected more of the drug into my I.V.

I struggled to fight off the effects, but the need to sleep overwhelmed me. My thoughts were too scattered. I just needed to stay awa…

Friday September 24, 2320

I came to again. I felt slightly better than the last… I couldn't remember how many times I had woken up… I threw-up on top of a puddle of dried puke. Gross.

I knew my captor would be coming down those wooden steps to drug me again any second now. I had to think quickly, but thinking was proving a challenge unto itself. I needed to be sharp and focused so I could figure a way out of this mess, that much my brain acknowledged.

What could I do? Could I use something dead? I searched the area for any spinning black hole I could find. Tons of roaches (eeeewww), a fly and…. Worms? I wiggled my toes on the ground. Dirt. I was in a cellar of some sort. I just needed something to tie off the flow of the I.V. into my veins without him noticing.

The door creaked open and the same slow clacking of footsteps sounded my doom.

My head still wasn't screwed on straight. I needed more time.

Instinctively, I reached out and connected to a dead worm's black center.

My captor's slow methodic pacing down the stairs made my skin crawl with the realization that this man felt very calm about keeping me tied up down here. He neared the bottom of the stairs. I could see his silhouette through my fuzzy eyes.

I made the worm move as fast as I could. I almost wanted to laugh at the absurdity of making an earthworm slither its way to my chair to perform some kind of rescue mission I didn't even know would work yet. It squirmed up the leg of the chair.

The man was within a few steps of me.

I needed to cause a distraction so I could try and make the worm tie off the I.V. tube.

The man was next to me now. He lifted my I.V. to inject it with the drug.

I looked up at him. I couldn't see any of his facial features. He was completely in shadow. "Who are you?" I tried to divert his attention from injecting me.

The worm slowly wrapped itself around the base of the I.V. squeezing off the flow of nutrients to my body.

"Not now, little one." He stroked the top of my head and I wanted to puke again.

I snapped off both ends of the worm (its dead it can't feel anything!) to disguise the cinch from my captor.

He released the toxins into my I.V. "Sleep." He sounded like the wicked witch in *The Wizard of Oz*.

"N...no... please." I tried to slur my words as much as possible so he'd leave. I didn't know how long the worm restraint would last. The liquid drug was shoving up against it, just waiting to enter my blood stream.

I dropped my head as if I was out cold.

I could feel him standing over me, watching. Please don't notice, please don't notice. I breathed slowly trying to convince him that I was properly drugged. What was he looking at? As the minutes passed by and he remained immobile I found it hard to keep up the charade from sheer terror. His presence felt like a pillar of mortifying psychosis that wouldn't leave. Slow deep breaths. Let the sicko watch me. He obviously wasn't looking at my worm ring or he would have done something by now which meant he was staring at me and only me. I couldn't tell you how scary it was being tied to a chair; helpless, knowing some psychopath stood within inches of you, just staring. He could slit my throat, shoot me, anything, and I wouldn't be able to stop him.

LEAVE!!

It took every bit of strength I could assemble to keep my breathing even and normal.

Finally, he walked away. The sensation of relief I felt was so overpowering I wanted to cry. I was still tied to a chair, but having him leave felt like a physical weight being lifted off my body.

He walked up the stairs in the same slow, even pace he had walked down them. When I heard the click of the door shutting closed I wanted to scream with joy, but I knew I had to keep silent.

My mind was almost completely clear of drugs and I wanted to keep it that way. The sensation of feeling almost normal again was a high I couldn't explain. I wanted to get out of there.

I knew I had to be as quiet as possible. I had to assume that he would hear any sound I made. Or maybe see… There could be cameras…

On the chance that I was being watched, I lolled my head back as if I still slept soundly. I peeked through slitted eyes to gain a better view of my surroundings.

The ball of light that illuminated the room was, in fact, the light of a holo-camera. It wasn't hanging as I first thought; it was resting on a six-foot tri-pod. Okay, he could see me *and* hear me. Good to know. The rest of the room was empty. The walls and floor were dirt, a plywood staircase was against the wall to my right, and a few roots dangled from the ceiling. My only concern would be what was beyond the door at the top of the stairs. If I managed to get that far. I couldn't think like that. My shoes!

The realization that Ryan had put a tracer in my shoes hit me hard. The man who kidnapped me must have had some kind of detector device and that was why he removed them. I guess I couldn't expect help from Ryan. Maybe Jason had some way of tracking me? Oh man, I hope they didn't think that I ran away again! Taking off the shoes would be a sure indication that I didn't want them following me! I wanted to throw-up again and not because of the drugs in my system.

I'd have to rely completely on myself. What else was new?

I rolled my head forward feigning sleep for the holo-cam.

First things first, I needed to get this I.V. out of my arm. I made what was left of the worm slowly tug up. The I.V. popped out of my vein and the fluid poured out onto the floor. I tried to keep it situated so it appeared to still be in my arm, but there was no way to tell if I was successful.

No opening of the door, so I was probably okay.

Next, these bonds.

Cockroaches, get ready to eat.

I connected to about a few hundred dead roaches. He must have had an exterminator down here recently because I could sense from the roaches strength that these troopers were freshly killed. Better for me.

I could hear the skittering and clacking of the hard shells making their way toward me over the dirt floor. Thank goodness they were darkly colored, *he* would be hard pressed to see them on the holo-cam. I tried not to think about the fact that I was making hundreds of the most foul disgusting bugs crawl up the back of my chair and behind my ankles. They were chewing within seconds of my connecting to their spinning centers. I could feel their chitinous mandibles gnawing their way through the leather bonds that held me to the chair. Tiny legs tickled my wrists and ankles as I made the roaches bite and chew. Gross.

SNAP!

The leather ties securing my hands dropped to the floor. Since the camera was only pointed at my front there was no way he could see the bonds fall.

SNAP!

My ankles were free now as well.

I stayed put, still pretending to be asleep, still acting as if I were out cold.

I made the cockroaches crawl far away from me. Never wanted to do that again! I thank the little fellows for freeing me, but yuck!

Next step was to stand up out of this chair. I knew as soon as I did my captor would be down here in seconds, so I had to think of an advantage I might have over him. I knew more than I'd known anything in my life that the man that kept me hostage was a killer. And not the military type of killer who attacked Jason and I at the Virtual Reality bar, no, this was a

213

man who *enjoyed* killing. It was like breathing to him. I could still feel him standing next to me, staring for ages. This was nightmare stuff.

There was nothing for it.

I stood up and smashed the holo-cam to the ground, grinding it into the dirt with my bare foot.

The room went black.

The latch sounded and the door swung open in a rush. The faint glow from the doorway was the only source of light anymore, but it was just enough to see my captor's body hit the stairs at a run. At least I managed to make him move at a speed above turtle status.

It was terrifying not being able to see anything and knowing that this person was with me in the dark charging toward me. I moved slowly and cautiously to a corner of the room, the dirt floor hiding the sound of my footsteps.

The man groaned in what I could only describe as ecstasy. He enjoyed this cat and mouse game. Then he pulled out his one advantage.

A flashlight.

Great.

He found me quickly with the glaring light. The brightness nearly blinded me. Like a bull he rushed at me.

I called on my little roach friends once more and made hundreds of them race across the floor and crawl up his legs, chest, arms and face. He screamed. It was the first time I sensed any fear from him, but cockroaches were harmless, he'd realize that soon enough.

I ran past him before he could grab me and practically flew

up the wooden staircase. My heart was racing, my head was pounding, I didn't know what I'd find when I ran through the door.

I could feel him brushing off the bothersome roaches. The flashlight flared in my direction as I reached the top of the stairs and ran through the doorway.

He was already on the steps, taking two at a time.

I slammed the door shut and searched for a lock on the knob, the door frame, anywhere!

Nothing.

BOOM!

The door hit me hard against my chest as he slammed it open, flashlight blinding me. I fell on my backside and tried to get back up to run.

"You're a bad little girl," I heard him say and his voice sounded almost pleased by that notion.

I scrambled to my feet and whirled around to run when I realized…

…I was in a small metal hallway with a steel door at the opposite end that was locked shut.

I turned around to face my attacker…

SMACK!

Ouch.

My head.

Everything went black.

Saturday September 25, 2320

"My little bug girl." I awoke to the excited whisper of my kidnapper. "All the roaches fell to the floor when I hit you over

215

the head." He was beside himself with glee.

Fantastic. Now he knew my gift. At least a part of it anyway.

I tried to move, but I was strapped to what felt like a metal slab. I couldn't see my captor. He was behind me and I could hear his heavy breathing as if he were about to burst out into laughter. I wanted to cry in terror, but I knew it wouldn't do any good. I was stuck here with this man and he had me tied up. Again.

The room I was in was metal, no windows, one ventilation grate and no furniture except the table I was on. Florescent lights on the ceiling made the whole room a greenish hue. I barely recognized the faint outline of a door as it blended with the wall so perfectly.

I wasn't drugged. That was an improvement at least, but the bonds that kept me strapped to the table weren't budging. I searched the area quickly for anything dead. Only one cockroach and from its location I knew that my kidnapper was holding it.

"I didn't want you at first. He made me take you, but now you'll be my biggest prize of all." He heaved with joy.

My eyes welled up before I could stop it. I had never been so scared in my life. I saw dead things every day. I thought it would make me tougher than this. I didn't want to let him observe me in this state. Somehow I knew that it would only make him more excited. I tried to focus. If I was going to get out of this I needed as much information as I could from this man.

"Who made you take me?" I asked.

The man finally stepped into the light and I saw my captor for the first time. I was shocked to see how normal he looked. He was average height and weight, blond wavy hair, cut short, aquiline features, wearing a dress shirt and slacks. I would have thought he was a teacher or a businessman if it weren't for his eyes.

They burned with an intensity that made my heart stop. There was no doubt in my mind.

This man was insane.

Which wasn't much of a leap considering my experience with him so far, but still, knowing I was dealing with *Cuckoo* might help me formulate a plan of escape.

"You know who." He smiled manically. "He lets me do my work without interference and I help him take out the filth of this world."

I tried not to show my fear.

Serial killer. The words played in my head like a broken record. Impossible. There hadn't been a serial killer in over a hundred years, or at least none that the public knew about. No one wanted to risk the death sentence or life imprisonment without Age-pro. There were medical facilities for people with these tendencies to go and get help. *He lets me do my work without interference...*

Another form of population control sanctioned by good 'ol Gramps.

Serial killers? How many were out there? How many innocent lives were taken by the man I was related to? Hundreds? Thousands? More like millions. I now knew of two methods he used: extermination with gasses and turning a blind eye to murderers. How many other ways was he taking out the human race while the world went on thinking everyone was going to live forever? How did he keep these deaths so secret? If people knew how easy it was to die on this planet, religion would still be practiced!

A horrible thought hit me.

No one ever saw Christian Coalition towns. They kept themselves segregated from the rest of the world. Turner could have wiped them all out and no one would have ever known. Were there any left? Had he killed all the people that no one would ask about and now had to move on to the general population? Was over-population really that bad? Or was he like the man who held me prisoner, a murderer who enjoyed killing. Probably a bit of both.

The man placed the dead cockroach in my face. "Your little pet, my pet." His creepy grin wouldn't budge. "Bring it back to life."

"Did Turner tell you *why* he wanted you to take me?" I ignored his request to gain more information.

This made the man's smile fade a little as if he were contemplating the matter. "Bring it back to life." He changed the subject back to the roach.

"I'll bring it back if you answer my question." If I remembered my studies about serial killers, most of the battle would be about who was in charge. I already knew he was *forced* to take me as opposed to a victim he would normally choose on his own.

"BRING IT BACK!" his voice boomed angrily.

I shuddered involuntarily.

Okay. He definitely needed to be in charge, and I was too frightened to fight it.

I made the roach crawl gently up his arm and back down again into his hand. His eyes never left mine.

He smiled, "Your eyes dilate when you do that. Did you know that?"

"No," I admitted truthfully.

"I didn't want to take you," he said flatly, and I couldn't sense any emotion from him, good or bad.

"Then let me go." I tried the honest approach.

"No. I don't think I'll do that. He'd take it all away from me if I did that." The killer didn't sound as if he was opposed to the idea of letting me go, only of the fact that he wouldn't be allowed to continue his murdering spree if he did. "Besides. You're too precious a gift to let go. It's in your eyes. They dilate when you bring the bugs to life."

"Yes, you told me that." I stayed as calm as I could, hoping to talk him down.

"Is it just insects you can bring back?" he wondered curiously.

"Yes," I lied. The less he knew the better.

"I wasn't sure what to do with you at first, that's why I kept you in the basement. I only take filthy girls. You didn't seem filthy to me, but you *are*. You're the filthiest of them all, I think." His eyes widened with a thrilled kind of look. "He must have known that. That's why he wanted me to take you." He was talking to himself at this point, as if rationalizing in his head why Turner would want me dead.

"Turner is my grandfather," I said just loud enough to interrupt his thoughts.

It worked. He turned to me a slight raise of his eyebrow. "Sometimes it's hard to rid the world of filth, especially when it's family. I understand now. He wanted it done special. It's your eyes, you know. I take the filthy parts away from the girls so they can be pure again. Don't you worry, I'll make you clean."

And the way he said it made my stomach drop.

He was going to gouge my eyes out.

And who knew what other body parts he had taken from girls like me.

"In time," he said and walked over to the door. He waved his hand over a seemingly blank surface, it lit up green and the door swung outward. Walking through the doorway, he didn't look back at me. He was planning to *cleanse* me forever.

The door clanked shut and I was alone once more. Well, me and the cockroach. I guess he wanted me to have company. I connected briefly to the roach and realized my captor had snapped off its mandible. He didn't want a repeat of my escape from the basement. I released the roach and ran scenarios through my head. He had stripped me of any help I could rely on. Sad that whenever I was in a dangerous situation (which happened a lot these days) my only way out of them was the use of dead things. How pleasant. Well, you work with what you have, right? And right now all I had was Larry. (I decided to name my mutant roach Larry after my first pet goldfish.) Anything to keep my mind straight. If I gave into the terror, I'd be frozen and useless. I needed to do *something* and Larry was the only one who could help.

I tapped into Larry's swirling core, made him skitter off the table and up the wall into the ventilation grate. That was where it became tricky. I needed to see through Larry's eyes like I had with Bruce and the corpses at the Virtual Bar. I hoped bugs weren't any different than humans. I focused all my energy on Larry and his tiny little eyes and…

...I could see. And surprisingly, I could see very well. And whoa! It felt as if I had a billion points of view. When I stared straight ahead I could also see behind me, beside me, above me, below me, all at once. Cockroaches had ridiculous eye-sight, who knew? Viewing my surroundings in Larry's body, I realized there was a light ahead of him at the end of the ventilation shaft. I made him run to the end of the shaft and peer through the second grating.

My captor was there, sitting at a round dining table eating a bowl of cereal. The room was small, sparse and very orderly. No one would ever know that this was a house of a serial killer. From Larry's angle I had to make him climb out of the grate to gain a better view of the door that led to where I was being held. It seemed like an ordinary wooden door from the killer's side. Nothing special about it, one would think it was to a closet or to a bedroom, not to a sealed off sterilized metal prison. There wasn't a phone in sight. I made Larry hurry back to the shaft for fear of the killer noticing him. He seemed very concentrated on his cereal, he chewed each bite over thirty times. Meticulous and methodical, there had to be some kind of advantage I could gather from that.

And then I felt it.

It was strange having to rely on another creature's senses so I wasn't sure I was actually feeling what I was feeling. But through little Larry I swore I could feel at least seven swirling black chasms coming from the killer's back yard. And these were human. Something about these metal walls prevented me from sensing them myself. I tried to probe the bodies as much as I could through Larry, but I could barely pick up their essence as it was. If there were really corpses back there I'd just need to get through the doorway to access them.

It struck me as funny that I could be so analytical about using dead bodies as weapons. The thought never would have occurred to me before until Gramps had actually tried to kill me. If he hadn't gone after me, I never would have discovered everything I had learned about my gift.

I kept Larry stationed at the grate to be my eyes on the killer's movement. I disconnected from him temporarily so I could clear my head and focus on how I was going to convince my kidnapper to let me into that room. Or at least into the doorway.

Four straps pinned me on the metal table: around the chest, abdomen/wrists, knees and ankles. There was a little wiggle room in the head, elbows and stomach. Question was: how heavy was this table? I needed to tip it over. It would hurt like no one's business, but it might loosen me up enough to scooch to the doorway.

It was a gamble I was willing to take. At this point my options were try something or die.

Like a swing I used my body to lean back and forth. The grating sound of metal was loud and I knew my captor would come through the door any minute to check on me.

I connected to Larry's eyes. Bad guy was still eating his Wheaties.

I swung harder and faster.

KA-KLUMP! KA-KLUMP!

So loud! Why couldn't metal be quieter?

My kidnapper heard that last one. He stood up with an

expression of pure hatred and anger etched on his face.

Not much time.

KA-KLUMP!

BAM!

The table fell on its side and it jolted the chest strap loose.

Oh man!

The door opened.

I freed my hands.

Like an enraged animal, the killer swooped down and grabbed my arms to re-secure them. He was so much stronger!

I just needed to get to the doorway.

It was open! So close!

I smashed my head against his in the most painful head butt imaginable. I couldn't tell if it hurt me more than him, but it did manage to make him loosen his grip. I punched his face as hard as I could, he reeled back from the shock of it.

I quickly untied the rest of my bonds and tried to make a crawl for the door.

But this guy was pumped full of adrenaline and he tackled me from behind.

I searched for the seven black holes of hope.

Not close enough.

I kicked wildly and managed to connect with his groin area.

He gurgled in anguish, but his grasp was still tight.

I inched closer.

No black holes.

Come on. Just a few more inches.

He started pulling me back into the room. How was he so strong?

My pure animal instincts kicked in and I whirled around and shoved the base of my hand straight into his face. The effect was enough. He reeled back from the instant explosion of blood coming from his nose and his eyes looked at me in shocked anger.

I had simply angered the beast.

I hoped Larry was right, I was betting all of it on the faith that there were seven corpses out there that were raring for a fight.

I leapt through the entryway and shut the door on him before he could pummel his way through. I knew I only had seconds before he simply swiped his hand over the sensor and came after me. He wouldn't hesitate this time. I was a dead woman if I didn't act fast.

Taking a deep breath, I searched for my seven girls and found them instantaneously.

The door burst open.

I grabbed a chair from his dining table and smashed his chest with it as soon as he was visible. He fell back into the room and I slammed the door shut on him again. I knew this wasn't a permanent solution. He'd just open the door again, but maybe this time he'd be more cautious, all I needed was a little time.

The girls were in varying degrees of decomposition. I know, gross, but as I learned from the virtual bar and Jason, the fresher the better. I squeezed my eyes shut and slammed myself into their swirling black chasms. They were buried, but shallowly. I made them dig as fast as they could. One only had one arm, ewwww. It made me realize what this monster had done to innocent girls and I was filled with such a rage that I wanted to make him suffer like he made these girls suffer before he ended their lives.

And that was my plan.

He was about to have a reunion he'd never forget.

The door creaked open.

I stood aside, second chair in my hands, ready to smash his face in a second time.

The girls were through the dirt and on their way to the house.

I was about to slam the door shut again when he shoved the metal table through the entryway keeping the door open.

I saw him then, his eyes wide with excitement and glee, blood on his nose, lips and chin from where I had hit him. He looked like something out of a nightmare. This man was the physical incarnation of a monster.

And he was coming for me.

The back door was locked. I made the girls shove hard against it to break it down.

This made his head turn from surprise, then he smiled wickedly at me. "Police won't help you, girl. Your grandfather keeps me quite safe."

I held the chair in front of me as a barrier between us. "Not the cops, a-hole."

His only response was a raised eyebrow, but his eyes were still filled with the thrill of the chase. "More bugs?" I could tell he welcomed that idea. He had adapted from the first time I sent the cockroaches after him. He wanted to live the experience again and defeat it. He fed on his own fear.

"Something like that."

BAM! BAM! BAM!

Almost through.

"Big bug." He leapt toward me.

I swung the chair at him, but he caught the leg with his hand.

He managed to yank the chair out of my hands and throw it across the room.

We circled each other. He salivated with delight, ready to pounce. I felt like I was a gazelle cornered by a lion.

BAM! SNAP!

The door flew open.

And in poured the most grotesque vision I'd ever seen in my life.

The seven girls were naked and mangled beyond comprehension.

He had stripped off what made these girls human. One had her lips ripped off and her teeth and jaw were visible beneath. One had no nose. One had her hands removed. One was missing her arm. One had her skin removed as if she had been boiled and peeled. One had no eyes. And the last girl was missing her entire face, just sinew and bone left.

I wanted to scream but I also wanted to cry. These girls had been tortured and murdered in the most horrendous way imaginable. There was no way of telling if he took these parts from their bodies while they were still alive or not. I couldn't imagine the kind of pain and torment they must have gone through before they were finally killed. I stared at the girl whose eyes were ripped out. It would have been me if I didn't have my gift.

The killer had stopped dead in his tracks as he watched the

seven girls walk through his back door.

"No," he muttered so quietly I could barely hear him.

"Yes," I said with so much emotion I almost choked it out.

Time to make them talk.

I controlled the eye-less girl first. She walked up to him so they were within inches of each other. He was still paralyzed by the sight of his victims. "What can we collect from you?" I made her say. Her vocal chords were deteriorated from rot so her voice was gravelly and low.

"Impossible." The killer dropped to the floor and held his knees to his chest. All his momentum and fire gone.

I knew it wouldn't last long. I needed to get him tied up.

I made the girl with no face kneel down to his level. "I want my face back," she spoke in the same rough voice as the other girl.

I had the girl with no mouth run into the metal room and grab the fallen straps from the table. Once in hand, I made her come back and place the killer onto one of his dining chairs, tying him in place. He still didn't struggle. His eyes kept moving from one girl to the next as if daring himself to wake up from a terrible dream.

His head was down and he shook it back and forth mumbling, "Impossible. Impossible."

I made all seven girls surround him in a tight circle just in case he came to his senses and managed to break free.

"You keep saying that, but here we are and I want my arm back." I made the armless girl speak.

"I just wanted something to remember you by. It was your wickedness that made me take those things from you. I made you all pure." He sounded like a child trying to explain why he broke his toys.

"Do we look pure now?" I made the skinless girl speak and bend down so close to his face that he actually flinched. Without lips, her words were garbled and lisped.

He rocked the chair violently, screaming in anguish. I realized that this may be too much for his warped mind. He sounded like a rabid dog, barking and yelling, snapping his jaw together and biting the air.

It was so much more frightening than when he was calm. I had provoked the monster within and it was coming out. Suddenly, the seven girls were exactly what they appeared to be, empty shells, nothing more. I felt more exposed and petrified than I did when I was strapped to that table.

His eyes met mine.

"YOU DID THIS!!!!" he howled in excruciating fury.

I backed away unconsciously. I was up against a whole other species of human being here and I was way out of my league. Being clever and wanting to exact revenge on this psycho may have cost me my life.

"MEAT PUPPETS! JUST LIKE THE BUGS!"

The way he said meat puppets made me instinctively gag. What had I been thinking? I should have just ran and left these girls to stall so I could escape. My own sense of self-righteousness had kept me there so I could see this man suffer. Selfish! Egomaniac! Stupid! All these words applied to how I felt about myself in that moment.

I needed to find a phone. If I couldn't call the police I'd call the gang. Jason could by-pass the police. He was a reporter. He told me that the more public I made things the easier it was to stay alive. Advice I should have remembered earlier.

The killer broke out of the bonds that held him by smashing the wooden chair to the floor. Along with the snapping of wood a very distinct crack came from his body. He had broken something.

Good.

Maybe enough to distract him while I escaped.

I was so shocked by his sudden transformation from crying mess to raging bull I had let the girls go lapse.

Tongue hanging loose and eyes bugging out, the killer came charging at me with a guttural roar.

I acted fast and made all seven girls tackle him to the ground. He struggled as if his limbs were made of chainsaws, tearing and ripping into the corpses. If he broke something his adrenaline and rage prevented him from slowing down on any level.

And then I ran.

Straight out to the backyard.

It was closed off with a six-foot oak fence. I could see over a hundred feet ahead of me the loose dirt where I had made the girls dig their way out to my rescue. I could feel the killer rip through their flesh to get to me. He was pinned down for the moment, but I knew it wouldn't last long.

I ran to the side of the fence and climbed over the top, landing on the neighbor's yard next door. No fences here, so I kept on running, running up the grass street as fast as my legs would carry me. I was instantly tired, days of being locked up and starved were taking its toll, only adrenaline kept me moving.

I was at least a block away, but I didn't want to stop. If I stopped he'd be there like a bad cartoon. All my fears from being locked up in that monster's house were bubbling to the surface in ways I couldn't control.

Tears flowed freely down my face. I could barely move forward as the tears turned to sobs, but I didn't stop. I had to keep going. I choked and bawled and gasped for breath. My run had turned to a sluggish zombie walk. I threw-up all over my clothes, but I kept walking. Nothing could stop me. The farther I moved, the closer I was to freedom. And I still didn't feel free.

I had dropped the connection to the girls without even realizing it. I was so focused on getting out of there I hadn't kept my concentration up. He was probably contacting help to get me back. Turner would appease him instantly. He wouldn't want it to get out that a serial killer still existed in our "perfect utopia" of immortality.

The neighborhood was barely above a trailer park in terms of social status, which meant they were poor, but not the lowest rung of poor. I was scared to knock on anyone's door for fear of them working for my grandpa. I wished there was a payphone I could use, but then again, Turner probably had those tapped in case I escaped. I made a split second decision and turned to the first "normal" looking house I could find. White picket fence, yellow paint, wrap-around porch with a swing set. Please let someone be home.

I was on the verge of collapse as I reached the front door. I tried not to think about the fact that I was covered in vomit, blood and dirt. I must have smelled pretty ripe. I knocked on the door and waited.

A few moments later a plump woman who appeared as if she was in her early thirties opened the door. One look at me and she gasped in horror.

"Please, help," I said through my tears.

"Oh my! What on earth happened to you?! Come in! Come in!" She shooed me inside. "Are you hurt? Of course you're hurt, sit down." She ushered me to her couch and sat down next to me examining each and every wound. Which really wasn't that many considering I managed to get out of there before he could start cutting me up. She had a round and friendly face with a splattering of freckles across her nose. Her hair was dark and pulled back in a messy bun and she wore a worn-in running suit with white socks. She looked like she'd always be in a state of "frazzle" no matter what the circumstances. At this point just seeing a friendly face made me want to collapse from relief.

"I just need to use your phone. I was kidnapped and I escaped, but I think he's looking for me." I wanted to warn her. The last thing I wanted to do was get her killed.

"It's that Brady man, isn't it? I knew it! Here let me get you a phone." The woman quickly snagged a cell phone from the next room and handed it to me. "I've reported him before, but they never do anything. I knew he was up to no good. That man is at least a hundred years old and he looks twenty. What is a richy up to living on our block in that hovel of his? Nothing good, that's what. What did he do to you? You call the police, maybe they'll listen to you," she rambled on and I suddenly understood that if she had her suspicions of the man that took me and called the police...

...Turner would have her phone tapped, or at least redirected to his people whenever she contacted the police.

She continued her rant, "I've seen him take girls in, but they never come out. One night I had my binoculars and saw him digging in his backyard! The police told me his pet dog died and he was burying him, but unless his dog was a Great Dane, that was a body, I'm sure of it!" She re-focused her attention back on me. "Listen to me ramble on. My name is Doris."

"Chelsan," I said quietly. "Do other people in the neighborhood pay attention to this guy?" I wanted to get a feel for the size of Turner's web on this block.

"They do, but they keep quiet, ever since Franny Lerner walked straight up to his house demanding she see inside. The police came and arrested her and when she came back she was... different." Doris looked like she didn't quite know how to explain herself.

"Different how?" I asked. Though I thought I knew the answer.

"I don't know. Just funny... off. Like she wasn't herself. She said that Brady let her see his house and that everything was fine. He was just a shy, quiet guy. Everyone was a little freaked out by her strangeness and some people said she was replaced by a robot. If you believe such nonsense. Anyway, it scared all of us silly, so after that no one said anything about Brady. *Utopic denial* is what I call it. They'd rather believe everything is just fine than actually have to admit that horrible things still happen in this world. Everyone on the block thinks I'm crazy to keep calling the police like I do, but we all know something is wrong with that man, and I can't just sit by and let him do whatever it is he does in there." She eyed me curiously, "What did he do?

Did you see any other girls in there with you?"

"Listen. I need *you* to make this call. I think your phone may be bugged and I don't want whoever is listening knowing that I've escaped. Can you do that for me?" I looked her directly in the eye to make sure she was on the same page as me. And I wasn't ready to answer her questions just yet.

"Will we be able to take that son of a bitch down?" She was very serious.

"Yes, but we have to be careful," I said. "I'll dial the number and you ask to talk to Ryan. Tell him you found his friend's shoes and give him your address so he can pick them up." I hoped Ryan would get the reference to the tracer he planted in my shoes. I wished I could talk to him myself, just to hear his voice. Everything I had been through… seeing him again seemed unimaginable.

Doris was on it. I dialed Ryan's number and handed her the phone.

Doris sounded like a mother when she answered the phone. "Yes, hello dear, is this Ryan? Oh good. Listen, I found your friend's shoes. Yes, yes. Why don't you come here and pick them up. Oh good. My address is 5522 North Glosten Street. Yes. Okay dear, I'll keep them safe until you get here. Bye, bye." Doris patted my hand encouragingly. "He's on his way and he's bringing friends. What a nice young man. He seemed beside himself when I mentioned the shoes. Are you sure they can help?"

"I'm sure. Thank you, Doris."

BAM! BAM! BAM! BAM!

"Is that your friends already?" Doris turned to her front door.

233

SMASH!

The door shattered as the killer kicked it in.

"Brady!" Doris screamed. "I'm calling the police right now!"

"DO IT, BITCH! *YOU'LL* BE THE ONE IN JAIL!" Brady laughed manically. He was covered in his own blood, his clothes were shredded, his right arm was limp and useless, but he was alert and enraged.

When he saw me he howled like a wolf and charged.

I was so weak. I didn't have much in me to fight back. I tried to connect to any black swirling hole I could find, but I couldn't seem to make anything move. I was completely drained. I wanted to run, but I knew he'd kill Doris. I couldn't leave her alone with this man. I had to make a stand.

I picked up one of Doris' lamps and smashed it onto Brady's broken arm just as he was about to tackle me. He shrieked in agony, but grabbed my throat with his uninjured hand despite the pain he was in. He tried to squeeze the last bit of life I had out of me. It was almost as if I stepped out of my body. I could see the faint stirrings of my own black spinning core growing stronger by the second. I was dying. I took my last bit of strength and clawed my fingers into his arm and tore.

Brady screeched so loudly my ears started to ring.

He let go and I came away with blood and skin in my fingernails.

CRACK!

Brady was silent as he dropped to the floor unconscious.

Behind him was Doris with a five-iron golf club in her hands. She bashed him over the head again for measure as if making sure he was really out. Her hands were shaking and she dropped the club to the floor. Then she ran to me and held me close. "You're okay now. He won't hurt you anymore."

I let her hold me. I was too weak to move, or cry, or anything but lie there.

And to see my captor *Brady* in worse shape than I was didn't give me any satisfaction like I thought it would. I was still scared of him, unmoving, unconscious and all. I think I'd always be scared of him. Forever.

Sirens and hover-fans became almost deafening from outside. Apparently, the cavalry had arrived.

"It's them, Doris." I looked up at her and managed a smile.

"Well, we just took care of ourselves, didn't we?" she chuckled and gave me a warm hug of support.

"Thank you," I said and tears came to my eyes.

"Oh nonsense. I've been wanting that monster out of this neighborhood for years." She tried to make things light for my sake. I could tell. I wanted to do something for Doris, protect her somehow. I knew Jason would have the answer.

My heart leapt.

Ryan came bounding through the door, eyes searching until he found me.

I was never happier to see anyone in my life.

When he saw me his face went from relief to utter worry in about a half a second. He raced to my side on the floor and Doris smiled and moved aside to let him hold me. I clung to him like he was a lifeline. And in that instance, he truly was. He didn't have to say a word, he just held me as if he couldn't believe I was really there. I could barely believe I was alive. And then I realized in horror that I really, truly must stink.

"I'm smelly," I said, my face in his chest.

"I don't care. I'm never letting you out of my sight again." He kissed my forehead.

"Chelsan! Thank goodness!" Nancy's voice rang out like sweet music to my ears.

Nancy and Bill came racing to our side. Doris stood up at that point and sat on her couch.

"Are you okay? What happened?" Nancy glanced at Brady. "Is that the guy that took you? Geez, Chelsan, he looks pretty F'd up." Nancy examined my face and saw the lump forming on my head from where I head-butted Brady. "Uuuck! You seriously stink!"

"Shut up, Nancy." Bill rolled his eyes. "Are you okay? Is this the guy?"

I nodded, not wanting to give Brady any acknowledgment. As if saying anything would wake him up again.

"Guys, this is Doris. She saved my life."

All three of them immediately turned to Doris as if seeing her for the first time. Bill and Nancy practically tackled her in a group hug repeating thank you over and over. Ryan didn't leave my side, but he nodded his thanks.

"Oh, mine just happened to be the door she knocked on. She escaped all on her own." Doris deflected taking any credit.

"Well, the five-iron to his head made sure he didn't finish the job." I wanted to make sure they all knew what a hero she was.

"Sweet. You golf? You now are a standing member of the LA Golf club. I'll send over new clubs, too." Bill obviously felt like he needed to give Doris a reward and I was extremely grateful.

"Oh, my." Doris blushed.

The buzz of hover vehicles and sirens caught my attention once more and I looked over at the shattered doorway.

Nancy followed my gaze. "Jason is out there taking care of the press. I better give him some details. Do you know anything about this guy? Was he just a thug for Turner?"

The memories were too fresh. I didn't want to talk about it yet, but I knew I had to. To protect Doris and myself. "Guys, he was a serial killer."

"Nuh, uh!" Nancy was in shock.

Ryan held me tighter.

Bill was actually speechless.

"Like a real one?" Nancy apparently couldn't wrap her head around it, and I couldn't blame her.

"Like a real one. Tell Jason he'll find seven dead girls' bodies at this guy's house, and a whole lot of proof," I informed her quietly.

"His name is Brady Johnson and he lives ten houses down on this side of the street." Doris gave the details. "And see if you can wrangle up some police officers to get this *thing* off my floor."

"Will do." Nancy ran out to tell Jason everything.

A roar from the crowd a few minutes later.

"I guess he told them," I said, knowing that I'd be a media frenzy unto myself yet again.

Jason and Nancy ran in after that with two police officers. The officers handcuffed Brady and dragged him out the front door to the onslaught of reporters wanting to get a holo-pic of the first serial killer in over a hundred years. The first one that was caught anyway. How many others were there?

Jason sat on the couch next to Doris. Doris's face had turned bright red at the sight of Jason. Apparently, she was a fan.

"This is Doris. She saved Chelsan's life," Bill told him.

Jason shook Doris's hand. "Then let me save yours. We have to make you as famous as can be. Are you ready for that, Doris?"

"Well, I… uh.. sure." Doris was starting to be overwhelmed by the last twenty minutes of her life.

"Then let's get you out there." Jason turned to me. "Chelsan, you're going to have to talk about *exactly* what happened to you. Do you think you can do that?" He was being gentle with me, but I could tell he'd push the issue if I said no. He was genuinely trying to save our butts.

"I'm ready," I half-lied. I really didn't know if I was or not.

"Are you sure?" Nancy had her hands on her hips. "Don't listen to this creep. If you're not ready, we're not going out there."

"This *creep* knows how to stay alive." Jason rolled his eyes at Nancy.

Apparently, problems had arisen in my absence. This didn't feel like flirting to me.

"Chelsan's been doing a damn good job of keeping alive herself." Ryan held me closer.

"I'm not questioning Chelsan's skill of keeping herself breathing. I don't know *anyone* who could have survived what she has. I'm just thinking of ways to keep Turner from trying to kill her again." Jason was being the level-headed one of the group.

"Vice President Turner?" Doris's gossip button had been pushed. "Is he behind all this?"

I stood up before this became ugly. Ryan stood up with me and held my hand. "I'm going out there. I trust Jason." I wanted to make that clear. If Nancy was having personal issues with him that was one thing, but when it came to the safety of my friends I'd do anything to protect them. Even if it meant re-living the last few days. Or.. wait a minute.... "How long was I gone?"

"Five days," Bill said as if he had counted the minutes.

Whoa. Five days? It felt like two, maybe three, that was almost a whole week! I suddenly felt woozy. I stumbled slightly and Ryan caught me. No wonder I was so weak! "He had me on an I.V. for a while, but I'm feeling pretty tired."

"We'll get you to a hospital as soon as we're done here. Let's do this quick." Jason took me away from Ryan and ushered me to the front door and the awaiting press. "Doris, you too," he called over his shoulder.

Doris stood up from the couch as if she had been poked by a cattle prod. "Coming."

Nancy, Bill and Ryan positioned themselves behind us like bodyguards.

The press corps was about ten times the size of the group that covered the *tornado* at the trailer park. It was like standing in front of an ocean of flashing holo-cams and screaming reporters, there was no end to them, just miles and miles of people and hover-cars.

Jason placed his hands up to quiet the crowd. It was instantly silent. "Chelsan has been through a lot these last five days so we're going to keep it brief people. She needs medical attention so most of your questions will have to be answered after her release from the hospital. That being said, Chelsan will give her statement. Chelsan."

I swallowed hard and fought off the feeling of fainting. "I was kidnapped from my best friend Nancy's house five days ago and taken to that house down there." I pointed to Brady's house, which I now noticed was swarming with police-hovers and officers. "He kept me locked in his basement and drugged so I didn't know how long I had been there…"

I was having trouble talking. I felt detached from my own voice, as if someone else was doing the speaking. I knew I couldn't tell them about how I used my powers on the cockroaches and the girls' corpses, so I had to skip over that part. "I managed to break free and we fought. There were bodies everywhere. I hit him with a chair and tied him up and then I ran. I ran until I decided to get help and knocked on Doris's door. She helped me call my friends and they called the police. Then he broke into her house and Doris knocked him out with a golf club. That's it. That's all I can remember." It sounded so mundane and boring when I said it out loud, nowhere near how horrific it actually was to live it. The press seemed to eat it up though. Especially, when the police took out the body pieces left from the girls.

Jason stepped in and steered Doris to the forefront. "Here's our hero of the day folks. Doris Hornbacher! Without her courageous whack of her five-iron, Chelsan would just be another victim in Brady Johnson's collection. Let's all give a round of applause to Doris!"

The roar of the crowd greeted Doris as she stood red-faced in front of the press. "Well… I…" She adjusted her hair and sweat suit to look more presentable. "It was nothing really. I did what

I could for the poor girl." Doris visibly began to relax as she continued. I think she was really starting to dig the attention. "When I saw that man strangling Chelsan I grabbed my golf club and hit him as hard as I could! I barely use my clubs anymore, it's so expensive to play, but this young man," she pulled Bill up next to her, "he offered me a free membership to the LA Golf Club! Sweet young thing." She turned her attention back to the press. "I have been calling the police non-stop for over three years now about Brady, but they did nothing! Nothing! We all knew it! I saw him digging, but they did nothing! Unfathomable! If Chelsan hadn't escaped, he'd still be on the loose killing young girls and no one would be the wiser! And if you think for one instant that there aren't others like him out there, then you are all delusional! Mark my words, I will find these killers!" She looked directly into the holo-cams for emphasis. "Your days are numbered." Doris had such conviction and intensity in her voice, it gave me goose bumps.

Jason was extremely impressed. I could tell by his lopsided smile. He turned to the press. "We're taking these girls to the hospital. The police will be making a statement at Brady Johnson's house in three minutes."

The mass of reporters moved like a swarm of bees toward Brady's house.

Doris leaned down to my ear. "That's her. That's Franny Lerner. The robot."

I glanced over to the woman Doris pointed to, and sure enough she wasn't a robot. She was dead. Another one of Grandpa's spies. Watching us carefully from afar.

I took my last vestiges of strength, covered in puke and blood and walked over to Franny. She stood there, black hole swirling, staring at me with hatred.

"Turner, if you're listening, you're going to have to do better than that if you want me dead. You lose. Again." I would have kicked the girl except I knew she wouldn't feel anything and neither would he. I just wanted him to think he hadn't broken me down, even though I wasn't sure if that was true.

"We'll see," was all Franny said and then she collapsed in front of me. She began to rot instantaneously as Turner released her body from his power. I knew if I didn't scream people would suspect me of either being crazy or somehow responsible. So I did. I screamed loud enough that half the press came running from Brady's house to my side. Once they saw the rotted mess that was Franny, all holo-cams captured the grotesque scene.

Ryan and the others hurried to my side. I turned to Ryan as he embraced me and whispered in his ear. "Get me out of here."

As soon as we stepped inside the holo-ambulance I lay down on the bed. My head hit the pillow and all the sounds and chaos disappeared as I passed out.

Pitch blackness. It was everywhere. So dark it felt like black fog. Where was I? I was somehow aware that I was dreaming, but no matter how hard I tried I couldn't make myself wake-up. I was stuck in this utter darkness.

"You can't hide from me forever, you know."

I heard a voice from the blackness. It was my grandpa. His voice a nightmare come to life.

"You're just a dream," I said, though I didn't know why. If it really was a dream why was I telling a figment of my imagination that? Something made me unsure of myself. Something in the tone of his voice.

He stepped forward and revealed himself. There was a faint reddish glow around him, emanating power. As if he were trying to intimidate me. "Really? Are you sure?" he replied, as if reading my thoughts.

I wasn't.

I didn't want to say anything.

"I have a friend with me. Would you like to see him?" Turner smiled at me as if anticipating my answer.

"Not really," I said.

"Oh, but he wants to see you. He insisted on it." Turner gestured to his left and Brady appeared next to him.

Dream or not, the memories were too fresh, I jumped back in spite of myself.

Brady didn't move, didn't talk, simply stood there.

"Notice anything special about our friend?" Turner stared at me with a penetrating gaze.

I forced myself to glance at Brady a second time. I noticed a black hole swirling in his chest. He was dead. Which meant Turner had killed him.

Dream. Dream. Dream. I reminded myself, but it was becoming clear to me that this was something else entirely.

"It will be the trial of the century by the time I'm done with it. Serial killers in this day and age? I was shocked to find out that Brady tapped Ms. Hornbacher's phone so that when she called the police it went directly to his home phone. No wonder LA's finest couldn't catch this monster. The scandal!" Turner snickered with delight. "Isn't that right, Brady?"

Brady's eyes came alive and he laughed evilly. "I killed them all! I just wish that last little morsel hadn't got away." Then his eyes went dead again.

"He'll say whatever I want him to say." Turner's gaze turned hard.

"And then I'll make him say whatever *I* want him to say." I crossed my arms protectively.

"We'll see." Turner repeated Franny's words. He looked neither miffed nor happy at the prospect, just contemplative. "Time to wake up now."

I awoke with a start. I was in a hospital bed with an I.V. plugged in my arm. I almost yanked it out on instinct, but I knew I was reacting to my dream. It felt like more. I didn't even know if that was possible. But then again I didn't know half of what Geoffrey Turner did was possible. He was like a giant steel safe with no combination, and it was starting to bug me.

"Oh good, you're up," came Jason's voice from the seat next to me. "Don't worry, your friends are outside. I needed a moment alone with you."

I sighed and ran my hand through my hair. Tangle city. I'd deal with that later. At least I was in a hospital gown and bathed. Small favors. "I should tell everyone what happened all at once." I really didn't want to repeat everything twice.

"That's fine. I want this to be between you and me." Jason was very serious.

"Okay. Weird. What is it?" He was kind of freaking me out.

"I don't know if I can protect you. I'm doing the best I

can, but Turner seems way more determined to kill you than I originally thought. I mean he had a *serial killer* kidnap you! And you're his granddaughter. I can't seem to wrap my mind around that."

"You and me both."

Although I was feeling about a bagillion percent better, Brady lurked in the shadows of my brain like a deadly stalker. And I realized that Jason blamed himself. For everything. "You know, Jason, none of this is your fault."

"Yes, it is. It's *all* my fault. If I wasn't so damned arrogant giving you my contact info at the tornado site you never would have called me and you never would have been at the virtual bar and you never would have..."

"Jason," I interrupted his guilt-ridden rampage. "Once he saw me on holo my fate was sealed. He's not stopping until I'm dead, everyone else that's with me is just in the way in his eyes. Listen, I don't blame you for anything, in fact, I thank you for helping me, anyone else would have ran by now and I really appreciate you sticking around and helping me see this through, okay?" I meant it. Without Jason I would have really been screwed. Then I thought about it a moment and a sudden flash of insight came to me in a rush. This wasn't about me. He just wanted to make sure he knew how I felt about him. "What is this really about anyway?"

Jason's eyes widened as if he weren't expecting me to call him out on his crap. "What do you mean? I..." He placed his hand over his face in exasperation. "Who am I kidding? Nancy hates me and I don't know what to do about it."

I knew something was up with them! "Trust me, she doesn't

245

hate you."

"A lot has happened since you were taken. I think Nancy is with Bill now," he admitted miserably.

I wanted to roll my eyes and slap him silly. "Bill? Really? You're a hundred years old and you still can't tell when a girl is trying to make you jealous, moron!"

"You think? Because if that's the case, it completely worked. I can't see straight I'm so crazy." Jason was as gloomy as I'd ever seen him.

In his moment of vulnerability I remembered why I had a crush on him. He really was cute in a dismal puppy dog kind of way. "Listen, Jason, just tell her exactly what you told me, that you're miserable without her and she'll be yours in a heartbeat."

Jason straightened up in his seat, appalled. "I can't do that. If she knew how I felt she wouldn't be attracted to me anymore. She'd think I was a pathetic loser. Trust me, after a hundred years, this is a universal truth I *know* about women."

"Uuuggghhh! You're such an idiot." I really did roll my eyes then. "Fine. She does hate you, and her and Bill make a great couple, so yaaaay!"

His face fell again in anguish.

Jason was exasperating, and if he didn't have the balls to tell Nancy he liked her, he didn't deserve her.

There was a knock at the door.

"Wait, don't call them in. I need more advice," Jason started.

"COME IN!" I yelled across the room.

Let Jason deal with his issues with Nancy head on. I knew he just wanted me to tell Nancy he liked her anyway. That was the real purpose of our conversation. Jason sure hadn't developed past the grade school level of relationships yet in life.

Nancy, Bill and Ryan came into the room with concerned smiles on their faces. I wanted to jump out of my bed and give them a group hug, but I was still feeling exhausted from my experience with Brady. And the dream made me not want to go back to sleep again, so I was stuck being tired and wanting to stay awake all at the same time.

Nancy barely glanced at Jason as she came to my side. She really was mad at him. Jason tried to hide his disappointment, but now that I knew how he felt it was easier for me to see his despair. Bill seemed indifferent to all of it and kept his eyes on me. His goofy smile made me feel happy he was there.

Ryan was instantly at my side. He pulled up a chair and held my hand. "How are you feeling?"

"Better." And I told them everything that had happened to me. From the drugs, to the worm, to the cockroaches, to Larry, to making Brady's victims attack him. They all sat in stilled silence, listening to me as if they were hearing a campfire story of horror and mayhem and not actually something that *really* happened.

"They didn't find a holo-cam in his basement. That means Turner has it. He'll have his team scour that footage to see everything you did." Jason was the first to break the quiet. "You're an amazing girl." Jason looked at me with awe and I noticed the same look in the eyes of Nancy, Bill and Ryan as well.

"I don't feel amazing." Their attention made me feel awkward. It was pure survival instinct down there and more than that, it was desperation. I was so terrified, in the dark…

"Well, you are, so don't argue." Ryan reached over and kissed my forehead. "Turner isn't going to stop. Making Chelsan famous only gives us a few weeks max. People will forget and when they do, Turner will strike again."

"It's personal now." Bill nodded in agreement with Ryan.

"It was always personal," Nancy said with genuine fear. "He holds you responsible for your father's death, and now you've made a fool of him more than once. Someone like him will *never* let that slide."

She was right. "He wants me dead so he can control me. The public wouldn't know any different. He could attack tomorrow or now and it wouldn't mean anything. Being famous won't protect me. We're not safe." They needed to hear the truth. Jason's bold plan of keeping me in the lime light meant absolutely nothing. Turner could care less if I was dead because then he'd have all the control. It was preferable.

Jason looked miserable.

In fact, all of them had a kind of helplessness about them.

"I don't mean to bring everyone down, but these are the facts. Turner is after me. He wants me to be his corpse puppet. The only way to stop that from happening, is to stop *him*." I realized I was the leader of this pack and I needed to take the reigns of control.

Jason's eyes lit up. "Then that's what we need to do."

Chapter Six

We talked out our plan late into the night until we all had to sleep. Everyone crashed at the hospital. I could tell it was because they were worried Turner would try something, but they all said they wanted to get an early start on our mission.

When I woke up it was about seven in the morning and everyone in the room was sleeping and snoring. Bill's parents made sure they all had beds brought in so no one would be sleeping in chairs or on the floor. His parents made large donations to this particular hospital, so the staff was very obliging. Someday, I would finally meet Bill's parents and thank them profusely for everything they had done for me.

I had a moment of serene contentment watching everyone sleep. Up until a couple of weeks ago the only person I was *sure* that loved me was my mom. Nancy and Bill were my close friends before, but now they had proven themselves to be much more than that. And Ryan had a crush on me! Ever since last year! That still made my mind reel. I was so sure he thought I was a freak, but come to find out he felt the same way about me as I did about him. Jason was the biggest surprise. A reporter who was as famous as could be and whose holo-pics I had plastered on my wall ended up being my champion and partner.

This was the gang.

And they would either be in my life forever or I would be the means of their destruction. I hated thinking that way. I already felt responsible for my mother and father's death, I didn't want to be responsible for getting my friends killed as well. I knew it was wrong to keep them involved in all this, but I needed them, selfish as it was, I wasn't willing to let them go. I also knew that if I tried to cut them off again they would just find me and scream at me for trying to. They were here for good. No matter what that meant for their well-being or their safety.

Jason was the first to wake up. I saw him glance over at Nancy briefly. That boy was so far gone it was almost funny, but I knew what it was like to have a crush on someone and live with the possibility that they could care less about you. I was lucky. Ryan turned out to like me back. According to Nancy, more than that actually… Aaack! This was the last thing I should be thinking about! I needed to focus on the task at hand.

We had a plan.

And the plan was simple.

We were going to break into Geoffrey Turner's headquarters.

Even thinking it made my stomach turn.

With the help of Bill and Jason's connections we'd arrive in two groups (we figured two groups were better than one, just in case one of us failed). Bill's group was the "tourists," it consisted of me, Ryan, Bill and Nancy. Like all places of power, there were tours of the facility open to the public daily. Jason would use his *reporter* card and enter the building that way.

Our goal: To find the real footage of what happened at my trailer park. If we could expose the exterminators, maybe we could take Turner down and put him behind bars.

Slowly, everyone started to wake up. Ryan was completely adorable as he yawned and smiled at me. I wanted to crawl up next to him and have him hold me all day.

As if reading my mind, Ryan came over to me and crawled into my bed. "How are you feeling?" he whispered in my ear. I wish he wouldn't do that. It made my brain flutter.

"Better now," I said.

"Except he's lying on your I.V. which can't be good," Bill grunted from the other side of the room.

"Whoa! Sorry!" Ryan immediately jumped out of my bed as if it were on fire.

Ah, man. Bill!

"You have to take it out anyway. I'll get the nurse in here." Nancy punched Bill's arm on the way out and Bill looked slightly ashamed, but not enough for my taste. I'd say the ratio of guilt to satisfaction was a good 2 to 10.

Ryan didn't seem to notice. He was so upset that he might have hurt me. "I didn't give it air bubbles, did I?"

"Don't be paranoid." Jason made a familiar expression on his face. I was beginning to recognize its meaning. It was the, *I'm with a bunch of kids,* expression.

Nancy came back with the Nurse.

"You ready to leave?" The Nurse talked to me as if I was

twelve-years-old.

"Yeah," I replied with as little attitude as possible.

The Nurse didn't even care if I had said *yes* or not as she walked over to me and pulled out the I.V.

She handed me a hospital electronic reader. "Thumbprint there and there and you'll be all set."

I thumbprinted in the places she told me to and the screen flashed green.

"Okay. You're good to go. I'll have some nurses take these beds away, don't you worry about it." She directed her *over-kindness* towards Bill who awkwardly smiled at her.

"Thanks," I said, then a thought hit me. "How is Doris Hornbacher?"

"She's just fine. On the news today." The Nurse grabbed a remote and turned on the holo-tv. Doris stood in front of the press, all fire and passion, talking about her mission to take down Brady Johnson. They showed a clip of Brady being taken to prison and my breath caught in my throat. My dream was real. Turner had killed Brady and now he was under his control. Brady's black swirling chasm taunted me through his holographic image.

"Good old, Doris. She's really taking to the limelight." Jason smiled in spite of himself.

Nancy had her arms crossed and purposely ignored him.

The nurse didn't. She smiled the most flirtatious smile she could. "She doesn't look as good as you do, Mr. Keroff."

"You haven't known him long enough," Nancy practically guffawed.

Jason played it as cool as a cat and ignored Nancy's barb. He smiled at the nurse and kissed her hand in farewell. "Thanks for watching."

Vomit.

This was Nancy's cue to roll her eyes at me and we could share a moment of disgust for Jason's cheesiness, but Nancy was livid. Her eyes bulged and she looked like she wanted to punch Jason in the face. She grabbed Bill's hand and dragged him toward the door. "Come on, Bill, let's MAKE OUT!" And they were gone.

The nurse was oblivious to it all, she was still enamored with Jason. "Call me." And she left as well.

Jason's face was riddled with misery and Ryan couldn't hide his enjoyment at the whole situation.

"I don't mean to be the interrupter of high school drama here, but we have another snag." I told Jason and Ryan about my dream with Turner and Brady.

"I've heard about astral projection. Another one of Turner's experiments. From everything I know it should be harmless, just a way of communicating," Jason shared with thoughtfulness. "It works both ways though. If we could get into his dreams... let me research it some more."

"We better find Nancy and Bill," Ryan said through a grin of amusement. "I hope they're not in the supply closet again."

I elbowed Ryan playfully. He was having way too much fun making Jason squirm. He knew as well as I did that nothing was going on between Nancy and Bill, but he liked watching Jason turn into Hamlet every time he mentioned the two of them together.

Nancy told me everything that happened in my absence

before we went to bed last night. I guess as soon as they discovered I was gone, Ryan went on a rampage. I was relieved to hear that no one thought I had run away again, but everyone's first thought was that Turner had me somewhere himself. So, unfortunately, all the searching went into Turner's holdings and properties and where the most likely place he'd take me would be. By the time Ryan remembered my shoes with the tracking device he had implanted inside, Brady had already destroyed them. They were flying blind and completely destitute.

Ryan and Bill went out everyday trying to find any sign of where I might be, but it was like looking for a specific grain of sand on a beach.

Nancy and Jason undertook the other approach of searching the net and following Turner like a hawk to see where he was going at all times. They even checked out a few places they thought might be likely candidates for where he was holding me, but it always ended up being a dead end.

According to Nancy the first few days of working together were *brilliant*. She said Jason was so polite and sweet, he even held her hand. In fact, that was how the whole mess started. When he held her hand, Nancy took that as a cue and tried to kiss him. Jason, apparently, freaked out and said she was far too young for him and that he saw her as a younger sister. Nancy was embarrassed and furious. (I would be too. It was *obvious* to anyone that had eyes that Jason was head over heels for the girl.) So, she decided to test the *little sister* theory and flirted as hard as she could with Bill. (She informed Bill of what she was doing beforehand and he became a willing participant. I think he liked the attention.)

At first, Jason didn't seem bothered by their flirting, but when Nancy planted one on Bill, Jason stood up and left the room. Nancy confided that she felt completely vindicated by his reaction, but when he came back, he acted as if everything was fine and even patted Bill on the back and wished the couple good luck. Good luck? For a hundred year old, he sure was acting like an immature idiot. But then again, he was a lab man for most of his life and being a famous reporter was still fairly new to him. I'd cut him some slack if it wasn't Nancy he was screwing with.

Ryan stayed out of the entire mess according to Nancy. She said he could care less about anything that didn't involve me. Apparently, he even slipped and said he loved me. (This made my heart leap all over again.) Everyone was upset and searching for me like mad, but Ryan was on a whole other level of torture. Since he was the last to see me, he felt as if it was his fault that I was taken. He kept on saying that he should have gone into the room with me and then it never would have happened. I somehow doubted that, and I made sure I told him that I didn't blame him one bit all last night.

So as things stood now, Jason had to live with the torture that Nancy may have moved on, and Nancy had to deal with the torture that... well... that was Jason Keroff. I didn't envy either one of them!

Poor Bill was the pawn in the middle, but he seemed to enjoy being the guy that made Jason jealous. Maybe it was some perverse way of dealing with his own jealously toward Ryan and me.

We left the hospital in two hovers. Nancy, Ryan, Bill and I in

Bill's and Jason in his own.

The drive over to Turner's headquarters was uneventful except for the three tirades about Jason and his moronic behavior from Nancy. We just let her vent. I was sure similar conversations were going on in Jason's head.

Turner's headquarters was fifty miles outside of Los Angeles. Its official title was "Population Control Center and Research." I know, very fancy, but the facility was HUGE! As we came within view of the building I realized why there were tours of this place. It was a spectacle unto itself. It looked as if someone took a handful of white crystals and placed them in the middle of a red maple forest. It was truly breathtaking. On closer inspection the building itself was made of a white metal that was shaped in every way imaginable from jagged spirals, to three-hundred foot cylinders, to different sized pyramids, to plain square boxes with no windows or doors to be seen. It was a big jumbly mess of shapes and sizes taking up a good square mile of space and that was just the surface. Jason told us that there was an entire underground department that was twice as big (underground equaled the *research* part of the building).

The ego on my grandpa was just starting to sink in. He really felt like he was untouchable. To have such a fortress that you allowed the general public into everyday was almost like rubbing his power in everyone's faces. And the crazy architecture to boot felt like an extension of Turner's twisted mind.

"The metal is used as a transmitter, look at the four corners of the space, their design is old school. Probably to protect information flow." Ryan pointed to the latticed metal towers at each corner of the building. They looked like mini Eiffel towers, but I had no idea what he was talking about.

"What do you mean?" I asked, genuinely curious.

"The building is used to determine what information goes in and what information goes out, but in the case of your grandpa I'm assuming, it's the *what goes out* that matters to him," Ryan surmised. He was so cute when he was thinking.

"Is that common knowledge, I.Q. boy? Will Jason know?" Nancy asked, a little too pointedly. Jason was obviously still on her mind.

"Probably not. The technology is old, like three-hundred-years-old. It hasn't been used since the early two-thousands. I did a history paper on it sophomore year and Mr. Gratsby thought I made it up. It wouldn't surprise me if Turner took it out of the school curriculum hundreds of years ago so he could hide it in plain sight," Ryan surmised.

"Another point on the agenda of things to check out." Nancy sighed heavily. I could tell she was growing more nervous by the second.

"We'll be okay." Bill tried to soothe all of us as we reached the public parking area of the building. There were hundreds of people coming for the scheduled tours, which made all of us a little less anxious. We could blend in nicely. "You got the thumbprints?" Bill parked and turned around in his chair to see Ryan.

"Yeah." Ryan pulled out a small rectangular metal box and opened it.

Inside were four ultra-thin thumb-shaped sheets of material. Ryan had been experimenting with making false thumbprints for the last five years and today was the day we were going to try them out. He programmed them to be four people that didn't exist which took a lot of time to create their histories and to fake thumbprint records. The only nice thing was that all four of our aliases were seventeen so he didn't have to make too long of history since you couldn't thumbprint until you were fifteen anyway. Genius.

"I just hope they work," Ryan admitted nervously.

"Let's find out." Bill smiled at Ryan supportively.

I still couldn't figure out their friendship. One minute they were at each other's throats, the next they acted like the best of buds.

Ryan offered the box to me first. "Take that one." He pointed to the one farthest to the left.

I picked it up and it felt like really thin rubber. I placed it on my right thumb and it instantly formed to its contours. After a few seconds it blended so perfectly, I couldn't even see the fake thumbprint at all. "Cool."

Everyone took their respective thumbs and put them on.

"Here we go," Nancy said through a nervous smile.

We exited the car and walked over to the admissions *cavern*, is the word I'd use to describe it. It was like the opening to an ice cave with fake stalactites hanging from an arched fifty-foot entryway. Even the surface of the archway looked like ice and rock, all an illusion to distract people's attention to what was really going on inside the building. A metal fence blocked off the opening to the cave, but directed people to a small booth for entrance.

Bill decided he'd be the first to try out the fake thumbprints. If anything went wrong the rest of us could take off, with Bill's

258

money and station, he'd be able to squirm out of trouble easier than we could.

Bill placed his thumbprint on the scanner.

"Thank you, Mr. Jaloux." The attendant smiled at Bill.

Bill walked through and waved. We all followed closely behind. No flags. No problems.

First hurdle: check.

We entered the cavern, which was pretty realistic even up close. It was as if we entered into the abominable snowman's lair with rubber snow and rocky surfaces. Ryan pointed to one of the stalactites. "Cameras. Keep your head down."

We all did as he said, hoping our faces weren't on some recognition program of Turner's. We couldn't rule anything out, but at the same time what could we do? We couldn't go back. Moving forward was the key. The alternatives were too scary to think about.

At the end of the cavern was a rotating glass door, which led to the waiting area. We walked through and entered into a large square room that was completely yellow. The walls, the furniture, the floor were all some shade of yellow. It was as if the sun puked all over this room. The contrast from the blue and grey cavern to this bright explosion of color was made purely for show. The people entering with us were full of ooohhhs and aaaaahhhs and were beyond excited to see the rest of the building.

"Tours over here, please." A petite woman dressed in a grey jumpsuit waved us over to the back of the room. With her blonde hair and make-up perfectly in order, she looked like a living mannequin. And the smile that was permanently plastered to her face indicated that she had been doing this job way too long. "Make sure you stick together, it's a big place in there, we don't want you to get lost." All her words sounded rehearsed.

We made sure we were in the back of the group so it would be easier to slip away. Ryan had memorized the floor plans of the building, but we still had to take in account that Turner's floor plans were probably hiding a few secrets that we'd have to figure out for ourselves. Hopefully, nothing that would sound alarms of any sort, but like I said, we had to keep going. Eventually, Jason would join us, we'd steal the tornado footage, go back to our tour and leave without anyone knowing we were here. Famous last words. I just hoped this time it really would be that easy. For once. Please?

"Through this door, ladies and gentlemen." Our guide pressed a button and a door slid open for us to enter.

There were about thirty other tourists in our group and, in awe, they all walked through the doorway. I pretended to do likewise while at the same time keeping my head down.

The long hallway we walked into was made entirely of black metal and lit with tiny runner lights on the floor and ceiling. It felt like yet another slap to our senses. There had to be some rhyme or reason to all these extreme décor decisions. From what I had learned so far of my grandpa, a lot of research probably went into the psychological effects of color and lighting. I found it interesting, whereas the general public seemed genuinely amazed.

"After this hallway should be the main assembly hall. We can take the south exit to get to the holo vaults," Ryan whispered to me and I nodded.

"Unless Jason gets there first," I reminded him. We might not have to split from the group at all if we received a text from Jason that he already had the footage. We weren't sure if Jason could access the vault. He was going to claim that he needed the holos from his newscast on virtual reality bars and that his news station erased it by accident. (Turner's headquarters had pretty much *all* the holo-footage in existence.) Supposedly reporters did it all the time, but we weren't sure if the footage we were looking for would even be stored there. If we didn't get Jason's text, we were going to try to get the holo ourselves and wait for Jason there. All good in theory, but we had no idea what security was going to be like. Probably high, but we didn't have any other choice. It was either do something pro-active or wait around for Turner's next attempt on my life. No thank you.

Our hostess turned to the group and began walking backwards while motioning to the strip lighting and metal walls, "This hallway is made with a special type of metal used specifically for transmission waves. All of Population Control's information is sent through hallways like these throughout the entire facility." Then she winked at a little girl as if sharing a joke. "We can't see it, of course, but even as we walk, billions of messages and transmissions are flowing along side us. Think of these hallways as veins and the information traveling through them are the blood cells of life."

Nancy couldn't help but roll her eyes. "Is she for real?"

The door at the end of the hallway slid open on cue and our tour guide didn't even have to turn around. She walked backward with an ease that was actually a little frightening, and waved us into the monstrous assembly hall.

Four walls, a set of ivory pillars and marble staircases lining each. The theme of this room was smooth marble stone. It felt like entering into Ancient Greece but with air-conditioning. There were stone statues and benches throughout the room. It was almost as if we were in an old graveyard. The more I thought about it, there had to be some kind of sense to all this architecture madness, each room so different from the next, but aside from reading Turner's mind, we were only guessing.

Several of the people in our tour were gawking over the statues. Nancy and Bill made some private joke and Ryan carefully examined every inch of the room. He leaned into my ear, "Back there, behind that faun looking thing."

The door.

Our exit.

We were pretty far from our escape, but our tour guide was at least herding us in the right direction. I nodded to Nancy and Bill and they stayed close behind us, letting Ryan take the lead. My grip on Ryan's hand tightened and he squeezed back reassuringly. I was so happy I wasn't alone in this. After my experience with Brady I found that I never wanted to be by myself *ever* again. I knew that would change over time, but honestly, the thought of being alone terrified me at the moment. Although, getting caught in my grandpa's headquarters was quickly rounding off the top of the fear factor list.

"Any word from Jason?" Nancy whispered behind me.

I shook my head.

We were going to do this.

"I hope he's okay," I heard her mumble under her breath.

The guide veered us away from our escape door and on to the next part of the tour.

"Now." Ryan pulled me behind a particularly large statue of a naked guy and Bill and Nancy followed. "Cameras on the left wall." As long as we couldn't see it, it couldn't see us. "Don't run, walk casually as if we were still on tour. We don't want to cause any alarm and running would be an instant red flag."

We all nodded and walked as relaxed as possible to the next statue. One more to go and then our exit.

Last statue. No problem.

Ryan smiled at me, a little excited. I smiled back though the last thing I felt was excitement.

"You guys ready?" I turned to Nancy and Bill.

They held hands as well and nodded.

"Please don't let that door have a siren," Bill said even though Ryan had assured him about fifty times before we even entered the building that according to the plans the door was for maintenance and had no alarms attached to it. I think this was another case of Bill trying to undermine Ryan.

Ryan's response was to ignore him, reach over and open the door.

No alarms.

Ryan raised his eyebrow at Bill triumphantly and held the door for all of us to walk through. Bill tried to appear as innocent as possible to me and I gave him an encouraging nod. He was putting himself on the line for me and any conflict he had with Ryan was between him and Ryan. I didn't want to have anything to do with it (although according to Nancy the only conflict they had was *me*, but I was ignoring that for the time being).

We walked through and Ryan shut the door behind us.

Finally, this place looked like a regular building! We were in a hallway painted plain white with cheesy holo-pics of daisy fields and sailboats on its walls.

No cameras.

That we could see anyway.

"There should be a door up here to the right." Ryan guided us forward. It amazed me that Ryan memorized the entire floor plan. No wonder Turner wanted his brain. He must have known Ryan's potential and wanted it all for himself. It scared me to think of how many kids were taken by Turner.

Sure enough the door was exactly where Ryan had indicated. He opened it and a gust of hot air blew in our faces. Once we entered the next room we stood on a metal grated walkway of a four-story labyrinth of stairways and platforms. Sporadically, a worker would enter from a doorway, walk up or down a flight of steps and enter another door. It felt almost factory-like with worker bees going to and from their destinations.

"Second doorway down on the opposite side." Ryan led me with his hand and Bill and Nancy followed.

We tried to hide the clank clank clanking of our footsteps, not wanting to draw any unnecessary attention to ourselves. So far no one was paying any attention to us, which didn't exactly put my mind at ease. It felt odd that we were able to walk freely through all these rooms. On one hand, this building was a public building and hundreds of strangers came through here every day, but on the other hand, it was my grandfather's headquarters and I *knew* what kind of a man he was which meant bad things were most likely happening here. Bad things that he wouldn't want the public to know.

We reached the door and Ryan pulled it open.

There were people everywhere!

It reminded me of the hallways at school, hundreds of workers moving in both directions trying to reach their respective destinations.

Ryan took us to the left and we entered the fray as if we belonged there. No one cared. No one noticed. Talk about zombies, but so far no spinning black holes here. Though after seeing that Turner's staff was dead I was expecting a few at least. The thought honestly scared me a bit. After my last encounter with Grandpa's staff, I was worried that I wouldn't be able to break through their wall of protection around their black centers. I did it once, but it was under the threat of death and I wasn't sure if I could do it again.

Another fear was that even if I *was* able to do it again, would Turner be alerted somehow? I just didn't know enough about my power to know any of the consequences of using it. It was all so confusing to me.

We shuffled along until Ryan took us through another door. It was another four-story metal melee of catwalks and staircases.

"We're deep in the underbelly now," Bill said almost to himself. Most of his excitement for adventure had been replaced by stress.

"The holo-footage vault is down three flights. We're almost there." Ryan tried to be re-assuring.

"Has Jason texted you yet?" Nancy asked.

"No," I answered softly. I could tell she was trying not to

show how concerned she actually was about Jason. Like it or not, the girl was hooked.

The four of us went down the metal steps and finally arrived at our destination door.

"It's through here. I'm not sure what we're looking for, but we'll have to be quick," Ryan told us all.

"Let's do it," Bill said, followed by a deep breath to steady himself.

Ryan opened the door.

Crap.

The room was shelf upon shelf upon shelf of holo-storage. It was intimidating. Each row was almost five-hundred feet long and had millions, maybe billions, of data slots on each side, and there were hundreds and hundreds of rows. There was *no way* we'd be able to find the holo-footage of my trailer park. I didn't even know where to start.

We entered the room, all of us with the same beleaguered expressions. There was no one to be found anywhere and no cameras. I was beginning to think that if there were holo-cams we just couldn't see them. I couldn't imagine a place like this not having visual security, but maybe Turner was that cocky. I hoped so, but I somehow doubted it.

"Um," I said out loud.

"Yeah, *um*, sums it up." Nancy shook her head. "Please tell me *Genius Boy* has some clue as to how we're going to find this footage."

"Give me a sec. Let me think this through." Ryan let go of my hand and walked over to one of the storage shelves. He ran his hand down the side and examined it every which way.

"You mean this footage?" With an overconfident smirk and holding a small metal chip, Jason stepped out from one of the rows of storage.

When Nancy saw him she forgot all caution and threw her arms around him in a great sigh of relief. "I was so worried, you jerk!" She kissed him quickly on the lips and Jason's arrogant stature turned into dumbstruck slush in about a split second.

"Hi," Jason said lamely.

"Hi." Nancy pulled away and gave him a small smile.

"You found it? In this mess?" I asked. My heart sang with relief.

"I know holo-storage like the back of my hand." Jason was starting to get his swagger back. "But we better get out of here before they realize the footage I took is not the footage I checked out." Jason tucked the metal chip in his shirt pocket. "I can't leave the way I came. They'll scan the chip and I won't be able to leave with it. I hope you have an alternate route?" He raised an eyebrow to Ryan.

"Yeah. Of course." Ryan took us through the door we came in. Hopefully, we could catch up to our tour and no one would ever be the wiser.

"Why didn't you text us if you had the footage?" Nancy, for the moment, was still being nice to Jason though one wrong word from him and he'd be back in the doghouse.

"Like I said, I needed an alternate way out. I knew Ryan would get you guys safely to the storage facility. I just had to wait." Jason tried not to make eye contact with Nancy. He was obviously still struggling with how he felt about her.

Nancy picked up on it immediately. "You're such a baby,

really!"

"Guys. Not now." Bill sounded like a dad quieting his rowdy kids.

It worked. Both Nancy and Jason kept their mouths closed as Ryan led us through the grated metal maze.

We were on the bottom floor of the four-story room, making our way up to the top floor.

Nancy pulled me back against the wall. She motioned for the others to follow.

"What?" Ryan whispered.

Nancy pointed upward. "Jill's dad," she answered as quietly as possible.

Oh boy.

Jill's dad, Owen Forester, was Turner's number one man. I had never seen him before and I admit I was curious to see the man who created the monster that was Jill. What kind of a man would take orders from someone like my grandfather and do the things he most likely had to do in his name? I had to see him. It was becoming a craving I couldn't control. It was almost like if I could see Jill's dad, I could see why Jill was the way she was. Just a peek.

I poked my head out slightly to see.

Owen Forester's spinning black chasm almost winked at me in greeting.

Even though I didn't want to, I suddenly felt a pang of sympathy for Jill. How long had her father been dead? Constantly vying for daddy's approval, but never getting it because he wasn't alive anymore. It didn't excuse her being the *nasty* that she was, but it did give some reasoning behind it.

I was about to tell everyone about Mr. Forester's condition when I caught a glimpse of Turner joining him on the causeway.

"Door?" Jason mouthed to Ryan.

Ryan shook his head and pointed up one flight of stairs.

"We're screwed." Nancy leaned against the wall in frustration.

"Of all the staircases in this monstrous building, they had to come to ours," I groaned.

It felt very fishy to me. Especially since it didn't look like they were going anywhere anytime soon. Yet at the same time they made no show of acknowledging our presence. They were just talking, or Turner was anyway, zombie-man was probably just listening to orders.

It made me think of how Turner kept these corpses animated. It was obviously a different process than mine because he looked genuinely shocked when I grabbed control of his staff. Some kind of spell, but what were the results of the spell? Did the dead people retain all their memories and sense of self? Were they simply puppets like mine were? *Or* were they truly back from the dead under Gramps's spell? Whatever it was, it was some serious mojo.

Turner almost gained control back over his corpses by rolling his eyes and spouting out his power words. And what was up with all the eye color changes? First, in my mother's vision with Grandma, then with Grandpa, was that a part of the spell? Brady told me my eyes dilated when I activated the cockroach. Was there some connection there? I had so many questions racing through my brain and the only man who could possibly answer them wanted me dead. Good luck with that.

"Are they going to move, or what?" Bill started to sweat. All

269

the pressure, excitement and fear bubbled over in a whirlwind of panic.

I placed my hand on his arm. "We'll be fine."

Bill's shoulders relaxed visibly at my touch. He nodded.

Ryan squeezed my other hand tightly. I could tell he didn't like me comforting Bill very much, but he didn't say anything because he knew Bill needed it. Extra points in my book.

Before we could react, at least a hundred soldiers stepped out of every door from all four stories. All black spinning holes. An army of dead people. And all of them started marching down toward us.

No wonder Turner had been standing there *forever*. He was waiting for us to try and escape to the door on the second floor. His master plan of having his men enter the room and grab us... not working out so well for him. As usual, his impatience overruled his good judgment. Good. Maybe we could escape from this. I tested the men's black centers and they were just like his staff. Walls of resistance like bulletproof vests.

"Did you really think fake thumbprints would work?" Turner's voice echoed off the metal. He sounded amused.

"What do we do now?" Jason asked Ryan. We weren't near any doors, which was most likely why Turner decided to act impulsively.

"We go down." Ryan nodded to the cement floor about ten feet below us. "There's a vent opening that leads to the lower level of the building."

The first of the dead soldiers jumped down to our platform and grabbed Jason's arm.

I took a deep breath and smashed through the invisible

barrier like it was made of glass. It was crazy at how easy it was. I was expecting some kind of opposition, but my mind remembered the sensation of ripping through the protective wall. I made the soldier release his grip on Jason. I slammed through all of the soldiers' invisible barricades and connected to their dark chasms of death. I tried to disconnect them from their black holes, but something was stopping me.

"Not this time, little one," Turner's voice boomed from above.

I looked up and his eyes were the same crimson as they were in Principal Weatherby's office. He had more time to plan this time, to figure out how to prevent me from destroying his minions. And apparently it worked because I couldn't disconnect the corpses from their swirling centers.

I'd have to settle for controlling them.

I made them all stop in their tracks.

I could feel the struggle Turner was experiencing trying to make his soldiers move again.

"Maybe you should have researched that a bit more, huh Gramps?"

Turner fumed. He began chanting loudly.

I could feel my grip on the soldiers lessen. They started to twitch with movement.

"I say we jump," I said to Ryan and the others.

It was the first time I noticed them all staring at me.

I realized they had never really seen me in action aside from a dead plant or small insects. Only Jason was slightly unfazed since he was with me at the virtual reality bar, but even he seemed a little dumbfounded.

"Guys, seriously, he's gaining control of them. I don't know how much longer I can keep them disabled." I needed them to snap out of it.

"Right." Ryan grabbed my hand and we jumped to the floor followed by the others.

Ouch.

And oops.

It was just enough of a distraction for Turner to regain control over his boys. They started dropping like super humans to the floor next to us.

Ryan grabbed the vent grating and flung it open. It was another drop, but only about five feet and it looked like a tunnel entrance to the right. "Everyone in!"

Jason didn't need to be told twice, he was the first to hop down.

Nancy huffed in annoyance at Jason's lack of chivalry. "Typical." And she jumped in as well.

One of the soldiers grabbed Bill and put him in a choke hold.

I connected to the soldier's black hole at about half power. Turner somehow blocked me out of the other half, but it was enough for Bill to fight back. He kicked the soldier back into the others and jumped down the vent.

"You next," I instructed Ryan.

"No way is that *ever* going to happen." Ryan said with so much conviction I almost dropped down the vent.

"I can actually slow these guys down, Ryan," I pleaded.

Ryan reluctantly nodded and jumped down to join the others.

The soldiers came at me. I had enough power over them to make them move in slow motion. It was surreal seeing hundreds of soldiers running toward me at a snail's pace as if I was watching an instant re-play on the holo-tv.

I looked up at Turner and our eyes met. Though they were solid red I could still see something I had never seen before in them.

Glee.

I hopped down and joined the others.

Ryan slammed the grating shut.

"Come on. Through here." Ryan wrapped his arm around me for support.

"I'm only half-controlling them. I can't seem to take them over completely. Turner is too strong and knows *way* more about this stuff than I do," I admitted weakly. Connecting to over a hundred bodies was taking its toll on my brain. "He'll send in live ones soon."

As if in unison to my statement I felt Turner release all his soldiers from their black holes, letting them die for real this time, and essentially making them useless to me. The stink was already wafting through the ventilation shaft's opening.

I finally paid attention to where we were. The shaft we jumped down was huge! I was standing and still had about two feet of headroom. A metal tunnel opened before us... dark and foreboding, but our only way out.

"This leads down four more levels. That's where the main power generators are. If we get that far, there's an elevator shaft we can climb up that leads directly to the front gate," Ryan said as bravely as possible, but I could tell he was as nervous as

273

everyone else.

Nancy pulled out a flashlight from her purse with a shrug. "I was hoping we wouldn't need this, but…" She let that hang in the air, not needing to finish the thought, not wanting to. We were in big trouble and none of us knew how we were going to get out of it.

"One thing at a time." I gave Nancy a reassuring look.

"Right," she said, swallowing her fear, but not masking it completely.

Nancy handed Ryan the flashlight and he took the lead. I had a moment where I felt like Larry the cockroach as we made our way through the giant man-sized shaft. Ryan guided us through the maze of twists and turns with ease. Nancy's small flashlight was the only source of light to show the way. So far, we couldn't hear any signs of pursuit, but we knew it was only a matter of time before we did. Jason took up the rear and Nancy, Bill and I were in the middle. I stayed as close as I could to Ryan for his protection and for mine.

"Why didn't Turner just shoot us?" Bill asked, breaking the intense silence.

I hadn't thought of that.

"It would be definitive proof that he could bring the dead back," Jason pondered as if he *had* been thinking about it the whole time. "If we all came back to our families riddled with bullet holes, but alive and well, there would be questions, investigations, you name it. He can't take that kind of press or attention."

"So we can use that to our advantage. Knowing he can't shoot us, he can only kill us with no marks essentially?" Nancy

274

mused out loud then turned to Jason. "You have family?"

Jason ignored her second question. "Let's not kid ourselves. If we cause him too much trouble, he will take us down anyway he can and spin it so that we were somehow attacked by terrorists or something. For now, he wants Chelsan. *Dead* or *alive*, but luckily for us *dead* means he's not using bullets. As for *us* I'm not sure what he's willing to do." Concerned, Jason glanced briefly at Nancy, but when Nancy returned the gaze he looked away.

She grunted in annoyance.

"No alarms either," Bill observed as if he were running through a check list of possible snags.

"No. Maybe he doesn't want any of the tourists to panic or word to get out," Nancy suggested.

"Or maybe he's so confident he'll get us there's no need for alarms." Bill was spiraling and I needed to snap him out of it.

"Let's just get to the main generator room, okay?" I said, turning to look at him.

He nodded once and averted his eyes. I don't think he wanted me to see him scared.

We moved farther down into the bowels of the Population Control's headquarters. Though I knew it was only four floors it felt as if we had gone miles underground. Still, being that we were already three floors down at the start of our mission, seven floors underground was a bit intimidating.

"Up here," Ryan informed us.

When we turned left we could see light looming in the distance through another grate about a hundred feet away. Ryan motioned us to stay while he checked it out. I watched him move slowly to the vent opening and peer out. Ryan's whole body went slack, arms dropped to his side, not moving, as if something had stunned him.

Danger or no, I ran up to him as fast as my legs would carry me. When I approached him he turned to me and his eyes were so full of terror and anger I nearly flinched at the onslaught of emotion glaring at me.

"What is it?" I asked and touched his arm as if that might help him snap out of the nightmare he was obviously in.

Ryan just nodded toward the grate.

I peered through and I understood immediately.

The vent opening was about eight feet above the ground so the entire room was visible. It was the biggest room I had ever seen. Almost as big as the hangers that held the skyscraper-sized hover-trucks from Clean-Up.

It was exactly as Ryan described to me that morning before school.

This was the place he had been taken all those years ago by Turner.

An I.Q. Farm.

Hundreds of kids at computer stations, virtual reality mats, holo-games, all focused and ignorant to everyone around them. It was a frightening spectacle watching these hunched, hollow-eyed children working on their invisible projects. I pulled Ryan in closer and he hugged me with all of his might. I could feel his emotions pouring into this one embrace. His fear, his sadness, his relief, his anger all jumbled together in a tangled mess. If he hadn't been as quick witted as he was, he would have been one of those kids below.

Ryan pulled away, his eyes clearer. He looked down at the

room again. "The main power generators should be at the other end of this room, through that door there."

The others had joined us from behind, not sure of how to react because of Ryan.

"Is this really an I.Q. Farm?" Nancy asked tentatively.

"It's the same one I was taken to. I remember it now," Ryan explained so everyone would know his personal stake in all this.

"Whoa," Bill said softly. I could tell the protective side of him wanted to reach out and give Ryan his support, but the *jealous guy side* of him wouldn't allow it.

Ryan grabbed my hand suddenly.

"What is it?" I asked. His face had gone another shade paler, if that was possible.

"I recognize a few of the kids." Ryan swallowed hard. "They're the same age." Ryan turned to me, eyes wide. "Turner is giving them Age-pro."

We all stood in stunned silence.

Giving Age-pro to kids was an unspeakable act. And it was a double whammy to think that Ryan could have been eight-years-old *forever*. I guess it wasn't a surprise that Turner was capable of such perversion, but it rocked us all just the same.

"They look like they're in comas, it shouldn't be too hard to get past them," Jason observed callously.

Nancy punched him in the arm. "Way to be sensitive, jerk."

"I'm sorry if I don't want to die, but reminiscing on what could have been isn't helping our escape here. Just because there's no alarm doesn't mean they're not after us." Jason rubbed his arm from Nancy's blow.

"He's right," Ryan agreed, though his eyes were still staring at the children below. "This vent is on hinges and swings outward." Ryan reached over and popped the vent opening. "If we move it slowly enough, hopefully no one will see."

I placed both hands on the hinged side of the grate making sure the rate of movement was as slow as possible. Ryan was at the other side and moved the slab of metal as far as he could without falling to the ground below. I clasped my fingers through the metal slats and stopped the grate before it could hit the wall.

None of the kids seemed to notice.

All five of us were now as exposed as could be standing over the entire room like a framed picture.

Jason jumped down first, his patience almost gone. I shouldn't really be surprised. He *did* cry like a baby at the virtual reality bar. Why should being in my grandpa's lair be any different?

Everyone else followed him down, Ryan was the last. It was my turn to be the *comforter* in this relationship and I found that I felt more helpless than I ever did when I was being attacked by Turner's lackeys. What could I possibly do to make Ryan feel better? He was in the very room of his nightmares and it was all because of me. If he had never liked me he would have never had to see or think about this place for the rest of his days. I should have seen this coming. I should have known better. Now Ryan had to face his personal demons, not in a healthy-let's-talk-about-it kind of way, but in an in-your-face-welcome-to-your-own-personal-torture kind of a way.

Yeah. I was a *great* girlfriend.

"The entrance to the generators is on the other side," Ryan informed them quietly and I squeezed his hand supportively.

No matter what, I didn't want him to feel alone in all this.

We walked as casually as possible, not wanting any of the children to notice. We didn't even know what they would do if they *did* realize we were there. Would they scream? Would they hit an alarm? Or would they do nothing?

Nothing. It seemed to be the answer for the moment. The kids were so involved in what they were doing I think I could have sat on one of them and they wouldn't care.

Better for us.

Ryan and I in the lead, we were half way across the room when a woman stepped in front of us. She came out of nowhere and I nearly leapt back a few feet from the shock of it. So much so that I didn't even realize who she was until it was too late.

Roberta. My grandma. The Feline.

The last time I saw her was in my mother's vision and a giant snake was coming out of her mouth! If I thought she was scary in a dream, in person she was downright terrifying with her stretched and frozen face. She stared at me with such venom in her eyes I almost expected her to hiss. I wanted to look away. The only reason I didn't was because I was afraid she'd eat me or something. She was taller than I expected, but everything else was the same as Mom's vision. Even her black hair was pulled back in the same tight bun and her skin had that strange plastic shine. Her eyes were so dark and so intense they reminded me of the swirling chasms I saw in the dead.

"Finally! Someone who can help us. We were on our tour and got incredibly lost! Could you tell us how to get back?" Jason came up from the back of the group with a friendly smile, although I could tell seeing a Feline was making him uncomfortable.

I realized then that no one else knew who she was. Only Gramps was on holo-tv. Roberta wouldn't want the world seeing that she was a cat lady. Although, even if she looked like she did when she was twenty, she'd probably still look harsh and nasty. It came from the inside and she didn't even try to disguise it.

Roberta answered Jason in a silent stare that made his smile fade instantaneously.

"We're leaving now," I stated boldly and stepped in front of the group in case she tried anything.

"Oh really?" Roberta smiled wickedly, though nothing else on her face moved. It only added to her creepiness.

"We really did get lost…" Bill tried to back up Jason's story, a little too naïve to realize we faced a foe, and apparently in shock at seeing a Feline in person.

Roberta's eyes turned white as she looked at Bill and he grabbed his throat from pain. Bill bent over coughing uncontrollably, his face turning red, eyes bugging out from lack of breath.

Don't mess with my friends.

I punched her in the nose.

Pretty hard, too, because she actually took a few steps back from the hit.

But it worked.

Bill stopped coughing and rubbed his throat in the aftermath.

They all knew they faced real danger now.

I didn't want to look at them. I didn't want to see the fear in their eyes. I kept my attention on Roberta.

She was livid. She took a step toward me and slapped me

hard on the cheek.

That whole side of my face tingled from the blow, but I didn't let my eyes leave hers.

"How dare you!" Roberta hissed at me.

"Get out of our way," I hissed back.

"Just like your mother," she accused malevolently.

"Thank you." I couldn't help but truly hate this woman standing in front of me. How could someone like my father come from two of the most despicable human beings on the planet? There was nothing nice about her. Not even an inkling. Not even a shred.

"Geoffrey told me about you. Told me how much like your mother you were. How stupid and filthy you were. Now I can see you are so much worse," Roberta spat.

"Thank you," I repeated, not wanting to give her an ounce of a response.

Roberta's monstrous face grimaced and she narrowed her eyes. "Geoffrey and I tried for two-hundred years to have a baby and we finally had Franklin, a beautiful, wonderful, brilliant boy. I nearly died during his birth and it scarred me so I couldn't have any more children. He was perfect for a hundred years until he met your mother!"

Roberta's eyes rolled back again, but I was on top of this trick now. I slapped her and her concentration was broken. She shrieked in rage, sounding more animal than human.

"You killed my only son and you *will* die for that," Roberta rasped from being jolted out of her spellcasting.

"Like I told Gramps, *you* killed your own son and took away my only chance at a normal life. So, I'd be watching your back if I were you." I was livid. No matter what I did I couldn't seem to calm down.

Roberta didn't seem to hear, as if what I had to say meant nothing to her. Or everything, and she didn't want to listen.

"These are my children now." Roberta motioned to the room. "Some of them for almost two-hundred years." It was the first time I had seen anything other than loathsome hate from her.

She finally noticed Ryan standing next to me. "Ryan," she said and there was genuine love in her eyes. "You've come back."

Okay. She was nuts. A grotesque caricature of a human being.

Ryan was frozen. I hadn't realized it until now. He recognized her from the start. She must have been involved in his kidnapping and it was all bubbling to the surface upon seeing her.

Roberta turned back to me with malice. "You've taken another one of my children. He'll be mine again soon. The guards are on their way. Ryan will live, the rest of you won't." She said it so matter-of-factly it was worse than when she performed her Voodoo eye stuff.

BAM!

Roberta dropped to the floor with a thud.

Nancy stood behind her with a metal chair in her hands and a look of pure rage. "I was tired of listening to that cat bitch." She turned to Ryan. "Can we get out of here now?"

Ryan broke out of his trance. "Yeah," he spoke quietly and started at a run to the other side of the room. All pretenses were down. No more trying to blend. If the guards were on their way then the kids freaking out wouldn't matter anyway. The creepy part was, the children didn't budge. None of what just happened, the yelling, the whacking, fazed them for a second.

They continued their drone-like behavior uninterrupted.

The guards busted through from the side and middle entrances of the room. They carried stun clubs and among the comatose kids we were easy to spot. Not one of them dead. Turner was leading the charge and our eyes met. Then I did what I knew was a horrible thing to do, but I couldn't help myself. I glanced over at the still form of Roberta and then back at him. It worked. He followed my gaze and saw the crumpled form of his wife in the middle of the room. He howled in rage and screamed at his men to capture us at all costs.

We were all at a full sprint now, following Ryan like frenzied rabbits running from the wolves. I hoped he knew where he was going. It would be just my luck if this were the one time he had the directions wrong. Ryan reached the elusive door first and swung it open with his full might. And sure enough the room inside was filled with hundreds of twenty-foot fuel cell generators and a set of elevator doors on the far wall. After everyone was inside, Bill and Nancy slammed the door shut and set the bolt lock.

"That's gonna hold them for about ten seconds." Nancy managed a small worried glance in my direction.

As if hearing Nancy, the pounding on the door began. The hinges were already starting to squeak from the amount of force being applied.

Ryan was halfway across the room, heading for the elevator doors. We all followed in a huddled pack finding it hard to keep up with him. Roberta spooked Ryan more than I realized. Maybe it was because of the way she looked at him after so many years. Whatever it was, Ryan wanted out, and he wanted out *now.*

I reached the elevator doors with the others.

BOOM!

The guards broke down the door and were pouring through in waves of uniformed gray, heading straight for us.

"Get to the other end." Ryan nodded to Bill.

Bill and Ryan pulled open the elevator doors with some exertion. We were going to have to climb, taking the elevator would be too risky. Turner could radio for a shut down and we'd be sitting ducks.

"Move. Move. Move," Bill yelled through gritted teeth.

I didn't need to be told twice let alone three times. I ran through the pried open doors and into the shaft. A security ladder leading all the way to the top was on my right. Just like Ryan had said. Thank goodness for his brain. I made Jason and Nancy start the climb first. I intended to go last.

Bill and Ryan counted to three and leapt inside the elevator shaft.

One of the guards that was way ahead of the others shoved his arm in between the doors, stun club flailing, just before they closed. I knew within seconds they'd have the doors open and we'd be gonners, so I grabbed his club and whacked his arm with it. His hand and arm went limp and Ryan and I stuffed it through the door as the rest of the guards arrived at the scene.

Bill started up the ladder behind Nancy and Jason.

Ryan turned to me. "We're not going to make it."

"Go! I have a plan to stall them. I'll be right behind you!" I said and shoved him toward the ladder. I had no such plan, but I didn't want Ryan to suffer for my sake. All of this was my fault and I couldn't live with myself if anything happened to my friends. Not if I could do something about it.

The guards clasped on to each door, trying to pry the doors open like Ryan and Bill had.

Ryan reluctantly started up the ladder, keeping his eyes on me the entire time.

I glanced at him briefly and smiled. "I'll be okay. Hurry."

Ryan shook his head and stopped mid-rung. "No. I'm not leaving you." He jumped back down and joined my side. "What's the plan?"

"Ryan!" I shouted, not wanting to admit that I, in fact, still did not have a plan.

"If we go down, we go down together. I'm not going to abandon you like I did last year." Ryan kissed me quickly and even with the doors being lodged open to our doom, my stomach still did the proper flip flopping.

"I appreciate you feeling guilty about ignoring me in school, but we could die here." I gave him my serious face though I secretly wanted him to stay right where he was.

The doors were almost open and we could see the hundreds of soldiers ready to pounce on us. Luckily for us the soldiers were trying so hard to get through they were stacked on top of each other making a traffic jam at the doors.

Okay. Maybe we should have tried to make a run for it. I looked up at Nancy, Bill and Jason. They weren't that far away. If I didn't do something fast, we'd all be screwed.

I concentrated. How sad was it that I was wishing and hoping for *any* kind of dead thing in the vicinity?

Relief flooded through me. Rats. Hundreds of dead rats

ranging from newly trapped to been-there-a-while rot. All in the walls. Blek.

I'd be revealing to Turner that it wasn't just people I could bring back, but he may have already found that out from Brady anyway. It was worth the risk. It was our only chance. I hoped these soldiers could scare because rats wouldn't cause any lasting damage. I was about to find out.

"Here goes nothing," I said to Ryan and he gently embraced my hand for support. "I hope you're not afraid of rats."

"Oh man." Ryan took a deep breath preparing for what was to come.

I took one of those myself and just as the first soldier had almost wriggled his way through the crowd I slammed into all the rats I could reach.

I would have loved to see the stampede of rodents racing across the floor. A melee of decomposed corpses to freshly killed, all scraggly, all vicious.

And…. Contact.

I made them attack the guards with all their strength. Running up their bodies, biting any piece of flesh I could find, jumping, leaping, snarling, biting monsters.

Screams of terror filled the air and it made my skin crawl, but I didn't break concentration, I kept the battle of the zombie rats going full force.

SHUUUNK!

The elevator doors smashed shut.

We could still hear the cries of terror through the wall.

"I'll keep the rats on them as long as possible. Let's get out of here," I said and found it awkward to walk over to the ladder and control the rats at the same time. I could feel their tiny teeth tear into the fabric of the soldiers' uniforms. I wanted to keep them occupied, but I didn't want to do any serious damage. The soldiers were only doing their jobs even if they were working for pure evil.

Ryan and I started our long climb up, me in front, Ryan in back. After doing the math, we had to climb about ten stories. I hoped I could keep the rodent onslaught going that long.

The elevator whizzed up and down next to us giving a little extra cover just in case the guards decided they wanted to fight with rat corpses as their new uniform.

I tried to pin point Turner's location, give him an extra bite or two in the face (see how he explains that on holo), but I couldn't differentiate between the men down below. I could only see the tiny swirling black masses of the rats. *Just keep them fighting.* It was taking all my energy to climb and control and I was draining fast. We still had eight floors to go and I was breathing heavily like I had already run a marathon.

Up ahead I could barely see Nancy and the others. They were almost to freedom. I needed to give Ryan and I a few more floors before I could let go of my hold on the rats. I just didn't know if I could do it. I had just been released from the hospital! What was I thinking?

"Ryan," I barely croaked out. Wow. I was fading quicker than I thought.

Ryan climbed up beside me faster than I could think. "What is it? Are you okay?" His face was full of concern.

"I'm keeping the connection, but climbing... both... too hard... I don't know if I can make it," I sputtered.

287

He just nodded. "Climb on my back. You keep the rats up, I'll take *you* up."

I didn't have the strength to argue. I limply crawled onto Ryan, piggy-back style, until I rested comfortably. Much better. It was still a difficult task using all the energy I had left to keep the rodents attacking the soldiers, but manageable. I leaned my head on his shoulder. I knew being six foot three Ryan could easily carry me, but climbing seven more floors with an extra hundred and ten pounds on your back had to take its toll at some point. I did my part. I kept my connection to the rats. And feeling Ryan's muscles expanding and contracting as he climbed up the ladder was somehow more comforting than a hug. Although I could have used one of those, too.

Still no alarms, which I found extremely odd. Turner must truly want to keep everything hidden under the rug. It made me wonder where exactly I was on his priority list. The scope of my grandfather's empire left me breathless. I was just a flea on a Great Dane. How important was I in the grand scheme of things? He could already raise the dead, so aside from a personal vendetta, why did he even care about me? That look in his eyes, in Roberta's eyes. That was my answer, I guess. They were insane with grief and anger and I was the living representation of it all. Although, Roberta looked genuinely crazy, anger or not. Maybe it was her cat-like face, with that frozen rubbery skin. I'm not usually one to judge on how someone looks, but seeing her face up close like that, with the stretching and the shining. Ick.

My eyes felt so heavy... I lost my power over at least half of the rats. I could connect to them, I just couldn't seem to make them move. Hopefully, the little guys I did control could still keep the guards occupied. I glanced up. The others were already on the surface. Ryan was sweating from the exertion of climbing with the weight of two people, but we were only two floors away from freedom.

"Almost there," I heard myself say though it sounded like it came from someone else.

And then my arms slipped from Ryan's neck.

I would have fallen all the way to the bottom if it weren't for Ryan's quick reflexes. He caught my wrist before I plunged to my death.

That woke me up.

I climbed back up to Ryan's back with as much effort as I could muster.

The elevator doors cranked open down below and soldiers began to flow through. They were rodent-free and moving up the ladder faster than I could imagine.

The near fall jolted me out of keeping the rats active, and my exhaustion made me forget to reconnect.

"Don't worry about the rats, just hold on." Ryan began climbing like a mad man.

One more floor.

The first soldier was only two floors away from us. Man they were quick.

I tried to get a good look at the guard closest to us. His clothes were shredded and he was sporting quite a few scratches and bites. He looked severely pissed.

Ryan reached the opened grate. Hands reached down and lifted us to the surface.

"Are you okay?" Nancy was all over me. I must have looked

really bad.

I could hear Jason and Bill slamming the grate shut from the outside.

No matter how hard I tried, my eye lids were made of lead. We were on the outskirts of the building about a few hundred feet from the parking lot. "I'm fine. Just tired."

"Not too tired, I hope?"

My eyes flew open from Turner's voice.

We all turned to see my grandpa standing with a few guards. He didn't have one scratch on him! Not even a nibble. He must have escaped as soon as he saw the rats coming. Or something else? I knew so little about my grandpa, his powers, his capabilities, it was frustrating. And worst of all, it was dangerous. Not knowing your opponent could mean fatal consequences.

Turner nodded to one of his soldiers.

The obedient man walked over to the metal grating and opened it for the climbing soldiers to exit. They started to file out one at a time forming a circle around our party. Ryan held me close as if he alone could protect me. The guards from below were shredded from head to toe. Maybe I went a little crazy with the rats. Bill and Nancy on the other hand appeared extremely impressed.

Nancy whispered in my ear with a hint of amazement, "Did you do that?"

I nodded and tried to make myself smile, but it just ended up being some sort of grimace.

Turner walked boldly up to Jason. "Give it to me."

"Give what to you?" Jason smiled that half-smirk that used to be the basis of my crush on him.

"Now." Turner wasn't in the mood for Jason or any of us for that matter.

We weren't going to make it out of here alive.

Jason reached into his shirt pocket and pulled out the holo-chip. He reluctantly handed it over to Turner's aged hands.

"Can't blame a guy for trying," Jason said off-handed.

"Yes, I can." Turner handed the holo-chip to one of his guards. "Search him, make sure he didn't make a switch."

The soldier patted Jason down thoroughly, searching every pocket, nook and cranny on his body. "Nothing."

Turner nodded. "Good. Destroy it."

The guard placed the holo-chip on the ground and used his stun club on it. The holo-chip sparked and fizzled until it went completely dead, a charred black fleck on the cement.

Jason's face stayed in that half-smirk, frozen in time, as if he couldn't decide if it would help or hurt his cause to act scared.

Turner turned to me. "You're free to go."

What?

"What?" I realized I hadn't said that out loud.

"You look exhausted. Get some rest." Turner's face revealed nothing.

What was going on?

"That's it?" I couldn't believe my ears. Maybe I was asleep already and this was all a dream.

"You came here with a mission and you failed. Now go," he stated way too calmly.

We began to walk away toward the parking lot and sure enough the soldiers stepped aside to let us through.

"Wait," came Grandpa's voice from behind.

Here we go.

"You guys get to the car. Don't wait for me," I said and shoved them away.

"Yeah right," Nancy, Bill and Ryan all spoke at once. I did notice that Jason had no arguments.

I turned to face my grandfather.

"Yes?" I asked, waiting for the worst.

"I'll send a car for you tomorrow at Nancy's. Three o'clock. You'll be safe, I assure you. We need to discuss a few… matters." Turner treated me as if we had been colleagues for decades.

And with that, he turned and left with all his guards. They headed toward a private entrance not wanting to draw unnecessary attention to their tattered state. Within seconds Turner was gone. The five of us alone in the parking lot, exactly where we started out at the beginning of this trip.

"Let's get out of here," Jason said with some urgency. I don't think he felt that Turner was on the up and up.

We all walked toward the lot.

"You're not really going to meet him, are you?" Bill asked with a boomingly over-protective tone.

"Yes, I am." I thought I hadn't made up my mind yet, but when asked directly I knew the answer had to be yes. If I didn't settle this with Turner, it would just continue on and on until one or both of us was dead, or worse, someone I cared about. "And don't try and talk me out of it." I knew the protesting would ensue.

"You're way too tired to listen to reason anyway. We'll argue with you tomorrow," Nancy said.

We all arrived at Bill's hover-car.

"Where's your car?" I asked Jason.

"I'm going with you guys. I'll have an intern pick up my car later." Jason replied, and I could tell he was trying to hide some of his fear. "No worries, I'll ride bitch."

No one had the energy to argue. We all piled into the hover-car, Jason sitting between Ryan and I in the back seat. Uggh! I'm sure there was some other way to arrange everyone so we could all be happy, but we were so ready to get out of there no one said anything.

Bill whizzed away from the monstrous structure and it felt as if we were flying away from a funeral. We were all silent. No one wanted to re-live what we had gone through, or maybe they didn't want *me* to have to, and I was grateful. I wanted to lean against Ryan and go to sleep, but Jason separated us. He was fidgeting like a crazy person.

"Would you stop that?" Ryan had apparently had enough of Jason's squirming.

"No. Let's get to Nancy's as fast as this hover-car will hover." Jason's knee wouldn't stop shaking.

Something was up and it wasn't just escaping Turner's grasp. Jason was hiding it from all of us and he wanted to be under the blanket of George's magic-red-orb-of-silence to tell us.

"Sure." Bill read between the same lines I had. We picked up some speed and flew to Nancy's house in no time.

Bill landed the car and George and Vianne came out to greet us.

Jason went straight to George before he could hug his daughter. I stayed close to him, not wanting to miss anything. "Your info-blocker still in tact?"

George was all business. "Had to make a few adjustments, Turner's guys have been trying to break it daily."

Vianne had done all the hugging for George and looked over at Jason and I with curiosity.

"Let's get inside." George nodded to his wife and she nodded back.

We all headed inside Nancy's house.

I grabbed Ryan's hand as we sat down on the couch. I didn't want to be separated from him any longer than I had to. He was becoming a continual source of calm for me lately and I wanted to be the same for him. I could tell seeing those kids really shook him up. His life would have been a comatose state of imprisonment if he hadn't got away. His hand shook slightly and I leaned in close feeling him physically relax. At least I could be some help however small it was.

Jason stayed standing, in fact, he was pacing. This boy needed to calm down!

Bill, Nancy and her parents all took their respective seats and all eyes turned to Jason.

"I have the holo-footage," Jason confessed, his eyes crazed.

"Okay, he's losing it." Nancy was concerned.

"No. I gave Turner a fake holo-chip, well, it wasn't fake, it was some footage I picked up after I stole the tornado footage, but I knew we'd need a decoy, just in case." Jason was babbling out his story now.

"But, they searched you." Bill tried to be the voice of reason to Jason's apparent insanity.

Jason continued to ramble. "They didn't search *inside* of me. I swallowed the chip. It's covering should be enough to protect it from my digestive system, but I need George here to retrieve the data just in case. Nancy's place is the only safe haven we have from Turner, as long as he's in the dark about us having the holo-chip, we could still get it on the air." Jason was excited now.

"You swallowed it?" I asked, as a surge of hope coursed through me. Maybe we could still take Gramps down before he could do any more damage.

"Yup." Jason acted like the cat that ate the canary. And I guess, he actually did.

"So what? You're going to poop it out?" Nancy's face cringed in disgust.

"Well, yeah, but I got it out of top security. Turner was just being lazy, he should have had me scanned but he was too obsessed with Chelsan to be thorough." Jason side-stepped the issue of how the chip was going to re-surface.

"But you're pooping it out?" Nancy wasn't letting it go. "That's disgusting."

"When is it coming out? Are you... regular... or..." Bill suddenly found himself too embarrassed to finish the conversation.

"Would everyone stop obsessing about my bowel movements and start congratulating me on accomplishing our mission. It's not easy shoving a piece of metal down your throat." Jason seemed very put off by the disturbed reaction of the others.

"I think it's brilliant," George beamed. "As soon as it... well... as soon as you clean it up, it'll be no problem retrieving the data. I'll have it transferred on a new chip and read to go... when you are." George apparently didn't want to mention the method of extracting the chip either.

Jason turned to Vianne and held his arm out for her. "Let's make a concoction that will speed this process up, shall we?"

Grinning, Vianne wrapped her arm in Jason's. "I'm sure I can put something together, load you up on fiber."

"This is so gross." Nancy's arms were crossed and she was extremely disgusted by the whole ordeal.

"Hush," Vianne scolded her daughter as she and Jason left for the kitchen.

Once they were gone, George turned to the four of us. "You kids should get some rest, Chelsan looks like she's about to pass out. Bill, Ryan, you better stay here tonight. I'll call your parents and let them know. You all have school in the morning."

Ugggh. School. Did we really have to go to school after everything we'd been through? Apparently, the answer was yes. But George was right about something. I was ready to drop. I only had a few minutes left in me. Just enough time to snuggle up to Ryan before wondrous sleep overtook me.

There were no arguments on anyone's part. We all said our good nights to George and headed up stairs. Bill and Ryan were to sleep in Nancy's guest bedroom, but there was no way I was letting Ryan out of my sight. Bill obviously didn't want *that* image stuck in his head so he left for the guest room.

Nancy decided to join him, giving me a wink and a nudge toward Ryan. "And besides, it'll make poop boy jealous. Mom and Dad won't care anyway. I think they're secretly hoping I'll marry Bill." And with that she joined Bill in his room.

Ryan and I entered Nancy's room still holding hands. It was like walking into a safe haven of awesomeness. I checked the

296

room once over for anyone lurking about. Once clear, Ryan and I plopped down on Nancy's phenomenal bed of comfort. It was just about the softest most amazing sensation ever.

Ryan and I faced each other forehead to forehead. His hand rested comfortably on my hip while I placed mine on his waist. I was about to nod off into dreamland when Ryan suddenly leaned in and kissed me. It was like an electric charge surged through my system and I kissed him back empowered by this newfound energy.

His lips were tender and firm at the same time and my head went dizzy with the feeling. Kissing him was almost like a drug taking over all my senses to the point of explosion. I couldn't seem to stop. I didn't want to stop. The more we kissed the more I wanted it to keep going. The thought of stopping was actually excruciating to contemplate. His hands pulled me in tighter to his body with just enough force to make the butterflies in my stomach go insane. I held onto him as if he were my salvation from all the craziness. His hand now cradled the small of my back with agonizing tenderness. This boy was going to be the end of me! So much adrenaline, hormones, emotions, everything was becoming too much to bear all at once.

I pulled away breathless.

He was slightly out of breath as well.

"Too much," was all that came out of my mouth.

Ryan nodded, though his hand still cradled my back, which made me want to kiss him all over again.

He was so freakin' hot!

We sat there for about five more seconds before Ryan pulled me in and started to kiss me again.

Oh boy.

It was even more intense than the first time. I found myself wanting more of him. Wanting more than just kissing. I wanted *all* of him. I started to pull off his shirt when he drew back.

His hand cupped my cheek. "We should wait. I want to make this special."

I had to take a minute to calm my brain down from all the excitement. "You're the human equivalent of a brain-fry," I laughed a little.

Ryan smiled back and kissed me gently. "I just want you to know…" Ryan was suddenly very serious.

I had a surge of panic. Was he going to break up with me? Was I terrible? Why was he looking at me like that?

"I love you," he said and there was genuine fear in his eyes.

And I realized the fear was because he didn't know how I felt about him. He was completely putting himself out there and I was officially letting him hang.

"I love *you*." I kissed him again.

We couldn't seem to control ourselves. It was becoming harder and harder to break away. I was filled with a genuine glow of happiness I had never felt before. Ryan loved me. I guess I already knew that from the way he looked at me to his actions over the last week, but to hear him say it made my heart swell uncontrollably. He pushed in closer to me and I was so besieged by this onslaught of sensations I couldn't even keep a coherent thought.

This time I had to rip myself away from him. "Whoa," I said and I felt like laughing again. These past days were filled with one extreme to the next. From the devastating death of my mother, to constantly fighting to stay alive, to the awe-inspiring loyalty of friends, to Ryan. I was shocked that my heart was still beating.

"Yeah, whoa is right," Ryan said with a genuine grin. "I really meant for you to go to sleep," he admitted sheepishly.

"Sure you did, perv." I tickled his side.

Ryan squirmed and laughed, then his eyes met mine, intense. "Everything that we went through today... I just wanted to tell you how I felt... In case..."

"Don't start thinking that way. I'm going to meet with Turner tomorrow, Jason is going to release the holo-footage and everything is going to be fine. I promise." I hoped I wasn't lying.

Ryan held my face in his hands and kissed me lightly. "You're right. Everything will work out. I have complete faith in you." Ryan positioned himself so he could cradle me from behind. He kissed the back of my neck. "Go to sleep. We'll talk more in the morning."

Ryan's arms felt strong and welcoming as they held me close when exhaustion finally claimed me. I was asleep in seconds.

Chapter Seven

Monday September 27, 2320

I became aware of the fact that I was dreaming when I realized I was flying over Nancy's house. It was strange because I felt completely awake, but I was soaring through the air like a bird. I could even feel the wind on my face and all the sounds of nightlife chirping and hooting as I sped past. I had no control over my destination. It was as if I was a fish on a hook being reeled in.

I was above it all; houses, buildings, hover-cars, almost in the stars themselves. I viewed the city below. Tiny glowing strings of light weaved together like a tapestry of luminosity. One thread radiated brighter than all the rest and I was immediately drawn to it.

When I looked down at my body, I saw that the light was actually connected to my chest and was the source that pulled me forward. Up close the string was bright yellow and seemingly had no substance, it was made up completely of light, and yet it was strong like a rope. It tugged me down toward its end.

Once I gave into the pull, I soared at a thrilling speed to see where this cord of light led. My surroundings whizzed by me lightning fast. It was such a rush I didn't want to wake up. I could feel my adrenaline course through my body and it was exhilarating.

The roof of an enormous twenty-acre mansion rose up to meet me like a wall of doom and I flinched, ready for impact. Instead, I flew straight through it as if it were made of air. The thread of light was so bright it was almost blinding as I entered a master bedroom the size of Nancy's house and I suddenly stopped, hovering over the source of light. I was drawn to it like a moth to flame. I was connected to it as surely as I was connected to anything. It felt right. It felt warm and inviting.

Through the glow I could tell it was another person who was emanating this cord of light. I squinted to see who I was so drawn to. To see who pulled me out of my body to bring me here? I could barely see their face…

No.

The cat-like features of my grandmother glowed brightly from the string of light that bound us together. I tried to break free. I wanted to wretch from the realization of who was lying in front of me. I could see Turner sleeping soundly next to her then. He just looked like an old man, snoring loudly, thinning hair tousled. Not nearly as scary as when he was awake, but Roberta was just as terrifying asleep, with her pulled back skin and frozen features. Truly a monster in the darkness. I would have thought she was dead if I hadn't seen her chest moving up and down.

The string started to rein me in once more. I tried to put on the brakes. I couldn't believe there had even been a second of comfort from this wicked woman. The last thing I wanted to do was be sucked inside her vortex of evil, but the pull was too strong. I was going inside her head. Just like Turner did to me that night in the hospital. This was the astral projection thingy that Jason talked about. I must have a natural instinct for it. Or, when Turner did it to me, it opened up that part of my brain so I could do it myself. Whatever the reason, I was here in Roberta Turner's bedroom, about to jump inside her brain.

And it suddenly occurred to me: that might not be a bad thing. Maybe I could find some things out. Maybe I could convince her to leave my friends and me alone. It was worth a try.

I closed my eyes and leapt in like I did when I flew through the roof. It was as if her body was insubstantial and only the light was real.

I opened my eyes...

I was alone in total darkness.

I didn't panic like I thought I would. I was actually quite calm considering I was in feline freak's head. Trying to figure out how this whole thing worked was my biggest concern. Do I walk around? Will things just appear in front of me? Is there some version of her in here like when Turner visited me? He was much more experienced than me when it came to this *out of body* ordeal, but so far I'd been figuring this kind of thing out just fine.

"Memories," I said aloud, hoping for some result.

And sure enough a long hallway opened up in front of me

with doors on either side. It seemed to stretch out for miles and miles as if there were no end. I walked over to the first door and opened it.

Inside was blurry, like seeing through a pair of someone else's glasses. No matter how much I squinted my eyes to get a clearer picture, it stayed the same fuzziness. From the blurred scene, I could make out a couple. It looked like Turner and Roberta when they were younger, in their twenties, but it was hard to tell for sure. It was outside in a park, Turner kneeled down on one knee, holding Roberta's hand. A proposal no doubt. Blek. I was glad it was blurry. Seeing them happy and in love made me want to puke. I closed the door.

I skipped ahead a few doors and opened a second one. This one was as clear as crystal and I nearly leapt back from the shock of it. It was the actual facial surgery that made Grandma a feline. I could barely watch as they lifted her skin off her skull and began cutting off the excess…

I shut the door as quickly as possible. Gross.

I walked down the endless hallway until I found a door that was partially open. Maybe it was something she wanted me to see? Curiosity got the best of me and I opened it the rest of the way.

It was a birthday party. Streamers, balloons of every color, and a sign that draped over the table that said, "Happy Birthday Franklin." My heart nearly stopped. My dad's birthday! Turner and Roberta came from the other room, looking the age they were today. Roberta carried a cake with two candles spelling out eight-five. I felt a thrill of excitement. I'd get to see my dad again, probably right before he met my mother by the happy expressions on Grams and Gramps's faces (definitely pre-Mom era). They still had that un-tainted pride for their son in this memory. The kind of look I'd seen in parents where they truly believed their kids could do no wrong.

"Franklin! Come blow out your candles! You can play with your toys later!" Roberta called out.

Toys?

I wanted to cry.

My dad ran in the room and he looked eight-years-old.

They gave their own son Age-pro! Eighty-five-years-old and he was still a child! It was grotesque. It was so wrong on so many different levels. My dad was forced to be a kid for almost a century! Maybe longer! This was just one memory and I had no idea how old he was when he died. My head felt as if it was going to explode from a mixture of intense feelings I couldn't even fathom.

And he looked so happy.

That was the hardest thing to watch.

They were a family.

A real honest family. And they loved each other.

I stepped out of the entryway and practically slammed the door.

I didn't want to see that.

I liked thinking of my dad hating his parents as much as I did. They killed my mother, they killed him, they tried to kill me!

So what if they had a few moments of humanity in them! Hello?! He was an eighty-five eight-year-old! I didn't care how cozy they looked, they were still psychotic.

I couldn't seem to shake the sparkling glow of contentment in all of their eyes. It was haunting me worse than anything.

I decided to walk a few doors down. This one was harder to open, but after a large tug it finally gave.

Roberta waited in her gold living room. (I recognized it from my mother's vision.) Her face wasn't as stretched as it was today, but I could definitely tell she had started the madness that ended up being her face. A man entered the room with trepidation. He looked very familiar, but I couldn't quite place where I knew him. He had small furtive features, almost mouse-like, very fitting for the feline standing over him. He seemed to be a doctor of some sort, at least the white lab coat suggested this to be true. His hair was gray and he had crinkles around his pale brown eyes and a large two-inch crease between his eyebrows as if he were perpetually upset.

"John, come in," Roberta said to the man.

John Fortski!

The man who invented Age-pro! Of course, my grandparents knew him. I should have known better.

"Do you have it?" Roberta's eyes were wide with anticipation, and this was quite a feat considering the paralysis drugs injected into her expression lines were doing their job very well.

"Yes, but it's in its very early stages. I can't promise that there won't be side effects." John was down right jumpy as if he knew how Roberta would react.

"I don't care about side effects! Does it work or not?" Roberta went from excited to angry in about a millisecond.

"It should work, yes, but I haven't figured out the proper dosage for the way the drug effects brain chemistry. A couple of the test subjects have had severe brain damage. They've become erratic and even dangerous." John couldn't look Roberta in the eye he was so leery of her response.

"All I care about is the wrinkles, Fortski. Does it stop those?" Roberta seemed unfazed by John's warning.

"It should, yes, but…" John began to argue.

"Give them to me." Roberta was on him, grabbing his lab coat, searching his pockets. John just stood there, frozen, letting her do as she pleased.

"Not yet, my dear." Turner entered the room. He was probably about ten years younger than he looked now.

"Geoffrey, don't start." Roberta let go of Fortski and whirled to face her husband.

"Let's give it a few more tries before we start down that road." Turner was calm and steady as if he'd had these kinds of discussions with Roberta before.

Roberta backed off of Fortski with what I think was a pout (it was so hard to tell from all the injections). "Fine, but if it's not finished within the year, you're buying me another face lift." She shook her finger at Turner.

"Deal, my love, though you hardly need it as beautiful as you are." Turner reached his hands out and Roberta took them lovingly.

Barf.

I walked out and kicked the door shut on my way down the hallway.

I was getting the hang of this and started to feel more at home inside the head of Grandma. I was sure I could find something that would help save us, if I just picked the right door. I'd stay all night if I had to, and the next night, and the next, I'd know everything about Gramps and Grams and all of their evil plans. I couldn't wait to tell Jason and the others about this, just a few more doors and then I really needed to get some honest to goodness sleep. I was sure this was paying a toll on my psyche and I didn't want to be exhausted in the morn....

I stopped dead in my tracks.

Roberta stood about ten feet in front of me in the hallway.

All the doorways disappeared in wisps of smoke.

Uh oh.

"Well," was all she said, but in that one word *so much* was packed into it and none of it good.

We were in utter darkness, but somehow both of us were visible to each other.

"Well." I tried back, but mine was completely lame. Could I just leave? How did I do that? I was still dreaming, right? My body was back at Nancy's so could she really hurt me?

"You thought you could nose about in my memories, did you?" Roberta wasn't pleased.

"It was sort of by accident. I thought I was dreaming and I saw this giant beam of light and it kind of pulled me in and it was you." I was seriously stalling at this point. I may have been asleep, but she still scared the living crap out of me.

"The unfortunates of being related. We're connected you and I, more than I care to admit," Roberta confessed.

Yuck. I wanted to break that connection more than I'd wanted anything in my life. I couldn't stand thinking of being linked to the woman who was responsible for killing my mother and father.

"You kept my father a child for eighty years." I don't know why that came out, but I was glad it did. Her face winced.

"A hundred to be exact, and he'd still be my child today if it weren't for your mother." Roberta was livid now, but I couldn't help my morbid curiosity. I wanted to know more about my parents and she was my only shot at finding out anything.

"How is that even possible? I saw my mother's vision, Dad was an adult. They met when he was twenty," I repeated what I had been told by Mom.

Roberta laughed which was really grotesque to watch. "Is that what she told you?"

"It's the truth." I did that to provoke her. Mom had obviously fibbed a bit and the only way to get anything out of this feline was to hit her anger buttons. And I was really good at hitting people's anger buttons. I had years of practice with Jill.

Roberta snarled in fury.

Okay, maybe I pressed too hard. I had to remind myself that I wasn't really there. But somewhere deep down I knew that wasn't true. I knew on some basic level of understanding that if I was jolted out of her head, or if I broke the connection between us, I might wake up damaged somehow.

"Lies. Everything that came out of your mother was lies!" Roberta's hands were shaking from the venomous anger coursing through her veins. "Your traitorous mother was our Nanny!"

What?

No, seriously.

What?!

Oh crap.

"When she found out Franklin's true age she kidnapped him

and stopped giving him Age-pro! She let him grow up! She kept him from us for ten years! Ten years of not seeing your own flesh and blood! I hadn't been away from Franklin for more than a day in all one-hundred years of his life and then to have him ripped away from me like that!" Roberta said, pain in her voice. I'd almost feel sorry for her, if she wasn't *crazy!* "Geoffrey and I will never forgive your mother for that. For turning our Franklin against us and kidnapping him. Your mother was worse than trash! She fell in love with an eight-year-old!"

My mom would have been about twenty at the time and my dad a hundred, but on some level I was repulsed by the idea myself. This must have been the part that Mom didn't want to tell me. It made more sense why she picked a man like Bruce to be her husband. It wasn't just the guilt of losing my father, it was the guilt of falling in love with a boy who looked eight-years-old. Even logically knowing he was eighty years older than her, the inherent *wrongness* of the situation probably haunted her until the day she was killed.

"Okay. I get it. You're right, it sounds gross, but how is that my fault?" I hoped I could reach her on an emotional level. Even though I wanted to say that I thought it was even more horrifying and repulsive that she kept a human being eight-years-old for a hundred years. But I wanted information and since her *doors of memory* seemed to be out of the question now I needed to nurture her anger for my mother. I went a step further. "Look at my eyes, my lips, they're his, you can see it." I stepped closer to her, trying not to show my fear.

There was a flicker of recognition in her eyes, then it turned to rage. "Get away from me, devil!"

309

Devil? What on earth was a devil? Some Voodoo thing? Whatever it was, it wasn't good. Even though we weren't *really* facing each other, I was still petrified of what she could do to me in my sleep. Turner and Roberta had already proved their magic was powerful, I didn't need any more examples.

"I said OUT!" she screamed and her whole body glowed a bright green.

My blood froze and I suddenly couldn't take in air no matter how hard I tried. The bright string that kept us bound together flared up between us and…

SNAP!

Severed.

Everything blurred, twisted, exploded until…

SLAM!

I crash landed back into my body like a skydiver without a parachute.

Air came flooding through my lungs and I sucked it up in large gulps.

Instantly, Ryan was awake with his arms wrapped around me. "What happened? Are you okay?" He was all concern.

I fell into him, still breathing in as much air as I could, afraid it would somehow be sucked out of me again.

"I did that thingy," I heaved. "That… astral thingy… get Jason." I could barely speak. I was freezing and shaking uncontrollably. Ryan wrapped the comforter around me tightly before he left to get Jason.

In a few minutes the whole gang (minus George and Vianne; I didn't want to wake them) was in Nancy's bedroom surrounding me like a pack of mother hens.

310

Jason sat on the edge of the bed and rubbed his hands over my covered arms to generate some heat. I immediately started to feel better.

"You warm yet?" Jason asked.

"Yeah." I took a deep steadying breath.

Ryan crawled on the bed behind me and wrapped his arms around the fluffy blanket that was me. I started to feel down right toasty.

"We have to be quiet, my parents are still sleeping," Nancy whispered.

I told them everything.

Jason seemed the most interested in what I had to say. He asked me the specifics of how everything worked, but I wasn't *sure* how everything worked, so I just told him what I saw.

"This is fascinating," Jason said with animation.

"I was thinking, *terrifying*, but what do I know?" Nancy had her arms crossed and was looking at Jason angrily.

I liked them better when they were in crush-mode instead of this…wait…they were at each other's throats when they liked each other, but I tended to agree more with Nancy on this particular topic.

"In any case, I don't think I can go back, she'll be waiting for me next time," I admitted, hoping to prevent Jason from even broaching that subject.

"I wonder if she ever took the experimental Age-pro. It would explain why she acts like Looney-Mcloon-Pants." Bill seemed the most interested in the fact that Roberta and Turner knew Fortski and were directly involved in the creation of Age-pro.

"When I saw her she was pre-second or third face surgery,

311

so she must have taken it later." I wasn't sure if Bill's suspicions were true.

"Let's assume that both of them took the experimentals, just for the simple fact that it gives us something to work with. If we know were dealing with brain damaged psychosis, we can better prepare for how to act." Jason tried to think strategically. "I should be getting the holo-footage sometime tomorrow, hopefully in the morning."

"Eww," Nancy chimed in.

"*Eww* or not, I can get it on the air and hopefully take Turner down." Jason ignored Nancy's jibes at this point.

"Do you think you can sleep?" Jason turned to me with concern. "It's only one in the morning, you could squeeze out a few more hours of sleep before school."

I couldn't believe it was so early in the night and now that the adrenaline was beginning to wear off, I *was* feeling sleepy again.

"Yeah, that sounds good," I said and opened up the covers for Ryan.

Nancy winked at me in approval and grabbed Bill's hand. "Come on, Bill, let's get back to bed. Night, Jason." She gave Jason a satisfied smirk and left with Bill.

Jason stood up and shook his head. "They make a good couple." His face was crestfallen and hurt.

I rolled my eyes. "You really are an idiot, Jason. Go to bed."

Jason didn't even hear me. He was lost in his own misery. "Night." He left without another word.

Ryan snuggled in close behind me. "He really has no idea she likes him, does he?"

"Not a clue, no matter how many times I re-assure him. He just wants to be miserable." I held onto Ryan's arms and smiled contentedly.

He kissed the back of my head. "Good night."

"Night." I closed my eyes and drifted off into blissful blackness.

When I awoke the sun's rays poured into Nancy's room like a friendly visitor. Everything always seemed more positive and hopeful during the day. Then I remembered I was meeting Turner and my good mood was sucked out of me. Not even the sunshine helped.

But…

…Waking up with Ryan next to me was definitely a plus.

Speaking of which… He opened his gorgeous brown eyes and gave me a sleepy smile. "Good morning."

I couldn't resist, I leaned over and kissed him. He gently held the back of my head and pulled me in closer. Here I go again. Breathe. Focus.

I drew back. "Behave."

"You started it," he said, smiling.

I wished he wouldn't do that. He was ridiculously cute when he did that.

I grabbed a tank and jeans from Nancy's closet and went into the bathroom to change. When I came back into the room Ryan was already dressed. (Nancy's dad let Bill and Ryan borrow some of his casual clothes, jeans and t-shirt kind of stuff.) The pants were a little big on Ryan, but he'd look good in a potato sack, so there you go.

We went downstairs and joined George and Vianne for breakfast. Bill and Nancy joined us soon after, followed by a very peppy Jason.

"Morning everyone." Jason exuded cheeriness.

"Did you? I mean, did it?" Vianne was a little leery of the topic of Jason's digestion at the breakfast table.

Jason waved his hand in the negative. "No, not yet, I'm just pumped about what happens when we have it. This could be it. My lifelong dream of taking down Turner could actually happen *today*! I'm just a little excited." Jason was simply beaming.

"Aren't you getting ahead of yourself? What if the chip is broken, we are talking about *your* bowels." Nancy smirked.

"Nancy," George scolded, "Jason is our guest so treat him with some respect," he finished authoritatively.

Nancy shrugged apologetically. "Sorry, just don't want anyone to count their chickens before they're hatched." She eyed Jason with annoyed disdain.

"There's nothing wrong with a positive attitude, you might want to try it sometime," Jason retorted.

Nancy stood up in a huff and left the room. "Bill."

Bill shoveled in the last of his breakfast and followed Nancy out of the room.

Nancy called out from the foyer, "Let's get to school!"

I stuffed my eggs in my mouth. "Great breakfast, Vianne, thanks so much." I stood up to join Nancy when Jason caught my arm.

"This meeting with Turner will be the perfect stall tactic. I need you to keep him busy until I can get the holo-footage on the air. Are you going to be okay with that?" Jason made sure our eyes met.

I nodded. "Yeah. He won't hurt me. He just wants to talk," I said, but didn't believe a word of it. After last nights rendezvous with Roberta I wasn't sure what Turner would do or say at our little meeting today. I tried not to think about it too much, otherwise my imagination would paralyze me.

"I don't want her to go." Ryan stood up beside me and grabbed my hand possessively.

I tried to give Ryan the most reassuring look I could muster. "I have to. I told you yesterday don't try and talk me out of it. I'm going."

"We'll see." Nancy's voice sounded from the other room.

I rolled my eyes and almost laughed. A lioness 'til the end, even if I made it extremely difficult for her.

"I hate to be the bad guy, but you *need* to go. This thing will be ten times easier knowing that Turner will be occupied with you." Jason looked genuinely sorry that he had to be the voice of reason in all this.

"I'm going. Don't worry. Just *do your thing* and then do your thing," I said and Ryan and I left.

George and Vianne walked us out and made sure we were all safe in Bill's car before they went back into the house.

The ride over was somehow comforting. It was nice to be around the three people that I trusted and loved. I didn't want to be all gloom and doom, but my meeting with Turner today was like a black cloud hanging over me and I wasn't sure if I'd ever feel this warm and fuzzy with my friends again. We didn't even talk about anything important. Mainly it was just Nancy trying to fool everyone that she had absolutely no interest in

Jason Keroff whatsoever. But in the end even she admitted she was full of crap and then proceeded to ask us all our advice on what she should do.

Bill and Ryan went pretty silent on the topic and I fully admitted to being a complete idiot when it came to boys, so the conversation ended up with Nancy in a huff.

We arrived at school and to my great relief there wasn't hide nor hair of any news reporters.

"Looks like Turner's making things easier on you. Show of good faith maybe?" Ryan sounded hopeful.

"Or he doesn't want anyone watching," Bill said what I was thinking.

"He doesn't trust you." Nancy agreed with Bill.

I always said I wanted honesty, I guess I was getting it in spades now.

"Chelsan!" I heard Jill's voice like fingernails on a chalkboard.

I knew her dad was dead, and I knew she had no clue, but as sad as that was I still couldn't stand her. With her intense, bright green eyes filled with annoyance, she came running up to me in her designer clothes and bouncing black curls.

"Yes?" I greeted her with as little emotion as possible.

"Don't give me attitude, I like this less than you do." Jill smiled at Bill kindly. "Hi, Bill."

"Hey," Bill acknowledged. He reached down and grabbed Nancy's hand. Looked like he wanted to play the same game Nancy was, but instead of trying to make Jill jealous, he was trying to subtly tell her to stay away.

Jill received the message right away. She turned back to me and snarled, "Daddy wants me to take you to Nancy's after school. He says if you don't come with me, Nancy's parents will be charged with a Landscaping Code Violation."

"What?!" Nancy was livid. "Your dad said he cleared that like ten years ago!"

"Well, paperwork gets lost, doesn't it?" Jill was enjoying this.

Before things got out of hand I looked Jill in the eye. "Fine. I'll meet you in the parking lot after class."

Jill's face showed her disappointment at the lack of a true fight, but she shrugged. "Be early. I don't want anyone seeing us together." She whirled around and was gone.

Bill seemed the most upset. "Turner is making sure you go."

"I was always planning on going, it's no big deal." I tried to calm everyone down. I could tell Ryan was livid. I think they were all secretly thinking of a plan to stop me and now it was foiled. Turner really didn't trust me. After everything we'd been through, I couldn't blame him. And he used the one thing he knew I'd never put in danger: my friends. Nancy's parents were practically adopting me and I'd die before I let any harm come to them.

The rest of the day seemed to fly by. I was really hoping I could savor these last few hours of freedom, but as always when you have some horrible thing to do, time goes by too fast.

I probably wasn't walking away from this encounter, but as long as my friends were safe I was okay with that. I couldn't help but think it would have been easier on everyone if Turner had succeeded in his plan that day at the trailer park and killed my mother and I both. But I didn't want to think like that. I was here and I wasn't going to give up. I was learning more and more about my powers each day, which on the one hand made

317

me a force to be reckoned with, but on the other, made me a target. Only time would decide which one I would be today.

The last bell of the day rang like a harbinger of death.

Ryan waited for me outside the classroom. He had that look. That look that said, *I'm not going to argue with you, but I don't like it.* He just took my hand and we walked toward the parking lot.

"I have another job offer from one of the best companies in the world. One that Turner *doesn't* have a stake in." Ryan tried to lighten the mood. "I'm meeting with their VP at Nancy's house. George seemed really excited when I told him, maybe the guy will like George and offer him a job there."

"You did that on purpose, didn't you? For George." I smiled with approval.

"Maybe," Ryan replied slyly. "He deserves it after everything he's done for you. For us."

"Do you think you'll take the job?" I asked. I was secretly hoping we could go to college together. If I made it that long. Ugggh! Stop!

"Naaah, but I always listen to their offers. It'll be pretty boring, but at least I'll get a free meal out of it." He smiled.

"Well… be careful." I couldn't think of anything else to say I was so nervous about what was coming.

Ryan squeezed my hand and pulled it up to his lips, kissing it gently. "Nancy's parents will just have to pay a fine. They'll understand. You shouldn't go."

"I'm going. I'm just a little nervous is all." As much as I wanted to agree with Ryan, I needed to get this over with.

We arrived at the parking lot and Jill was waiting there with her scowl of greeting.

"Let's go." Jill started walking away without waiting to see if I was following.

I turned and kissed Ryan. "Love you."

Ryan kissed me back. "Love you."

I couldn't look at him anymore or I'd chicken out. And where were Bill and Nancy? They were probably tied up in class. I wanted to wait to say goodbye to them, but Jill was almost out of view. I ran after her like an idiot.

I caught up to Jill and walked next to her, hoping we wouldn't have to talk. *Just drop me off at Nancy's and leave me alone.* Maybe I'd see Nancy and Bill before Turner's car came to pick me up.

Jill's hover-car was a top of the line, ridiculously expensive BMW. "Get in," she barked.

I opened the door and slid into the car. I really didn't want to fight with her, and thankfully it appeared she didn't want to either. The interior of the car was to be expected, lots of expensive bells and whistles, including a holo-GPS and auto-pilot.

"Don't touch anything." Jill wanted to make sure I knew my place.

"Jill, just shut-up." I tried to keep quiet, but she was so good at provoking me.

"I'll make you ride in the trunk." Jill's eyes flared angrily.

"I'd like to see you try." I gave her a look that suggested she should back off.

Jill grumbled something under her breath, turned on her car, and took off out of the parking lot. The way she drove we'd be there in no time. Thank goodness.

The holo-GPS projected the three-dimensional map in the middle of the dashboard and led Jill to Nancy's house.

"I could just tell you how to get there," I offered. As soon as I did I knew I shouldn't have.

"Yeah, right. Like I'd take directions from trailer trash. My dad warned me not to listen to anything you say. *Most of all* directions. He said you could lead me into a trap." Jill smirked egotistically.

"A trap? What? Where I beat the crap out of you and steal your car?" Now that I said it, it sounded like a good idea, in dreamland that was. But the more obvious point of Jill's rant was Turner's paranoia that I wouldn't show up for this reunion.

"Exactly. Your seat is rigged to taser by the way, so don't even think about trying anything." Jill actually sounded scared so I wondered at the validity of her threat.

"I'm not going to do anything. Just get me to Nancy's so I can get away from you." I stared out the window trying to ignore her.

"I'm not the freak in this situation, you know." Jill wasn't letting go. It was like now that we were alone she could let out all of her frustration on me. "You're the one who intruded in a life you had no right to. You don't belong with the rich, you belong with your own kind." Jill sounded like she believed the hate she spouted.

I was tempted to destroy her world and tell her about her dad, or worse let him die naturally by disconnecting him from Turner's control, but as annoying and cruel as Jill was, I just couldn't do that to another human being. No matter how tempting.

"Why should you care? What possible difference in your life could it make to have someone who doesn't have any money go to your school? Really? Are you that bigoted?" I sighed, already exhausted from this conversation.

"I am *not* a bigot." Jill seemed horrified by the notion, which was weird because she so obviously *was*.

"What would you call it then? Let me quote: *You don't belong with the rich, you belong with your own kind.* How is that *not* being a bigot?" I stared at her profile as she kept her eyes on the airspace in front of her. I had hit a nerve.

"I hate you," Jill seethed and said nothing more.

Good. Now I could concentrate on… uuuggh… what? How my grandpa was planning on finishing me off? My argument with Jill felt like a vacation compared to what was in store for me.

And then out of the blue Jill said, "I'm sorry I made you cry the other day, when I brought up your mom."

"You have reached your destination," the GPS announced.

I turned to Jill as if my ears had played tricks on me. Was that an apology? She stared straight ahead as if she hadn't said anything, but I could tell there was *actually* some emotion there.

"Look, Jill…" I started.

"Don't," Jill stopped me. "I just need you to be my enemy right now." She still couldn't look at me. "It's the only thing that makes sense to me."

And as weird of a statement as that was, I actually understood it. She needed something stable in her life and I guess her hatred for me was it. Maybe that would change in time. I could only hope. It would make the last year of high school a whole lot easier, but then again I might not make it past the next couple of hours so I simply nodded.

Jill landed the hover-car and opened my door from her side.

"Get out," Jill said quietly.

I exited the car and before I could turn around she had shut the door and lifted off.

So much for Jill Forester.

Almost within seconds a steel box of a hover-truck landed in front of me. It was solid silver like a bar of tin with spinning fans. I couldn't even see where the driver would sit, the metal was so continuous. *Where were the windows?*

"What the...?" My heart sank. This was Turner's "ride."

Two heavy doors swung open and a man dressed in an all white three-piece suit was there with a large grin. "Chelsan, come in." He looked as if he was in his mid-twenties so he either *was* in his mid-twenties or he was middle class and had been Turner's slave for centuries. His hair was short and perfectly in place along with everything else about him. He could have been a doll with his aquiline features and perfectly constructed body.

The inside of the hover-box was as white and sterile as the guy who greeted me. It was devoid of anything except two benches built into the walls facing each other. I sat down on one of them and the spongy white surface wasn't any kind of material I could recognize. I felt way out of my depth in this situation, which was exactly the way Turner wanted me to feel, I guessed. I gritted my teeth in frustration because I was letting it work. I was letting him win even on the smallest of levels and that was unacceptable.

The man in white shut the doors and sat across from me with

that same annoying grin. "All set here. Let's go." He seemed to be talking to the air in front of him.

But the hover fans churned in response and we were off. Away from my friends. Away from safety.

What was this place? It was like a quarantine facility... Oh.

It *was* a quarantine facility, and I was the thing that needed to be quarantined. Nothing dead in this spotlessly clean metal box. No swirling black holes here. It was amazing how comforting they had become to me since meeting my grandpa. Something I used to consider a curse ended up being the one thing I could depend on.

"Where are we going?" I asked fruitlessly.

"We'll know when we get there." The man in white said with a smile.

Can we get a little more vague? Probably, so I kept my mouth shut and took deep calming breaths. As we whizzed over Los Angeles I leaned my head back against the wall of the truck and closed my eyes. I knew there was no way I could even guess where we were headed, but since I was stuck here in this sterile box I thought I could try something. I concentrated on the ground below us and sought out any and every black hole I could find. Mostly bugs, ants and houseplants. Okay, that meant we were still in the burbs. That was helpful.

The longer we drove the black holes turned into larger animals, opossums, coyotes, lots more bugs of every variety imaginable (blek), birds, heading over a forest, but which one and where? It was impossible to tell there were so many now because of Population Control's laws. It didn't matter, there were enough animals I could use in my arsenal if I had to. Of

323

course, that was assuming we were going to land sometime soon! Where were we going?! So frustrating!

I was so zoned into all the black swirling chasms, I nearly jumped when they all turned into at least five square miles of giant dead oaks. No dead animal or insect or any kind of corpse that I could sense. Just the blackened roots of lifeless trees.

The hover-truck landed in the center of the dead forest. I couldn't for the life of me remember any place like this. You'd think we'd have learned about places like these in geography class or something, but it must be just another one of Turner's secrets he kept from the people.

The man in white opened the doors of the truck and smiled at me. "Out, please."

I stood up and jumped outside of the metal box.

Burnt, charred earth greeted me like an apocalypse. It made me a little dizzy with the swirling holes of the dead trees and the blackened ground beneath me. The only proof that there had been any kind of life here was *me*.

"This way, please." The man in white was a startling contrast to the darkness of the land.

I followed him around the hover-truck and I gasped.

Turner stood in front of an army of hundreds of soldiers with nothing but scorched earth for miles. It was a surreal moment to see so many men dressed in full army gear, holding automatic weapons, all pointed at me. Turner had a smug look on his face. He was only about twenty feet away, which was way too close for my taste. And *way* too close for those guns to be aimed in my direction. Who did he think I was? Some kind of living bomb? I wish I were at this point. Maybe I could take him down with me. I just hoped Jason would have enough time to get the holo-footage on the air and hopefully save my butt. It didn't look good at this point in time.

The driver of the hover-truck was one of Turner's soldiers and he exited the vehicle with his own gun raised, stepping into line with his fellow combatants.

"Did you enjoy your adventures in my wife's head last night?" Turner had an edge of fury to his voice.

"Yes," I said. A part of me wanted to goad him on. It was like playing Russian Roulette. I felt like I had nothing to lose. If he was going to kill me, there was nothing I could do about it.

"Tell me what you saw?" He took a step closer and something in his eyes warned me that something was off.

"No." I kept my answers as brief as possible and noticed that the less I said the more agitated he grew. I had seen this kind of behavior before. He was stalling. But for what? I needed to find out more. "You brought a firing squad?"

"Possibly, that depends on you. Nothing dead for miles. I wasn't sure how far your reach was, so I made sure five square miles was free of any corpses for you to *surprise* me with." The look on Turner's face was infuriating. He was so proud of himself.

Interesting.

He had no idea I could control dead plant-life.

The dead roots might just become my best friends.

I wasn't sure *what* I could do with them, but it was starting to look like I'd have to figure it out soon.

"Why am I here?" I asked, trying to fish out the truth from him.

"Why indeed," Turner smirked.

He was definitely stalling. It was driving me bonkers and it started to scare me.

The man in white walked over to Turner and whispered something in his ear.

Turner smiled as wide as I'd ever seen.

My heart sank. Something just went his way and anything that went his way was never good.

With a sparkling glint in his eyes, he turned to me. "You, my dear, are no longer useful to me."

Hundreds of guns clicked and clacked in readiness to mow me down.

My whole body shuddered.

I was really going to die if I didn't do something right now.

Now it was my turn to stall.

"Can't you tell me what just happened?" I asked desperately.

Turner laughed at my horror, reveling in it as if I was a swimming pool of retribution. "It will give me great pleasure in telling you how you were duped before I kill you."

Duped?

"You thought you were this special creature that I had an ounce of interest in? I've wanted you dead since you were born. Your mother was very clever in marrying the one man I couldn't track. *Bruce Lenton* one of my first experiments in tracking devices. It was a complete failure and ended up making him and anyone in a two-mile radius of him disappear entirely from the map. Franklin knew about Bruce and must have told your mother before she killed my son. My only tiny bit of satisfaction was knowing that Bruce was a violent man and I hoped that he beat that murderer regularly," he seethed.

Sudden realization brought tears to my eyes. Mom didn't marry Bruce to punish herself, she did it to save me. That day I killed him it wasn't disappointment or judgment in her eyes, it was fear that Turner would find us. A love even deeper than I could ever imagine surged through me. *Everything* Mom did was about saving me.

"When my scientists finally discovered how to find Bruce they were very surprised to find that he was, in fact, dead, and yet living. It wasn't hard to figure out that one of you was keeping him that way," he gloated.

While he rubbed in his superiority, I took the time to connect to every tree root I could underneath him and his army.

"I can do everything you can do with Vodun and Wicca, but what I *can't* do is solve complex formulas and theorems," he said as if revealing something wicked.

What? I can't do that either.

Ryan.

It wasn't me he wanted. It was Ryan.

Duped was an understatement.

I should have realized it when I saw how Roberta was salivating all over him.

The parking lot of the Population Control Headquarters was *way* too public to kidnap Ryan. Turner had to come up with this elaborate ruse just to separate us, knowing I'd never let him take Ryan without a fight.

"Ryan," I whispered in shock.

"He's ours now, I just got word. He should have been ours years ago, but he was more clever than we gave him credit for.

He can't replace our Franklin, but it's a start. And we won't have history repeating itself by having his whore take him away from us again." Turner was simply beside himself with happiness. "It's over now. You lost."

He motioned his men to take aim and suddenly all the guns were pointed at me.

"Wait!" I yelped. (Yes, I would actually categorize what came out of my mouth as a yelp; I sounded like a thirteen-year-old boy in puberty.) "I'm about to die anyway, just tell me he'll be okay." I felt the roots of the trees beneath them as if they were an extension of my own limbs, but I needed to trick Turner into giving me some clue as to where Ryan was being held.

Turner actually sighed as if I was an annoying fly he couldn't swat. "Of course he's fine. He'll be treated like a king as he should be. He's ours now."

Ours. Roberta's and his. Replacing Franklin.

Ryan was at their house. I knew it from the depths of my soul. I'd find him there.

"One more thing," I said with confidence this time.

"You're stalling now." Turner's eyes narrowed with sinister glee. "This will be the last thing that comes out of your mouth, so make it good," he almost cackled with triumph.

"It's not just corpses I can bring back, *Gramps*."

BOOM!

The ground shook as hundreds of thick gnarled roots burst through the ground beneath Turner and his boys. I made them wrap around their bodies like vises. The guns clattered to the dirt as I squeezed the black roots around the soldiers until they couldn't move an inch.

I had fallen from the force of the dead trees bursting through the soil, but stood up and brushed myself off.

I walked up to Turner whose face fumed from betrayal and anger, but his body was ensnared like the others so he couldn't touch me.

I smiled. "I guess you don't know everything about my powers, now do you?"

His eyes flashed with the same curiosity they did in Principal Weatherby's office. I surprised him. *Again.*

I whirled around to see the man in white standing by the hover-truck, terror in his eyes. His hands went up in supplication before any words had come out of my mouth.

"Please, don't kill me," he uttered in panic.

"I didn't kill *him*, why would I kill you?" It was taking most of my energy to keep the roots sturdy and in place, but I tried to sound as strong as possible. "Get the keys."

The man in white practically jumped at the command and hurried over to the ensnared driver, grabbing the keys from his pocket. He ran over to me and handed me the keys. Just to be safe I exerted more of my energy and brought up dead roots to capture him, too. He squealed in fright, and proceeded to whimper once the cage of limbs was in place.

I turned one last time to Turner. "I'm going to get Ryan."

"Good luck with that," he said with such a condescending attitude that I wanted to squeeze the life out of him with one of the roots. It was the second time I had the chance to kill him. It would mean the safety of the people I loved and mine as well. So easy. Thirty seconds ago he was going to kill *me*. His soldiers had been about to mow me down with bullets. Why couldn't I do it? No one would blame me. They'd probably congratulate me.

But I couldn't.

I just couldn't.

It would be the worse mistake of my life. I might regret it later with every fiber of my soul, but right now, I couldn't do it. My grandparents were the only tie I had left with my father and even though that meant nothing to them, it meant something to me. It made me nauseous to admit that, but a part of me wanted Turner and Roberta alive. A very small part, but still. I wasn't ready. Honestly, I hoped I never would be.

But in this case, for Ryan's sake, I did need to bluff.

"Oh, I won't kill you, dear Grandfather, but Grandma is expendable. No one knows she exists anyway the way you keep her ugly cat face out of the media. You killed my mother, I'm killing your wife. Even-steven." And then I grinned in the most vicious way I could contort my face.

It must have worked because Turner looked downright terrified. "You wouldn't."

"Really? Remember, I am *your* granddaughter." And I turned and walked to the hover-truck before he could figure out I was deceiving him.

"NO! I'LL GIVE YOU ANYTHING! ANYTHING! I PROMISE I'LL NEVER TRY AND HURT YOU AGAIN!" Turner screamed and his voice was laced with anguish.

I whirled around before I entered the truck. "We'll see." I threw back his own words in his face and he roared like a caged lion.

I was about to vomit as I sat in the driver's seat. Thank

goodness there was auto pilot. I turned on the holo-GPS, gave it Nancy's address and whizzed away from the scene. I knew my connection with the tree roots would end as soon as I hit the four-mile mark, but at least they'd stay in place. I hoped it would take a while for the soldiers to break out of the crusty old branches, but I didn't want to delude myself. It bought me some time.

Hopefully, the team was at Nancy's and we could rescue Ryan together. I needed all the help I could get.

As the car followed the holo-GPS's directions, I tried not to think about what I just went through. I needed to keep focused on saving Ryan. I had absolutely no idea how that was going to happen and frankly, I was secretly hoping that the team would have some suggestions. At full speed the car landed in front of Nancy's house in about twenty minutes.

I flew out of the vehicle and ran to the front door and stopped dead in my tracks.

The steel door was off its hinges and laying inside the house.

This was where they kidnapped Ryan.

I ran inside the house.

"Hello?!" I called out, hoping to hear *anyones* voice.

Silence.

The house looked like it had been hit by a hurricane. The couch was flipped over, glass and wood splinters everywhere. *Please let everyone be okay.* If my adrenaline hadn't been at full throttle I would have broken down right there.

"Hello?! George! Vianne!" I called out again, frantic for any response.

"Chelsan?" It was George and he sounded like he was in the

kitchen.

I hurried as fast as I could and practically fell into George on his way out to find me. He embraced me in a desperate hug. "Thanks goodness you're all right. They told us…" His voice started to break up, "They told us you were dead."

I pulled away and wiped the tears from my face I hadn't even noticed were there.

"I almost was," I admitted with a lump in my throat. "What happened? Turner said they took Ryan."

Vianne came hurrying out of the kitchen and nearly toppled me over as she drew me in for another embrace. "Oh Chelsan, we were so worried." She let go of me to inspect me thoroughly. "Any injuries?"

That was when I finally noticed the two of them. They were covered in small cuts and bruises. I held my hand to mouth in shock. "Forget me, are you guys okay?"

Vianne held my hand warmly. "We're fine, dear, nothing that won't heal, but Ryan… he put up such a fight." Tears came to Vianne's eyes. "They took us by surprise. The man who said he was here to offer Ryan a job turned out to be one of Turner's soldiers. He had a whole team with him. We made Jason take Nancy out the back before things got too ugly. He has the tornado footage, Chelsan, he's on his way now to get it on the air. Bill's been hysterical trying to find you, he's pretty beat up as well. You should have seen him trying to protect Ryan…" She trailed off, trying to hide her emotion.

"I need to call Bill." I tried to keep my head clear.

George handed me the phone almost immediately after the words came out of my mouth.

I dialed quickly.

Bill picked up before the first ring had finished its chorus. "George? I'm going to Jill's to see where she dropped Chelsan off." Bill's voice sounded determined through the phone.

"Bill, it's me," I said before he could continue.

"CHELSAN!!! Where are you? Are you okay? Tell me where you are, I'm coming!" Bill went from composed to frantic in about a millisecond.

"Bill, calm down. I'm at Nancy's, come pick me up. We'll go to Jill's together. I think I have a plan." The seeds of an idea were starting to form in my brain.

"Okay, I'm on my way." Bill sounded elated to hear from me.

I hung up the phone and handed it to George. "He's on his way."

"Why Jill? Do you think she knows something?" Vianne asked as she touched up one of George's wounds with a damp cloth.

"No, it's her dad I'm interested in." Man, if this plan was going to work, Jill would hate me forever. But, there was nothing for it.

The whirling fans of Bill's hover-car were louder than normal since the front door no longer existed. I turned to George and Vianne. "Are you guys going to be okay?"

"We're fine, just go. Get Ryan back." Vianne kissed my cheek and sent me on my way.

I ran out to greet Bill and slammed into his six-foot frame like I had smacked into a tree. A tree that grabbed me and squeezed me in a bear hug that nearly popped my lungs. I hugged him back with just as much force; we nearly killed each other from affection.

Bill drew away first and his eyes were watery, but sparkling at seeing me. He kissed my forehead. "We all thought…" He trailed off, not able to finish the sentence that ended with me dead.

His lip was cut pretty badly and his eye was black. "Oh Bill."

He shrugged his wounds off like a badge of courage. "It's nothing."

"It's not nothing. This is all my fault."

"Chelsan, we have to get Ryan back," he said as he took my hand and yanked me to his hover-car.

We were in the air faster than I could think. He kept on glancing over at me, relief etched in every feature. "I tried to stop them, but they eventually had to stun me." I could tell that was hard for Bill to admit.

"Stunners only?" I asked, trying to get a better idea of what we were up against. I just hoped Jason and Nancy's mission would prove successful. It was our only bargaining chip for long-term safety. Without that footage, rescuing Ryan would be a futile effort since they could simply re-take him again. We needed to take Turner out of power or at least bump him down a notch. Enough where it would make it difficult for him to target us. Us. Ryan and me. Somehow we both ended up being Grams and Gramps's obsession. It was difficult enough when they were after *me*, but now they were after my *boyfriend*. In fact, it seemed like they wanted Ryan a lot more than they wanted me. I didn't know if I should be offended or not.

Although after showing Turner that I could control dead plants may have put me back on the top of their list.

"Yeah, just the stunners." Bill answered my previous question. "I don't think they thought we'd fight as hard as we did. If you think *we* look bad." He actually smiled and then it quickly turned to a frown. "When I woke up, Ryan was gone. I'm really sorry, Chelsan. I did everything I could to save him."

"I would *never* blame you for that. Don't ever think that." I wanted to re-assure him.

"You think Jill had something to do with all this? Where did she drop you off anyway?" Bill changed the subject after a moment of quiet.

"She dropped me off at Nancy's. I don't think she knows anything," I said.

"Then why are we going to her house?" Bill asked.

"For her dad."

"Oh boy." Bill swallowed hard figuring out my intent. "Is she going to find out? Or... are you...?" he asked as if wanting to know but not really *wanting* to know.

"Hopefully, she won't know a thing, but Mr. Owen Forester is coming with us. He's our only way in." I tried to muster as much confidence in my plan as possible for Bill's sake, but I secretly worried that making Jill's dad come with us might backfire if Turner warned Roberta that I'd escaped. I was going in blind. I had no idea what to expect of Jill's dad. Did he have thoughts of his own? Was he constantly controlled by Turner and his people? Would they know that I had taken over? I just didn't know, but he was literally *it,* in terms of a plan. I couldn't show up at Roberta's mansion, I'd be taken immediately. Mr. Forester was going in and he was going in alone. Worse case scenario, they break their ties with him and he'd finally die his proper death instead of this half-life he was living. Which was for the best, I knew, but Jill wouldn't see it that way. I'd always be the person who killed her father even though I had nothing to do with it.

"We're here," Bill announced as we landed in front of the most stunning mansion I'd ever seen. Architecture dating back to the early two-thousands, it was made mostly of metal and glass. Five solar panels on the roof were curved like walnut shells reaching up to the sun. They were gigantic, at least two-hundred feet tall and a hundred feet across. The base of the house was bright silver metal and sparkled in the fading daylight. In startling contrast of the metal base, the trim of the house was all colored glass from the doorknobs, to the window frames, to the sculptures on the bright green lawn. It was like a museum or spectacle, I couldn't decide which.

The hover-landing pad was encircled by the most amazing collection of rose bushes I'd ever seen. Every color imaginable in perfect bloom reaching out to greet you as you exited your vehicle. It was extremely unfair that someone like Jill lived in such a castle, but then again Jill had other disadvantages that I didn't envy. Like her dad.

Bill and I left the car and walked up the marble steps that led to the front door.

Jill opened it in a fury. Apparently, she saw us coming. "What on earth are you two doing at *my* house?!" She could barely talk she was so angry.

"Is your dad here?" Bill asked, knowing that anything that came out of my mouth would be met with rage.

"My dad?" This threw Jill off completely. "Why?"

"Is he here or not, Jill?" Bill said brusquely.

"He's here," I confirmed, seeing his swirling black hole in the back of the house. "He's in the back of the house."

"How did you…?" Jill went from fury to shock to suspicion all in a span of a second.

"It doesn't matter, Jill, the less you know the better." I tried to be as nice as was humanly possible.

"GET OFF MY PROPERTY!" Jill slammed the door in our faces.

"That went well." Bill rolled his eyes. "You shouldn't have said anything."

"It doesn't matter. I'll get him myself." I closed my eyes and slammed through the barrier that kept me from Mr. Forester's black hole. He was mine now. And I knew as soon as I connected to him that he was just like anything else dead. Nothing upstairs. Just an empty shell for me to puppeteer. "Just a few seconds." I made him walk to the front door and open it.

Jill was standing next to him, terror, suspicion, fury and sadness all rolled into one heartbreaking expression. She wasn't stupid, she knew something was going on, and she knew I had something to do with it.

I tried to smooth the situation and made her dad speak. "It's okay, Jill, I'm just going to go with your friends for a bit."

And instead of making things better, it seemed to make them a whole lot worse. Jill started to cry hysterically. I made her dad touch her shoulder to comfort her, but she flinched and pulled away, wiping away her tears. She stared at me with resentment and revulsion. "He hasn't spoken to me except to give me orders from the Vice President in three years."

Ooops. And ouch. I couldn't control how awful I actually felt for Jill in that moment.

"I'm sorry, Jill, but Ryan's in trouble." I couldn't begin to explain everything to her now and I didn't know if she was ready yet anyway.

Jill didn't know how to respond, so she fell back to her usual annoying self. "You're an evil disgusting excuse for a human being, Chelsan Derée, and I hope you die. If my father doesn't come back, I'm holding you fully responsible and if you think your life was torture before, you haven't seen anything yet." And with that she stalked off, leaving Bill and I alone with Mr. Forester.

"Bye Jill, see you at school." Bill tried to lighten the moment.

"I don't really care what Jill thinks right now, let's just get Ryan." I made Jill's dad follow us to the hover-car.

I had him sit in back and we were off toward Turner's house. We only had my dream to go by so I made him drive to Nancy's house since that was my starting point in my vision. I closed my eyes and visualized the landscape in front of me and instructed Bill where to go.

"I think we're here. That's got to be it," Bill said.

I opened my eyes and looked down. "That's it." There it was in the flesh. My grandparent's house. The house where my mom rescued my dad, where they came back when she was pregnant with me, where my dad lived for over a hundred years, and where Ryan was now held captive. Hundreds of years of my own family history in *that* house. It almost took my breath away with the enormity of it. The property was ginormous, all twenty acres of it. It was a classic Victorian, brick and wooden trim, ivy

338

growing up the sides. It looked like a mansion version of my high school and Turner's namesake. He must love that era of architecture.

"Park here, away from the house," I told Bill and he quickly landed on a grass street a block away from the house.

I made Mr. Forester step out of the car. "Okay, here comes the hard part. I have to really concentrate here, so keep an eye out for any trouble."

Bill was more than up for the task. His eyes were still filled with wonder as he watched me make Jill's dad move. I kept on forgetting how new my power was to everyone. I held my secret in for so long, and to find out I could have confided in Bill and Nancy from the beginning without judgment, made me wish I'd shared my burden earlier.

I closed my eyes and concentrated…

…And I was in. I was seeing through Mr. Forester's eyes now. I made sure I could move all of his limbs by doing a quick shake down. This made Bill cringe a little, but I couldn't help that now, I needed Mr. Forester to be as fluid as possible when entering the house. I knew that as soon as Roberta saw him the jig was up, but I was more concerned about the guards and making a route for Bill and I to break in.

Through his body, I made my way across the grass-covered road and through someone's lawn to reach my grandparent's house. The gate and fencing surrounding the mansion was black wrought iron and loomed before Mr. Forester like the bars of a prison. Ryan's prison. My father's prison. Soon to be *my* prison if this didn't turn out okay. (That was if I was lucky, knowing Gramps, he was still on his "murder Chelsan" mission.) I erased those thoughts from my mind as they were making it difficult for me to maintain my control over Mr. Forester. Directly to the left of the two-way gate was a small guard station with two men on duty. One sat next to a screen that had hundreds of camera angles from inside the house, while the other leaned against the wall, bored. I made Jill's dad walk up to them.

"Evening. I'm here to see the Vice President. He's expecting me." I tried to sound as monotone as possible taking a few cues from Jill's comment about how her dad had only given her orders over the last two years. If Turner's people were used to Mr. Forester a certain way, I didn't want to act differently than what they expected. I figured *neutral* was my best course of action.

"Of course, Mr. Forester. Word was just sent that he's on his way." The guard sitting at the monitor screen smiled up at him. "I'll let the doorman know."

I tried to keep Mr. Forester's face as cool as possible, but it was a hopeless undertaking. I could never tell what *my* face looked like, so how was I supposed to know *his* looked like? "Sounds good. Tell him I'll wait for him in the study when he arrives." I seriously hoped there was a study in that house.

"Will do. Good day." The guard nodded in a friendly manner.

"We're through," I informed Bill, though my eyes were still closed. I couldn't quite master the art of seeing two different perspectives at once so it was just easier to keep my lids shut. I hoped I would *never* have to do this again! Keeping Bruce alive was one thing, but controlling my enemy's father and sneaking into my grandparent's lair was another.

The guard sitting inside the booth hit the button for the

intercom. "Mr. Forester is here to wait for the Vice President."

"Copy. We'll have refreshments ready," came a friendly voice through the speaker above the guard's head.

"Thank you," the guard responded then turned to me. "You're all set, Mr. Forester."

"Thank...." I started to make him say.

BBBBZZZZT!

BBBZZZZTT!

Out of nowhere Bill was there with a stun club and both guards were down.

He turned to Mr. Forester with a smile, but his eyes were full of determination and bravery. "Get your butt up here. We're getting Ryan together."

I opened my eyes and it took me a second to make my own perspective the more dominant one. I couldn't believe Bill! I was shocked, proud, scared and little excited by his aggression. He was right of course; three was better than one dead guy. Once we were in, who knew how many dead servants they employed that I could use to my advantage. Spiders and flies would work too in a pinch.

I followed the same route I made Jill's dad travel and was next to Bill and Mr. Forester within seconds. I disconnected from Mr. Forester's eyes, but remained linked to the rest of his body.

"Get that stun club ready," I advised Bill.

Bill grinned at me.

I looked up at his bruised, cut face and his silly smile and I couldn't help myself. I hugged him. "Thank you, Bill."

Bill gently pushed me off, eyes sparkling, still smiling. "Hug me *after* we pull this off."

"Right," I said and took a deep breath, head back in the game.

I made Jill's dad walk up the long cobblestone footpath that led to the front door. I followed next, with Bill behind, hiding his stun club. As far as I knew our plan was to stun the crap out of everyone until we found Ryan. The more I thought about it, the more nervous I became. This house was HUGE! Too many people, too many rooms. I put out my feelers for any corpses inside.

One.

Okay. Not ideal, but workable. I quickly popped into the dead person's eyes.

My heart skipped about a million beats.

Ryan sat in front of me, chained to a metal chair that was bolted to the floor. The room was a small square of white, walls, linoleum floor and ceiling. No windows and just one single white door. I nearly crumbled when I could see how beat up Ryan was. I thought Nancy's parents and Bill looked bad, Ryan apparently didn't stop fighting the entire time. Two black eyes, bloody nose, swollen lip, bruises and cuts all over his arms and who knew where else. His worst nightmare came true, he was back with my grandparents and this time it was for keeps.

The body I was in slapped him hard across the face. So much for treating him like a king!

Ryan spit out blood and refused to make eye contact with his tormentor.

And then it occurred to me.

When I connected to this dead person, Turner's usual barrier hadn't been in place. This particular corpse didn't have any defenses against me.

Odd.

Why?

A trick most likely. But what kind of trick?

I immediately took control of the rest of the dead person's limbs. I looked down at the body. A woman. Clothes and skin ragged and dirty. Who was this person?

I made her bend down and whisper in Ryan's ear. "Ryan, it's me, Chelsan, Bill and I are at the house. Sit tight and we'll be up in a few."

Ryan's head whirled around so fast to look in the corpse's eyes it frightened me. "Chelsan, don't! Leave me here, please!"

WHAM!

I was bumped out of the dead woman's body.

"Roberta knows we're here. We have to hurry," I said as my head was spiraling. Why didn't Ryan want us to rescue him? He couldn't possibly want to stay. Maybe they were brainwashing him. I didn't care. I was going after him whether he liked it or not.

Taking full control of Mr. Forester we opened the front door without waiting to knock.

It was empty. The foyer was all dark wood paneling and polished flooring. From the brightness emanating in front of us, I saw the glints of gold from the living room. It was hard to forget the gold gaudiness from my mother's vision and apparently Roberta and Turner hadn't changed their décor in the last twenty years.

The eerie stillness made my mind scream the word *trap* over and over. I finally understood why people in horror movies always *investigated* when every instinct in their bodies told them to run. It was as if someone was controlling me and there was nothing I could do to stop it.

Roberta stepped in front of us out of nowhere with five guards behind her. She smiled her stiff, stretched smile. "Chelsan."

"Roberta." I wondered where on earth this was going. She wasn't having the guards attack. She didn't even look like she was mad that I was there. What was going on?

"Come with me. All of you." Roberta turned and walked up a flight of stairs, her guards following dutifully. "You're outnumbered, dears, please," she called over her shoulder.

"Should we?" Bill asked. I could tell he was thinking the same thing I was.

"Ryan told me to leave," I confided in Bill.

"Maybe we should." Bill was a smart guy. He knew something was wrong, too.

"I just can't, Bill. I can't leave Ryan here. They'll never let him go." Even though I knew I was most likely being an idiot and walking straight into the lion's den. I couldn't abandon Ryan. I'd never be able to live with myself.

"Okay. I'm with you." Bill leveled his stun club, ready to use it despite the odds.

"And besides, there's a dead bee hive on the west wing," I whispered to Bill, sensing it as we followed Roberta and her men up the stairs. I didn't know what I'd do with a bunch of bees, but at least it was something. Other than that, Roberta appeared to have had the house cleansed of anything dead aside from a fly here or there. A rush cleansing job. Which meant

Turner must have informed her of my escape and they knew I'd be coming here for Ryan. I kept Mr. Forester with us as well, he was more of a shield now than anything else. Somehow, I didn't think I'd be able to keep Jill's dad safe, but my choices were slim and living was way more important than dying to keep my enemy's *dead* dad in good shape.

Bill and I kept a good distance from the guards just in case they tried anything funny, but they seemed very disinterested in us. Their main concern was my feline grandmother who strode down a long hallway with a slight bounce to her step. The flight of stairs was as tacky as the rest of the house with its gold-inlaid carvings of lion heads on the top and bottom of the railings to the silver and gold Chinese-style runner on the steps. But deep dark brown wood was the main attraction of the upstairs, just like the foyer the walls and floor were the same color. The few pieces of artwork hanging from the walls did little to lighten up the space. There wasn't a window in sight, the only light source being the inset bulbs evenly spaced out on the ceiling.

Roberta stopped at a white door at the end of the hallway and turned to me with a large grin. "Here we are," she practically purred.

I was sure that this was the door Ryan was behind. Sure, because of seeing through the dead woman's eyes and sure, because I knew I was walking into the snappy part of her mousetrap. I looked over at Bill and the expression on his face matched what I was feeling.

Roberta's guards stood next to her like statues, void of showing any emotion whatsoever.

"Shall we go in and see your lover?" Roberta cackled. Like a kid who had a surprise that they couldn't wait to reveal.

"Keys, please. I know he's in chains." I decided that whatever she had planned for me I could handle, I only wanted to free Ryan and get out of there.

Suddenly we heard Ryan scream from behind the door. "CHELSAN! DON'T COME IN! GET OUT OF HERE! PLEASE!"

Hearing his desperate plea made me want to help him even more. I knew this was a mistake, but my heart was stronger than my head at this point. She handed me the keys a little too happily for my taste, but I took them anyway.

I shoved past Roberta and her guards, Mr. Forester in tow, and swung the door open.

There was Ryan just as I had seen him through the corpse's eyes, chained to the metal chair. Tears streamed down his bruised face as he looked at me. He was devastated to see me, as if I had sprung the trap and it was too late. All I saw was him, nothing here that could hurt me.

One step at a time. I ran over to his chains and started to unlock him.

"Chelsan," came a woman's voice from behind me.

Chills ran down my spine and I froze in place. It couldn't be. No. No. No. No.

I looked up at Ryan and his eyes confirmed my worst fear.

"You should have left me here." His face was wracked with sympathy.

I slowly turned my head.

I couldn't breathe.

I couldn't think.

346

I couldn't react.

Standing in front of me was the corpse I had controlled.

Mommy.

I started to shake violently, dropping the keys to the floor.

Roberta's cackle of delight was the only sound that reverberated off the walls.

Mom.

Mom.

Mom.

No.

She was barely recognizable, she was beaten to pulp, her eyes freshly gouged, her skin left to rot. She looked like a zombie out of horror film. Her black swirling hole was invisible to me. Somehow Roberta had found a way to block me from even seeing if a body was dead or not. This was her trick. This was her plan. She brought my mother here to torture me. To punish me. To watch with utter happiness as I suffered. And it was working like a charm.

I couldn't even cry. I was frozen. Literally frozen.

I hardly noticed Bill as he picked up the keys and continued to unchain Ryan.

My mother walked forward and looked at me with her empty sockets. "Such a failure."

I tried to rationalize that this wasn't my mom, this was Roberta making my mom talk, move, function, but the words were coming out of her mouth, with her voice... even with her torn-out eyes and her rotted skin, she was still Mom.

"Stop," I whispered.

"Stop what? Stop telling you the truth? I can finally tell you what I really thought of you," my mother laughed. And it was her laugh.

Tears flowed freely. My body was shaking so badly I could barely stand.

I tried to find her black hole. To disconnect Roberta from my mother's body. To make her stop myself, but it was as if a real live person stood in front of me. If it weren't for her condition I might think she was actually alive...

"Please," I sputtered.

Mom walked up to me and placed her hand against my cheek lovingly. "You were nothing but a burden to me. You killed your father and forced me to marry Bruce. I'll hate you forever, little one."

Roberta and my mom laughed hysterically at the anguish on my face.

Ryan and Bill were both by my side now.

"Let's get out of here." Ryan tried to lead me out of the room.

Roberta nodded to her guards.

Her men quickly grabbed Ryan and Bill before they could even react. They were both so focused on me they didn't have their defenses up. They both struggled to break free, but they weren't strong enough for the...

...wait a minute...

I could sense something in the guards, something off.

Like flashes of light, it was flashes of dark. They were dead, and their swirling holes were hidden like the one in my mother. My emotions clouded me from seeing it in her, but the guards were another story. Just when I started to gain some kind of stability my mom smiled down at me.

"Every second of my life, I wished you were dead instead of your father. Maybe now I can get my wish." She laughed again.

And then she started to dance. It was grotesque and humiliating.

Roberta stepped forward simply thrilled with the events taking place. "I can make her dance some more." She grinned, looking like the cat she was.

I noticed Roberta's eyes were bright solid green.

"Chelsan, she's not your mother! Your mother died! Don't listen to her!" Ryan screamed.

And I suddenly realized he had been screaming this whole time.

I had blocked him out, I was so focused on my mom and Roberta.

I started to break out of the spell.

Roberta made my mother dance and jerk and slam herself against the wall. How long had she been torturing my mother's body like this? How long had she gotten her kicks out of degrading her and beating her up? Roberta used her corpse as a form a therapy to satisfy her thirst for vengeance on my family.

My mom began to scratch and tear flesh off her arms, laughing manically the entire time, continuing to slam herself into the wall.

It made me enraged beyond anything I had ever felt before. All I could see was red. How dare she? How dare she?

I closed my eyes from the fury. In the depths of my soul a scream started to rumble from the very core of my being. A scream so powerful, I could feel my whole body arch backwards from the force. It poured out of my mouth and filled the room with deafening impact.

I could see then.

Even with my eyes closed, I could see everything.

All the things that Roberta kept hidden.

All the corpses roaming the hallways of this giant mansion.

All of their black raging chasms, welcoming me like their true master.

No more.

I connected to each and every one of them.

I felt their last force of life left to them in this world.

And I obliterated it.

BOOM!!!

The whole house shook from the force.

I opened my eyes and I was covered in blood and chunks of flesh.

What had I done?

Rather than see my mother tortured, I had annihilated her entire body. There was nothing left of her. Nothing. Just blood and pieces of rotted flesh splattered everywhere. I didn't know if I could live with myself after that. It felt like I had killed her, even though I knew that wasn't the truth, it felt true and it was consuming me like a wave of guilt I had no way of surviving.

I realized then that the guards had also exploded.

No more black holes.

No more bodies.

I had destroyed them all.

Roberta's eyes were clear as they stared into mine. She was shocked and scared at first, but when she recognized the shame I felt, it was like I had given her the best prize of all. She started to laugh in triumph again, even covered in her own guards' blood, even knowing she was completely alone against me.

She had won.

And I couldn't take it.

I couldn't take that look of victory in her eyes.

I wanted to rip them out myself.

I wanted her to die.

"See how you like this!" I screamed at her.

I connected to the hundreds of dead bees in their fumigated hive and made them fly through an opened window.

Ryan and Bill stood next to me, holding each of my arms.

"Chelsan. Let's get out of here," Ryan pleaded.

But I didn't want to listen to him.

I wanted to see Roberta suffer.

We heard the buzzing before we saw them.

Roberta's face fell slightly as she recognized the sound.

"Let's see how you handles bees, Grams!" I smiled myself.

The swarm of dead bees entered the room like the cavalry. I made them sting her over and over, just to wipe that triumphant smirk off her face. She screamed in anguish and tried to cover her feline face from the bee blitz.

At that point, Ryan and Bill physically dragged me away.

"Chelsan, come on." Bill's voice was laced with concern.

I followed willingly, but I kept the bees attacking Roberta while we headed toward the front door. With each sting it took away some of my guilt and hatred of myself. It felt like the more I hurt her, the better I would be.

I knew it was wrong.

And yet I didn't stop.

We slipped and slid our way through the blood soaked house. Every servant, guard and maid all appeared to have been dead people that couldn't escape my attack. It made me sick to my stomach. I, literally, made all of these people blow up into a million pieces and now the three of us were covered in it and slipping on all that was left of them. What was I?

The more my head spun with the terror of who I was the more I wanted to punish Roberta. It was her fault! Her fault I was the way I was! They performed the ritual to kill me! They had been trying to kill me non-stop for the last two weeks! They had murdered my mother and my neighbors! They had tried to kill my friends! Neither one of them deserved to breathe! Making each bee sting every part of her I could reach was a small penance to pay for what she'd done.

That woman made the last image of my mother a nightmare! She knew I'd never be able to erase that from my mind. And that was precisely why she did it. She wanted me to remember the rotted, beaten, puppet of my mom forever. And I would. And I hated her for it.

She had fallen to the floor now, the bees too much for her.

I didn't care.

Jill's father.

He had exploded like the rest of them.

I pushed it from my brain. He was already dead. I didn't kill him. But why did it feel like I killed everyone in there?! Roberta made me feel like I murdered my own mother! The hate that seethed through my blood was like an addictive poison I couldn't get rid of and a part of me didn't want to. The hate felt right.

It felt good.

The three of us ran out the front door and we stopped dead in our tracks.

Turner was there with a handful of his armed soldiers.

Turner raced up to me, already knowing what I was doing. "Please, take them off of her. Please!"

I shrugged away from him. "I warned you!" I wanted to set the bees on him as well, but something in his eyes made me pause.

"Please, she's all I have left in this world. You took my son away from me, don't take her away, too. I can't stop them! I tried! Please!" Turner was desperate.

And instead of feeling good (like I thought I would) he was actually making me feel bad.

No.

She deserved it!

And so did he!

They killed my mother.

As if from nowhere an onslaught of Police-hovers and Press-hovers flooded the front of Turner's house and started landing all over his property.

The hover-van nearest to us opened its doors. Jason and Nancy spilled out and hurried over to us.

Nancy's eyes were wide with horror as she saw the three of us covered in blood and people bits. Her hand went to her mouth. "We need paramedics!!" she screamed.

"Nancy, it's not our blood. We're okay," Bill reassured her.

One look at us and Jason approached Turner with a serious and condemning expression. "We have the footage of your exterminators killing Chelsan's trailer park already on the air."

A particularly burly policeman handcuffed Turner and started to drag him away toward his hover.

The press was screaming at Turner and screaming at us. I couldn't concentrate, but I couldn't stop making the bees attack Roberta either.

Turner kept his eyes on me, terrified. "Chelsan, please!"

I could feel that Roberta's body wasn't moving as I made the bees continue to sting her.

Ryan whispered in my ear. "Your father died to save you. He could have killed his parents instead, but he didn't."

My head froze up.

My knees gave way as Ryan caught me.

A wave of reality washed over me.

I dropped the bees.

What was wrong with me?

"Upstairs." I grabbed the first policeman I could find. "Roberta Turner was attacked by bees. She needs medical help."

Nancy embraced me tightly. "We thought you were dead. Again." She pulled away smiling, although she groaned when she realized that she now had blood all over her as well. "Oh great."

I tried to smile back, but it wasn't in me. "Can we just go home?"

She picked up on the mood of the moment and figured out pretty quickly that the last thing anyone of us wanted to do was celebrate.

"Of course." Nancy gave me another hug, stains be damned.

"My car is over one block," Bill said and we started to walk through the throng of reporters and police officers, all asking us why we were blood-soaked.

None of us answered them. What would we say anyway? Jason would think of something, like he always did.

Roberta was taken out of the house by hover-gurney. She was alive. I was surprised at how relieved I was about that. With everything that had happened, I let my rage get the best of me. It made me hate myself all the more.

As Turner was being placed into the police-hover he nodded to me then turned away.

Maybe there could be a truce between us.

I doubted it.

I just hoped they'd be able to keep him in jail.

As we made our way back to Bill's hover-car, Ryan held my hand and squeezed it. "You going to be okay?"

I shrugged.

I honestly didn't know.

The ride back was silent. No one wanted to say anything that might cause anyone any pain.

George and Vianne were waiting for us in the front yard. They freaked out when they saw all the blood, but as soon as they realized it wasn't ours they were all hugs and smiles. Their house was back in order and aside from the front door everything looked like home again.

George gave us all robes to change into while Vianne made us a quick meal. The only thing we washed was our hands, we were too tired and hungry to do a proper job. We all must have looked a fright with our hair and skin covered with dried blood, not to mention the cuts and bruises Ryan and Bill were sporting.

I scarfed down my entire plate and even had seconds.

Nancy did most of the talking, telling us of her and Jason's escapade to air the footage. They managed to sneak into the International News Building and through clever maneuvering, Jason snuck into the main server room and aired the footage on all stations across the globe. Nancy explained that Jason didn't want to risk telling his producers about the chip for fear of them working for Turner. "You can't trust anyone. Jason's right about that." Nancy's eyes fluttered. I guess they had worked things out. But knowing them, that could last all of five minutes.

"Turn on the holo." Jason walked into the kitchen and we all jumped slightly.

"You scared us to death." Nancy stood up and grabbed his arm with a flirty smile. Yup. They were definitely on good terms again.

"Just turn it on." Jason wasn't happy and that made my stomach sink.

Vianne clicked the holo-tv on.

The news anchor was at his desk with footage of Turner behind him at a press conference.

Turner had his usual *public face* on. All concern and heartbreak. "It appalls me that Mayor Bradfield could be responsible for such acts. It is a violation of what Population Control stands for and it a hideously cruel act of murder and man-slaughter. Our hearts go out to the victims of this horrendous crime and Population Control will do everything in its power to make restitution for Mayor Bradfield's actions. I'd especially like to thank Jason Keroff and Chelsan Derée for bringing this footage to light. If not for the heroics of those two individuals, Mayor Bradfield would have succeeded. The city of Los Angeles thanks you, the world thanks you, and I thank you..."

Jason turned the holo off with a grunt. "The bastard got away with it. Every bit of footage, equipment and logs were all under Bradfield's name. We should have known when he let us go so easily at Headquarters. It wouldn't hurt him either way if we actually succeeded!" Jason was fuming now.

I should have been more upset by this news, but somehow it seemed expected.

This was a small respite from my grandfather. I didn't know how, but I just knew it in my heart.

"Make him set up a memorial," I said to Jason, interrupting his rant.

Jason stopped and he nodded. "First thing."

Ryan leaned over and kissed my cheek. It was the first feeling of good that I felt since leaving Turner's.

Jason was already on the phone making demands and it made me smile a little as I looked around the kitchen. My new family. Everyone with a few bumps and bruises but otherwise just fine. I felt my emotions course through me as I realized how much they were a part of my life. As difficult as it was to think of my mother after everything that happened, I knew she'd be happy for me. I couldn't let my grandparents have that kind of power over me. I wouldn't let them destroy the beautiful memories I had of my mom. She loved me with everything that she had. She stayed with a man that beat the crap out of her just to keep me safe. She would always be my hero.

Ryan reached over and wiped the tears from my cheeks. I didn't even know I had been crying. I had been doing a lot of that lately. And probably a lot more in the days to come. I needed to heal from all this and it was going to take time.

Ryan held my face in his hands and kissed me. It was filled with just as much passionate, toe-curling craziness as all of Ryan's kisses, but there was something more to it this time. I wasn't nervous. It felt right. I finally felt like we loved each other equally. I never wanted to be with anyone else and I knew Ryan felt the same way.

"You all need showers," George said with a crinkle of his nose.

It was such an obvious statement that we all laughed. It was good to release the tension. And for once in a very long time I felt like everything was going to be okay.

"I hate to be the bad guy here, but school *is* tomorrow." Vianne gave us a look that made it clear she was just the messenger.

Really?!

I couldn't believe it was only Monday! But the more I thought about it, the more welcoming it sounded. Normal. Calm.

Then I thought of Jill's threat: *If my father doesn't come back, I'm holding you fully responsible and if you think your life was torture before, you haven't seen anything yet.*

Well, at least she wouldn't try and kill me.

Who was I kidding? School was going to suck.

Uuggh!

Other Books by Becca C. Smith

The Riser Saga:

Riser

Reaper

Ripper

The Atlas Series:

Atlas

Grigori Returned

Alexis Tappendorf Series

Alexis Tappendorf and the Search for Beale's Treasure

The Black Moon Saga (with F.M. Sherrill)

Black Moon

Black Sunrise

Bio

Born and raised in Seattle, WA, Becca C. Smith fell in love with storytelling at an early age. The first book she read was The Lion, The Witch and Wardrobe when she was four and she's been looking for the door to Narnia ever since!

Becca is a passionate reader, consuming anything that has an element of sci-fi or fantasy. Mix it in with YA and Becca is a fan for life! So it's no surprise that she writes in these genres as well! From her YA sci-fi horror series The Riser Saga featuring a teenage girl who can control the dead, all the way to her urban fantasy books, The Atlas Series, where Becca mashes magic, science and mythology all into one. And being a child of the 80's she's a sucker for crossovers, so both book series share the same universe as well as some of the key characters!

When Becca isn't writing, she's a total fangirl! Being a super fan of something means she's going to sew about it. It's how she shows her nerdtastic love for whatever it may be! From adorable little Supernatural plush dolls, to elaborate Firefly/Serenity bags, Becca simply loves to create!

Becca lives in Los Angeles with her brilliant husband, Stephan Fleet, and their two cats, Duke and Snake Plissken.

Chapter Zero

Year: 2320

I was dreaming.

It was the only way I could explain the darkness.

It felt as if I stood in outer space where someone forgot to add the stars. It had to be a dream…

…Or maybe something else.

My gut screamed that this was something more. Something all too familiar.

The last time I had a "dream" like this my friend (and super famous reporter) Jason Keroff told me it was called astral projection. Yeah, sounds pretty weird, but actually it's quite terrifying. It basically means that I've either traveled to someone else's brain or they've traveled to mine.

Either way, not exactly my idea of a fun time.

I might be jaded though. The only three times I've ever experienced astral projection were pretty horrific. The first time was my mother telling me that she was being murdered. The

1

second and third times were with my grandparents. Which I know for a normal eighteen-year-old girl might not be a problem, but for me it was terrifying since my grandparents wanted to kill me.

Yes, I said kill me.

What's crazy is that I didn't even know who my grandparents were two months ago! But suddenly they were in my life and ready to take me down. In fact, they were the ones who murdered my mother in the first place!

My grandfather is Geoffrey Turner, the Vice President of Population Control, which basically makes him the most powerful man on the globe. With the world's population out of control due to a tiny pill called Age-pro, which stops the aging process and makes you young forever, he definitely has his hands full. Before I knew him as Gramps I thought he was a pretty decent guy, but that was before I found out *how* he actually controlled over-population.

Unbeknownst to the public, he exterminates them, and my mom was one of the casualties. He gassed our trailer park and made the world believe it was a tornado. If it weren't for my besties, Nancy, Bill and Jason (and my unbelievably amazingly gorgeous boyfriend, Ryan), the public would never have known about what really happened to my mom. Of course, sneaky man that my grandfather is, he completely framed the Mayor of Los Angeles and got away scot-free. So *my* mission wasn't over. I vowed to expose my grandfather for the mass murderer he was.

I still intend to accomplish this.

The first time Gramps visited my dreams he flaunted the fact that he had Brady, (the serial killer he hired to kill me) under his control. (Yes, he employs serial killers for his methods of "fixing" over-population. Serial killers who were supposed to be extinct for a hundred years!) I could see the black swirling hole spinning in the center of Brady's chest and I knew he was dead, and that my grandfather controlled him.

Did I forget to mention that's how I see dead people?

Actually, anything dead. If it had life, and now it doesn't, I see a black churning hole in its center.

Oh, and I should also probably mention that I can control the dead, too. Like they were puppets. Seriously, I know how it sounds, but it's something I inherited as a baby when my father sacrificed himself to save my mother and me from the deadly curse dear old Grandpa and Grandma placed on us. (Another story for another time. Let's just say that Dad's side of the family has some serious conflict-resolution issues.) Anyway, I quickly found out my grandparents have the same power to control the dead that I have, but they use rituals and Vodun spells to do it. I guess that gives me an advantage because my power over the dead is innate, but not much. Turner still manages to be a step ahead of me at every turn.

The third time I experienced this "dream astral thingy" was with Roberta, my grandmother. She's what society calls a *Feline*. Someone who was around when Age-pro was invented in 2020, and had so many face-lifts they resembled cats. Age-pro "freezes" you at the age you're at when you start taking it, so she was stuck with *stretched frozen face* forever. Turner keeps her out of the public eye since Felines terrify the youthful public. The main difference between my third dream and the earlier ones was the fact that it was actually *me* who traveled to *her* head. I saw all sorts of things in Roberta's twisted brain. The worst being that she and Turner kept my father eight-years-old for a hundred years by giving him Age-pro! So horrific, I still can't stop thinking about it.

So, yeah, astral projection, definitely lame.

I looked around in the darkness, hoping that I wasn't in either grandparent's head. Maybe I lucked out and I was in Ryan's brain.

I immediately wished I hadn't thought that. What if I saw that he didn't like me as much as I liked him? Or he was going to break up with me? Or he secretly liked someone else? I knew I was being paranoid, but I couldn't help it. Ryan was just about the smartest most amazing boyfriend EVER. And I didn't want to find out I was completely delusional in thinking that he actually liked me.

I took a deep breath. I had nothing to worry about. Ryan had proven how much he liked me over and over. I needed to grow some confidence!

And I needed to figure out where I was. Or more importantly, *whose* brain I was in.

"Chelsan?" A child's voice called out in the darkness.

My heart skipped a beat. The voice sounded terrified.

"Hello?" I answered back. The blackness was so complete I couldn't even see my hand in front of me.

Suddenly, I started to glow like my skin was coated with phosphorous. I became the light source in the inky shadows.

That's when a girl about seven years of age stepped into the luminosity my skin radiated. She was stunning to look at, with porcelain skin, bright lavender eyes and long black hair almost as dark as our surroundings. I couldn't stop staring at her eyes. Aside from their over-large kewpie doll size, they were filled with sadness and fear, but mostly hope.

"You are Chelsan, aren't you?" she asked tentatively.

"Yes," I kind of mumbled. I was still trying to figure out why I was in this girl's head or more likely why she was in mine.

"I knew it." The little girl closed her eyes and took a sigh of relief. "I've been searching for you since I first saw you."

"Um…" Wow. I was full of words of wisdom. I couldn't seem to help it. Even though this girl was maybe eight tops, she intimidated the crap out of me. She just held herself in a way that radiated power. I felt out of my depth and I couldn't figure out why.

"I saw you." She stepped forward and her lavender eyes pierced through me.

I felt like I was being probed or something. It scared me enough to take a step back from her.

"Who are you?" I blurted out.

The girl immediately placed her hands up in supplication. "Don't be scared of me. I need your help, and you're the only one with the power to do it."

"Look kid…" I was about to try and break our brain-dream connection. This girl was freaking me out on a core level, even worse than Turner had when I first met him. She was just… well… scary. And I had *zero* reasons to give why. It was just instinctual. Something was very off.

"I'm ninety-eight."

Oh.

Oh man.

Of course. That's what was off. Her eyes were scary because she was almost a hundred years old and stuck in a child's body! She said she had seen me before.

"The I.Q. Farm." I suddenly realized.

"Yes. I saw you use the rats." She looked up at me with desperation. "I saw you bring them to life and attack the guards. You escaped and left us all there." She nearly choked from emotion.

I remembered all too well. When the gang and I snuck into Turner's headquarters I connected to hundreds of dead rats and made them attack Turner's army so we could escape. It was a terrifying experience especially when we stumbled into one of Turner's biggest secrets: I.Q. Farms.

Turner kidnaps kids whose test scores rank above the genius level and brings them to facilities known as I.Q. Farms. The public has no idea these farms even exist, and Turner's goons keep the children's parents silent. The only reason I had even heard of these farms in the first place was because Turner took *Ryan* when he was eight. Ryan pretended he had cheated on his test scores and Turner sent him back home. Three years later my grandparents were furious when they realized that Ryan had tricked them when he solved Trilidon's theorem. (A math problem that hadn't been solved in centuries!) But Ryan never forgot how terrifying the I.Q. Farm had been. And when we discovered one as we were escaping from Gramps's headquarters, Ryan realized that some of the kids were the same age as when he'd left them.

Yet another distortedly repulsive thing my grandfather does. Using Age-pro to keep these kids children forever. I still didn't know why these farms existed, but seeing this girl in front of me

6

and knowing she was eighty years older than me made me want to throw-up a little.

"I'm… I'm sorry." That's all that I could say. The kids had looked like they were in technological comas when we were there, all of them strapped into devices and focused on holo-screens.

But the guilt hit me like a ton of bricks.

I had left hundreds of kids locked in a basement of technology against their will.

I could have done something…

Couldn't I have?

I just didn't know. I was so focused on saving my friends at the time, I hadn't even considered helping the kids.

"Don't be. If you had been captured, you would have been killed. But you can help now." The girl managed a small smile. "My name is Elisha Stearne. I was seven when I was taken. I've been in the main facility ever since." Elisha looked around with sudden paranoia as if someone was about to appear in front of us. "He's coming. I don't have much time. Turner is monitoring my brain activity. He knows I left…"

"What can I do?" I asked. My guilt made want to do anything I could to help this girl or lady or… gross! I didn't want to think about it too long.

"You need to help me and some others escape." Elisha's eyes were round with fear and determination. "We're guarded by Turner's dead army. You can break through your grandfather's defenses. I need you Chelsan. I have to go."

"Wait!" I didn't want her to leave. I felt like I needed more to go on.

Elisha's beautiful face was contorted with terror. "You only have two days, after that it won't matter."

"Why?" I was already getting in panic mode.

"Turner has scheduled my execution for Thursday morning."

SWOOSH!

Elisha flew out of my sight like a giant vacuum cleaner had sucked her back into the black void she came from.

CPSIA information can be obtained
at www.ICGtesting.com
Printed in the USA
LVOW12s1540091216
516587LV00003B/505/P